Magic Man

Magic Man

RON BASE

Thomas Dunne Books
St. Martin's Press
New York

This is a work of fiction. All of the characters, organiza-
tions, and events portrayed in this novel are either prod-
ucts of the author's imagination or are used fictitiously.

THOMAS DUNNE BOOKS.
An imprint of St. Martin's Press.

www.thomasdunnebooks.com
www.stmartins.com

Library of Congress Cataloging-in-Publication Data

Base, Ron.
      Magic man / Ron Base.—1st ed.
         p. cm.
      ISBN-13: 978-0-312-32809-2
      ISBN-10: 0-312-32809-5
      1. Magic—Fiction. 2. Hollywood (Los Angeles,
Calif.)—Fiction. 3. Love stories. gsafd

PR9199.3.B3757 M28 2006
813'.54—dc22

                                      20060404192

First Edition: August 2006

10 9 8 7 6 5 4 3 2 1

For my darling Kathy,
who helped me find that which cannot be found

Acknowledgments

The discovery of Brae Orrack's supposedly lost account of his Hollywood adventures has already been well documented. The story of how the manuscript was found in a forgotten cellar below the oldest sound-stage on Paramount's lot among the papers of the late producer Louis Payne has been the subject of no small amount of media attention. Less known is the intense effort that has gone into authenticating his memoir, particularly in light of allegations from some quarters that the handwritten manuscript is a fraud.

Certainly Orrack hardly looms large in the early history of movies. However, diligent research turned up references to him that verify much of the information contained in his curious story. In the archives of the Los Angeles Public Library, for example, there is the *Los Angeles Times* report of the *Lilac Time* premiere dated July 17, 1928, that makes mention of him. More evidence was uncovered at the Margaret Herrick Library of the Motion Picture Arts and Sciences in Beverly Hills. Many thanks to the library's staff for their patience and kindness. Also, the staff at the Monroe County Public Library helped unearth details of Orrack's movements in Key West, Florida. As well, Ric Base not only asked probing questions, but was kind enough to chauffeur his brother around Key West and environs.

Even with the manuscript's authenticity finally established, it was apparent that Brae Orrack was nothing if not verbose. Thus the talents of editor Peter Wolverton and his assistant, Katie Gilligan, proved invaluable in shaping and focusing the story. Sabrina Soares Roberts did an amazing job of fact-checking the edited manuscript.

In the end, however, ultimate credit for the existence of the Orrack manuscript must go to my agent, Frances Hanna, along with her husband and partner, Bill Hanna. When no one else could, these two saw the possibilities inherent in Orrack's chronicle. For that, I am unendingly grateful.

Despite all this work, however, there remain those skeptics who insist that Brae Orrack is at worst a liar and at best a teller of tall tales. My only recourse then, is to present the manuscript much as Orrack wrote it and let the reader decide. Be warned, however: If one is to embrace his story it is best to believe in magic—and in love. Otherwise, one is advised not to read further.

PART ONE

Cinemaland

✴

Chapter One

Reluctant as I am to begin this tale on a sour note, knowing how a reader likes a cheerful story, I nonetheless must report that on that particular Sunday evening in 1928 I was five weeks short of the time my father's curse would kill me.

On that evening in question, arriving on the pier in Venice, California, wearing my dad's fancy tux, desperate for rent money, I was in trouble as only a young fellow can be in trouble when he's closer to dying than he is to living.

My cousin Megan, a witch who knows of such things, says there is always a way around a curse. All I had to do was find that which cannot be found. So there you go. A little optimism. Find what cannot be found. No problem at all.

What's that you say? How do you find something that cannot be found?

Well, that's the problem, isn't it?

But not to dwell on these things. I am here to tell a story, not to make you feel all miserable, although a little sympathy for yours truly wouldn't be out of place, I don't think, since what I am about to relate doesn't always put me in the best light. Better to get you feeling sorry for me right off the top, I would say. That way, further down the line, you'll be more willing to overlook my considerable shortcomings.

My first customers happened along a few moments after I set up the small sign I'd had specially painted. It's not every night a fellow shows up on the pier in white tie and tails. It's like my dad always said, you look at a man in a tux and everyone sees a gentleman—and everyone takes a gentleman seriously.

They had to be sisters, ten and twelve I would say, not great prospects, but better than nothing. They looked like they'd just been ironed, and they both had dark hair done up in luxurious ringlets, cheeks rosy, and eyes bright with fascination, willing to believe anything.

Well, just about anything.

"You really a magic man, like the sign says?" asked the older and more forward of the two.

"Why would I say such a thing if it wasn't true?" I demanded, adding the twinkle to my eye. "Don't I look like an honest fellow to you?"

"Not exactly," said the older girl.

I chose not to take offense, for if the truth were to be told, I am not such an honest fellow. But that's the point, is it not? To convince folks you are what you aren't.

"On this pier they don't allow us to tell lies," I reassured her. "You are in luck, for I am indeed a magic man. Brae Orrack by name, magic man by trade and inclination. What's your name, sweetheart?"

"Pauline, but I ain't your sweetheart. Mom says I'm too young for sweethearts."

"Right she is about that," I said. "And what about your sister here?"

She was the smaller of the two, and shy, given to gnawing away at her knuckle as she stared up at me through thick eyelashes.

"How do you know she's my sister?"

"That's why I'm a magic man, you see. I know these things."

"Then you should know her name," Pauline replied reasonably.

"It's Annie," I said.

The eyes of the little girls grew larger, and the revelation had the effect of drawing Annie out of her shyness, and even convinced her to cease gnawing on her knuckle. "How did you know?" Annie asked.

"Magic," I said. And good eyesight that allowed me to see the name on her charm bracelet. But they didn't need to know that. Much of my largely misspent life was caught up with persuading folks young and old that I knew a good deal more than I actually did. It's a talent often overlooked, but one that should never be underestimated, particularly in a young fellow untried in the world, but meaning—with the help of smart evening clothes—to give the opposite impression.

"Okay, so you're a magician," said the older girl, Pauline. "Like the guy Annie had at her birthday party last year."

"He made eggs come out of kids' ears," affirmed Annie. "Can you do that?"

"And he wore a scarf around his head, too," chimed in Pauline, as though that were the clincher.

"You must understand, there is a great difference between a magician and a magic man," I said in my most authoritative voice.

"There is?" said Pauline.

"Indeed. A magician knows tricks, sleight of hand, how to deceive the eye. A magic man, on the other hand, is a highly trained individual knowledgeable in the dark art of conjuring."

"What's conjuring?" demanded little Annie.

"Turning stones to bees, that's conjuring," I said.

"You can turn stones to bees?" Pauline sounded dubious.

"Where I come from, that's about the first thing you learn."

"We're from Encino," said Annie. "They teach us to mind our manners and not to speak until we're spoken to. Nothing about turning stones to bees."

"That's the difference," I said. "I come from the land of magic and superstition, a place where the power of Satan and the evil eye transfix everyone, where always it's the funeral plumes and never the bridal roses, where the curse on souls and the getting of revenge endure over love. It is the land that ruined my youth and haunts my life."

"Boy, that doesn't sound much like any place around here!" Pauline said.

"Is that why you left home?" demanded Annie. "Because it was so awful?"

"That was one of the reasons all right. But I also left because I had to find that which cannot be found."

"What's that?" Pauline wanted to know.

"Love," I said.

They both wrinkled their faces. "Is that something you can find?" asked Pauline.

"I have to believe it is."

"Doesn't sound like much fun," said Annie.

"So far it hasn't been," I admitted. "In all honesty, I'm not even sure what I'm looking for. Alls I know is that I have to find it in the next month."

"Why?"

"Because if I don't, the curse my father put inside my body will kill me."

They stared at me for a long time. Annie spoke first. "Your daddy doesn't sound like a very nice person."

"I'm afraid he's not," I said.

"Is your father here?"

"Thankfully, no," I said.

"Where is he?"

"A long, long way from here."

Indeed John Orrack, or, as we knew him, the Great Orrack, was so far away it might as well have been another planet. And I wasn't exaggerating when I said it truly was a place of darkness, where the funeral plumes smothered the bridal roses every time. It haunted my life, haunts it to this day, in fact. I was lucky to escape, although, of course, I did not really escape at all.

Still, being cursed and on the run had led me to this wondrous place, and so I couldn't be too bitter, I suppose. Before arriving in Venice, California, I had barely even heard of a roller coaster, let alone actually seen one. In fact, before I got here I thought the only Venice in the entire world was the one in Italy, and I'm willing to bet Megan thought the same thing. Fancy my surprise then upon arriving and finding there was a second Venice, for all I knew more impressive than the first.

Here, they had roller coasters everywhere, and from what I hear the Italian Venice has no roller coasters at all. The roller coasters had names such as the Giant Dipper, Some Kick, High Boy, and the Chute. There were fun houses, miniature auto speedways, roller-skating rinks, flying planes, Ferris wheels, and carousels. There was the Toonerville Fun House, a Glass House, a whip ride, and a Dragon Bamboo Slide. There was billiards and bowling and you could dance all night and on Sundays, too. Dancing on Sundays. Impossible. I'd never heard of being able to do *anything* on a Sunday, let alone dance. Mind you, at the Venice Ball Room, beneath the big American flags, the hanging lights, and the red, white, and blue bunting, attendants kept a sharp eye. Any couple on the polished hardwood floor spotted with their cheeks together was politely tapped on the shoulder and ordered to move apart.

In this fantastical Venice, I had rented a room on the second floor of a pink boardinghouse that backed onto the Cabrillo Canal, part of the network of waterways created by a cigarette manufacturer named Abbot Kinney. He wanted a California Venice just like the Italian Venice, and since he was richer than anything imaginable, he could damn well get what he wanted. Imported gondolas glided along canals forty feet wide, filled four feet deep with seawater forced in by the high tides and retained via a series of locks. There were arching footbridges and an elegant hotel called the St. Marks with columns and arcades reminiscent of a doge's palazzo, where hot salt water was piped into each room. Not that they would ever have allowed the likes of me into them, of course, but these are the stories you heard, and I had no reason to discount them. There was also a restaurant shaped like a Spanish galleon, where each night an armor-suited trumpeter appeared to sound the end of the day.

On the weekends, thousands packed themselves onto the beach under umbrellas, luxuriating in the sand and a broiling sun, awaiting the evening and the good times to be had in such abundance on the Venice and Ocean piers. Now they swarmed past, headed for the farthest reaches of the pier. Particularly popular that summer was the Some Kick that dominated the far end. Everyone wanted a ride on it. The young men and women dressed formally for the occasion, the men wearing jackets and ties, and a hat of some sort. Straw boaters were popular that year, although the fedora remained a staple. The women, too, almost invariably wore a headpiece, silly little straw hats being popular, perhaps to match the straw boaters of their male escorts.

By now I'd attracted a few more customers; a guy in one of those straw boaters, trousers held with suspenders, a smile a little too crooked, and eyes a little too bright. His corpulent girlfriend was all done up in rouge and lipstick so that her face in this light looked as though it was made of wax. There was an elderly couple; him rail thin and slightly stooped so as to more easily talk to his tiny wife, who tottered like a windup doll. I liked the elderly couple. They looked as though they might believe anything, even a magic man on a Venice pier. These were curious things of which I spoke, things not generally heard amid the clang and clatter of roller coasters.

"He can turn stones to bees," little Annie announced to the crowd.

"Let's see you do it," said the guy in the straw boater.

"Ah, you see," I said, "that's the part of all this that costs."

"This is crazy," said the guy in the straw boater. "This guy's got as much chance of turning stones to bees as I do of turning my farts to gold."

Exactly what I wanted to hear; a man who sees easy money in the offing is the man with whom I can do business. "You may be right, my friend. But one dollar says you aren't."

"A buck, huh? You don't turn that stone into a bee, you pay me a buck, that it?"

"My misfortune to have encountered a formidable mathematician this evening," I lamented.

"I'll take some of that," said the old gent. He slapped a one-dollar bill down on the table.

"Guess I will, too," said the guy in the straw boater.

"We don't have any money," said Annie mournfully.

"Don't worry about it," I said, giving them a sympathetic smile. "I'm

sure there are lots of other well-heeled folks here this evening delighted
to finance such an amazing spectacle."

That created a general murmuring among my listeners. One thing to
hear a fellow go on when it's not going to cost; another to lay money on
the line. Still, there was the prospect of reward if I failed to deliver. And
after all, when you think about it, who in the world could ever turn a
stone into a bee? It began to look to most of these folks like that easy
money you always hear about, the stuff the movie stars and railway ty-
coons are always showered with, but never the ordinary fellow like you
or me. Three other gents soon plunked down their hard-earned dollar
bills.

I reached into my pocket and withdrew three round stones, placed
them in the palm of my hand, and held them out to little Annie. "I want
you to pick one of the stones."

She hesitated, and then grabbed the middle stone. "Good," I said.
"Now I want you to toss it as high as you can into the air."

"Hold on," said the guy in the straw boater, stepping forward and
snapping at those suspenders of his like he was the most important gent
in the world. "How do we know this isn't some sort of setup—you in ca-
hoots with these here kids?"

The overweight doll-face with him looked tremendously impressed. I
gave them one of my best smiles.

"All right, sir, then by all means, take the stone from the child's hand,
and toss it into the air for me."

"How about I pick another stone?"

"You'll disappoint a sweet little girl, but go ahead."

He chose another stone from my palm, turned it over in his fingers a
couple of times so as to ensure it contained no bees, shrugged, then
heaved it into the air.

The stone looped up into the starry California sky, and then started
to arc downward. It wasn't necessary for me to do anything, since all
these things are accomplished by the mind, but a little showmanship
never hurts. After all, it's all show, isn't it? You don't really believe a fellow such as myself, cursed and dying as I am, could actually turn a stone

into a bee. 'Course not. You're smart enough not to buy such a preposterous claim on your common sense, I'm sure. I'll fool these other suckers, not you.

So I threw out my arm, and the stone exploded in a tiny puff of smoke. There was the sound of buzzing, and the bee zipped past the end of the nose of the guy in the straw boater, causing him to jump back in alarm.

A series of gasps and squeals went up from my little audience, accompanied by delighted applause from Annie.

"Well, I'll be damned," said the guy in the straw boater as I collected my money.

A slim woman, the perfectly dressed type who would only tolerate perfectly dressed daughters, appeared and called out to Pauline and Annie. "We have to go now, mister," said Pauline. She took her sister's hand, and started off toward their mother. Annie pulled away long enough to say, "Good luck, mister. You know what?"

"What, Annie?"

"I really do believe you are a magic man."

"Then you've made me a very happy man indeed," I called after her. Their mother took her daughters' hands and whisked them off to what I hoped would be a life for them as perfect as their clothes. Alas, that's not quite the way it works, now is it? But one can live in hope.

The other onlookers began to drift off. The overweight woman pulled at the sleeve of the guy in the straw boater, but he didn't want to move. He snapped at his suspenders, and watched the bee as it continued buzzing around. "There's a trick," he pronounced. "Got to be a trick. There's always a trick."

He showed me another dollar bill. "It's yours. All you got to do is tell me how you do it."

I smiled. "Maybe you should consider this, my friend: maybe the trick is, there's no trick at all."

"What are you trying to say, all this hooey you been feeding us is true? You really can turn stones to bees?"

I allowed my smile to grow wider. That only served to agitate him.

That's when the cop appeared; a skinny guy, the brass buttons of his hip-length blue tunic done right up to his chin despite the evening heat, the big badge flashing on his chest, the midway light reflecting off the visor of his cap positioned just so atop his fat head. Ah, for a world where the flatfoot doesn't make his appearance when you least want him. I would actively campaign for such a world myself, and I suspect I would quickly gain many supporters.

As soon as the guy in the straw boater spotted the cop, he started waving his hands. "Hey! Over here! This son of a bitch is trying to cheat me!"

The cop had the face of a weasel and the suspicious eyes of his kind. "What's going on?"

I tried to look as innocent as I possibly could, an impersonation that in the past I have not proved to be very good at.

"This guy swindled me out of a buck, that's what's going on."

I might as well have been caught red-handed holding up a bank. The cop gave me the up-and-down with those suspicious eyes before inspecting my little sign.

"Right, you're a magic man," he said with a sneer. "You got a permit to be out here on the pier?"

"Didn't know you need a permit," I said.

"The guy got five bucks from me and a couple of other poor suckers," the guy in the straw boater said. "Police should be out here protecting people from this sort of shakedown."

I still had the money in my hand. The cop helped himself to it. "Better let me have that," he said.

"That's my money," I said in an agitated voice.

The cop knew of these things. He immediately saw the desperation on my face, and knew that he was about to win this nothing encounter, and I was going to lose, as guys like myself always lose. He touched at the shiny peak of his official cap. "You want to spend the night in jail, pal, open your mouth one more time."

And, of course, I did not want to spend the night in jail and therefore I kept my big yap shut. I longed to brain the bastard, let them both have

it, and there was a day when I would have done just that. But that was
another day, not today at all. Today, I kept quiet and contented myself
with a suitably sullen look.

The cop had seen lots of sullen young fellows like myself, and could
not have cared less. He handed the money over to the guy in the straw
boater. "Shouldn't allow shysters like this out here, shaking down decent folks," the man in the straw boater snarled.

The cop was looking at me in a different manner, seeing that something had happened to my face. "What's the matter with you, pal? It's
like all of a sudden you're not here."

The bitter taste of almonds filled my mouth. The air went out of me
and I found myself down on one knee, holding my stomach, trying to get
my breath back, a pain so deep and abiding that it took on a life of its
own, as though it were happening to someone else. I rolled onto my side,
going into a convulsion so intense my soul floated away from my body, at
least that's how it felt. I peered down at myself twitching away and mar-
veled at my dad's vengeful brilliance, the endlessly slow way in which he
had decided to kill me. The cop bent over me and the shine of the brass
buttons of his uniform seemed blinding. From a distance I heard him
say, "You all right there, fella?"

"He's faking it." The guy in the straw boater was tensed forward so
that his belly folded out over his waist, hanging between those suspenders like a beach ball. His girlfriend held her hands carefully on
either side of her face, so as to seem shocked without disturbing her
makeup.

The cop's sympathy was short-lived. He only had so much to give out
each night, and he was unwilling to waste much of it on me. He said,
"On your feet. Hear me? On your feet!"

I reentered my body in time to be jerked upright. The almond taste
melted away and the spasms began to subside. I felt tired and confused,
not sure where I was. But here was the cop to remind me. He was tough,
this cop, particularly when it came to handling the poor and the sick.
"Get off the pier. I don't want to see you here again, understand?"

He shoved me and I staggered away. I saw the old gent and his wife, curiously fragile now, as though they might break apart right there on the pier. They quickly turned their backs.

Then, unexpectedly, the almond taste returned. I clung to the railing as I went into another convulsion, gritting my teeth, no choice but to ride it out, lamenting my misfortune at having ever been born. My father's curse was inside me. The attacks would only grow worse. I was a dead man.

Chapter Two

The next thing you'll be wondering is, what does this curious lad Brae Orrack look like? After all, I'm about to embark on an adventure with him, so best be clear on his physical dimensions in case I should spot him on the way home or something. Well, here's all you have to know. All you have to know is that at the ripe old age of twenty-six, Brae Orrack is the most devilishly handsome creature you are ever likely to come across. Women take one look at my perfect physical beauty and they become transfixed. Why, it's all I can do to walk down a street without hordes of young beauties charging after me, anxious to feast upon my lithe, sculpted body.

If you believe that, you might also believe I turn stones to bees. Ah, but you say, I just saw you turn a stone to a bee. Well, you did indeed. Or did you? You can't be too sure about me, can you? Where my truth ends and a little fable-telling starts. That's all right. I prefer to keep you off-balance just a wee bit.

Fact is, despite my best efforts to see otherwise when I stare into the mirror, I'm big and awkward, a bit of a lumbering soul, and fearsome some would say. I see myself more as a gentle lad, but a lad who doesn't care to be pushed too far, and not always entirely responsible for his behavior when he is. I'm sorry if I scare you, don't mean to do it, maybe it's that damned scar scrawled across my chin and wandering along my neck, a souvenir of an unpleasant encounter I'd just as soon not talk about; or the way my eyes can go dark when the funeral plumes get the better of the bridal roses. Certainly, it wouldn't be my hands, them being long, delicate things, graceful you might say, the most elegant part of me. The hands of a piano teacher, my mom used to say. Or of a magic man, added my dad.

The sign that spelled out Venice in bright lights was strung across the intersection at Windward Avenue and Pacific. Feeling as lonely and miserable as I could remember since arriving in Cinemaland, I stood beneath the lights for a while and began to feel better. I can't explain what caused this. Could have been the electric energy, I suppose. That's what you want to believe, isn't it? That there is a rational explanation for everything in the oh-so-modern world of 1928? Well, you go right on with the believing, even if I might care to argue the point and say that maybe things aren't always so rational, no matter how hard you want them to be.

I felt stronger now and so I left the Venice sign behind and walked farther along Windward, still not able to shake off my depression. The Venice lights could do a number of things for me, but I had long since discovered they could not cure loneliness. I was beginning to wonder if anything could.

I crossed one of the footbridges and made my way past the Antler Hotel, heading toward the pink boardinghouse. From across the lagoon came the happy screams of roller-coaster and Dragon Bamboo Slide riders, folks without a care in the world. I longed to be one of them, but I was cursed and they were not. Curse or no curse, thanks to that cop I was down to my last fifteen cents, and with not a whole lot of prospects for improving the situation.

The boardinghouse where I lived stood along the Cabrillo Canal, or rather it sagged against it, as though tired of being adjacent to the railroad tracks behind the house, and ready to fall into the water. Its paint had long since faded and chipped, and the porch running its length was in need of repair. However, the landlord, Bing Reilly, preferred to drink away the boarders' eight-dollars-and-fifty-cents-a-week rent money at the speak in the basement of the Antler Hotel or over at Menotti's Buffet rather than address the house's woes. Meanwhile, his lovely wife, the redoubtable Peg Reilly, clung to the kitchen, rolling foul-smelling cigarettes and conjuring up new ways to make her meals inedible while she complained about everything, particularly the unreliability of her lodgers.

One of the gondoliers who worked the canals lived at our boarding-house. His name was Lucca, he was from Italy and barely spoke English, miserable away from the real Venice, he said. He dreamed of the day when he could return to the square of St. Mark at sunset, push his gondola across the Grand Canal and once again see the marble palaces and the majestic facades of the churches and museums. This new Venice offered nothing, he said, no culture or literature or civilized discourse, only farm boys in search of roller coasters and freak shows.

A real estate salesman down the hall, Vernon Avery, always chewing away on the peanuts he purchased every day at the pier, advised that the most valuable land in all Los Angeles was to be found along Wilshire Boulevard. The man next door, Eddie Todd, said he was from Lone Pine up in the Sierras. He got himself into rubber: Los Angeles being the second largest rubber manufacturer in the United States, according to him.

Now, Meyer Rubin was an interesting gent. He never said anything about where he was from, and he looked like a bookkeeper with that crafty face and his bald head. In actual fact, Meyer was a bootlegger selling booze out of a suitcase. According to him, a car trunkload of commercial alcohol could make one-hundred-and-twenty-thousand quarts of bourbon or eighty-thousand quarts of scotch. These could be sold for ten dollars a quart so that a smart-thinking entrepreneur could make anywhere from eight hundred thousand to more than a million dollars. Meyer hinted broadly that he happened to be one of those smart entrepreneurs, although being a bootlegger sure wasn't getting any easier. The city was supposed to be as dry as a bone, and there wasn't a decent saloon between here and the Mexican border. Yet somehow, according to Meyer, eleven thousand people last year were arrested for drunkenness.

He had competition from everyone. Why deliverymen sold booze, and so did taxi drivers and newspaper boys, anyone who moved carried a suitcase or a sample case or even a trunkful of liquor bottles. The pressure of all that competition caused Meyer to drink a lot more of the product than he should have. Many nights I'd come home and find him passed out on the couch.

As for me, well, I was the poor bugger who went off to the pier every day in the badly fitting tux with my little sign to hoodwink the locals. They put me down as harmless and good-natured, even if I did claim to turn stones into bees. Maybe I could and maybe I couldn't, but it certainly wasn't making me rich, and as rent day approached they could see the tension as I worked to come up with enough money to keep old Bing Reilly from giving me the heave.

As I came around the waterside of the garage adjacent to the house, Lily Parker came down off the porch in a light dress fitted to her lush curves. Now I guess I forgot to mention Lily, didn't I? Well, I can get to her right now, since there she is standing in front of me and kind of hard to avoid. When I first laid eyes on her, I thought that was it, here was what I'd come all this way to find. But the sparks refused to fly, somehow. I didn't understand this curious love business at all. I would look at Lily and appreciate her, and we could talk endlessly, but there was nothing beyond that. Very odd how it works, and how you can't make something true that just isn't. She was a singer and dancer from Charleston, South Carolina. So far she had managed to play dance hall girls in a couple of Universal two-reelers. To while away the hours before stardom arrived, she worked as a ticket taker over at the Some Kick roller coaster, worked unhappily, beginning to realize she might not be the next Clara Bow. I couldn't understand this moving-picture business, and what drove all these people, Lily included, to want to be a part of it, but I liked her nonetheless. When I was broke, she often as not staked me to a piece of apple pie and a cup of black coffee. I loved the American-style apple pie, and Lily got a kick out of watching me devour a slice. I do believe I amused her, so strange and different was I from any of the other men who came nosing around.

"You scared me, Brae," she said.

"Did I scare you, Lily? I didn't mean to."

"Coming out of the dark like that." She had a curious little voice, a kind of breathless rasp that she seemed to have to exert a great deal of force in order to push out.

"Did you hear the news? Joan Crawford's engaged to be married to Doug Fairbanks, Jr."

"It's not possible," I said. "If Joan was going to marry, I'm sure she'd call me first."

"It was in the paper today. Doug says he's the happiest person in the world."

"Funny, I was just wondering who the happiest person in the world was. All this time it was Doug Fairbanks, Jr. He managed to keep that pretty well hidden, I must say."

She took my arm. "What kind of a night did you have?"

"Bad," I said glumly. "A cop threw me off the pier."

"Did you make anything?"

"It'll be all right."

"How can it be all right?"

"Somehow," was all I could think of to say.

A black-painted gondola, its iron prow riding high, bounced against the side of the canal, moored there for the night by Lucca, who could no longer tolerate the lowbrow inclinations of the American Venice. Lily stood beside the canal, a lovely vision by the light of a crescent moon. *Ah, Lily,* I thought to myself, *why can't I fall in love with you?* It would all be so simple if I could just fall in love.

"Tell you what. Let's see if we can get rid of that hangdog expression. Why don't I treat us to a cup of coffee over at the diner?"

"Lily, I can't always be taking things from you."

"You can take me over in Lucca's boat. He won't mind."

"He won't mind as long as he doesn't know."

"My generosity might even extend to a piece of apple pie."

"For that I would even steal Lucca's boat."

She lowered herself into the gondola, holding my hand. I untied the lines and climbed in. A canoe paddle was fixed beneath one of the seats. I pushed off, using the paddle to keep the gondola in the shadow of the canal. The craft leaned at an odd angle in the water because, according to Lucca, they were funny about things in Italy and so built their gondolas with the left side bigger than the right.

We headed north, away from the boardinghouse, the gondola moving forward with surprising swiftness. Behind me a porch lamp flared on. A ground-floor window blazed with light. The breeze carried voices that rose in—exasperation, anger? At this distance it was hard to say. *We are invisible,* I told myself. No one could see us.

We were half a mile from the boardinghouse, fleeing the world, I liked to think, always fleeing the world, but for what? Ah, that was the question, wasn't it? The one I could not answer. Not much time left for the fleeing, though—or the answering.

Dark shapes of pastel bungalows and wood shacks rose above us. Lily crouched on one of the seats. Presently, she sat up straight, and a few seconds later turned so that she faced me, wiping away tears. "Sorry."

"No matter," I said.

"I get so depressed out here sometimes."

"It's supposed to be paradise."

"Well, they do try to trick it up like that, don't they? Right down to the moonlight gondola rides. But it isn't, it isn't really paradise at all. You're new here, and you're slightly naïve if you don't mind my saying."

"Don't mind at all. Whatever it is, it's better than I've seen, so for the moment I'm satisfied with that."

She laughed and shook her head. "You and your magic. Do the rubes really buy it?"

"They do when they see me turn the stones to bees."

"And do you tell them you'll die if you don't find true love?"

"It's true."

"You're a bit of a confidence man, Brae, you know that? With your magic tricks and stories about curses. All that sleight-of-hand stuff. You bear close watching."

"Why, there's not a dishonest bone in my body."

"Don't give me that. You're a man and men are constructed of dishonest bones." She issued a sigh. "Well, I guess I know one thing."

"What's that?"

"I'm not your true love, otherwise you'd be just fine, wouldn't you?"

"Lily, Lily, you don't take me seriously at all."

I turned easily into Venus Canal, lights from a truck on Washington Boulevard briefly illuminating us. Above Washington, a red trolley car headed east along the electric railway line. We slipped under a footbridge, and the diner came into view. You could hardly miss the place, it being shaped like a gigantic hot dog outlined in lights, complete with a wavy yellow line to mark where the great hand of God must have applied the mustard that made the hot dog smile—God becoming a very curious artist indeed once he reached America. The hot dog–shaped diner shone in suspended triumph, hanging like a big nighttime grin between the canal and Washington Boulevard.

Lily laughed suddenly and pointed. "That's it! That's where you find love—straight ahead, south of the moon and east of the big smiling hot dog."

"Lily, I do believe you're making fun of me."

She looked back at me, her face sad. "Those directions are as good as any when it comes to finding your true love, believe me. You stand as good a chance finding it there as anywhere."

Inside the diner, Duke Ellington's "Black and Tan Fantasy" wailed from a radio. A curious ocher light illuminated a waitress waiting on a drunken customer, who was wearing a squashed hat and nodding in time to the music over coffee in a chipped mug.

"Duke Ellington," the drunk announced. "It's like listening to the sound of sin on silk."

The waitress was not impressed. She angrily announced that he had to eat something or get out. The customer gave her a vague smirk, as if he knew a lot more than she about Duke Ellington and sin on silk.

"Duke makes the sin exotic and humid," the drunk continued. "It's like you went down into some place you never should ever have gone into, and all the women are naked and available, and the possibilities are endless."

"Shut up or get out!" snarled the waitress. Sin was not so exotic, the possibilities more finite late at night beneath a big smiling hot dog sign. "Black and Tan" ended and was replaced by Helen Kane singing "I Wanna Be Loved by You." Unfortunately, the drunk knew one or two of the lyrics and wanted us to know he knew. The waitress scowled some more. The drunk was not deterred.

I sat across from Lily in a booth away from the big windows overlooking the canal, and ordered coffee black for the two of us. "And how about some of that apple pie," I said in my cheerful American voice.

"What apple pie?" The waitress seemed insulted by the notion of apple pie.

"You don't have apple pie?"

"We got a bad drunk singing. But we got no pie."

"Then the coffee will be fine."

The waitress made a face and drifted away as though borne along by the tide. Lily heaved a sigh. "Funny."

"Not funny at all," I said sadly. "I was lured here for apple pie, and now there's none."

"I was just thinking about something I read in a fan magazine back in Charleston. 'So all your friends say you're a natural weeper and should be in the movies. They use glycerin out here when they're stuck for tears, so I wouldn't leave home if I were you.' I should have paid attention, I suppose. But, of course, you never do."

"You've done all right for yourself—better than me."

She shook her head. "No, and I have to be honest about this. I'm not going to make it."

"Lily, don't say that."

"It's true. For a moment there, I thought it might happen, but it's not going to. And here I did everything you're supposed to, played by all the silly rules you think you have to obey in order to become a Hollywood starlet."

"What kind of rules?"

"You must be five feet to five feet eight inches tall. You must not be any more than one hundred and thirty pounds. You must not cut your hair or change its color without the studio's permission. You must take lessons— riding, sewing, dancing, and social etiquette. You must not smoke or chew gum in public places. Must not stay out late in public places. Must possess one long dress, one sports outfit, a formal dress, and a pair of dance shoes. Did it all, Orrack. I've been the perfect little starlet."

"Maybe we both got handed a load of bull," I said. "Me arriving here expecting to find true love on every street corner."

"Like I said, straight ahead, east of the moon and south of the big smiling hot dog. That's where you'll find it."

"Lily, you must believe me, it's not lies I'm telling you. I wish they were. I am indeed cursed."

"So are we all, Brae. So are we all."

"You just ask my cousin Megan. She knows of curses and things, her being a *buidseach,* and all."

"A what?"

"A *buidseach*—a word that means witch where I come from."

"Your cousin is a witch? Well, I have a brother who is a little bastard."

"I'm serious here, Lily. Megan is known as *Gorm-shuil* or blue eye because she has one black eye and one blue."

"And that makes her a witch?"

"No, no. Folks know she's a witch because the smoke from a witch's cottage always blows against the wind."

"Of course. For a moment there, I forgot."

"Now Megan's a white witch, you understand, an honest sorcerer who only tries to do good, not one of the black witches up to nothing but mischief, rising storms, drowning people, taking the milk from cattle and such."

"You haven't heard? The black witches all moved to Hollywood and are running the studios."

"It's Megan who told me about this place."

"You didn't know about Hollywood?"

I didn't need a lot of prying into what I did or, more embarrassingly, did not know about things, so I ignored the question. "She said this was the place where I could shake off the curse."

"She told you to come here?"

"She did indeed."

"Her sense of direction seems a little questionable, you ask me."

"She had all these movie magazines, full of stories about people falling in love."

"Just stories, Brae. They make that stuff up. That's why they call it make-believe. They make you believe things that aren't true."

"But that's all the movies are about. People in love." There was that sense of longing in my voice again. I had to do something about it, big strapping fellow like myself sounding all winsome and lonely.

"That's the movies, don't you see? More of the making-believe. Why everyone goes. Not because it's real but because it's a dream where everyone lives happily ever after. But it doesn't happen, not in real life, anyway. And certainly not in the real life around these parts. Not as far as I can see."

Now I was properly embarrassed. Here I was in search of love in a town that made moving pictures wherein everyone fell in love, but did not believe in it—and actually made fun of anyone who did.

The waitress put two coffee cups down in front of us. Gertrude Lawrence sang "Someone to Watch Over Me" on the radio. Another love song. Why did they write this nonsense if no one believed it?

At the counter, the drunk did not know the words and occupied himself knocking over a water glass. It crashed to the floor and broke. The waitress yelled at him to get the hell out. The drunk gave her another vague smile, but didn't move. The woman retreated behind the counter, making faces, deciding whether to call the police. Gertrude Lawrence continued to look for someone to watch over her.

"Better be getting back," Lily said. "My friend Slim Talbot's expecting you tomorrow at eleven sharp."

"I still don't know about this."

"Like I said before, rent's due and you didn't make a cent today plying your magic trade."

"I'll talk to Reilly," I said.

"Talk till you're blue in the face. Bing Reilly will still toss you out, and that witch of a wife of his will give him a hand. You won't have a place to stay. Keep an open mind about things, Brae, and don't be stubborn. You may be full of magic where you come from, but here in America you're just plain broke. So listen to what Slim has to say. Will you do that?"

"I'm thinking about it, Lily. I really am. I'm thinking about it."

Gertrude Lawrence stopped singing just as two cops came in carrying nightsticks. I recognized the skinny bugger who tossed me off the pier earlier. The other cop was a big, meaty brute with a neck so thick he couldn't get his collar properly done up, the sort you brought in for the rough stuff. They didn't even glance at us, but instead walked straight over to the drunk. The big meaty fellow used his nightstick to unceremoniously whack the drunk across the head. He collapsed to the floor. The anger rose in me and before I knew it I had started to my feet. The weasel-faced cop turned, his face frozen. "What's your problem, pal?"

"Don't do it, Brae," Lily said quietly. "Stay out of it."

"Did you hear me?" the cop repeated. "What's your problem?"

"No problem," I said to the cop.

His eyes narrowed. "You're the shyster from the pier, right?"

"I'm the honest young gent you lifted five dollars off." I gave him the sort of level look that says you're willing to put up with a certain amount of stuff, but then no more.

The cop got the look and decided not to push things. Instead, he shifted his gaze appreciatively to Lily and said, "Better get him home, if you know what's good for him."

"Oh, I know what's good for him all right," Lily said.

The cops then occupied themselves by dragging the drunk outside. She was right. I had enough trouble without trying to save all the drunks in Los Angeles tonight. Another tune started up on the radio. " 'In a Mist,' " said the waitress. I noticed she had tears in her eyes. "Bix Beiderbecke."

Lily went over, opening her purse and withdrawing a handkerchief. She handed it to the waitress. "Why are you crying?"

"That son of a bitch they just dragged out of here?"

"What about him?"

"I used to be married to the bugger." She angrily dabbed at her eyes with Lily's handkerchief. "He knows everything there is to know about music, but he don't know a thing about staying sober."

Chapter Three

Lt was late by the time we got back, and the pink boardinghouse stood in darkness. I tethered the gondola in its place against the side of the canal. Lily took my hand and led me to the back of the house. She softly hummed "Someone to Watch Over Me."

"We must be very quiet," she said, and I wondered what that meant, since people came and went at all hours of the night, particularly Meyer Rubin, his personal mystery deepened by virtue of the fact that he was a bootlegger. By now, Lily was leading me into the mudroom at the back of the house. She paused to take off her shoes, and I removed mine, and then she took my hand again as we went through the kitchen, which smelled of Mrs. Reilly's awful tobacco and overcooked cabbage, a specialty of the house. Dirty dishes were piled in the sink. A leaky faucet dripped water onto them, making a loud plunking sound. We came out of the kitchen, and the snorts and sighs and grunts of the other boarders in uneasy sleep rose up. It is my opinion that no one ever sleeps well in boardinghouses, the walls are too thin and perfect strangers are too close to one another for their own good. My opinion was nothing but strengthened by the cacophony of low animal-like noises filling the air.

Lily had my hand again. From the parlor came loud smacking and snorting sounds. I peered in and there, laid out on the sofa, was Meyer

Rubin, fully dressed, his hands folded over his chest like he was a corpse comfortable in his coffin. He snorted a second time, a demonstration of life, if nothing else. "Sampling the product again," Lily whispered into my ear. Meyer did a lot of that product sampling.

We moved together up the staircase. Every step seemed to have its own unique creaking sound, all the creaks sharing one thing in common: their loudness. The more we tried to move quietly, the more noise we made. Finally on the upper floor, its scuffed hardwood a dull gleam in the light from the window above the landing, Lily stopped, and I could see her sweet profile in the darkness. She appeared to be trying to decide something.

"Come along," she said finally.

"Where are we going?"

"South of the moon and east of the big smiling hot dog," she said, drawing me into my room and closing the door.

Moonlight streamed through the single window, outlining the miserable iron bedstead with which the generous Reillys provided their guests, and the flowered wallpaper done in tiny blue roses, the roses fading like everything else in this house. Jesus hanging upon his cross stared balefully at us. Depending upon my mood, I could read the expression on the Nazarene's face in any of a number of ways. Tonight he looked vaguely shocked, his eyes bulging slightly, unblinking, not wanting to miss a moment of the drama currently unfolding before him. Lily faced me and in the darkness, leaned forward and kissed me on the lips. Should I tell you that was the first time in my twenty-some years of life on Earth that I had been kissed? Would you believe that? Would you believe I had to travel all the way to Cinemaland in order to find a kiss? Kisses weren't in abundance around the place I come from, I must tell you, most girls not being much interested in kissing an outcast lout such as myself. But then that's why I was here, wasn't it, not for the movies or the sunshine or even the peculiar brand of magic. No, I was here for this, the warmth of skin upon skin, the moisture of lips as they touched yours, all the things Megan intimated might be found in this place, and now here they were, in the person of Lily Parker from Charleston. Why had it taken me so long to make this journey? The question rose dimly in the back of my mind. No time for answers now. No time for anything but the wondrous kissing.

"There, you see, that's magic. Better than turning stones into bees any day, don't you think?"

"Yes," I agreed, trying to keep the excitement out of my voice. I kissed her eagerly again. She put her arms around me, and drew me even closer, and we kissed for a long time, until we both grew breathless, and she began to unbutton my shirt.

"What are you doing?" I managed to ask.

"More magic," she said, as she helped me off with my shirt and pushed me gently back onto the bed. We kissed some more and she ran her hands over me. I must confess to some confusion at this point. If I did not love Lily, surely I shouldn't be doing this with her. But I wanted to do it so badly, every fiber in my being strained for the touch of her, and she was being very accommodating, touching me all over in that particular way she had, and me trying to touch her right back.

She lifted my shirt away so that my torso was naked in the moonlight, and she moved her hand along my rib cage. Her fingers drifted to other places as she kissed me again. I pulled away. "What's wrong?" she asked.

"I think the world of you, truly I do, but I must be honest and say that it's not love I'm feeling. I'm not sure what love is supposed to feel like, but I doubt this is it."

"Brae, you don't have to love me. At least not after tonight. Tonight's tonight. Let the rest take care of itself."

"But I'm wondering if I should wait until I find my true love."

"Then being able to turn stones to bees won't be much help," she said. "Now what I'm going to show you is very important. It's about how a woman wants to be loved, the things you must know."

I confess I had not considered how to love, just the challenge of finding it. The fact that there was unmapped territory beyond the mere finding filled me with confusion. "But do all women want the same thing?"

She laughed again. "I'm sorry, it's just that I've never encountered anyone quite like you. Believe me, what I'm about to show you will work with just about anyone."

"You're sure of this?"

"Let me show you," she said.

And she did. Valuable lessons; where to move and how; when to use the mouth and employ the hands; mysteries of touch and sense explained; patience and endurance put to good use; lessons of the heart and of the head that can so easily elude you unless you happen upon the right night and the giving woman who spreads herself so unselfishly and envelops you with knowledge you can carry across a lifetime.

Later, she began to weep softly, and I held her in my arms and asked her what was wrong. She said everything was fine, just fine. *Then why is she crying?* I wondered.

"Be quiet and listen. You don't know anything about women. Do the things you just did and you won't need any other magic."

"But why aren't we in love, Lily? When it's so wonderful as this, why aren't we in love?"

"Who can say about these things, Brae? Things are just the way they are and there's no getting around them. We're not in love. I'm not a movie star. Life's not fair. But right now we're here together in the darkness, and everything else is a long way off. Now come here, my lovely magic man, there's something else you should know, and we have time so I'm going to show you."

And she would have done just that, I have no doubt in the world— except at that moment I saw the Serpent stone, and the air went out of everything. "What's wrong?" she said.

Why had I not seen it earlier? Wasn't paying attention, of course. But there it was, hanging from a silver chain draped over the bedpost as neat as you please. I pulled away from Lily and reached over to retrieve it. The stone was about the size of a rifle bullet, a hole through it from end to end, indented along the sides, brilliant color streaks swirling about its surface. Unusual, you might say.

"What is it?" she asked.

How was I going to explain it to her? And what would I say about how it got there? "It's nothing," I said, allowing the stone to drop to the floor.

"You look suddenly very pale, Brae."

"The exertions of the unlikeliest and most wonderful evening of a young man's life," I said, pasting on my best smile. "Now there was something you were going to show me, was there not?"

There was indeed. She almost made me forget about the stone.

Almost.

I lay beside her later, thinking, *there is only one person in the world who could have placed the Serpent Stone in my room.*

My father.

Somehow he had found out where I was and he had come to make sure the curse did its job and put an end to me.

And yet it was not possible. My father could not be here and thus could not have put the stone in my room.

You see, my father was dead.

Chapter Four

The crowds had packed away the bathing suits, the picnic lunches, and the laughter, and emptied out Venice. The pier was like a big complicated play toy left unattended at the edge of the Pacific. Seagulls circled the skeletal curves of the Giant Dipper and Bob's roller coasters as I came along Windward Avenue toward the terminal. The Venice sign was just so many unlit lightbulbs this morning, beneath which toiled gangs of real estate salesmen intent on enticing customers to settle down under a sun they swore never stopped shining. I dodged past them, making my way to the streetcar stop on Pacific Avenue. A camera on three legs was mounted atop a platform poking out of the Venice Lagoon. A man wearing a homburg and a tweed suit stood upon the platform, his head bent to a young woman in a summer hat, sweater, and jodhpurs. Another man, barefoot, his trousers rolled up to his knees, pointed the camera toward twenty bathing beauties knee-deep in the water, who were trying not to shiver in the morning breeze. The real estate salesmen seemed much more interested in watching the beauties than they did in selling the future of Venice.

I spent the last fifteen cents I had in the world so I could ride into town on one of the crimson streetcars of the Pacific Electric Railway. "The greatest electric railway system in the world," the company boasted. The cars were the pride of the city. Everyone rode on them, delighted to have access to such a unique transit system. Big red cars capable of speeds of up to sixty miles per hour from Santa Monica, near Venice Beach, to downtown Los Angeles in less than twenty minutes.

The Los Angeles of 1928 was still pretty much a village. At night you could fire a cannon straight down Hollywood Boulevard and not hit anything. A lot of folks arriving in dreamland to seek their fortunes, professed to be disappointed at the sleepy nature of the place, not exactly the glamour spot of the world, what with one traffic cop at the corner of Hollywood and Vine to control the rush hour traffic between five and six o'clock each night. But to me, given the dark place from which I hailed, it was plenty magical enough, sun-drenched, the clear desert heat rising to a sky as deep and blue as imagination itself. Mountains rose in the distance so unreal in the bright sunlight, they seemed like cardboard cutouts. On the far side of those mountains lay an unexplored place called the San Fernando Valley. Few people I'd talked to had ever been out there.

The trolley car passed olive groves, and streets lined with eucalyptus trees and royal palms. Oil derricks rose in the distance. Closer to the city, the houses became more elegant with deep wide lawns and pepper trees. An orange grove dominated the corner of Hollywood and Vine, and farther along the boulevard, horseback riders were a common sight since many people kept stables in back of their homes.

Two passengers on the seat ahead of me were deep in conversation. "Can't stand the idea of going all the way downtown on this thing," one man in a bowler hat said. "No choice, though. Car broke down this morning."

The other man, bareheaded, turned to him. "Traffic gets worse every month, what with all the cars."

"I hear they may build a subway."

"Nah, too expensive," said the bareheaded man. "Elevated train, that's the ticket. Trains come downtown, they don't ever touch the ground."

"Don't hold your breath," replied the man in the bowler hat. "My sister works at the new City Hall. She said Harry Chandler, owner of the *Times,* doesn't want elevated trains. Read the *Times,* they're *screaming* against the idea."

"Harry Chandler? What's some goddamn newspaper publisher doing telling the city what to build or not to build?"

"Chandler and a few other people like him got this city by the short and curlies. What they say goes." He lowered his voice. "You know, twenty years ago, Chandler and all those guys got together to control the water coming down from the north. They bought up most of the land out in San Fernando Valley. Made them rich and powerful. That's the truth of it. Better get your car fixed, pal. There aren't going to be any elevated trains in this town."

I got off at Bronson Avenue. By now the trolley was packed with shabbily dressed anxious men and women. They swirled off the streetcar, too, streaming along the street toward the main entrance of the Paramount studio. No one said a word. Only the sound of shuffling feet broke the silence.

At Marathon, my fellow passengers joined hundreds milling in front of Spanish-style gates. A man in shirtsleeves bellowed, "Haven't got a voucher, you don't get paid today." He handed out white pieces of paper and then passed people through the gate. He regarded me coldly when I approached.

"Fella, you're too big."

"I've got an appointment inside," I said.

"Who you going to see?"

"Slim Talbot."

"Sorry, thought you was one of the extras. See the guard over there."

I went to a tiny office just inside the gate and announced myself to the guard, who checked a clipboard before waving me through with a mumbled burst of directions.

Inside, the extras, clutching their vouchers, were being herded across the lot toward a wrought-iron stairway that ran up the side of a two-story building. Others, apparently finished for the day, filed toward the gate, lining up in front of a cashier's window. The cashier passed each man and woman a five-dollar bill, two ones, and a couple of quarters. *I could use that money right now,* I thought, and wondered what these people had to do to get it.

I stopped a kid in a cloth cap. "What's going on?" I asked.

"Got some period drama going, need lots of extras today," he said. "Good day, yes sir. Up there is Makeup and Wardrobe. Better get yourself a voucher, pal. Ain't got no voucher, you ain't going to get paid."

Out the other side of the building tumbled seventeenth-century gentlemen and their hoop-skirted ladies. The shabbily dressed extras were being transformed into rich and prosperous noblemen and women from another time; the poor were playing the rich, at least for a day. Brightly painted and hung with false braids and curls and wigs, they shuffled toward a mustard-colored airplane hangar, heads lowered, as though to the slaughter. Whatever was to happen to them today in the moving-picture business, there didn't appear to be any joy in it.

I turned a corner and found more costumed extras, these in creamy white uniforms with lots of gold braid. They stood in a cluster at the entrance to one of the soundstages, smoking and chattering among themselves. A stagehand, his sleeves rolled up to his elbows, a cigarette dangling from a corner of his mouth, pointed down a narrow street and said Slim Talbot was to be found at the end.

Let me see, we got Pola Negri here, and we got Clara Bow," Slim Talbot said. "Why, Paramount is the most powerful motion-picture corporation in the world."

"Is that a fact?" I tried to sound impressed.

"That is indeed a fact. Mr. Adolph Zukor, who built this place up from nothing, has studios here in Hollywood, and in New York. Why, they even got a studio in Paris, France."

"Why would they have one there?" I asked.

That seemed to stop Slim in his tracks. "Well, you'd have to ask Mr. Zukor about that. But he must know what he's doing, because he also owns the world's largest chain of theaters and a fella owns that many theaters, he ain't no dummy. So if he wants a studio in Paris, France, that's the end of it."

Slim Talbot, an aging elf with a big belly and a walrus mustache, wore a black suit, a white shirt, and a string tie. He also wore the sort of shiny cowboy boots I'd previously only seen in movies, and wire-rimmed glasses that made him look forever surprised. Perhaps that's why he kept removing the glasses, and polishing them with a white linen handkerchief. He occupied a small windowless office smelling of old cigarette smoke. It contained a wooden desk and two straight-back chairs. I sat on one of the chairs in front of the desk, while he sat behind it in the other.

"Tell me, Mr. Talbot, what is it you do around here?"

"I'm the repairman," he said promptly. "When something's broke, I fix it."

"I see."

"I also make sure certain folks know what it is they have to know. So here's another thing you should know, Mr. Orrack: This is basically a workingman's town, okay? Forget all that crap about glamour and riches and orgies and all that."

I must confess I had heard little if anything of orgies, but then I was not the most informed individual who ever came down the road.

"Folks out here, they work for a living, go to bed early, get up early. Very few folks go to orgies at night."

He paused, as though expecting me to comment on the orgy situation. I didn't know what to say, and so I said, "That's good to know."

"Now there's something else," Slim continued. "Lot of folks, rich and poor alike, are plain scared."

"Scared?" That surprised me. "What have they got to be scared about?"

"It's this thing called sound."

"Sound? What do you mean by sound?"

Slim looked exasperated. "The movies are starting to talk, in case you hadn't heard."

I hadn't heard and I wasn't sure what he was getting at. "Talking pictures. Why would anyone be interested in hearing people talk?"

"Your guess is as good as mine. It's a novelty, no doubt about it, and who knows how long it will last. In the meantime, though, people don't know what to make of it, and when folks don't know what to make of something, they tend to get real scared. So right now, until we see how this deal is gonna play out, everyone's a little on edge."

He studied his wire-rimmed glasses as he carefully wiped at the lenses with a handkerchief.

"What brings you out to Southern California, Mr. Orrack?"

"I'm here to find true love," I said.

He looked at me for a long, silent moment, then leaned forward and inspected his glasses yet again to see if they'd changed in the past few seconds. "Well, that's one I ain't heard before. How's the search going?"

"Nothing so far," I said.

"Don't want to do nothing to discourage you, but you may be in the wrong town."

"Lily tells me the same thing," I said. "But I'm a persistent fellow, and an optimist added to the bargain. I don't give up so easily."

"An optimist, huh? Well, there's no shortage of them in these parts, that's for damn sure. Town rides on optimism. It's the electricity that keeps things humming." Talbot readjusted his glasses on the bridge of his nose, as though unsure of what he was seeing across his desk. "Lily uses the word 'impressive' when she talks about you. She likes you a lot."

"Impressive woman herself."

"That she is, Mr. Orrack, that she is." He sat back in his chair. "Unfortunately, like everyone else out here, she wants to be a star of the moving pictures. How about you, Mr. Orrack, got any ambitions along those lines?"

"I told you why I'm here," I said.

"Indeed you did, and I admire your honesty. You're kind of a tough-looking hombre, and that's certainly what I'm looking for. Mind if I ask you about that scar?"

"A disagreement that got out of hand," I said. *No need to go into the miserable details,* I thought to myself.

"So you're a man accustomed to a tight spot now and then."

"Now and then," I said agreeably.

"Okay, so maybe you fit the bill for what I've got in mind."

"And what is it you have in mind, Mr. Talbot?"

"Keeping a young fella's ass out of trouble. Think you can handle something like that?"

"It's a possibility, right enough."

"See, another thing you should know about this town, Mr. Orrack, it's full of con men and grifters and charlatans—only they don't call 'em those things. This is a place where no one wants to be what he is. You come here to be someone else. Lot of folks are running away from things, arriving out here to start over fresh and forget what it was they left. The town's ready-made for that. So this fella I'm talking about, young fella, he's a bit of a con man like the rest, and he's got good looks to boot. His name's Cooper, comes from my neck of the woods, in Montana. He was known as Frank back there. But as I said, you don't come out here to keep being what you were, so now he calls himself Gary."

"Gary Cooper?" I said.

"You know him?"

"Never heard of him. Why did he change his name?"

"They do that out here. They change your name."

"No one's changed my name."

"Stick around." Slim Talbot leaned back in his chair. "No reason you should know Coop by any name. He was doing some stunt riding for me, and then someone decided he might look good closer to the camera; crazy idea you ask me, but then I've discovered one of the problems out here is that no one tends to ask me much of anything.

"Anyway, I like Coop okay. He's a little wild and impulsive, a country boy masquerading as this urban gigolo character, not an impersonation he's very good at, you ask me. He's a little too caught up with being seen with the right starlet, but there isn't a cowboy collecting eight dollars a day falling off horses out there in the Valley wouldn't trade places with him."

"What's any of this got to do with me?" I asked.

Slim Talbot studied his glasses again. "Big as this place is, and as important, it's had its fair share of trouble. There was that whole Fatty

Arbuckle thing a few years back that gave everyone a black eye. Then one of the directors on the lot got himself murdered under mysterious circumstances. Had another young fellow who turned out to be a drug addict—Wallace Reid, supposed to be our all-American boy. The sumbitch was hooked on cocaine."

"This Cooper's on drugs?"

"Nah. Nothing as simple as that. Coop's problem is women. He can't keep his hands off 'em."

"Why would Paramount care about that?"

The question did not please the repairman at all. "Ain't you listening? No one wants any more scandals around here, particularly if they're started up by a young no-account probably ain't gonna amount to anything, anyway."

"All right," I said, attempting to show the right amount of deference.

That seemed to settle Slim somewhat. "Coop's got a part in a new Colleen Moore picture, something called *Lilac Time*."

"Never heard of it."

Slim shrugged. "I hear it ain't much, but the studio wants to make sure young Cooper keeps his nose clean until the picture's opened. There's a kid here at the studio, rat-faced little German, but a nice guy. Name's Georgie Raft. From New York. Well, you know, you come from New York, and you know guys in the mob. They say if Owney Madden was short a man to ride shotgun on one of his beer trucks, well, Georgie was always available."

Who was Owney Madden? What did Georgie Raft matter to what we were talking about? None of these names meant anything to me.

"This is headed somewhere, I suppose," I said impatiently.

"Georgie was around the other day whispering in my ear. Apparently Coop's got himself mixed up with a fox named Lane Farrell. She likes to get into trouble with men. Unfortunately, she's also married to Al Howard, owner of the *Johanna Smith* and he doesn't like her hobby one bit. Coop came shambling along and Lane decided she could fit him into her lineup. You can imagine what her husband thought about that."

"What's the *Johanna Smith*?"

"Brother, you are new in town, aren't you? It's a gambling ship been causing all sorts of fuss around these parts. It's moored outside the twelve-mile limit, so the cops can't get at it. Lane spends a lot of time and money out there. Apparently, she couldn't keep her mouth shut about Coop. Al Howard didn't like the idea of sharing, and when Al doesn't like something, he can get pretty mean. He's put the word out that Coop's about to have his pretty face rearranged."

"What is it exactly you want me to do?"

"Drive Coop around. Make sure he hangs on to his face—and stays out of the kind of trouble that could upset Paramount. At least until the picture opens. After that, they're gonna get rid of the boy so he won't be our problem anymore. But for now, well, you think you can handle something like this?"

"I suppose I could."

Talbot leaned forward again, sweeping the glasses up from the table, poking them up on the bridge of his nose. "I'll pay you fifty dollars for working tonight, and maybe tomorrow if he still needs a driver. That's more than these cowpokes over at Gower Gulch bring down, only you don't suffer no broken bones for your troubles. You make sure Coop stays out of trouble. Failing that, you get him out of the trouble he strays into. You do it quietly so that it don't get into the papers. How about it, we got a deal?"

My stomach was beginning to hurt again. And I realized that I had absolutely no way out of here. I either took what Slim Talbot was offering or I was finished anyway. I was at the end of my string. I had less than five weeks to break my father's curse, with little or no idea how to do it, and no money.

"I'll need some money in advance," I said.

"Twenty-five dollars now. The rest day after tomorrow. Maybe more if Coop decides he wants to keep you on. How's that?"

Before I could get my mouth open he had peeled off two ten-dollar bills and a fiver and spread the money in front of me. It was more cash than I had ever seen in one place. I scooped the money off the desk.

"Now what?"

He adjusted the glasses one more time, and rose from behind the desk. "We stop off at Wardrobe, get you properly outfitted for the job, then I drive you over and introduce you to the man himself."

He took me down the street and a young woman, earning good-enough money to be smoking factory-made cigarettes, measured me, then went through long racks, and found a smart gray uniform, complete with a cap and gleaming knee-high brown leather boots. I tried it on, and she nodded approval. On the rack was a cowboy outfit, complete with a hol-stered six-gun dangling from it. I stared at the outfit, and then turned to the full-length mirror and studied myself in the chauffeur's uniform.

I did not like what I saw.

Chapter Five

According to the repairman Slim Talbot, this town they called Beverly Hills not so long ago was nothing but fields of lima beans. An oil company leased the land, and when no oil showed up, it was decided to develop the area for real estate. No one paid much attention to the place until those two sweethearts of the screen, Mary Pickford and Douglas Fairbanks, bought fourteen acres on a hilltop and called it Pickfair. Then all the swells and the newly rich movie stars, who didn't have a clue what to do with their money, couldn't wait to move in.

The house Talbot pulled his beat-up Packard in front of was hardly luxurious by the standards of Beverly Hills, a quaint one-story affair, painted white, bounded by hedges, and a white spiked fence.

"Okay, there you go," said Slim.

"You're not coming in?"

"Let's see how you do on your own. Just go on inside. He's expecting you."

"A test, is it?"

"Sure, Mr. Orrack. Put it down to that."

I got out of the car. Talbot leaned over and said, "And Mr. Orrack?"

"What's that, Mr. Talbot?"

"Cheer up. You may even enjoy yourself."

"How do I get back?"

"Pick you up at that corner back there. In about an hour. How's that?"

"Fine," I said.

I waited until he drove off before I went up and knocked on the door. Beyond the boulevard, the magical kingdom that was Beverly Hills glittered through the afternoon haze. From this vantage point, above it all, everything was perfection, not a blade of grass out of place. Curiously, I could hear the sound of a pipe organ coming from one of the adjacent houses. Down the street, a slim Chinese lad in a white jacket wearing white gloves watered the lawn with a garden hose. He swung the hose smoothly back and forth so that the water sprayed the perfect lawn in a perfect geometrical pattern. The Chinese fellow saw me staring at him and he stared back as he continued to water the lawn.

I knocked again. Silence. Except for the strange sound of the pipe organ, and the swish of the garden hose held by the Chinese fellow. I wondered if anyone was home. Then from the inside, the sound of insistent whispers: voices hissing and arguing. Again I knocked, very hard and official this time. That inspired more whispering. I tried the door handle. It swung down, and the door eased open.

I stepped inside and found myself in a narrow wood-beamed sitting room, its stucco walls decorated with animal heads: a couple of antelopes, a lion at full growl, and a glassy-eyed zebra. Silk-shaded lamps flanked two easy chairs positioned near a table and an overstuffed chintz sofa. Beside the sofa, a surprised young woman with the purest white skin I'd ever seen stood, clutching a robe around her. Glossy golden hair with just the hint of red tumbled around the face of a decadent angel.

"Someone's playing organ music up the street," was all I could think of to say.

A tiny cupid's bow of a mouth was open and saying, "I'll bet there's a joke, but it's too early in the morning to talk dirty."

She spoke in a high, slangy drawl, the way the natives of that borough of New York that is called Brooklyn tend to speak, a surprising voice that somehow did not suit her.

"You're not his mother," she said.

I shook my head. "No, I'm not."

She turned and called, "Coop, it ain't your mother."

She stared past me out onto the street to verify that a mother did not lurk behind a tree. "Big brave cowboy, he's afraid his mother is going to find him in bed with a bad woman." She called, "Coop, come out here, you big lug."

"Clara, don't call me a lug!" an angry voice came back.

"There's a guy here. He's big and he's wearing a uniform. What should I make of that, Coop?"

I looked at her incredulously. Her black eyes—the most arresting black eyes, I should say—danced flirtatiously. "I'm Clara Bow," she said.

Now I'd been long enough in Hollywood to come to know that in this land of dreams, certain people inspired more dreaming than others. Those that did the inspiring were deemed to have been summoned from the heavens, like the stars, and therefore were known as moving-picture stars. Clara Bow was one of these stars. Maybe Colleen Moore was bigger at that moment, but she was pretty much Clara's only competition. I'd seen her in a couple of pictures, and, like most men, I thought she was it, which is I suppose why they tended to call her the "It" girl. I guess it is the polite word you would use to describe her. Me being a polite fellow, and not wanting to rile anyone, that's the word I'll stick with. Other gents undoubtedly would use rougher language where Clara was concerned, and she might even appreciate it.

"Orrack, ma'am. Brae Robert Orrack. I just saw you in *The Fleet's In*."

"Did you now?"

"One of your best pictures ever, I would say."

"Well, in that case, you should say it often. I'm impressed, Mr. Orrack, and it's not often I'm impressed by anything coming out of a man's mouth this early in the day." She shook my hand. "Why do you keep looking at me like that?"

"I guess I'm trying to figure if I'm in love with you."

That assertion did not seem to phase her one bit. "Of course, you are." She grinned. "Are" came out *ahr*. "Don't even think about it. I start to get twitchy if at least one man a day don't confess he loves me."

Frank Cooper sauntered into view, a black silk robe loosely tied over his slim nakedness. He said, "There are one hundred thousand miles of paved roads in America, did you know that?"

He paused and looked around, as though seeking verification of this fascinating observation. When none was forthcoming, he frowned, trained his gaze on me, and said, "Who the hell are you?"

"His name's Brae Orrack," Clara volunteered. "He's not sure whether he's in love with me."

"That's the one thing I don't like about you, Clara. Too many uniformed fellas show up at the door announcing they love you."

"Makes me want to find you a uniform, Coop."

I took a good look at him and no doubt about it, he was a grand-looking man, the kind of fellow you might choose to look like if you had any say over such things; tall and lanky with glistening jet-black hair, possessed of a long thin face, beautiful in its way, with smoothly chiseled hollows beneath the cheekbones. The face had petulance to it, as though on the verge of hearing it could not have its way and not liking it. But that was a tiny flaw, quickly forgiven. Overall, you'd look at him and wish the gods had been kinder to you. But the gods had not been kind, and now looking at him you knew for certain what bastards they could be.

He threw himself into one of the easy chairs, and reached for a cigarette from an engraved silver box on an end table. He tapped its end against the box, then inserted it in his mouth, and glanced at me.

"Wouldn't happen to have a match, partner?"

"Sorry," I said.

"A chauffeur without a match." He glanced sharply at Clara, as though somehow she was responsible for this.

"That's as good a place as any for me to make my exit," she said. "You boys play nicely now."

As soon as she was gone from view, Coop leaped from the chair, disappeared for a few seconds, and then reappeared with the cigarette lit. He plopped himself back into the chair, drawing heavily on the cigarette. "How come Slim didn't come in with you?"

I shook my head. "No idea."

"Slim handles these situations for me." His voice was low and lazy, as though it didn't have a care in the world. I envied him that voice. I envied him being him. He was young and beautiful, and he didn't have to worry about rent money or the streetcar fare back to Venice, demons that sprang out of the darkness as soon as you closed your eyes, or wild curses, and Black Death, or much of anything else. He would be driven through life, he would not have to do the driving. I would do the driving. He would sit in the back, comfortable as can be.

"Got to be honest with you." He frowned. "I don't know much about chauffeurs or what to do with them."

"I think how it works is this way: I drive, you ride in the back. Anyone waves at you from the street, you smile and wave back."

"A chauffeur who don't have a match, and don't know anything about being a chauffeur. Tell you what, partner. I don't think I like you."

"Sometimes I inspire that emotion in people, no question. But usually they're horses' asses so I don't worry about it too much."

Cooper put his cigarette down, and said, "Well, partner, that's all they wrote for you."

"I'm sorry?" I said.

"Thanks for dropping by, but I don't think I'm going to be needing your services."

"You didn't think for a moment I was referring to you, did you?"

"So you can let yourself out the door there."

I started out as Clara Bow floated back into the room. Her hair looked soft and fluffy, like a baby's, and her small white body was clad in a trim navy-blue sport suit with splashes of red that matched her red socks.

"Where are you going Mr. Orrack? The party over already?" "Party" came out *pah-tee.*

"I believe I have just been fired," I said.

She stared in disbelief. "For what?"

"He's disrespectful," Coop said.

"I'm glad my mother can't hear you saying that. She raised me to deeply respect those that deserve respect—and to cast a wary eye in the direction of those who don't."

Coop squinted at me through his cigarette smoke.

The telephone on a nearby end table rang. Coop grabbed at the receiver. "Oh, Mother."

He showed us his back. Clara rolled her eyes. "Alice can *smell* it when he's got a woman over here."

"Uh, look, Mother, it's difficult to talk at this particular moment. Well, because I'm interviewing the new chauffeur." Pause. "Right at this moment, I don't have a chauffeur."

Clara Bow insinuated herself between me and the door, those black eyes trained on me, more arresting than ever. "He's a spoiled brat, I'm afraid."

"Yeah, but you know, Mother, it is Colleen's picture, so a lot of the attention's going to be on her," Coop was saying, "I'm kind of just along for the ride."

"A louse, no doubt about it," she added. "The trick is, Brae, not to take him too seriously."

"Is that what you do?"

"My problem is I take him too seriously." She added with surprising solemnity, "Don't you go making the same mistake."

"Well, I don't know what I'm going to do about getting to the theater," Coop was saying. "I just don't happen to like . . . well, yes, Mother . . . no, ma'am, I don't want to look like a fool driving myself to the premiere. . . ."

I went past Clara and out the door. Now I'd be dishonest if I said I wasn't worried about this turn of events. But then that's my problem in a nutshell, you understand. I am not capable of making the most rational judgment about things. I rile people, then get angry and storm away, and I should not do that. *Well,* I told myself as I reached the gate, *at least I've got enough to pay the rent*—that is if Slim Talbot didn't demand his money back, seeing as how I got myself fired within five minutes of meeting Gary Cooper.

Clara Bow called, "Hey, Mr. Orrack!"

I can't tell you how relieved I felt at that moment. However, I tried not to show any emotion as I turned and said, "What is it?"

"Come back here a minute, will you?"

Clara being a hard woman to say no to under any circumstances, I went back up the walk.

"He—he's real s-s-s-scared right now, okay?" The black eyes gave me an imploring look. I realized suddenly that she was anxious, and that anxiousness was making her stammer. "He—he's heard that the movie's a disaster and that Paramount is thinking of dropping him. He's not t-t-t-taking any of it real great, so you gotta be a little patient with him, Mr. Orrack. P-p-p-patient with all of us right now."

"Okay," I said.

"So come on back inside, will you?"

I allowed her to lead me back into the house. Coop was off the phone and once again pacing. He had lit another cigarette. He didn't look at me.

"What are you doing here?" he demanded.

"I a-a-asked him to come back," Clara said.

"Well, you shouldn't have done a fool thing like that."

"I—I wanted Mr. Orrack to have a chance to see you s-s-s-start acting like a mature human being. Something I'm sure you can do if ya put your mind to it."

"I don't even want to go to the damned thing," Coop groaned. "Everyone will be fawning over Colleen Moore, and she'll get all condescending, and treat me like"—he shot a glance at me—"like her damned chauffeur."

"You have to go tonight, baby boy. So just make the best of it. Mr. Orrack is here to help you. Right, Mr. Orrack?"

"Helping the weak and afflicted, what makes my life worthwhile," I said brightly.

Coop made a production of issuing a deep sigh and throwing up his hands. "I guess so."

Clara said, "Better get here early, Mr. Orrack. About six-thirty."

"That's fine."

"As long as you drive the car, and stay out of my way," Coop said.

"My poor mom listed getting in the way among my most grievous shortcomings."

Neither of them said anything. Coop sucked on his cigarette, the

smoke floating around that beautiful head. Clara Bow looked visibly relieved, and that surprised me. Here was this big Hollywood movie goddess, nervous and anxious on a sunny morning.

Made me think that maybe Slim Talbot was right, everything wasn't
so perfect in paradise after all.

Chapter Six

I felt a combination of anger and relief as I walked down to the corner where Slim Talbot said he would meet me. The arrogant bastard named Gary Cooper riled me, no question, even if he was scared for his future. Well, I was scared for mine, too. He was going to be out of work; I, on the other hand, was soon to be dead. I hated to admit it, but I needed this. There was nothing else on my horizon. Driving around a spoiled young movie star was better than nothing.

I waited around for a half hour before Slim came along. He leaned over and opened the door and I got in beside him.

"How did it go?"

"Well enough, I suppose."

"What's that supposed to mean?"

"It means I'm driving him tonight."

"Good enough," he said. "Two of you get along okay?"

"Like I say, I'm driving him to the theater in my brand-new chauffeur's uniform."

"And mighty handsome you look in it, too, Mr. Orrack." Slim allowed a chuckle. "Well, I do believe Frank's a bit carried away with himself. He'd better enjoy it while it lasts, 'cause he ain't going to be around for long."

"Guess I'm having trouble understanding what it is anyone would see in him."

"That's two of us, Mr. Orrack. Coop's good-looking enough, I suppose. Leastwise the girls seem to think so. But there's lots of good-looking fellas out here. They say the camera just plain loves certain people. They make magic up there on the screen that most others just can't pull off. No explaining it, I guess."

"And you think this Cooper has the magic?" It made my blood boil to even say the words. Magic. I had the magic. What was he doing with it?

"Maybe if the talkies hadn't come along. But now I reckon he's finished."

"Why would talking finish him?"

Slim once again looked impatient. "Because he can't do it. Leastwise, he can't do it proper. Certainly not like one of them Shakespearian stage-trained actors from back East. That's who they want out here now. Guys like Coop, all they can do is look pretty, and that's not gonna be enough."

Slim dropped me off in front of the boardinghouse. "You can get back to Coop's place by six-thirty okay?"

"I'll be there, Mr. Talbot, don't worry."

"Make sure you keep that uniform clean. You want to make a good impression tonight."

I gritted my teeth and said, "I'll make sure I do that, Mr. Talbot."

He drove away and I went into the house. Two of the boarders had staked out space in the grim little parlor dominated by a sepia portrait of the good landlord Bing Reilly and his missus at their wedding. Mrs. Reilly had put on a few pounds since that particular miracle day; so had Mr. Reilly, come to that.

Meyer Rubin flipped the pages of the evening edition of the *Los Angeles Times* from his perch on a sagging easy chair. "How do you like that? Mrs. Amelia Earhart crossed the Atlantic, the first woman ever to do it. Traveling at one hundred and ten miles an hour."

Nearby, Eddie Todd leaned against a scuffed sideboard fidgeting with the brand-new Philco radio landlord Reilly had recently purchased. He was trying to tune in his favorite radio station, KFWB, which had started broadcasting three years ago and was now all the rage. "Damn thing don't work," said Eddie angrily. "Who cares what a woman does anyway?"

"Admiral Byrd says it weren't no stunt as far as he's concerned. He says it was, quote, 'a necessary pioneering effort.' "

"Who cares what Admiral Byrd thinks about anything?"

"Landlord Reilly catches you fooling with his Philco and you'll be flying across the Atlantic," Meyer said with a laugh. He tossed the paper to one side and took a swig from the hip flask he always seemed to have available. "To help ease the pain of life," he said.

"Supposed to be some sort of minstrel show on now," Eddie said as static erupted from the Philco's tiny speaker. "I love the minstrel shows."

"Didn't you hear? They canceled the minstrel shows in honor of Amelia Earhart."

"Bet she didn't even do it," said Eddie. "Bet it's some kind of hoax."

They both looked amused when they saw me. Meyer made his flask disappear and Eddie gave up on the radio.

"Hey, hey, get a load of this character. Looks as though someone brought my car around just in time," chortled Meyer Rubin. "Did you hear about Amelia Earhart, Brae? She got across the Atlantic safely. One hundred and ten miles an hour."

"Glad to hear it," I said.

Eddie Todd said, "You gonna be chauffeuring our friendly landlord this evening, Brae? He's been looking for you. Even if you do drive him, I think he's still gonna want the rent money."

"Add Lucca to the list of people in search of young Brae Orrack," said Meyer Rubin.

"Lucca? What about him?"

"Appears someone took his gondola out for an unauthorized ride last night," said Meyer. "Maybe that's why you got that uniform on, eh, kid?"

"Do we have to catch you as Reilly tosses you out of the house?" asked Eddie Todd.

"Not a chance," I said. "Rent's all taken care of. What's more, I'm off to the moving pictures this evening with the rich and famous."

"Off to bow and scrape at the feet of those bastards is more like it," Eddie said.

I didn't like that, but I grinned easily. The two of them loved to pull your leg, and I suppose it was harmless enough.

"Is Rin Tin Tin gonna be there?" asked Meyer. "He's the only one of them stars I'm interested in meeting. Him and Amelia Earhart. I wouldn't mind slipping it to Amelia, comes to that. I wonder if she might be interested?"

"Least in the rubber business we don't have to take our hats off to no one," Eddie said.

Meyer rolled his eyes. "Yeah, right. The mavericks in the rubber business."

"Hey, it's legal work," mumbled Eddie. "Honest day's pay for an honest day's work. Did you see the paper yesterday? The Treasury Department says it arrested seventy-five thousand people this year alone for trading in illegal booze—fifty-eight thousand convictions."

"Yeah, well, no one's arrested me," Meyer retorted. "I mean, what's the Treasury Department gonna say? Everyone's drinking like a fish and you can make a killing selling booze? Of course not. They tell you how many arrests they made, and how they're defeating crime, but it's all bull."

"You'd better hope so," said Eddie.

Meyer focused on me. "Ah, but what I want to know, young Brae, have you found true love yet?"

I'd made the mistake of telling these two about my ambitions here in Southern California. Being typically cynical and shallow American men, neither of them married or ever likely to be, they'd never let me hear the end of it.

"Curious sounds coming out of his room last night," stated Eddie Todd, relieved that the conversation had now veered away from his status in the rubber business. "True love may well have been found—at least for the night."

I shook my head in feigned exasperation. "Don't know what I'm to do with you lads. Is our landlord around?"

"Bing's at the speak over at Menotti's," said Meyer.

"No way. Only the basement at the Antler Hotel is good enough for Bing these days," Eddie said.

"Guess he don't like my stuff," Meyer said.

"Maybe Bing wants the stuff they serve at the Antler that ain't made in a car radiator and won't kill him after the first swallow."

"Hey, watch that," admonished Meyer good-naturedly. "I provide the workingman with fine Canadian whiskey."

"Right. Canadian whiskey from Long Beach, California."

"That's close to Canada, isn't it?"

"Where's the good missus?" I asked.

"In the kitchen figuring fresh ways to poison us," Meyer said. He pulled out the flask again and took another snort. Eddie shook his head and resumed his fiddling with the Philco.

I found Mrs. Reilly bent over a steaming pot bubbling away on her wood stove. Even shorter than her husband was Peg Reilly, and her vast body was wrapped in a large apron stained with grease and dusted with tobacco. The wild bird's nest atop her head surely was the result of perpetually poking her finger into a light socket. As usual, she had a roll-your-own jammed into her mouth, ashes sprinkling the insides of the pot. I presented her with my friendliest smile. "Did you hear about Amelia Earhart, Mrs. Reilly? She got across the Atlantic okay."

"Guess that means she won't be helping me get this here dinner ready then, will she?"

She stopped stirring to give me the once-over. "What the hell you all dressed up for? Got yourself some honest employment that don't include fleecing the customers on the pier?"

"Indeed I have, Mrs. Reilly." I peeled off a couple of bills and slapped them down on the table in front of her.

Steam from the boiling pot rose up around her. Mrs. Reilly slowly removed the cigarette from her mouth. Men from the moon could have landed and she wouldn't have looked more surprised.

"A woman flies the Atlantic. You got money in your pocket. Two miracles in a single day. Who would ever believe it?" Her eyes narrowed as she studied the money. "This was come by honest, was it?"

"I can't think of another way to come by wages, can you?"

"Afraid I can, Mr. Orrack. Particularly when it's a strange fellow claims to be over at the pier turning rocks into bees."

"Study it as careful as you like, Mrs. Reilly. The money's good. Now if you'll excuse me, I have to speak to Miss Parker."

"Miss Parker ain't here." It pleased her no end to smack me with that piece of news. She celebrated by sticking the roll-your-own back into its perch at the corner of her mouth.

"Oh? I didn't know she was working tonight."

"She's moved." The words were rolled out like freshly turned aces.

I couldn't believe what I was hearing. I'd left Lily in my bed only a few hours ago. "Moved? How could she have moved?"

"Didn't pay the rent, so out she went." The old monster's eyes gleamed with the delight that comes when evil has loads of bad news to disseminate.

"How long ago did she leave?"

"Don't know. Ten or fifteen minutes."

I raced out of the house and onto the street. Mrs. Reilly's high-pitched yowl followed me, "We ain't holding dinner for you!"

Late on a midweek afternoon, the Pacific Electric Railway terminal that served the Venice Beach area was almost deserted, except for Lily. She wore a two-piece summer dress, the skirt printed with small red flowers, and a short jacket of dark blue. A hat was pulled at an angle over her blond hair. She stood with her feet together, hands clasped in front of her, hanging on to her purse, flanked by two small suitcases. She looked like an angel ready to ascend to heaven, properly dressed to travel, of course.

I came racing up, feeling vaguely ridiculous in my shiny chauffeur's uniform, but she only smiled in surprise and said, "Hey, Orrack, don't you look handsome."

"Why didn't you say something?"

"Maybe I was trying to avoid a scene like this. Or maybe I actually listened to myself at the diner last night, and I decided after you left this morning that this isn't the life for me. I gave it a good try, and now it's time to leave."

"Where are you going?"

"Back home to Charleston."

All sorts of emotions churned inside me, not the least of them guilt. "I feel like I'm somehow responsible for this."

She touched my arm. "It's just time, that's all. Let's face it, after you've spent the night with a real live magic man, what else is there out here? Why, a girl might just as well go home."

"Maybe if you stay we could figure out how to fall in love."

"I don't think it's something that you try to figure out, dear Brae. I do believe it's something that just happens. No. Let's leave well enough alone. The streetcar will be along in a moment. It'll take me to Union Station. I've a six o'clock train to Charleston. My dad's going to meet me. He's happy I'm coming home. So's my mom. So am I, when you get down to it."

"I'll go with you to the station."

"You don't have time. Not if you're driving Mr. Gary Cooper to a real live Hollywood premiere this evening."

"It doesn't matter."

"Yes, it does. You need the money so you can keep going. Remember, you're after bigger things, true love, and all that. Also, I gave Slim my word that you'd be okay, so don't let me down, all right?"

"All right," I said.

"And don't get mad at everything," she added. "There's all this stuff rushing around inside your head, Brae, and for the life of me, I'm not sure which parts are real and which parts aren't, but just be careful, please. Will you promise me that?"

A streetcar swung lazily into view and slid to a clanging stop not far away, disgorging a handful of passengers.

"Brae," Lily said insistently. "I want your promise."

Would that a promise could make the things inside me go away, but that's what she wanted to hear so I said "I promise, Lily," and I carried her bags onto the car while she paid the fare.

I kissed her one last time. There were tears in her eyes. "Good luck tonight, Brae. Good luck tomorrow, and the day after that, too."

"Maybe I'll come looking for you," I said.

"South of the moon and east of the big smiling hot dog, that's where you're bound to find me," she said.

The streetcar driver impatiently called out. There was just time to push the rolled bills from Slim Talbot into Lily's hand. She stared in astonishment as I made a leap for it, escaping the streetcar an instant before the doors hissed closed. Lily grasped at an overhead strap for support while she raised her other hand in farewell. I wandered back toward the boardinghouse pondering why, if I did not love Lily Parker, I felt so wretched.

Chapter Seven

An agitated Coop was waiting for me when I arrived promptly at six-thirty, the good manservant showing up when he was supposed to. Lily would be proud of me. Not that my new employer noticed. He was too busy being miserable. "Come in, come in, the whole evening's ruined anyway."

Dressed in an evening shirt open at the collar, he began pacing back and forth, running a hand through his dark hair. I watched him for a couple of minutes before I said, "Not that it's any of my business or anything, but what's happened?"

"I'll tell you how it is, Mr. Chauffeur. Goddamn Lupe Velez ain't coming, that's how it is."

"I thought you were going with Miss Clara Bow."

Coop wasn't listening. "The most important night of my life, and she lets me down."

"Why would she do that?"

He stopped pacing. "You know anything about ties?"

"Ties?"

He looked impatient. "Ties! You know, things go around your neck. You know anything about them?"

"You can't tie an evening tie, is that it?" There was no end to the man's helplessness apparently.

Instead of answering, he petulantly thrust the tie into my hand. "My mother used to do this for me."

"Well, I'm not your mother," I advised.

"You want to bring something new to my attention, partner?"

"Well, this is your lucky night because my dad did manage to teach me how to make a proper bow tie."

"Your dad tied bow ties, huh?"

"He was a magician. Wore a bow tie for every performance. It was part of his trade."

"Part of yours, too?"

"For a time."

"So you can do magic tricks, huh?"

"After a fashion."

"What sort of tricks? Cards, that sort of thing?"

"I use stones."

"Stones? What do you do with stones?"

"I turn them to bees."

He grinned and said, "See, Orrack? I knew you were going to be useful for something. Fella that can tie a tie and turn stones to bees, no end to his capabilities. Tell you what, let's begin with the tie portion of your talents and go from there."

He stood straight, his shoulders back, his chin up like a good boy while I stepped behind him and flipped the tie around his neck. I repeated the words I'd heard my father recite so many times.

"You start with one end about one and a half inches longer than the other."

Coop said, "Lupe is Mexican and crazy. One moment she is the most loving woman ever came out of the sunset, next moment she's trying to slit your throat with a wire coat hanger. Somehow she got wind of Clara being around here."

I knew that Lupe Velez was an actress, tiny and sexy in the sort of nostril-flaring manner that Latin ladies seemed to favor when they appeared on the screen. Now I also knew why he was so abruptly alone. "That's why she's not coming tonight?"

"And here I thought you were just another chauffeur."

"Not me. I'm plum amazing, I am. Cross the long end over the short end and pull it through the center."

"As for Clara, she don't mean nothing to me, not really, and I'm not so sure I mean a whole lot to Clara. But try telling that to Lupe."

"And how do you feel about Lupe?"

He made a dismissive snorting sound. "I feel like if I turn up dead, the police should immediately pick up Lupe, 'cause of all the people I know she is most capable of committing murder."

I concentrated my attention on the tie. "Next you form a single loop with the short end, making sure to center it where the knot will be. You bring the long end over it."

Coop watched my hands at work, his brow knit in what for him approximated chagrin. "Between my mother and Lupe, I'm about to go loco."

"What's wrong with your mother?"

"She don't want me sleeping with all the gals in Hollywood."

I thought fleetingly of what it might be like to sleep with all the women anywhere, let alone here. My mind could hardly begin to grasp the concept. "A conservative woman, I take it."

"Ma wants me in bed by seven with my milk and cookies. But this is Hollywood, partner, and it's hard to find a quart of milk after dark."

"Now, form a loop with the long end and push it through the knot behind the front loop."

I adjusted the ends, and stood back to admire my handiwork. Coop dashed in to the hall and studied his reflection in the mirror. He came back looking very pleased, as though some immense hurdle in his life had been overcome. "Got to admit, Orrack, that's not bad at all. Mighty impressive, in fact. Maybe Clara was right about you, after all."

"What did Clara say?"

He didn't hear me, having rushed back into the hall to once again inspect himself.

"No doubt about it," he called out, "I like them petite, and scream-ing bloody murder at me." For a moment I thought he was discussing bow ties. He said, "How about you, Orrack?"

"What about me?"

"Chauffeurs like women, too, don't they? What kinds do you like?"

I thought of Lily and her recent tearful departure. "I'm not sure," I admitted. "The more I think about it, the less I know about women in general."

"Well, partner, welcome to the club."

"It's confusing because that's mostly what brought me here in the first place."

Coop came back into the living room. "What?"

"Looking for a particular woman."

"Well, there are plenty of them out here to choose from. Maybe too many. Just ask my mother."

"Yes, but she can't be just any woman," I said.

"What kind of woman does she have to be?"

"She must be the kind I'm in love with."

"Oh," Coop said in a dull voice. "Now you sound like my mother."

"The problem is, I don't have much time left to find out."

"No? How's that?"

"I'm going to be dead in a month or so."

He looked at me as though I recently started speaking in tongues. "I'm sorry, what did you just say?"

What was the matter with him, anyway? Could he not understand simple English? "Back home, my father threw a curse in me."

"Your dad did this to you?" Coop sounded amazed.

I nodded. "The only way I can break it is to find the woman I love. Otherwise, I'm a dead man."

"What exactly do you mean by curse?"

"Curse. An evil spell inside of you. The kind of thing that makes you dead."

For a time, Coop remained silent. Then he cleared his throat, and said, "Partner, I'd keep a lid on that curse stuff I were you. Otherwise you might just find yourself clapped into the loony bin."

"Well, you asked," I said.

"You're kind of a strange character, Orrack."

I didn't think of myself as strange at all, but then I wasn't sure what to make of the folks I'd encountered out here, so maybe they felt the same way about me. "I come from a strange place."

"Not me," Coop said in a merry voice. "Nothing strange about Montana. No one attaching curses to you out there. The only thing my daddy ever cursed was a cow."

That hall mirror again proved irresistible. The sight of his own face appeared to please him endlessly. He ran his fingers lightly along its planes, as though he needed reassurance that his handsomeness was real and not just an illusion. Who could blame him? If you looked like that, perhaps you needed constant reassurance that the gods had not played some sort of cosmic joke, and what they had given you for seemingly no reason they could just as easily take away again.

His eyebrows suddenly shot up and he turned and looked at me. A smile played at his lips. "I've got a hell of an idea, Orrack." He studied me some more. "Yeah, I think this is going to work out fine."

I did not like the look on his face. "What's going to work? What are you talking about?"

He took me by the elbow and led me down the hallway into his bedroom. "The studio sent around an extra monkey suit, just in case." He opened a closet and pulled out a set of evening clothes. He held them against me. "Yup, I think it'll be just fine. You're finished with chauffeuring for tonight, partner. We're going to get you into this here monkey suit, so's you can be my escort."

"That's not what I was hired for."

"You were hired to play nursemaid, and that's what you're doing. You can protect me from any irate fans who don't like my acting. Why, you could have your hands full."

He saw that I was still hesitant. "Damned if I'm walking into

Grauman's Chinese by myself. I'll look like that horse's ass you were mentioning this afternoon. You can be my friend Orrack from . . . where the hell you from?"

"A place where always it's the funeral plumes and never the bridal roses, where the curse on souls and the getting of revenge endures over love."

He looked baffled. "Let's just leave it that you're from out of town."

No sooner had I stopped protesting than Coop had me out of the chauffeur's uniform and into the white tie and tails. I had to concede that I looked pretty damn good, nothing like him, of course, but not bad. My dad always said you look at a man in a tux and you see a gentleman. Also, there turned out to be an added benefit. Getting me into formal gear put Coop into a fine mood. He was boyishly direct and eager and you could not help but be drawn to his high spirits, the way a child's happiness makes him so much more appealing. I knew little of childish ways. I never felt I had anything like a childhood. Life demanded that I grow up pretty fast. Coop, on the other hand, never had to grow up at all. Hollywood removed that particular necessity, at least for the time being. No wonder he disliked the complications of women. They made him think like an adult. Getting me dressed up for the night required no adult thought at all.

We went out to the garage and there sat a sleek Rolls-Royce touring car. It was gleaming black, hairline stripes of red, ivory, and gold along the wheel cowls that curled luxuriously away to the running board, while the driving compartment was set back from a hood as long and graceful as a sweet dream.

"They call it the Phantom," Coop said.

"You don't say."

"Six cylinder in line configuration. Single dry-plate–type clutch. Four speeds, plus reverse. Does about eighty-nine miles an hour. They have cars like this where you come from, Mr. Orrack?"

"Somewhere there's got to be one, maybe two. But no one ever showed them to me."

"Never seen a car like that in Montana, either. But this is what you get for wearing lipstick and kissing pretty girls, and smiling when they tell you to."

I looked at him. "They make you wear lipstick?"

"And paint and eyeliner. Otherwise you look all white and pasty on film. It's all about pretending you're something that you ain't and getting away with it. All that stuff helps you pull it off."

He saw my uncertain look and grinned. "Your dad always wore a tux you say? Part of the pretending, right?"

"Absolutely," I said.

"There you go. We're all tricksters out here. Some of us just get better paid for it than others." He nodded at the Phantom. "They say it's the best car in the world."

"Can't see any reason to disagree."

"Tell me, Mr. Orrack, you think you can drive the best car in the world?"

"Mr. Cooper, I'm for giving it a try."

"Then we'd better be off. It's a beautiful evening. I think we can ride with the cabriolet down."

I climbed inside, noting the elegant polished mahogany capings, luxuriating in the feel of the deep-buttoned brown leather upholstery. My heart beat wildly. I felt like the poor kid who woke up rich on Christmas morning. Cooper slid into the passenger seat next to me. "You won't be riding in back?"

"Not tonight, Orrack. Tonight we're a couple of swells on the town, you and me."

I started up the engine, put it into gear, and backed out of the drive.

PART TWO

That Which Cannot Be Found

✳

Chapter Eight

I steered the Rolls around a streetcar moving lazily along Holly-wood Boulevard, my heart pounding a mile a minute, hardly able to keep the stupid grin on my face in check. I was a dying man saved for one night by the sheer pleasure of driving a rich man's automobile. And what a car! I only had to touch at the steering wheel and it responded as though caressed by angels. I glanced over at Cooper and saw that he shared none of my giddy exuberance. Instead he sagged against the passenger door, his head against the glass, that lovely face turned a sickly gray. He stared out at the lavish Spanish colonial hotels and the opulent apartment buildings, eyes wide and unblinking.

"You all right?"

He didn't respond.

"Did you hear me, Mr. Cooper?"

He turned and gave me a melancholy stare. "Feeling kind of sick to my stomach," he said. "Don't know what's wrong with me."

"You're nervous, that's what it is."

He scowled. "I ain't nervous. Must be something I ate."

"Right you are," I said cheerfully. "Something you ate."

He tucked himself deeper into the seat. He was a funny soul; one moment the happy kid getting me all dressed up for a costume party, the next the petulant boy about to face a firing squad. To hell with him. He wasn't going to spoil my night. For Coop there would be lots of other nights like this. Not for me, though. Whatever happened, whatever my future held, it certainly didn't include a lot of Hollywood premieres in a glittering car on a perfect night.

Everyone flashing past looked happy and young and excited to be alive. A red-coated doorman guiding a Pierce-Arrow Brougham into a parking space waved at me. I smiled and gave him a jaunty wave back. *Save me a table, bucko,* I thought to myself. *I'll be back with Clara Bow glued to my arm soon as the picture's over.*

Crowds formed on either side of the street, growing thicker as we moved along, so that after a few minutes they swarmed onto the boulevard. Folks stood on the roofs of parked cars to get a better look. A motorcycle cop swirled past, and then another and another. Ahead, I could see light beams cutting into the sky, sweeping the area in front of the most astonishing building I'd ever laid my eyes on. There was madness in the architecture out here, a belief that you could adapt the world to Southern California. Grauman's Chinese Theatre, which had opened a year before, with its soaring pagoda roof was nutty thinking, Oriental division, an imposing pagan shrine, all jade and red trim glowing in the Hollywood night.

"God almighty," Coop said, staring up at the edifice. "Not sure whether I'm ready for this."

I wasn't so sure either. I could barely swallow as I slowed the car. My hands trembled upon the steering wheel. The crowds were massive now, held back by dozens of police officers, straining to keep the restless multitudes away from a forecourt splashed with a searing white light thrown off by gigantic arc lamps.

I brought the car to a halt, and immediately a red-coated attendant, eager-faced, threw open the door. "You need her parked?" he called out at the top of his voice, startling me.

"You bet your life!" I said it with such force that he jerked back in amazement. I was out, past him, then hit by a blare of light and noise. The crowd surged forward as Coop came around the side of the car. The light flared even brighter so that the whiteness was like a scream that turned Coop into a pillar of salt. I squinted against the light and grabbed him by the elbow. "Get hold of yourself," I said.

A gasp of excitement went up from the crowd as a short man in a purple tuxedo appeared. "That's Tom Mix," said Coop. Sure enough, Tom wore a purple cloak matching his tux and a broad black sombrero. I couldn't imagine anyone being fool enough to show up in an outfit like that, but the crowd seemed to love it, particularly when Tom stepped over and began to shake hands. I noticed he concentrated on the teenage girls straining at the police lines.

Coop finally pulled himself together and we moved toward the forecourt. Pale faces blank and stupid with excitement stared at us. A couple of women called out Cooper's name; photographers loudly demanded that he look a certain way. Over the din I could hear the amplified voice of an announcer calling the names of arriving guests. Marie Prevost was there and so were Bessie Love and Wallace Beery, not to mention Rod La Rocque, Vilma Banky, and Harold Lloyd without his glasses. John Gilbert swirled by amid a party of similarly dressed gents. They looked like a gaggle of penguins. An Asian lad, draped in black, posed with his wife who was done up in traditional costume. A grim-faced reporter, notebook poised, intercepted the dazed Coop and fired off a question, "What do you think about sound?"

"Sound?" Cooper looked confused. The questions were coming at him like bullets to be dodged. He edged backward and seemed about to bolt. This was all for him, but he wasn't embracing it very well. I must say I could have done better, but no one was asking me.

I shoved him past the reporter, deeper into the forecourt. "Can't you think of something a little more entertaining?"

"Can't think," he gulped.

Another reporter approached, this one short and sweaty, furiously chewing gum. "Hey, Coop," he called out. "Any truth to the rumors you've had every broad in Hollywood?"

Before he had time to answer, a woman stepped forward and tugged at Coop's sleeve. A winsome thing with a pageboy haircut and a beaklike nose, she wore a hideous apricot chiffon gown and a coat trimmed with ostrich feathers. She looked like a big-nosed fairy princess laid off from a traveling circus. This was Colleen Moore, the beloved star of *Lilac Time*.

"There you are," she snapped irritably. "You're goddamn late as usual, Coop. Come and have your picture taken with me like a good boy."

He allowed himself to be led meekly away. I followed close enough to hear her whisper, "Who's the big palooka with you?"

"Old friend," Coop muttered.

"Kee-rist, couldn't you get a date? They say you've fucked everyone in Hollywood."

"Yeah, well maybe I should have fucked you, Colleen, that way you wouldn't be going around saying I'm a lousy actor."

"You should be so lucky—besides, I never told anyone you're a lousy actor."

"What's that mean? You think I'm lousy?"

"Honestly, Coop, you're such a baby."

A mass of photographers and reporters loomed before them. More flashbulbs exploded to mark their coming together. One of the reporters cried out, "Miss Moore, the police are saying twenty-one thousand people have come out here tonight for your first big premiere."

At this piece of indispensable intelligence, a cheer rang out from all concerned. Colleen Moore beamed. "Be still my fluttering heart," she gasped.

"I am so excited tonight to be here at Grauman's Chinese Theatre with my husband, Mr. John McCormick, the head of production at National General Pictures, and, of course, my gallant costar"—as she said this she squeezed Cooper's arm—"who really is wonderful in the picture!"

Someone brushed past my shoulder, and I turned at the same time she turned, a slender woman in a silver gown that shimmered and glittered as it caught the light. An oval face floated in that light, pale and smooth, framed with golden hair. I caught the flash of emerald eyes filled with hints of gold. Those eyes flicked across me momentarily, before she was swallowed in the crowd and I could dimly hear Colleen Moore saying,

"Now as you know, we here in Cinemaland are all concerned about the coming of sound."

I scanned the crowd, craning my neck, desperate for one more glimpse of her, but she was nowhere to be seen. Around me a snarl of discontent erupted from the wolves at the mention of the word *sound.*

"Yes, yes, I know, but for the moment the public seems to want to hear things when they come to the theater," said Colleen Moore. "So in *Lilac Time,* we do have sound, fabulous wonderful sound. It is called Photophone and I do believe it will revolutionize our beloved industry."

A reporter in a fedora barked, "Now that Ronald Colman and Vilma Banky have announced they won't make any more pictures together, what do you think? Could you and Coop become America's next big screen team?"

One of the heathens that built the theater must have decided to scale the jade roof because Colleen Moore became intensely interested in studying its farthest reaches. "That would be nice," she replied vaguely.

The comment provoked another fusillade of flashing bulbs. Then we were all being pushed across the court toward the main entrance, Coop glaring and muttering, "That cow!" The woman in the silver gown returned like a small miracle, directly in front of me this time. She delivered a dazzling smile and briefly I believed it was for me. Instead, it was aimed at Colleen Moore. The delightful Miss Moore elbowed me out of the way as she embraced the woman. "Nell! I was beginning to think you wouldn't come."

"Wouldn't have missed this for the world," Nell said.

Colleen swung the woman around and shoved her in front of Coop's nervous, strained, unappreciative face. "Nell, I want you to meet Mr. Gary Cooper, my costar in *Lilac Time.* Coop, this is Nell Devereaux, the famous woman flier and mountain climber."

"Mountain climber?"

"A person who climbs mountains, Coop," Colleen said with an exaggerated sense of patience.

Nell Devereaux, I thought. *Her name is Nell Devereaux. Remember*

*that name, remember the first time you ever heard it, record it for history,
set it down for all time.*

Nell Devereaux.

"Colleen," Nell said in a throaty voice that to my ears hinted at many
things, "you never said it was going to be like this, it's all so crazy."

"What can I tell you, dear? It's show business."

Nell looked me up and down. "And who's this?"

"Some friend of Coop's," replied Colleen in a way that suggested being a friend of Coop's meant that you were of no importance whatsoever.

Now was the time to get my mouth open, to dazzle them with my glib
tongue and witty way around the English language. But opening a bear
trap would have been easier. Nell Devereaux gave me a confused look.
While I stood there like a fool, a man dressed in a white dinner jacket
stepped forward and Nell said, "Colleen, this is my friend Gerardo
Machado."

Colleen smiled and said, "It's such an honor to have the president of
Cuba with us this evening."

"Tonight," he said, "I am only a fan of yours, Miss Moore."

Colleen beamed. What a charmer. Machado's face, framed by graying black hair, was round and comfortable, like a big, soft, slightly moist
baby. His eyes were large and protruded slightly and only added to the
sense of him as an overgrown child. He was a fellow who slept the night
through, uninterrupted by the cares that give poorer lads lines and gray
hairs. I noticed one thing, though: he kept his left hand, white and withered and short two fingers, against his trouser leg.

"I love being here," he said in a rich, happy voice. "Hollywood is the
capital of the world's dreams, no? That is why I love the Americans, they
have this wondrous ability to turn their realities into fantasies and show
them on the screen for the entertainment of millions. No other country
in the world can do this."

Everyone murmured something encouraging, Machado beamed, and
Coop took the opportunity to introduce me as his "pal." Nell's disinter-
ested gaze drifted across me an instant, reminding herself, no doubt, that
I was the deranged soul who could not open his mouth. I found myself

standing next to Machado. He never even glanced in my direction. I did not exist in his world. He turned and flashed a row of white teeth. "Come, Nell, I am looking forward to this wonderful American picture."

But I didn't care about Cuban presidents one wit. No, Nell occupied all my attention. Here was what I'd come here to find—the way around the curse, the woman who could save my life; love draped in a silvery gown in order to display its unconscionable beauty.

And love it was, sure enough. Without knowing what love was, I knew instinctively this was it. How could it be anything else?

Coop slipped up beside me. "Say, did you get a look at that Nell Devereaux? Isn't she something?"

Before I could tell Coop to lay off, that Nell was already spoken for by his chauffeur, there was a commotion behind us. Photographers and reporters suddenly stampeded away. I saw a frown of confusion cross Colleen Moore's face.

White light erupted anew as klieg lights shifted and photographers went to work firing away with their flashbulbs. A moment or so later, the crowd parted, and there stood Clara Bow dressed in a black taffeta gown complete with a flaming red cape to match her hair, gold evening slippers and diamond earrings glittering in the bright light. The police could barely keep back the screaming reporters and cheering fans. She seemed not at all perturbed by the small riot she caused. She wore her fame like a second lovely skin, the movie goddess receiving blissful homage from her adoring worshipers.

"Bitch!" I heard Colleen Moore hiss.

Chapter Nine

T hat was the thing, the walking into a darkened movie palace, as if slipping into a warm bath, having only to focus on the bright rectangle of moving light in front of you, watching in a kind of hypnotic trance a pattern of images appearing and disappearing like a dream. Folks crowded the theaters, hungry for transportation away from their own lives and into someone else's. This was the most powerful force in the world, I reckoned, the true magic if you want to know the truth. But like the magic my dad practiced, an audience of suckers was required, marks willing to put up with nonsense. You only had to sit through *Lilac Time* to see that.

Coop played a British flier in the Great War, while the breathless and pop-eyed Miss Moore was a French girl named Jeannine, befriended by the British airman. You could no more believe her the offspring of French peasants than you could swim the Indian Ocean. She conversed with her guardian angel, who turned out to be Joan of Arc. A few minutes later, Coop arrived on the scene. The locals never gave a second glance to this uniformed young man in their midst decked out in rouge, eyeliner, and a bright smear of glistening lipstick. Nor did they seem perturbed as he wandered the French countryside, rolling his eyes as if having a seizure, and wildly throwing his hands around. At the end, Colleen

Moore believes the young flier dead and sends lilacs to his room. She then saunters off sadly down the road not knowing Coop isn't really dead. He's at the window trying to get her attention. They provided him with an extra dollop of eyeliner and lipstick for the big finale.

Not being all that familiar with moving pictures, I suspected Coop would be in trouble as soon as the lights came up. I wasn't sure whether folks in the theater would want to lynch him or just satisfy themselves with a good beating. No wonder Paramount was anxious to get rid of him. I figured I'd better get him out of there, quick. He was young; there were other things for him in this world, maybe a return to Montana and hard work on a cattle ranch where no one would know about the wild-eyed acting or the lipstick.

Then the applause started.

What the devil are they clapping for? I wondered. The sound rose to thunderous proportions. Some fool, obviously drunk out of his mind, yelled, "Bravo!" And then I saw Colleen Moore rise and bow graciously to the throng, the queen acknowledging her adoring subjects. And just to show the queen had not lost her common touch, she lifted up a hand toward Coop, and the next thing, instead of running for the exit, he was on his feet and *waving* to the crowd. If he'd flown the Atlantic by flapping his arms, the applause couldn't have been more appreciative.

Women brushed tears from their eyes as the houselights went up and we began filing out of the theater. People slapped Coop on the back and told him he was a big star. I realized with a dull shock that Charlie Chaplin was actually shaking his hand. Surely, Charlie couldn't have thought Coop was up to much. Could he? What the devil was wrong with everyone? I caught sight of Nell ahead of me with Machado. She turned and smiled vaguely in Coop's direction. She didn't look as though she was brushing away any tears.

Clara Bow was at my elbow, that pure white skin glowing against the taffeta gown. An array of exotic odors swirled around her. *How can one woman smell so good?* I wondered. But then that's what movie goddesses were supposed to do, weren't they? Look wonderful and smell good. She squeezed my arm and said, "Excuse me, Mr. Orrack, but you seem to have lost your chauffeur's uniform."

"I'm Coop's date," I said.

"And a handsome date you turned out to be," she said. "But what happened to Miss Lupe Velez?"

I decided it would be the best thing to stay away from that particular question and answered, "I'm not so sure."

Coop loomed into view, frowning when he saw Clara.

"Hey, baby boy," she said.

"What are you doing, Clara?"

"C-c-c-come to celebrate your big night," she said in the stammering voice that denoted her nervousness. I noticed her eyes fill with what looked to me to be panic, but then she quickly hid her feelings with a hurried kiss planted on Coop's cheek. "C-c-c-congratulations, Gary," she said, and then hurried off into the crowd.

Coop stood there, obviously trying to contain his anger. "That don't beat all," he said. He glanced at me. "What did you think?"

"I think Clara would have made a better date than me."

"I'm talking about the movie."

"I liked the part where Miss Moore talked to her old pal, Joan of Arc."

"I definitely should have left you in the car," Coop growled. Then he spotted Nell. "Wonder what Nell thought of the movie. You didn't happen to see her reaction, did you?"

My sinking heart felt as if it was being packed in ice.

We fled the Chinese for a spectacular temple designed by a fellow named Frank Lloyd Wright. The walls were large concrete blocks ornamented with hieroglyphics. A monumental fireplace dominated a living room opening onto an interior courtyard, complete with its own fountain. Beautifully dressed guests, driven into an excited babble by the moving picture they had just seen, wandered through, making appreciative sounds, and looking greatly impressed.

Clara Bow made her entrance, surrounded by the world. She seemed so small and alone amid the rubberneckers and the well-wishers and the bulky security guards in ill-fitting evening clothes. Despite the crowd, she managed to insinuate herself beside Coop, who looked uncomfortable in her presence. Even though she smiled flirtatiously as the photographers fired away, I thought I detected a sad yearning in her eyes, particularly as Coop abruptly moved away, leaving her alone in the crowd. I remembered what she had said earlier about taking Cooper more seriously than she should. Coop was wrong if he believed Clara didn't care for him. She cared all right.

The bathroom was done in black marble, the lighting recessed. I stood at a urinal the size of a tomb, and thought some more about Nell. I thought about Nell and me together forever. A swim to Timbuktu seemed more likely.

The door opened and who should hurry in but Nell's date for the evening, Gerardo Machado, *el presidente* himself. Fate had sent him along to ensure that I received a good dose of reality. He positioned himself next to me and proceeded to go through a series of curious movements employing only his good right hand to unbutton his fly.

"I like the action pictures," he said, addressing the wall in front of him. "All those sentimental things, I don't like them at all."

A furtive glance revealed that indeed he had managed to open his fly single-handedly, an impressive feat even for a man not the president of Cuba. He glanced at me. My eyes flew back to the wall.

"I know little of such things, but I suppose it will make a lot of money, particularly because it has sound. That is what is necessary now, is it not? This sound?"

"I do believe it is," I said.

"Although I thought she was supposed to be funny. Is that not why Colleen Moore is famous?"

"Well, she certainly wasn't funny in this," I ventured.

Machado chuckled at the wall. "My favorite scene, when she talks to Joan of Arc."

We both laughed at that.

"The male lead, what's his name? I met him outside the theater."

"Cooper. Gary Cooper."

"Wooden," Machado said. "Like they say here, a cigar-store Indian." He stole another glance in my direction. "I hope he is not a close friend."

"No," I said. "Not really."

"And so much rouge and eyeliner. Or maybe that is how the American pilots looked during the Great War. Do you think?"

"Could be," I said, and again we laughed. I could hear the hollow sound as his pee danced against the marble, as if pissing inside a bell.

"I'm sorry," Machado said. "I did not catch your name."

"Brae Orrack."

Machado adroitly put his good hand to use to button his fly. Then he backed away a few paces and studied me more closely. By now we'd both finished and were old pals moving together across the black-and-white tiles to the sinks. "You know what else I like? I like the gossip about these movie people."

"Gossip?" I said, trying not to sound too stupid.

"For example, someone told me tonight that Douglas Fairbanks is very self-conscious about his height and therefore does not allow any actor to appear in his movies who is taller than him. Have you heard this?"

I admitted I hadn't.

"I am told this on very good authority," he said with a reassuring nod. The waterspouts at the sinks were shaped like black diving fish. Machado made a graceful ceremony of washing his hands, carefully covering them with soap, before brusquely massaging them beneath the rushing water.

"Could you hand me one of those towels, please?"

He held out his hands like a surgeon about to operate, making no attempt to hide his withered and deformed left hand. I grabbed a fluffy white towel from a nearby rack.

"Just drape it over my hands, if you don't mind. Thank you."

He proceeded to carefully dry his hands. He noticed me watching him. "As a young man I worked in a butcher shop," he said. "I make a mistake. You know what it taught me?"

"Not to make mistakes."

Machado broke into laughter. "You get the idea, my friend."

Again he looked me up and down. I had the uneasy feeling he was reading from a list of my virtues and deficits, noting that the deficits far outnumbered the virtues.

"Tell me, what are you doing here in Southern California?" He seemed to take it for granted I was not a native of the area.

"Looking for opportunities," I said. No sense alerting him to what I was really looking for. Obviously, as a result of meeting Nell tonight, I had to figure out a number of things, things my new friend Gerry didn't need to know about just now.

"Well, Señor Orrack, congratulations."

"For what?"

"I believe you are the first person I have met here who does not wish to be in the movie business."

"Maybe I do, maybe I'm just being careful."

"Or maybe you are being truthful."

"Yes, that could be a possibility I suppose."

He laughed. "Probably not a word I should employ out here. Why don't we rejoin the group? And, of course, we will say nothing but nice things about our friend Señor Cooper who wears rouge and waves his hands a lot."

He winked conspiratorially, and again we laughed together, and that's how we emerged from the washroom, sharing a joke, Machado and me, pals. He stopped laughing when he saw Coop with his arm around Nell. They looked as if they'd been together forever. I felt Machado stiffen beside me. Then his face regained its placid ease as Cooper dropped his arm. Nell appeared unperturbed, as though men spent their lives putting their arms around her, and other men spent their lives trying not to notice.

"Nell, I've just been talking to this young man," he said in such a way as to suggest this was the best thing that had ever happened to him.

Nell even blessed me with another look. "Isn't that interesting." Her voice did not sound interested at all.

Machado continued, "Señor Orrack and myself, we both agree that the best scene in the movie is when the lovely Colleen Moore speaks to the great Joan of Arc."

"What do you know?" Nell said. "That's my favorite scene, too."

Machado took Nell by the arm and drew her to one side. They spoke for a time, and she frowned while he waved a finger under her nose. Coop shifted around, trying to keep his eyes averted.

"What did that Machado character really think of the movie?"

"He wondered why Colleen Moore wasn't funny."

"See, everyone wants her in comedies. I didn't want to do this, I fought them tooth and nail over it," he moaned. "I ain't no English fly-boy. Not by a long shot. The studio made me do it because they're out to get rid of me. That's it. With this whole sound thing they see the chance to dump me."

"The audience seemed to like it."

"What do you expect what with Colleen sitting right there and every-thing? No, it's a disaster, and that's the end of it. Those studio boys, they're lying bastards, that's what they are."

Nell came back alone, still frowning, and said, "Gerry sends his apolo-gies. He had to leave."

"You ain't going with him?"

"What's this 'ain't' stuff?" Nell looked around. "Are all premiere parties this dull?"

"We could all go somewheres else."

Nell studied him. " 'Somewheres,' huh? How about the *Johanna Smith*? Is that 'somewheres' we can get to?"

"That's the gambling ship, isn't it?" I said.

"I don't like to gamble," Nell said.

"Then why do you want to go out there?"

"Because Gerry said he didn't want me going out to the *Johanna Smith* tonight."

Coop grinned. "Ain't that something?"

" 'Ain't?' " said Nell. "Am I really with a guy who says 'ain't?' "

"Let's get going," Coop said.

"Let's talk a minute in private," I said to Coop.

He followed me a few paces. I could see the obstinacy forming ranks.

"According to Slim Talbot, they're not exactly laying down red carpeting and popping champagne corks out there when your name is mentioned."

"That problem's been taken care of."

"Maybe so, but it's my job to protect your hide, and I can't do it if you go waltzing into the eye of the storm."

"Orrack, I only know one thing: that beauty wants to go out there, and I'm crazy about her, and I'm going to take her."

Chapter Ten

The pilot of the taxi boat taking us out to the *Johanna Smith* cut through the calm seas so that everyone aboard got sprayed with water. The lights of Long Beach faded away into the night. Ahead, long beads of red light glowed bright to mark where the *Johanna Smith* waited on its voyage to nowhere, as the locals referred to the destination of gambling ships. There were about a dozen of us huddled into the boat getting soaked. Everyone seemed oblivious to the spray, concentrating instead on laughter and the gulping of illegal champagne. The boat bounced hard over roughening swells and several of our passengers looked distinctly uncomfortable, beginning to realize that champagne and rough seas did not necessarily mix. Coop eyed the crowd sullenly, as though daring someone to tell him they liked the movie. No one took up the dare, maybe because no one aboard even knew he was in a movie, let alone the fact that we had just come from the big premiere. Every so often, he stole a glance at Nell, but she ignored him as she ignored everyone else, so that she could engage the pilot in conversation. He wasn't much older than me, with the face of an eager young puppy.

"Yes'm, made of wood she is, about four thousand ton. Used to be a lumber carrier. San Fran was homeport. They fixed her up real nice."

"Are there gangsters all over the ship?" Nell lifted her face to the stars so that she could receive the full force of the spray. "I hear the ship is crawling with gangsters. I hear if we win they'll kill us. Is that true?"

"They don't always kill you. Win a little bit and they only maim you."

She solemnly studied the pilot. "Are you a gangster?"

"Nope, not so far as I can tell," he said good-naturedly. "Wouldn't mind being one, though. Gangster or movie star, there's the jobs for you."

She jerked a thumb back at Cooper. "Coop here, he's a movie star."

The pilot turned and studied him, then shrugged. "Can't say as I recognize him."

"Go and see *Lilac Time*."

"That the one with Colleen Moore?"

"That's the one."

"I like her a lot, she's funny. Your friend there, he funny, too?"

"Naw," Nell said, "he's a cigar-store Indian."

I wondered if she had picked up the line from her boyfriend Gerry Machado. Everyone laughed. Cooper, in order to demonstrate his democratic nature, forced a grin.

"Well," said the pilot, "we had Charlie Chaplin out here, and Ramon Novarro, even Douglas Fairbanks himself, although Mary, she weren't with him. Don't reckon America's sweetheart comes to gambling boats."

"Coop thinks I'm America's sweetheart, don't you, Coop?"

She'd already had champagne in the car on the way out to Long Beach, so she was a little tipsy and playing it smart and sassy. Coop was trying to catch up to her, but he wasn't even on the same track.

She came back and threw her arm around his shoulder.

"You're slim and dark, and the hair falls across your forehead just so, and I'll bet every starlet in Hollywood wouldn't mind turning her heels up for you, and you wouldn't mind if they did it either, would you, Coop? Bet you wouldn't mind at all." She pecked him on the cheek. "But Nell's not going to be quite so easy for you. Nell doesn't have air between her tiny ears. Nell's a fight. Wonder if you're up to it."

She turned to me. The gold in her eyes was dancing. "What do you think, Mr. Orrack, do you think our boy's up to the fight?"

"The fight's one thing. But it takes a special kind of man to win a war."

Coop scowled in my direction. "What's that supposed to mean?"

She smiled impishly as the *Johanna Smith* loomed closer. Not much to look at, it crouched on the oil-black water as though trying to hide.

"You sound like a man of experience in these matters, Mr. Orrack."

Which of course I was not, and I couldn't help but wonder if she didn't know that, but nonetheless decided to let me off the hook. Coop was her victim tonight, not me. I wasn't a big-enough target. I wasn't any target at all. I plastered on my best smile and said, "I've done many things in my life, Miss Devereaux, but I've never won a fight with a woman, let alone a war."

The words came out sounding like tin, but if she noticed, she decided not to let on. What was wrong with me? Why was I acting like this? Why did every word out of my mouth sound so foolish? I was willing to bet Machado never spoke such nonsense. Surely he was a man of the world who knew exactly how to talk to a beautiful woman. I, on the other hand, knew nothing at all, as I demonstrated so painfully each time I opened my mouth.

A searchlight aboard the *Johanna Smith* picked us out of the water. The taxi boat pilot cut his speed and turned the boat into a wide curve so that it could come up smoothly against the hemp fenders of the landing stage. The pilot announced, "Okay folks, we're here. Now don't lose so much you can't throw me a tip on the way back."

A young man in a white mess tunic as eager to please as the boat pilot, helped the ladies onto the landing stage and guided them up the stairs to the main deck.

When we got up to the deck, Cooper yanked me to one side. We went over by the railing. "What the hell you up to?"

"What are you talking about?"

"Nell Devereaux is what I'm talking about."

"What about her?"

"I just want to make sure you're not getting any ideas, that's all."

"And what sort of ideas would I get? For instance, would I figure her boyfriend is the president of Cuba, and not a lad to be messing with? Would I be getting an idea like that?"

"Ideas like you deciding that somehow you ain't the chauffeur anymore. Any ideas along those lines."

"Nell's right. She is with a guy who says 'ain't.' "

"Hey, I loaned you a monkey suit and let you ride up front, but that's as far as it goes, Orrack, so just remember that."

He stormed off, leaving me at the railing, choking back anger and embarrassment. The little soldier Coop dressed up for the evening wasn't responding the way he should, so he had to be put in his place, and smartly, too. Why did I ever let Lily talk me into this? I took deep gulps of the cool wet sea air and that calmed me some.

Another pilot boat approached. The engines were cut so it could nudge against the landing stage. The young man in the mess jacket rushed forward to greet the single figure leaping nimbly onto the stage. He brushed past the young man and hurried up the stairs to be swallowed in the gloom of the main deck. From somewhere below, I could hear dance music and laughter. I was trying to decide whether to go down or to wait here for Coop, when I heard the scrape of a match against the bulkhead. The match light flared around the face of the lone figure from the pilot boat, a man whom I could now see had a white scar and yellow teeth.

In a couple of minutes or so a hatchway opened, and another man stepped out, this one short and dapper, beautifully dressed from the look of things, with spats and gleaming cufflinks. His black hair shone in the deck lights and those same lights allowed me a look at a ratlike face that featured hooded, almost Oriental, eyes. Even at this distance it was a hard face to take your eyes off of.

The two men met at the deck's railing, casual, but somehow tense at the same time.

"There you are, Kiki," the short dapper fellow said, pulling at his shirt cuffs so that they showed just right.

"Georgie," said the fellow called Kiki. "You always look like someone just gave you a good shine."

"Never leave the house with getting shined up first," said the dapper fellow named Georgie.

The man called Kiki said something I didn't catch. They talked for a while longer before Kiki said, "He wants her off the boat."

"Why don't you lay off for tonight? Al doesn't want any trouble over this, and neither do I."

The man who called himself Kiki said something else that was lost on the wind. Whatever it was, it did not sound very friendly. Something gleamed through the darkness, and the dapper gent stepped quickly back.

This was a situation with which I was all too familiar: lads with knives, the late-night threats dropping from their lips, and me somehow in the middle of it. The character named Kiki wasn't expecting anyone behind him so there was the element of surprise working in my favor when I grabbed him by the wrist of his knife hand. I pulled him around, twisting until the knife clattered to the deck. I pushed Kiki against the bulkhead and bent over to pick up the knife. It was a switchblade. I straightened and tossed it over the railing.

"It's a pleasant evening," I said. "No need to be anything but friendly-like, don't you think?"

Small and wiry, even smaller than the dapper gent, this Kiki character, and those are always the dangerous types, no question. But if it came down to a bare-knuckled fight, he lacked the necessary weight, and he knew it. He pulled himself up short and contented himself with a snarl. "This is none of your business."

"Knives are everybody's business," I said with a smile.

He swung around to the dapper fellow named Georgie. "You get her off the ship. Otherwise, there is big trouble."

"Sure, Kiki. Anything you say."

Kiki swung back to me. "I know you, hombre."

"I'm a likable-enough fellow, Kiki. Always interested in making new friends."

He took a step toward me and I shifted the balance around so as not to be caught by anything he tried to pull. Georgie said gently, "Hey, no more trouble, Kiki. I mean it."

That prompted Kiki to back off. "I'll talk to you later, Georgie." He said it like it was a threat.

"You do that, Kiki."

He went back down to where the pilot boat waited. The young man in the mess jacket rushed out happily. Kiki knocked him out of the way and jumped onto the pilot boat. Georgie calmly brushed at his jacket and said, "I don't think Kiki would have done anything. But you never know about a guy like that. Thanks."

"I'm a bit nervous around knives."

"An understandable human reaction to knives, I would say." He stuck out his hand. "George Raft."

"Brae Robert Orrack. Pleased to make your acquaintance, Mr. Raft. I think we both know a chap named Slim Talbot."

He looked at me in a different way, or as different as those fathomless black pools he called eyes would allow. The closer you looked at Georgie, even in the better light, the less you could see. His face was a mask, his clothes a shield. Who knew what lurked beneath the surface of him? Maybe he didn't know himself, but he wasn't going to reveal much to the world one way or the other.

"Sure, you're the guy Slim hired to baby-sit Cooper. He said you were a tough-looking hombre."

"Tough? I would say devilishly handsome."

Raft laughed a mirthless laugh, and said, "Well, Slim was hoping you'd be able to handle yourself in a tight situation. Looks like he was right." A ghost of a smile replaced the mirthless laughter. I was to see a good deal of that ghost smile. " 'Course you bring Coop straight to the place where he is most likely to get himself into trouble."

"I guess you must be something of an expert when it comes to trouble on boats, Mr. Raft."

"Yeah, it appears I am, all right. The guy showing me his knife, that's Kiki Diaz. Works for General Machado, the Cuban dictator."

"I know who Machado is."

"Kiki followed a certain young lady out here. She's dating his boss, and I guess she's not supposed to be aboard. He wanted to take her off. I told him it wasn't such a good idea."

"The lady wouldn't happen to be Nell Devereaux?"

"You know her?"

"I came out on the boat with Nell and Gary Cooper."

Georgie couldn't hide his surprise. "She's down below with Coop?"

I nodded.

"Well, give Coop credit. He can't act, but he sure knows how to keep getting himself into trouble."

We went together down a wide flight of stairs to a lower deck adorned with fishing nets and anchors. A snazzy-looking bartender kept stifling a yawn as he presided over a short glass bar with a lot of empty stools. A small orchestra played morosely for the dancing pleasure of a few disinterested patrons huddled in clusters at small tables. The gambling hall was down another flight, its entrance marked by a gilded arch, a smoky overheated hole thick with tobacco smoke that clung like a cloud to a ceiling so low the top of my head actually brushed it. No one seemed to mind. The place was packed with well-dressed patrons swarming the roulette wheel and the three crap tables, as well as the chuck-a-luck tables and the slot machines. The faro tables were piled high with enough yellowbacks so a fellow like myself would never have to work again. That's what they wanted you thinking, of course. You're in a place like this and they want you believing you might walk out of it rich.

A bar spread the length of the room, and featured hardworking bartenders in naval whites, complete with peaked officers' caps, and no inclination to yawn. The waitresses wore cute little blue and white sailor suits with sailor hats perched at a jaunty angle. This was the heart of the *Johanna Smith*. Never mind the music and the dancing, you could get that anywhere and save yourself a boat ride. But down here was heat and smoke, the sweat rolling down your starched collar, a languid lady on your arm, the silver dollars employed as chips jangling away in your pocket. Here was glamour, cheap and alluring, no question, and as intoxicating as the next glass of champagne. And here I was part of it, strolling about with Mr. George Raft himself, obviously a man about Hollywood, although exactly what kind of man I wasn't sure. Slim Talbot said he rubbed shoulders with gangsters, fascinating for me, seeing as how I'd never seen a real live American gangster, let alone rubbed shoulders with one.

Raft adjusted his shirt cuffs and handed me a card. "Any guy knows his way around a knife, he's okay as far as I'm concerned." To Raft that appeared to be the ultimate accolade. "I owe you, Mr. Orrack, and I always pay my debts. Anything I can ever do to help you, call me at this number."

"I appreciate that."

"Just keep an eye peeled for Kiki Diaz. I guess there are a couple of things he's not capable of, but I can't imagine what they might be."

"I'll do that."

"And watch out for Coop while you're out here. He may think he's out of the woods with Al Howard, but I don't think he is."

"Coop and common sense are strangers. Otherwise we wouldn't be here in the first place."

"Well, do your best is my advice."

"And I thank you for it."

He shook my hand and disappeared into the crowd.

"Looks like someone messed up your tie, Orrack." Nell Devereaux stood directly in front of me.

"I was upstairs on the deck taking on a rat with a knife."

"What is it about men, they all have to act so tough?"

"It's an awful habit that I'm trying to shake off," I said.

"Mind you, you do look sort of tough, Orrack, so maybe it's not an act."

"Oh, it's an act, all right," I said.

She stood very close, adjusting my tie. "My dad told me to never get mixed up with a man who can't tie a bow tie."

"What about General Machado? How is he with a bow tie?"

"I'll have to ask him," she said.

I could feel the heat coming off her. The tiny nose gleamed above the film of moisture along her upper lip, and I took in the sweet endless curve of her jaw and the gold in those eyes.

"Where's Cooper?" My voice sounded funny.

"Why are you so all-fired interested in him?"

"A gent named Al Howard doesn't like him."

Nell made a big face and turned her fingers into claws. "I hear he was messing with Al's wife."

"I just want to make sure Al didn't drop him into the Pacific."

"Not as yet. Coop's taking a leak. That's what you call it, isn't it?"

"No, ma'am, I would not call it that."

"You're different, huh? But men always think they are different, don't they? No, don't answer that, I think you are, and that's good. I like different. Different is what makes things interesting. So what do you say, Orrack, ever danced with a princess? You do dance, don't you?"

"How could a devil like myself not know how to dance?"

True enough. My mother having been a dancer before she met my father insisted I learn the finer points of the waltz. Perhaps keeping in mind my less-than-startling good looks and my unsavory reputation, she advised that dancing would attract the girls. Until now I had doubted the wisdom of that argument. But not tonight. Tonight the accomplished hoofer, I escorted her up the stairs to the bar, and swirled her onto the dance floor as the little orchestra right on cue started up on "My Blue Heaven." Never mind that the place was even now only about half full and the dance floor nearly empty and the band seemingly hitting more wrong notes than right. I was feeling more confident suddenly, the cotton out of my mouth, and a few sentences uttered that didn't sound totally asinine. I held her close, enjoying the firmness of her, and the soft swell of her bosom against my chest. All thoughts of saving Coop from a swim in the Pacific disappeared.

"You're so inscrutable, Orrack. What are you thinking?"

"I'm wondering how you got to be a princess."

"Silly, you get to be a princess by marrying a prince. I thought everybody knew that."

"Of course. With all this excitement tonight, I plain forgot."

"It was my first trip to Paris. Seemed like a good idea to marry a prince, so I did. Prince Dimitri Nicholas Goitzine. It lasted about two seconds. But I'm still a princess. That's why they fall all over me out here. Are you impressed, Orrack?"

"Don't be ridiculous. Back home, I dance with princesses all the time."

"Bet you don't. Bet I'm the first."

"Tell me about mountain climbing." *Tell me anything. It makes no difference,* I thought to myself, *as long as I can continue holding you in my arms.*

"Nanga Parbat, it's in the Himalayas. But I wouldn't exactly say I climbed it. Bastards wouldn't let me up past the twenty-thousand-foot level."

"Why?"

"Why do they stop you from doing anything? I'm a woman. What about you, Orrack? Who am I dancing with?"

"A man of magic," I said.

Her eyes lit up. "I knew it!" she exclaimed. "Makes sense. A magic man. Knew there was something special about you. A princess and a magic man—perfect. What are you doing here, among all these heathens?"

"I'm looking for you."

She gave me a curious look. "How did you know I would be here?"

"I didn't, not for sure."

The music stopped. Coop stood sheepishly at the edge of the dance floor. A slim, balding man glowered beside him, along with three goons.

"Who's that with Coop?"

"I do believe it's the owner of this tub," Nell said.

"Al Howard?"

"Aren't you supposed to be protecting Coop from Al?"

"That's what I'm here for all right."

Al Howard grabbed a handful of Coop's shirtfront and jerked him forward.

"It's probably time for you to spring into action," Nell said.

I walked over to Al Howard and said, "My name's Brae Orrack, Mr. Howard. A pleasure to make your acquaintance. I'm a friend of Mr. Cooper's."

"Good," said Al Howard. "Soon as I finish kicking Coop's teeth down his throat, we'll get to yours."

I turned to Nell. Her eyes were slightly narrowed, not watching Coop or Al Howard, but me.

"I'd like to introduce you to another friend. This is Miss Nell Devereaux, noted flier and mountain climber."

"Get them out of here," Al Howard said to his goons.

"Miss Devereaux," I continued, "is a close friend of the honorable Gerardo Machado."

Al Howard looked at Nell in a different way. "You know General Machado?"

"Gerry is a good friend, a dear friend," Nell said, suddenly losing the lazy drawl with which she ordinarily addressed the world. "Gerry and I were with Mr. Cooper at the movies earlier this evening. Grauman's Chinese to be exact. For the premiere of the new Colleen Moore movie, *Lilac Time*. Have you seen it? I suppose not, since it just opened tonight. Well, if you're expecting Miss Moore to be funny, you'll be sorely disappointed because it's a very serious drama." She was now speeding along as though fearful she wouldn't have time to get all the words out.

When she finally paused for breath, Al Howard actually looked relieved. "Yeah, well, General Machado ought to be more careful about his acquaintances." He pointed a finger at Cooper. "You've been warned already. You've got no respect for me. No respect at all."

Nell said to Al, "The president wanted more than anything to be here this evening. He really did. He had planned to come out here, and that is for certain." Talking a mile a minute now. "But you know what happened? Well, let me tell you. There was an emergency. An emergency in his own country. That's what kept him away. The only thing that would keep him away."

"Emergency." Howard looked her up and down. He then looked at Coop. "Get off my boat. Don't come back."

I pulled Coop past Al. His goons looked anxious to prove how mean they were, but for the time being restrained themselves. On the way out, I saw Georgie Raft leaning against one of the pillars, looking as casual as you please, that ghost smile fixed to his ratlike face. He gave me a little salute. I suspected nothing in the world ruffled Georgie Raft.

We came out onto the deck. The air was clean and no one jumped out at us with a gun. The pilot boat waited below, bobbing against the landing stage. Coop was already halfway down the stairs. He did not look happy.

"You talk fast," I said to Nell.

"I wasn't talking fast at all," she insisted. "What would make you say something like that?"

"I must have been mistaken," I said.

"I thought we made a pretty good team back there," she said.

Did we? "We did," I said out loud, as much to reassure myself as to answer her.

"Do me a favor."

"If I can."

"Make Coop bring you to lunch tomorrow. And don't call Machado honorable. There is nothing honorable about him."

Chapter Eleven

I could have handled that situation okay," Coop said in a sullen voice. "I didn't need you interfering."

I barely heard what he was saying, still dazzled as I was by Nell's words—words I continually reran through my mind as I steered the Rolls-Royce back toward Los Angeles. *Make Coop bring you to lunch tomorrow.*

That had to mean she was interested, did it not? Otherwise why would she say anything?

I thought we made a pretty good team back there.

How had I responded? Cleverly? I couldn't remember saying anything, let alone anything that could be mistaken for clever. Damn, what was wrong with me? I couldn't be tongue-tied in front of her. That would never work. The world was full of men without tied tongues. I had to become one of them, and fast.

"Did you hear what I said?"

"You said you could have handled those lads by yourself."

"So why didn't you say something?"

"What's there to say in the face of such irrefutable logic?"

Coop shifted uneasily beside me. He looked pale and tired. Al

Howard and his goons had made his big night small. He'd insisted on walking into the hornet's nest, and guess what? He'd gotten himself stung, as predicted. I felt a little sorry for him. He shouldn't have had his night ruined like that, not in front of Nell. But even as I felt sympathy, I couldn't help but think it served him right, particularly after what happened when we escaped the *Johanna Smith*.

By the time the pilot boat reached shore, Coop had regained his former cockiness. He summarily decided to leave me out in Long Beach while he drove Nell back to where she was staying in the Malibu. For one heart-sinking moment I thought she was going to go along with this fool notion. But when we came up from the docks, waiting for her was a car every bit as impressive looking as the Rolls.

The chauffeur announced he had orders from General Machado to drive Miss Devereaux out to the Malibu. Despite Coop's pleading, she decided to go. She didn't even look at me when she got in. What did that mean? Perhaps we weren't a team after all. Maybe she said that to all the young fools she encountered. The thought plunged me into a depression that I quickly yanked myself out of. I would not come to fast conclusions about anything that happened this evening. I would keep the memory of her close; that was real enough. Anything else was a foolish young man's fool speculation.

Or so I told myself repeatedly.

Coop shifted again and seemed to come to a decision about what he should say next. "Even though things were never out of control or anything, you did pretty good there, Orrack, stepping in the way you did."

"Well, I figured you could handle it all right, but just in case . . ."

"Yeah," Coop said. His mood lightened. "Turns out getting you to be my chauffeur wasn't such a bad idea after all."

"Glad to hear it," I said.

"Say, why don't you drive me out to the Malibu tomorrow? There's a luncheon I'm supposed to attend. Might as well have you along. What do you think, Orrack?"

Coop's way of inviting me to Nell's luncheon: I could be there, but as his driver, and nothing more. That was fine. The goal was to get out to this Malibu place. Never mind how it was done.

Coop was saying, "You be at my place around eleven, and we can drive out there for one o'clock. How does that sound?"

"Sounds okay."

"What's wrong with you? You sure don't have much to say for yourself. Least you could do is show a little appreciation since I'm throwing you another day's work out of the goodness of my heart."

"I'm tired, that's all."

"You're looking for an apology for the way I acted when we got on the boat, is that it?"

"I'm not looking for anything."

"Anyway, it's not you I have to be worried about."

"No?"

"Nell's not going to be interested in a fellow like you."

I knew things he didn't. I could afford to be generous, I reminded myself. "You're probably right."

"Probably? Ain't no probably about it. You know, you not being very sophisticated around women."

Not sophisticated around women? Well, I wasn't. But I thought I was doing a better job of hiding that sorry fact. If Coop could so easily detect my shortcomings, what could Nell see? Probably right through me to Nanga Parbat and back again.

"The problem is that Machado character," continued Coop. "I don't think she really likes him, but it doesn't look like she can shake him so easy."

"A smooth operator, all right."

"Smooth like oil," Coop said. "But he's my competition for Nell, not you. I should have realized that, and not been so tough on you. You're on my side, just doing the job you were hired to do."

"Glad you're able to see it that way."

"Funny. Every time I swear I'm not going to complicate my life any more than it is, I go ahead and make it more complicated. But this time it's worth it, the prize being a gal like Nell Devereaux."

Despite my limited knowledge of women, I suspected Nell wouldn't like being called a gal and that she was no man's prize. In order to win a woman like her you did not take possession. No, you won Nell, I suspected, by being her equal. I doubted I was up to the task, but at least I could take solace from the suspicion that neither was Coop.

By the time we reached his house, Coop was feeling sufficiently beneficent that he decided I should drive the Rolls home, and then pick him up the next day. Despite myself, I was on the verge of liking him. Wasn't I easily swayed? All a man had to do was give me his Rolls-Royce Phantom and I was his friend for life.

I cruised on home with the top down, the late-night breeze blowing over me, like one of the rich swells of Cinemaland in my fancy evening clothes. All I needed was Nell Devereaux beside me. It was easy to imagine the two of us driving through the night, young beauties on our way to one of those hilltop palaces where we would curl on silken sheets and make endless love. Wouldn't that be something?

It was nearly one o'clock by the time I got back to the boardinghouse. I parked the car near the canal where Lucca moored his gondola, out of sight of the roadway, but so that Eddie and Meyer couldn't miss it as they left for work in the morning. There would be more jokes about me driving the rich and famous, but envy, too. After all, I was the one parking a Rolls-Royce outside a pink boardinghouse, even if it was only for the night.

I tossed the keys into the air, caught them again as I strolled across the lawn toward the house. Two gents drifted out of the shadows, smoothies with slicked-back hair in double-breasted blue suits, smelling of cologne.

One of the men hung back, while the other started forward, cocking his head as though to get a better look at me. "Hey, hombre," he said in heavily accented English. "How you doing this night?"

He flashed a wide grin, and I could see by the shiny white scar slashed down the right side of his face and the broken yellow teeth that Kiki Diaz had come to visit.

"Kiki, you're up late," I said.

"So, Georgie tell you about me, huh?"

"Georgie told me all about you."

"So, no hard feelings, okay?"

"No hard feelings at all, Kiki."

Kiki's friend came nearer, and appeared to sniff the air, as though that might help him detect whether I was friend or foe. He had a droopy eye, made that way by the scar cutting down across his forehead, through his eye, and along his cheek. Two scar faces on a warm summer's night in Southern California. Three, actually, if I added my own facial deformity to the collection. The things you get to see when you travel far from home.

"Who's your friend?" I asked, trying to keep the fear out of my voice, for these fellows did scare me, no question.

"His name is Rodrigo. He don't speak English so good, but he's a real nice fellow."

"Glad to hear it."

"I tell you what—" Kiki started to say.

"Tell me anything you care to, Kiki. It's a beautiful night, and it so happens I have a few moments to chat before the chief of police arrives for a nightcap."

His face went blank then relit suddenly, like someone putting a match to the gas flame. "Hey, you're making the joke, eh? That's very funny. The chief of police coming for a drink. That's a good one." He turned to his companion. "You hear that?"

The man behind him said nothing. Kiki shrugged and turned to me again. "He don't get your joke."

"As long as you understand me, Kiki."

"Oh, I understand you, hombre," Kiki said. "The general, he like you. He say to me, Kiki, you go to this place and you wait for Señor Or-rack to show up. When he does, you bring him to see me."

"And where would that be?"

"Not too far. We got a car right over here."

"Well, thanks for the offer, Kiki, but I think I'll just be off to bed."

"The general, he's going to be very disappointed."

"Some other time."

"Hey, did I tell you? My friend Rodrigo, he got a gun."

Rodrigo grinned inanely, trying to give the impression he understood what was going on.

"Rodrigo has a gun? You don't say."

"This car we got, amigo, it's a big comfortable car, a Nash. You'll really like it, honest."

"Any other night I might have been impressed. But tonight, well, tonight I drove myself home in a Rolls-Royce. So a Nash would be something of a comedown for me."

"Why don't you just get in the car? That way we don't even have to think about my friend's gun."

"I'm not thinking about his gun, Kiki. I'm thinking about a good night's sleep."

"Here's some free advice: think about his gun."

I could make a run for the house, and that would force Kiki and Rodrigo to decide how much fuss they wanted to create in a quiet neighborhood late at night. Probably they didn't want any trouble, but it was hard to know. But then there was this other thing: I was not a fellow for running. Oh, I'd done it, all right, which was how I ended up in these precincts, I suppose. However, it's not something I'm inclined toward, particularly when it's a couple of lowlifes like these two. If I did happen to go off with them, what then? On the one hand, they could slit my throat and be done with me. On the other hand, maybe Machado really did want to talk—after all, we were old pals at the urinals, were we not? Could be interesting—could get me closer to where I wanted to be, which was with Nell.

"All right," I said. "Why don't we get going?"

During the hour-long drive in their flashy Nash, thick with sweet perfume odors, Rodrigo kept shifting around while Kiki, at the wheel, glanced back every so often, as though to remind himself of the interesting places into which he might stick a knife.

"Hey, that scar you got on your face, where you get that, my friend?" Kiki finally inquired.

"I'll tell you about mine, Kiki, if you tell me about yours."

Kiki flashed a grin in my direction. "A guy tried to kill me."

"What happened to him?"

"Only thing can happen when a guy try to kill you and he don't succeed—you kill him back. Right?"

"That's right."

"So what about you? What you do about the guy that did that to you?"

"I sent him off to college, made sure he got an education so he could make a contribution to society and wouldn't go around trying to knife innocents like myself."

Kiki gave me a quick blank stare. "You joking. Right?"

"That's right, Kiki," I said. "I'm joking."

"You tell too many jokes," Kiki said darkly.

"It's one of my shortcomings, no question."

Below the road, moonlight reflected off a white frame beach house. The sea sounded beyond and the sad wail of a fishing boat's foghorn rolled over the night.

The car went through a porticoed entranceway and into a cobbled courtyard flanked by flower gardens, surrounded by a seven-foot-high wall and stands of cypress trees.

An arched hallway ran the width of the house. My new friends led me past a sitting room with a beamed ceiling and a ten-foot-wide fireplace. The hallway opened onto a wide porch cast in the light from candles positioned along the balustrade. A garden of bougainvillea, hibiscus, and geraniums spread below the balustrade. A good-sized swimming pool rose out of the garden, surrounded by blood-red tiles. Machado was doing an impressive breaststroke in the pool, moving with admirable swiftness along its length. He was naked.

"General," Kiki called out. "I bring you Señor Orrack."

Machado stopped swimming, swept the hair from his eyes and rolled lazily over on his back to survey me as I came across the red tiles. It was like walking on a pond of blood.

"Do you know who has the biggest penis in Hollywood?" he asked.

I thought he was joking, but then his face appeared entirely serious. "No, as a matter of fact I don't."

"Who would you think it might be? Take a guess."

"It's not something I've thought a whole lot about."

"A wild guess. Who would you think?"

Machado seemed intent on getting an answer out of me and so I said, "How about Douglas Fairbanks?"

Immediately, Machado's face exploded with light and he stood up in the shallow end of the pool oblivious to his nudity. "You see? That's what I would have thought, too! But no! You are entirely wrong. You know who is is? This little fellow they call the tramp."

"Charlie Chaplin?"

"You are as amazed as me, no? Who would believe it? They say— and here I am quoting someone in the know about such things—that he is hung like a horse. That is what they say. Hung like a horse."

The phrase appeared to delight him. I just stood there, not sure how to respond. Was this why he had Kiki and Rodrigo drive me all the way out here in the middle of the night?

Still chuckling, he settled back against the side of the pool, spreading out his arms. "Why don't you get out of those clothes and come for a swim?"

"Not tonight, thanks."

"I do this every night before bed. It helps me sleep." He pushed away from the side and spoke to his bodyguards. "Kiki, you and Rodrigo give me a few minutes with Señor Orrack."

"Sure enough, General," Kiki said.

The two gunmen made their exit. Machado swam over to the edge of pool. Beyond the garden, lemon trees gave way farther up the hill to pine and eucalyptus.

"Charlie Chaplin," he said, as though still not able to entirely digest this piece of Cinemaland lore.

"Hung like a horse," was all I could think of to say.

He laughed and lifted himself out of the pool, his soft white body wet and glistening in the moonlight. He shifted around so that he sat on the pool's edge, his feet dangling in the water. "Take your shoes off and sit beside me," he said.

I did as he told me, rolling up my trousers to the knee so as not to ruin Paramount's expensive evening clothes, and then plopping myself down beside him, allowing my feet to dip into the surprisingly warm pool water. Machado appeared totally unconscious of his nudity, a man absolutely sure who he was even without clothes. I envied him.

He looked out across the pool for a time and then said, "What do you want, Señor Orrack?"

"I thought you might be able to tell me that."

"I don't mean, what do you want, like, 'I want a nice automobile or I want a beautiful woman or I want a better house or a raise in my pay.' These are small things, inconsequential. I'm talking about what you *really want.*"

"I guess I want to live," I said.

He gave me a curious look. "Well, your dream has come true, my friend, you are living and breathing. Congratulations. Now that you have that much, what is it you want next? What are your ambitions?"

I thought about this and said, "To go on living."

That brought a second look. "There is doubt about this?"

"Yes, there is," I said.

"You are a very curious young man," he said.

"Everyone says the same thing. I'm not from here. Maybe that has something to do with it."

He got up from the pool and padded over to a large towel draped across a chair. He picked up the towel and began to dry himself.

"Your father, what did he do?"

"He was a magician."

"A poor man?"

"Very poor. And evil."

"Evil?" Machado sounded surprised. "That is a curious word to use when you talk about your father."

"I am a curious young man, aren't I? You said it yourself, General."

"But then, if I am honest, and I had to use a single word to describe my father, I would say evil also."

"It took me a while to learn to hate my father," I said. "But he helped me along. Especially the way he treated my mother."

"Ah, you see. I never knew my mother. My father slept with whores. Your father did the same thing? Dishonored your mother?

"You might say that." Well, there was plenty more to be said on that subject, but not tonight.

Machado stopped drying himself and rejoined me at the pool, exuding that sense of confidence like a warm glow. You could not help but be attracted to it.

"I trust you, okay? You and me, we can talk. Men talking together, being honest with each other, that's a sign of friendship, don't you think?"

"I suppose it is," I said uncertainly, having no idea where he was going.

"This Gary Cooper," he said.

"Coop? What about him?"

"What is he? A gigolo? A man who feeds off women in Hollywood, I understand. A despicable man, don't you agree?"

"An actor," I said.

"I understand this Cooper plans to attend a luncheon in Miss Devereaux's honor tomorrow in the Malibu."

So that was it.

"Do you know about this?" He dropped the towel and began to shrug into the robe.

"I know he wants me to drive him out to the Malibu," I said carefully, taking the opportunity to stand as he came back toward me, wrapping the robe around his girth.

"Here is what I would like you to do, Brae. I would like you to drive Mr. Gary Cooper out to the Malibu, just as you planned. But now you do this as my friend."

"Which means?"

"You act as my eyes and ears. Report any activities that occur between Cooper and Miss Devereaux during the course of the afternoon.

"Naturally, I do not expect you to do this exclusively in the name of our new friendship. I propose to pay you two hundred dollars for your good work. One hundred dollars to be paid now. The other hundred will come when you report to me tomorrow evening—with the prospect of more money, depending on what we mutually decide to do."

"Just out of curiosity—I know we are friends now and everything—but for the sake or argument, suppose I said no?"

Machado looked genuinely shocked. "But why would you say no? After all, we are friends, and friends do not argue about such things."

So there it was. I would spy for love. Or I would be in deep trouble with my new friend General Machado. I would not report that I too loved. I would not say that mine was a more desperate love because I was counting on it to save my life. No, best to keep quiet about that while Machado fished a hundred-dollar bill from the pocket of his robe, as though he carried them in all his clothing. I plucked the money from him, staying calm, the way a fellow used to such amounts of money stays calm; the way a fellow takes money from a pal who's just hired him to do a job.

"Kiki and Rodrigo will pick you up at your boardinghouse tomorrow evening at about eight, and they will drive you out here," said Machado. "We will have a swim, a bite to eat, and we will talk like men who are friends, men who don't mind sharing secrets. It will be a good conversation, I'm sure."

To my surprise, he embraced me, a profound hug suggestive of our new friendship and burgeoning partnership, more meaningful than the trading of any Cinemaland gossip.

By the time Kiki and Rodrigo got me back to the boardinghouse it was almost dawn. I stepped onto the porch wondering about what I had done, and what sort of trouble it might get me into. No more trouble than if I had said no to General Machado, I suspected. Friendly as he seemed, and as much as I did have a sneaking liking for him, he did not strike me as a man anxious to hear the word *no.* So for the moment, it was probably wiser for me to go along.

I'd no sooner decided this when abruptly I was struck by a feeling of anxiety. My heart started racing and I had trouble catching my breath. I came along the darkened hallway, fearful, having to practically force myself to climb the stairs and enter my room. Immediately, the fear grew inside me. I had a sense that someone had been here, although nothing seemed disturbed. Not that there was a whole lot to disturb, this room standing as a testament to the miserable nature of my existence in Venice Beach, my total failure to attain even the most meager of material goods. My narrow bed remained unmade, a lasting and unchanging shrine to my exertions with Lily. Jesus still peered down from his cross on the wall, in obvious pain, but vaguely accusing, also, I thought, understandable considering what he had recently witnessed in this room. Then I had another thought. I went to the dresser drawer where I had placed the Serpent Stone and opened it.

The stone wasn't there.

I went through what clothing I had in the drawer. No sign of it.

The feeling of fear and foreboding rose like a tide. Someone had been in here. Someone had taken the Serpent Stone. I heard a noise from outside and started. Gathering my wits, I went to the door and opened it a crack. There, in the predawn gloom of the hall, amid a swirl of floating dust particles, Meyer Rubin leaned against the wall at the top of the stairs, trying to straighten himself. He wasn't wearing a suit jacket and his vest was open to show the button-straining bulge at his waist. "Hey, Orrack," he called in a slurry voice. "Whatcha doing up at this hour?"

"You haven't seen any strangers about, have you, Meyer?"

"Strangers?" Meyer snorted. "I see nothing but strangers, friend. I deal in strangers. That's all I see."

"But nobody in here, in the house?"

"I can't see straight, let alone a stranger." He said it with a gurgling laugh and lurched on down the hall. He waved a floppy arm in my direction. "I sampled the product tonight, Orrack. Always a mistake. You're a curious fellow, you know that? Mighty strange, but I like you all the same. G'night."

I closed the door. The almond taste filled my mouth and the pain in my stomach was like a sudden blow that put me on the floor. Once again, I found myself floating near the ceiling, staring down at this figure on the floor. That fellow did not look well. He looked like a man dying.

A moment later, I was that man again. I rolled over on my back, and saw Jesus looking down at me. Was that a gleam of sympathy in his sad eyes? Or disdain? Hard to tell from here. I tried to get my breath back and thought of Nell.

Ah, Nell. You can save me. You are my last chance in this world.

Chapter Twelve

Rancho Topanga Malibu Simi Sequit, otherwise known as the Malibu, was a twenty-seven-mile-long strip, running up the Pacific coast from Santa Monica as far north as Ventura County. The Spanish had named the place and the locals loosely translated that into "Where the mountains meet the sea." Until three years ago this land where the mountains meet the sea was privately owned, a feudal kingdom protected by high security fences and guards patrolling on horseback. Now, according to Coop, the owners, strapped for cash, had begun to lease ocean frontage to Hollywood celebrities in search of a quiet retreat from the city.

The road into the colony was private, the way barred by a gate. Near the gate stood a cluster of bulldozers and trucks, surrounded by uniformed troopers. The state was preparing to invade so it could build its own highway, Coop explained. We stopped by a guardhouse, and announced ourselves. The guard gave the car an admiring look, decided we weren't any danger to the Malibu's sovereignty, and waved us through. We came along a dirt track, the sun toasting brown the hills that ran down to the sea past grazing cattle and fields of grain.

"Did you see this morning's *Times*? They liked *Lilac Time*."

"What did they say?"

"They liked the tender love scenes and the idealistic sentiments."

I thought the love scenes ridiculous, but by now I had learned to keep such idealistic sentiments, as the *Times* might say, to myself. "What about you? Anything to say about you?"

"I'm a sincere and manly lover."

"Exactly how I would describe you."

Coop threw me a look and then settled into silence for a time.

"Couldn't sleep after I got home last night," he announced suddenly.

"I wouldn't have thought sincere and manly lovers had any difficulty sleeping."

"Yeah, well, there you go, Orrack. There is more to us manly lovers than meets the eye. I lay awake thinking about Nell. Now that never happens to me. Never."

When I didn't immediately answer, he frowned. "What's the matter? You seem awfully quiet today. Couldn't sleep either?"

"I slept just fine," I lied.

"See? You're not in love. I am."

Of course, he was wrong about that. But then he was wrong about just about everything, wasn't he?

"What does that mean? You being in love."

"You're in love with somebody, it means you marry them. Pretty straightforward, you ask me."

"You'd marry Nell Devereaux?" The thought filled me with horror.

"I do believe I would. Yes, sir. The way I'm feeling right now, I believe I would."

"But you were just telling me last night how women complicated your life."

"Well, that was before I met her. She has class, Orrack. That's what I didn't have until now, and that's what I need."

"You need class?"

"Fellow in my position, sure. Like I told you last night, it's all about pretending. Hell, I'm a hick from Montana, but that don't work so well out here."

"Doesn't it?"

"No, it don't. They like you smooth and silky so that's what I give 'em."

"Ever think you might do better by being yourself?" I ventured.

He gave me a sidelong glance. "You loco or something, partner? Being yourself ain't pretending. I wanted to be myself I'd have stayed on a horse in Montana. Nope, Nell's the ticket all right. Folks in this town would have to take me seriously. Clara don't have class. Neither does Lupe. But Nell, boy, she has it coming out her ears."

"I don't know much about class," I said. "But I don't think it should come out your ears."

"What do you know about anything?" He snorted dismissively. "Being yourself. There's how stupid you are about things, right there."

We dropped down to a long, gently arching cove choked with volcanic rock. The cove ran off toward a misty headland. The islands of Santa Catalina, Anacapa, and Santa Cruz were hazy outlines to the south. A tiny cottage was mounted above the cove, flanked by stables. We were visiting Leslie Carter and her husband, Louis Payne, who were hosting a luncheon in Nell's honor. Leslie kept herself busy being old and wealthy. Louis Payne was a producer at Paramount.

The interior of the house was cozy enough: an Indian rug was hung on the wall near a plain brick fireplace. Big windows framed by blue-and-yellow cretonne curtains opened out to the sea.

Handsome, sporty types sprawled upon the sofas and comfortable chairs. Their ladies this afternoon were arrayed in a variety of summer hats with dramatic brims, the fashion rage this year, apparently. Everyone succeeded in looking disinterested at our arrival. There was no sign of Nell.

Leslie Carter raised a hand from the easy chair in the center of the room where she held court. Her face was mottled and haughty, her tiny form swathed head to foot in black, topped by a wide-brimmed garden hat with a crown of what looked to be geraniums sewn flat against the crown.

"Coop, do find yourself a drink. Louis. Louis? Where the deuce is that man?"

A handsome ruddy-faced gent, thick in the waist, but with a full head of curling white hair, dashed forward. "Here, breath of my life, right here."

"Wherever were you, my dear?"

"In the kitchen, fondling the maids."

"Keep your hands off the help, pet. They'll run off, and out here they are so hard to replace."

Her eyes never left me as she spoke.

A winsome young thing said, "Beverly Hills, then. They say Beverly Hills is the place to be now."

Leslie finally tore her gaze from me and focused on the winsome young thing. "Ye gods, girlie, surely you're not suggesting Beverly Hills as an alternative, what with that dreadful Doug Fairbanks and his awful tan, and little Mary who refuses to grow old, and people throwing themselves off the top of the hills of Beverly because they haven't been invited up to Pickfair to be put to sleep. Spare me! Malibu is the place, believe me. What do you think, mister—"

"That's Brae Orrack, ma'am. I'm afraid I'm not from around here, so I wouldn't know."

"Brae Orrack." She said my name as though she was handling nitro-glycerin. "No, I didn't think you came from around here, young man."

Behind me someone said, "You know Raquel Torres, that tough little piece of business under contract over at Metro? They made her record her voice yesterday."

"They made her do this?"

"That's right. I hear they're going to reproduce everyone's voice, and put it on file. All the studios. They want you for a movie, they take out your record, and play it, and if they don't like your voice, well, that's it, you're finished, you don't get hired."

"Listen to this. I hear there are trainloads of New York actors on their way out here. You know, people who have acted on the stage, with trained voices. The studios are bringing them out."

"They've gone mad for talk. Anything's possible."

"It can't last."

"I'm not so sure. Some people argue that talking pictures are here to stay."

Coop said to Louis Payne, "Have you seen Nell, by any chance?"

"Not by any chance, Coop, certainly not by any chance. By design. I stop chasing the maids and starlets when she's around. The absolute adorable thing about her is she detests Hollywood, and movie people. In particular—and this is the best thing about her—she refuses to have a thing to do with actors."

Coop looked as though he had been slapped in the face. Honestly, the man took a joke like anyone else would take a bullet.

I noticed Leslie Carter staring at me again. What was wrong with the woman anyway? Why did she keep looking at me like that?

A large woman in a flowing lemon dress said to a gentleman with a small round face and smaller round glasses, "Get this, his defense is that his wife took arsenic as a beautifier for her complexion."

"She lost her life trying to look good," chortled the round-faced gentleman. "That could only happen out here in Cinemaland."

Already I was tired of the prattle—not to mention Leslie Carter's piercing, suspicious eyes. I went out on the porch at the rear of the house.

A great palomino raced across the beach at the edge of the surf, coming toward the house, its hooves throwing up sprays of water and clumps of sand.

As the horse grew closer, I saw that the rider was Nell. Of course. Who else could it be? Not for her anything but the dramatic entrance. If you fly airplanes and climb mountains, then you do not merely get out of a car. Even a horse becomes somewhat mundane. Maybe she should have jumped out of a passing plane. I don't believe it would have surprised me.

She reined up below the porch as a man ran forward and grabbed the bridle. She leapt from the horse and came toward me, carrying a riding crop. This early afternoon, Nell wore a white open-necked shirt and tan jodhpurs shoved into knee-high boots. She did not walk toward the house. This was a woman for striding; a long, fine, straight-legged gait that showed determination. She would reach her destination, no matter what.

Spying me on the porch, she produced a smile that immediately cut away the rest of the world. "Orrack, the magic man. How are you?"

She flung her hand out to me, and I took it in mine.

"Miss Devereaux, a great pleasure to see you again."

"You are a charmer, aren't you, Orrack? I suspected that last night."

Me? A charmer? The fool unsophisticated around women? The spy for Machado, safe because he was no more than a movie star's driver? None of it true: Nell Devereaux thought me charming, and she would know such things.

"I'm not here to meet charmers, though," she continued. "Bring on boring Hollywood. I've steeled myself for this. Did Cooper come along with you?"

That was not the question I wanted to hear, but I put on a brave face. After all, I was charming and therefore able to overcome such things.

"Well, not being here to talk to charmers, you'll certainly want a few words with Mr. Cooper."

"Careful," she said. "You keep talking like that, and I'm going to run away with you."

"Well, that's the idea, isn't it?"

"Is it?" She delivered a merry laugh before disappearing through the door. From inside came loud, welcoming sounds. Now the party could begin in earnest; light had entered darkness.

I trailed her inside as Leslie Carter actually rose from her chair and fluttered over to bestow a kiss on Nell's proffered cheek. If Nell hated Hollywood, and found Hollywood people boring, she did an excellent job of covering it up. She smiled, bussed cheeks, and shook hands, not at all abashed by the attention, accepting it as no more than the natural state of affairs.

Coop hung to one side, like a dumbstruck sheepdog, the dark

strands of his hair falling down his forehead. Nell went over and pecked him on the cheek. That upset me no end. I received no such peck, and here I was the charmer. So she only kissed the non-charmers? Boiling with jealousy I turned away and found myself face-to-face with Louis Payne. He held out a book. "Have you read this?" It was a novel called *The Virginian* by Owen Wister.

"Afraid I'm not familiar with it." The last thing I wanted to do right now was talk about books with this old man.

"It's been around for a while; a great story of heroism and chivalry in the Old West. I'm hoping to make it over at Paramount. It's been done a couple of times before, but now with sound all the rage, it could be even better. Problem is, I can't find the right actor to play the lead."

The next thing Nell and Coop slid past me and disappeared out the back door. With nary a backward glance, I might add. Louis Payne raised an eyebrow. "I wonder if young Cooper knows what he's getting into."

As casually as I could, I said, "And what is he getting into?"

"A very dangerous fellow named General Machado."

"You know him?"

"A former cattle rustler who made good. Learned the trade from his father, and then gave it up so he could produce live sex shows. Four years ago he was a likable rogue around Havana's fleshpots. Now he calls himself *General* Machado, and runs the island. He has charm, powerful friends, ambition, and he knows how to pull off a neat balancing act—playing on the Cubans' dislike of Americans, while at the same time making himself very popular at the State Department by denouncing communism. They like that sort of thing there. They manage to overlook the fact that he admires Mussolini, has suspended political parties, moved millions of dollars off the island into his Miami bank accounts, and with what time he has left, orders his secret police to shoot anyone who gets in his way. He is corrupt, immoral, and highly dangerous."

"And chasing around after Nell."

"I'm afraid I'm partially responsible for that, thanks to my relationship with an all-round fixer at Paramount, a fellow named Slim Talbot."

"I know Slim," I said. "The repairman."

"Is there anyone in town who doesn't? Among Slim's other functions, he runs interference for General Machado when the great dictator visits Los Angeles. Anyway, I made the mistake of introducing Nell to Slim, and from there I do believe Slim made sure Machado got to know her. Big mistake, I'm afraid."

"Louis, pet, where are you now?" Leslie Carter's voice cut through the rest of the conversation in the room. "I need you!"

Louis Payne winked at me. "Be right there, breath of my life."

I went outside. There was Coop aboard a mare, racing Nell toward the distant headland. He beat her to the top, and that surprised me. Given the quality of the horse he looked to be riding, it would have been his skill that got him there first. The acknowledgment that Cooper could do anything properly irked me no end.

"I didn't know Coop could ride." I turned to find Louis Payne standing behind me, still holding the copy of *The Virginian.*

"He's from Montana," I offered. "Used to be a cowboy out there."

"You don't say?" said Louis, keeping his eyes on the two riders.

I indicated the book in his hands. "Maybe he could play *The Virginian* for you."

"He's such a phony on the screen," Louis said. "Nothing natural about him. A lot of actors got away with murder doing silent pictures. Rolling their eyes, wringing their hands, all sorts of nonsense that won't fly with sound. I believe the studio's about to let him go."

Atop the headland, I could see that they had dismounted. Nell walked away toward the edge. Coop hesitated by the horses, and then when she turned, he walked over to her.

"Still," Louis said, "maybe I'm underestimating the boy. He's certainly good-looking enough. You never know. Everyone's in such a panic at the moment, anyway. Won't hurt to have a look at him, I suppose."

I could see them very close together, Coop towering over Nell.

Maybe she liked that, tall fellows able to take command. I squinted, using my hand to shield my eyes from the sun. Was he kissing her? No, he couldn't be. But they were so close, what else could they be doing? My stomach twisted in a knot, and for once it had nothing to do with my father's curse.

Chapter Thirteen

Sandpipers poked through kelp beds as gulls hovered above the cliffs of the headland, staying at a safe distance so I could ponder my various misfortunes, including the one featuring General Machado, not as my new best friend, but, if Louis Payne was to be believed, a murderous dictator, the last man in the world I should have anything to do with. Well, I'd known some no-accounts in my time, even been accused of being among that breed, but murdering dictators were new to me.

The sound of approaching hoofbeats drew me out of my reverie. I thought it was Coop racing Nell back, exultant after all that kissing. But when I turned, I saw Coop riding alone and I could not have been more pleased if they had named a day after me.

Well, it turned out I could be more pleased, because not only was Coop back, but miserable in the bargain. "What are you doing?" he demanded as he leapt down off the horse, and slapped it toward the stables.

"Sitting here contemplating life," I answered.

"Yeah, well, quit being so damned flippant."

"Flippant?" I couldn't imagine what he was talking about.

"Yeah, flippant. I'm gonna say good-bye to Louis. I want you to bring the car around and have it ready when I come out of the house."

"Bring it around to where? It's directly in front of the house."

"Just do as I goddamn well tell you, and don't argue about it," he snapped, storming off toward the house. I looked back at the cliff and thought I could see Nell, seated in the grass near her horse, staring out at the Pacific. Thinking about what? Me? What an amusing fellow you are, Orrack. Why would she ever be thinking of you? Because we're good together, that's why. She said it herself. Make sure Coop brings you to lunch. So I could see the two of them ride off into the sun together? For a wild moment, I considered going up there. But supposing she didn't want to talk to anyone right now, least of all me?

Coward that I was, I slunk around to the front of the house, climbed behind the wheel of the Rolls and started the engine. A couple of moments later, Coop came out and got in the passenger side, slamming the door. "What are you waiting for? Let's get going."

You can imagine what a jolly ride it was back to Los Angeles, Coop slumped into a corner, scowling out at the horizon, me wondering if I should say something to him, but then not knowing what to say, seeing as how I didn't exactly want to encourage his relationship with Nell. This falling out between them neatly played into my plans, although using the word *plans* in connection with Nell and myself was something of a wild exaggeration.

"Goddamn women," he mumbled finally. He sat up straighter in his seat. "I live forever I'll never be able to figure them out."

I couldn't resist. "Does this mean you're not going to marry Nell Devereaux?"

He looked over at me sharply. "Who said anything about marrying?"

"You did. On your way out here."

He settled back in his seat and didn't say anything for a time. "Well, I won't be marrying her, so don't go renting a tux or anything like that."

"Thanks for the warning," I said.

"Turns out she's in love with someone else."

That sank my heart like a ship. "General Machado?"

He shrugged. "That's what I figured, too. But she says it's not him. She wouldn't tell me who. Some guy she's met."

Was there no end to Nell's suitors? They were lined up for miles, coming from all points of the compass, so many that you couldn't keep track of them all. I was lost in the crowd, the poor fellow driving cars and spying for the rich.

By the time we got back to his house, dusk was gathering and the dying sun drenched the neighborhood in rich ocher shades. At this time of day Los Angeles was a beautifully lit paradise; despite all the miseries you might currently be experiencing you couldn't help but be thrilled to find yourself here. Everyone that is but Coop. He unfurled himself from the semifetal position he had adopted and said, "Partner, looks like we've come to the end of the trail."

"Well, you're home, no doubt of that," I said.

"No, what I mean to say is that I won't be requiring your services any longer, Orrack."

"I see." I said it in a noncommittal way, trying to keep the disappointment out of my voice.

"I gotta start to concentrate on my career and put all this other crazy stuff behind me."

"Sure, I understand," I said.

"Come on inside, so's I can call a taxi for you, and also give you a little something for all your trouble."

"You don't have to do that, Coop."

"No, no, you're a good man, Orrack. I know we got off to a rough start there, but I like you, so don't argue with me, okay?"

What is the point? I thought to myself. All someone like me ever got from these Cinemaland people in the end was their money, so I'd be crazy not to take it. We got out and I followed him up the walk. He saw that the door was slightly ajar and came to a stop as though trying to figure what might be waiting for him on the other side. I suddenly realized that's what I was being paid for. I stepped past him saying, "You wait here. Let me take a look."

Coop didn't seem to mind that suggestion one bit.

Inside someone had closed the curtains so that the mounted animal heads stared sightlessly in the dimness. For a moment I didn't notice the chiffon evening gown carefully laid out on the sofa beside a lady's handbag or the red high-heeled shoes neatly placed beside the sofa. I did, however, see where someone had thrown up on the carpet. I followed the trail of vomit into the bathroom.

There, lying naked on the floor except for several strands of pearls, her perfect white body curled on its side, was Clara Bow. Her toenails and fingernails matched her hair. She was not moving.

Coop appeared behind me. I could hear his sharp intake of breath as I kneeled down to her. I didn't have all the experience in the world with this sort of thing, but I knew enough to check to make sure she was still breathing, and to clear her mouth with my fingers, ensuring that she had not swallowed her tongue. The good news was that she was still drawing breath, but not a whole lot of it, not enough to keep her going for very long.

"What the hell's she gone and done?"

"I'm not sure," I said. "Maybe taken something."

"Oh, Christ." The words came out of him like a sob.

"Call an ambulance," I said.

Coop just stood there, staring at her.

"Do as I say," I told him quietly. "Call the ambulance."

Wordlessly he left the bathroom. I lowered my head until my lips touched that lovely bow of a mouth, and I began to give her artificial resuscitation. After a few minutes of doing that, she suddenly stirred and choked. Her eyes fluttered open, and she rolled over on her side, throwing up some more.

"Orrack," she managed to say as I helped her sit up. "You being here m-m-mean I'm still alive?"

"What did you take, Clara?"

"Shit. C-c-c-can't even kill myself proper."

"Clara, tell me."

"What any self-respecting actress takes. Sleeping pills, of course."

I held her for a minute and then she lay back and passed out again. Coop appeared at the door. He had gone as white as Clara's body. "Ambulance is on its way," he said.

"She took sleeping pills," I said.

Coop shook his head. "Thought Clara would be a little more original than that."

The statement sounded as mean-spirited as anything I could imagine. I glared at him. He didn't seem to notice.

Chapter Fourteen

The ambulance arrived in ten minutes. By that time we had wrapped Clara in a blanket, and she seemed to be breathing more easily. The attendants were two middle-aged characters dressed in white uniforms with hair clipped close to the ears and smelling of stale cigarettes. They could have been twins. They were professional enough, though, even after they recognized Clara. I told them about the sleeping pills and that didn't seem to bother them one way or the other. They quickly got her onto a stretcher.

"My wife loves her movies," announced the younger one in a neutral tone.

"Then let's get her over to Los Angeles General so they can properly save her ass," said the older one impatiently.

I went out ahead to hold open the doors of the ambulance while they got her inside. Coop followed. "I'm going to the hospital with her," he said. "I want you to phone Slim and tell him what's happened."

"Why would you telephone Slim?"

"Don't ask questions. Just do it." He sounded much calmer now, a little more like an adult having to deal with this. All to the good.

"Soon as you get hold of him, get in the car and come over to the hospital. You got that?"

I said I did. Coop climbed into the back of the ambulance with Clara. He looked as though he was climbing into the mouth of hell. The attendants closed the door and the next thing the ambulance went shooting off down the street. Across the way a hump-shouldered woman wearing a black dress appeared; a keeper of the crypt, unless I missed my guess. She frowned at me as though I'd ruined her day.

I went back inside and telephoned Slim. He didn't sound happy. "Where are you?"

"I'm at Coop's place. Clara Bow took some sleeping pills. They've rushed her to the hospital."

Silence on the other end of the line and then Slim said, "Say that to me again."

I repeated it more slowly this time. More silence. "Coop told me to call you," I added.

"Yeah, I'll just bet he did." Slim sounded angry.

"Coop wants me to bring the car over to the hospital."

"All right, you do that. Stick with him. And Orrack?"

"Yes?"

"Don't say nothing to no one, you got that? Absolutely nothing."

"Got it," I said.

The line went dead. I took a big deep breath and went out to the car.

It took me half an hour to reach the Los Angeles County General Hospital. At reception, they wouldn't tell me where Clara was, and so I guessed that she might still be in emergency and wandered in there like I owned the place. It was all but empty, a couple of lights illuminating gray walls and a lone nurse hunched over paperwork behind a desk. The ward was like a theatrical set for a horror movie, awaiting only the arrival of the monster. Well, here I was. Now where was everyone else?

Clara had a room to herself at the back of the ward. There was nothing in there but a hospital bed with her all but lost in it, a tiny bundle hooked up to various tubes, like a hastily abandoned experiment. She stirred as I entered and managed to rustle up a smile. "Orrack," she said.

"Just wanted to make sure you were all right," I said.

"They pumped my stomach and did other unmentionable things, so I suppose I'm gonna live." She did not seem enthusiastic about the prospect. "My momma was crazy, and I guess I am, too."

"No," I said.

"Is he here?"

"He came in the ambulance with you." I seated myself in a chair beside the bed. Her hand found mine. "Well, you certainly scared us all," I said.

"I didn't want to scare everybody," she said sadly. "Just him. Goddamn, and I had it all planned out. The dress I would wear, the pearls. Even bought a new pair of shoes for the occasion."

She blinked away tears. "Then goddamn it, I t-t-t-threw up. Spoiled everything."

I didn't know what to say in response so I just sat there, holding her hand, and after a while, she drifted off to sleep again.

I went back out to where the nurse was seated. She jumped when I appeared at the desk, as though ghosts haunted the place. She recovered and demanded to know how I had gotten past her, and then ordered me into the waiting room. That's where I found Coop talking to a perplexed Slim Talbot.

"Alls I'm saying, you shouldn't be here," Slim was saying. "It's gonna look bad."

"What was I supposed to do?"

Slim saw me approach and nodded in my direction. "You could have let Orrack handle it. That's what he's here for."

"She took the pills in my house, for God's sake."

"She wants to see you," I said to Coop.

"How the hell would you know that?" Slim demanded.

"I just saw her," I said.

"It ain't your job to be seeing anybody," he said angrily. "It's your job to stand there and do as you're told and keep your mouth shut!"

"Hey, ease off there, Slim," Coop said. "Wasn't for Orrack, Clara might be dead now, and then where would we be?"

Slim glared, but didn't say anything else to me. Instead, he spoke to Coop. "Look just get the hell out of here, will you? There's all sorts of reporters outside. Now I know those boys and I do believe I can take care of them okay, but just in case. Orrack can drive the car around to the back by the kitchen. I've done this before. The reporters don't ordinarily stake out that entrance. He'll pick you up there and take you home."

"I should see her, make sure she's all right," Coop said. He didn't say it in a way that made you think he actually believed it.

"Coop, you got a career to think about here," Slim explained patiently. "Twenty-four hours ago, I wouldn't have given a plugged nickel for your chances in this town. But now I hear that's all changed."

Coop looked surprised. "You did? What'd you hear?"

"Talk that they might just be thinking of some fool young cowboy for the starring role in *The Virginian*."

"Nobody's said anything to me."

"Apparently Louis Payne wants to have a look at you."

"Payne? You mean that old fart out at the Malibu?"

"If you weren't so dumb as soon as a pretty girl walks in front of you, you might actually pay attention to your business, like you're supposed to. He's the producer of that picture."

"I can't believe that old guy's in charge of *The Virginian*," Coop said.

"So from here on in, young fella, you got to go real careful. Walk away from this. Go home with Orrack. Clara's gonna be fine. I'll see to it myself. That's a promise."

More than anything in the world, I wanted Coop to tell Slim to go to hell or better yet just turn on his heel and walk the few yards it took to reach Clara. Instead, he hung his head like the beaten dog he was, and didn't say a thing. Slim poked me in the arm. His eyes were fierce. "Go outside. Get the car. Bring it round to the back. Make it quick."

The blood rose into my face. I was on the verge of losing whatever sense of control I'd been able to maintain what with everybody ordering me around. But you'll be glad to know I swallowed hard and did not show anything. Be polite. Do the job. Don't talk back. The good servant Orrack.

Outside, the night had cooled considerably. I let the breeze wash across my face. That calmed me some, that and the crowd of reporters gathered at the entrance giving me the once-over.

"What's going on in there?" demanded a sallow-faced young fellow in an oversized fedora lost in a suit that could have fit two of him.

"Sick people getting better," I said.

One of the reporters came over, a fat guy with a flushed face, breath laced with illegal whiskey. "You didn't see Clara Bow in there by any chance?"

"That's a joke?"

"No joke. She's in there."

"You're a princess like Clara, why would you come here?"

" 'Cause even princesses get sick," said the sallow-faced guy. The others chuckled: what a rube, they were thinking.

"Well, I saw my uncle Fred in there, but Clara Bow wasn't with him."

The reporters chuckled again. The flush-faced guy waved a dismissive hand and everyone proceeded to forget I ever existed, a not uncommon occurrence in my misspent life, but helpful this evening.

I got the car and drove it around to the rear of the hospital, found the kitchen entrance and parked. A few minutes later, Coop came slinking into view, looking like he had just escaped from Sing Sing Prison. I reached over and opened the door and as soon as he was inside, he hunched way down so that as I drove past the reporters, they couldn't see him.

After I had turned onto the street, he straightened and said, "This is the damnedest thing. I thought that *Lilac Time* was going to be the end of me. Instead, they're talking about putting me into a Western. If that don't beat all, I don't know what does."

"Funny, I thought you might be more worried about Clara," I said. "Guess that was kind of stupid of me, huh?"

He shifted around a bit. "Sure, of course, I'm worried. Why wouldn't I be? Pulling a stunt like that at my place. She's going crazy over this sound thing."

"I don't think it has anything to do with sound," I said.

"What else would it be?"

"She's in love," I said.

"Love?" The word exploded out of him as though he'd never heard it before and couldn't imagine what it was. "How the hell would you know that?"

"She told me," I said. "Told you, too, when it comes to it."

"She never said a damn thing," he insisted.

"Yes, she did. Everything that happened tonight, I believe, was her way of telling you."

That reduced him to silence. I glanced over and saw that in the light thrown off by the dashboard his face had turned the color of dough. A tear rolled down his cheek. I could not believe it.

Gary Cooper was crying.

I dropped him off at his house. He made some noises about me coming in, but I just wanted to go home, and I believe he wanted to be left alone, too. I parked the car in the drive and waited until he went inside and shut the door. I stood in the gathering darkness, watching the lights swirling in a golden glow down the Beverly Hills. No light went on inside Coop's house, though. It remained in darkness.

Eventually, I walked down the street and found a bus stop. I waited for twenty minutes until a bus came along that got me down to the streetcar line on Sunset and a trolley that took me back out to Venice Beach and the pink boardinghouse. I was about halfway home before I remembered I was supposed to meet with General Machado. In all the excitement, I'd forgotten about it. As I approached the boardinghouse I wondered if Kiki Diaz might still be waiting. But Kiki wasn't there. Instead, sitting on the porch was Nell Devereaux. She sat with her knees together, wearing a yellow summer dress, her hair loose around her lovely face. She looked wonderful in yellow. She undoubtedly looked wonderful in any color.

"You left without saying good-bye."

Well, I could have said something, only the words refused to form in

my head and when they did my mouth wouldn't release them in a timely
fashion.

"So I came to the lair of the magic man," she added. "Finding him
wasn't easy, let me tell you."

"So how did you?"

"Let's say I owe a big favor to a man named Slim Talbot."

"The repairman?"

"Your employer, I understand. Not a man you want to owe favors to."

I didn't respond, too busy wondering why Slim hadn't said something, thinking she knows I'm the chauffeur, not Coop's friend, just his
driver who lives in a pink boardinghouse in need of a paint job. She
frowned and said, "You have to help me out here, Orrack. It's not every
night I turn up on a fellow's doorstep, particularly when he takes his
time about showing up and most particularly when it doesn't seem like
the fellow is all that thrilled to see me."

"No, no," I hastily interjected, panic helping me finally discover my
voice. "Just surprised, that's all."

She stood and came over to me. "I'm sure women must show up all
the time, lusting after you."

Lusting after me? Was Nell lusting after me? What about this mysterious person she told Cooper about? The guy she loved. Did she lust after him, too?

"You're very quiet again, Orrack."

"I had to drive Coop home. That's why I left."

"Not a happy fellow, our Coop."

I thought of Clara Bow lying naked on his bathroom floor. "No, he
isn't."

"He thinks he's in love with me, but he's not."

I was simultaneously upset and relieved. He loved her, but didn't
really love her. "You can tell something like this?"

"He's so transparent, that boy. When you're Gary Cooper, and the
world is at your feet, you don't love anyone but yourself. How can you?"

"Well, I might give it a try," I said.

"Tell you what."

"What?"

"How'd you like to take me over to the pier and show me a swell time? Are you up for that?"

I was dead tired when I arrived home. But not now. Now I was a new man, ready for anything as long as it included Nell.

"I do believe I am, Miss Devereaux."

She took my arm. "Then let's be off, Mr. Orrack."

Chapter Fifteen

We strolled along Ocean Front Walk, part of the thronging crowds out for a night's excitement, but not part of them at all. We went through the arcaded walkways past the Owl Drug Company and the Billiards and Bowling emporium across the street, past one of the many barbecue places in Venice Beach, past the sweetshop and the Western Union office, past the Neptune Theater and the Potter Apartments where you could rent rooms by the day or the week. We ignored it all, lost in each other; Nell explaining that she was born in Port Huron, Michigan, me riveted to her every word. Her father was a mining engineer who decided his daughter would have the best possible education even if she was a girl and shipped her off to private schools and colleges in England and France. Much to her father's chagrin, none of it interested her, except the languages; she learned to speak five. Otherwise her preference was for speed. Anything fast: cars, boats, and horses. Especially horses. At a fair once in Detroit, they offered a cash prize to anyone who could ride a horse named Outlaw. The animal had thrown all comers. Nell didn't hesitate. She climbed aboard.

"Don't tell me you rode him," I said.

"You don't think I could?"

"That's the thing. I believe you could."

"Then you think too highly of me. Fact is Outlaw threw me like he threw everyone else. But I was the only woman who tried that afternoon, and I stayed on longer than anyone else. I swear I did."

Attending Columbia University in New York, she met Amelia Earhart. The two became friends and erstwhile rivals. Amelia decided she wanted to drive a car. An instructor taught her in forty minutes. The same instructor taught Nell in ten, she said. Amelia decided to buy an airplane and learn to fly. Nell went out and bought one, too. That was the real speed. Better than cars or horses. Better than anything. She could not wait to be airborne. She was one of only one hundred and seventeen American women, along with Amelia Earhart, who held a pilot's license. Flying got her the first whiff of notoriety—or rather not flying. The plane she piloted developed engine trouble, and she had to bail out. Thus she became the first woman ever to parachute from a plane, above Cincinnati in 1925.

Then, according to Nell, she got sidetracked in Paris: the prince who was a mountain climber made his appearance. Being from Michigan, she couldn't help but be impressed by royalty. That was her problem, she ruefully conceded, dangerous, powerful men with whom she had nothing in common too easily distracted her, Machado being a case in point.

"Makes me wonder where that puts me in the scheme of things," I said.

"Does it?"

"Not being a prince or running a country. Those shortcomings can make a fellow nervous when he's with you."

"Good," she said. "Keep you on your toes, Orrack. But here's the thing, you're a magic man, are you not?"

"That's me," I said.

"So in the scheme of things, that's much more interesting than being a prince. After all, the world is full of royalty. But how many magic men are there?"

"I hadn't thought of it quite that way," I conceded.

"Leslie doesn't know what to make of you."

"No?" I did not like the sound of that.

"She believes you're a warlock."

I tried to laugh. "And she knows a lot of warlocks, does she?"

"She believes in that sort of thing—the supernatural, witches and warlocks."

"Well, they don't really exist, do they?" I didn't sound very convincing.

"Leslie seems to think so."

"But you don't?"

"There is something entirely dangerous and fascinating about you, Orrack, no question. Something I should probably stay away from."

"That would be the best idea all right," I said.

She hugged my arm. "But then I would have no one to go to the midway with, now would I?"

"What about your friend General Machado? Doesn't he like to do this sort of thing?"

She studied me with great intensity before she said, "The princess and the dictator. You can't make this stuff up, can you?"

You can't make up the magic man and the princess either, I thought. Out loud I said, "I guess you can't."

"He wants me to go away with him."

"Go where?"

"Havana, I suppose. He'll make me a queen and I'll sit beside him on the throne."

"You could help him shoot people."

"Come on." She frowned. "They're rumors, that's all. No one knows anything for sure."

"Gerry would know, wouldn't he?"

"Yes, I suppose all I have to do is get up the nerve to ask him," she said quietly.

"So you'll go?"

"I don't know. I don't want to love anyone. Love's such a waste of time, and it complicates everything." She looked at me. "What about you?"

"What about me?"

"You don't want to fall in love do you?"

"Me? Never crossed my mind."

She studied me more closely. "You sure about that?"

"Absolutely," I lied.

A curly-haired strongman wearing a fake over-the-shoulder leopard skin yanked on a chain attached to a Model T filled with laughing teenagers as we came onto the pier. The teenage boys stopped watching the straining strongman so that they could give Nell the eye, me feeling proud as punch about it, with maybe a hint of jealousy thrown in for good measure. She ignored the stares and said, "So far you haven't been much of a date, Orrack, if you don't mind my saying so."

That devastated me. "I haven't?"

"You haven't taken my hand. A boy and a girl on a date. The boy's supposed to hold her hand, don't you know?"

I'm not sure I did, but she didn't need to know how lacking I was in knowledge of such matters. I quickly took her hand and she squeezed it and we held hands like that, allowing ourselves to be swallowed up in the noisy razzle-dazzle of the midway. That's when I heard the voice.

For a moment, I thought I was imagining things. But then I heard it again. There wasn't enough noise in the world to drown out those words: "I come from the land of magic and superstition, a place where the power of Satan and the evil eye transfix everyone, where always it's the funeral plumes and never the bridal roses, where the curse on souls and the getting of revenge endures over love."

No, it couldn't be. Impossible. I peered through the surging crowd, but couldn't see anything. Maybe it was simply my fervid imagination working overtime.

Nell was at my elbow. "I want a frog."

"What?"

"A frog. You're a magic man, aren't you? You can get me a frog."

I heard the voice again, clearer than ever: "You see, a magician knows tricks, sleight of hand, how to deceive the eye. A magic man, on the other hand, is a highly trained individual knowledgeable in the dark art of conjuring."

I swirled around, trying to see through the crowd. "Are you all right?" Nell's voice, directly into my ear.

"Never better," I said.

"Then what about my frog?"

What the blazes was she talking about? Then I noticed the Chuk-a-Ring, and understood. It was one of the midway games. Your prize was a stuffed frog. I'd been around the pier enough to know these games were rigged to keep the suckers from ever winning. But what was the use of telling her that? The lady wanted a frog, and I could do nothing but try to get it for her.

A pimply-faced barker no more than nineteen in a stained vest saw us approach and broke out a toothless grin, eyes gleaming with the restless knowledge that the marks had arrived. "There ya go folks! Win the lady a stuffed green frog. All you have to do is get one of these rings around one of them fellers three times and you got yourself a prize, yes sirree, Bob!"

"No problem for a magic man, I'm sure," said Nell. Was there the hint of a challenge? I believe there was.

"None at all," I said in a voice ringing with certainty I did not feel. I was terrible at this sort of thing, even if the game wasn't a cheat. Never in a million years was I going to get three rings around those stuffed frogs mounted at various intervals on fake water lilies floating in a tub of water seemingly miles away. I looked at Nell. She stared back expectantly at her knight in shining armor, the hero who would win the day—and the frog.

Damn.

I felt the sweat rolling down my scrawny worthless neck. The rings were made of light balsa wood, designed to be totally untrustworthy, certain of going in any direction but the one chosen for them. I raised one, narrowed my eyes, and leaned forward across the counter, trying to gauge the distance between the nearest fake water lily and me. Gently now, oh, so gently, I tossed the ring into the air. It looped up, seemed to hang for an eternity and then dropped. To my utter amazement, it fell neatly around a frog.

I couldn't believe it. The barker seemed as surprised as me. "That's the one," he said. Nell clapped delightedly. The barker removed the ringed frog from his lily. "Two more," he announced.

The second ring was by necessity aimed farther afield, but my confidence was high, my aim more sure, my throw a little smoother. For one sickening moment, however, I was sure the ring would miss entirely. But no—miracle of miracles—it settled around the second frog.

"One more, and we got ourselves a winner, yes indeedy," announced the barker sounding a trifle unsure as he removed the second frog.

Nell's gold-flecked eyes, so intense now, never left me.

The remaining frogs occupied a remote place far, faraway. As I stood there poised with that last ring, I realized my eyes had grown blurry. I was losing my eyesight. Going blind! That third ring was slippery in my fingers. It was all I could do to hold on to it. Wild rivers of sweat ran down my back. My stomach tightened into a painful ball.

Summoning what little confidence I could still muster, I raised my arm in what was supposed to be a graceful movement. Except at this point there was not a graceful movement in my entire body. The wooden ring jerked away from my fingers, spinning on a wobbly trajectory toward—what? I had launched the damned thing into outer space. I concentrated on that shimmering, uncertain ring, willed it—*willed it!*—it to land on one of those frogs.

Abruptly, the ring dropped as though hit by gunfire. Too late.

Far too late.

But then.

Sometimes there really is a *but then* in life. Not very often, just once every hundred thousand years or so.

The ring caught the frog, hung there, frozen, as though trying to get past so it could travel on forever. But that frog wouldn't let the ring go; it liked the ring that had arrived so unexpectedly, wanted that ring on its lily pad. And mostly it got its wish.

Mostly.

The ring settled indecisively, half on the frog and half off.

The pimple-faced barker peered at the ring, turning his head at an angle as though not quite believing what his eyes were telling him.

I heard Nell say, "He won! Give him his prize."

The barker didn't say anything, not ready to buy that argument before studying the situation with a great deal more care. He approached the partially ringed frog the way an Apache might steal up on a cavalry encampment. He bent down, peered again, and then said, "Well, I'll be damned." He straightened, turned, and announced in a bewildered voice, "We got ourselves a real live winner."

Nell threw her arms around me as though I had flown to the top of Nanga Parbat with her hanging from my clenched teeth. She was like a happy kid as she took possession of her stuffed frog from the sullen barker. As for me, well, I'm not quite sure what to make of what I did. There was palpable relief, I guess, accompanied by a sense that in a life where good luck hadn't exactly dogged my trail, it somehow found me at that moment. I don't know why winning the frog counted for so much, but it did, and I had, against anything I ever would have predicted, won the day.

And then I heard that voice again: "Here's what I'd like you to do. Just pick one of these stones. That's it, any one of them."

I swung around and this time through the crowd I could see the broad shoulders and muscular arms of a man in a tuxedo, his black hair glistening in the light thrown off from the Some Kick roller coaster. Just a glimpse, mind you, before the crowd closed in again and that momentary image was lost.

"Is something wrong?" Nell sounded concerned.

I forced a grin. "The pressure of winning. Kind of takes it out of a fellow."

"I can imagine the pressure must be enormous," she said with a laugh. "Why don't we get out of here?"

"All right."

I did not look back as we strode off the pier. I was on a real date. I had won the damned frog. I was not going to think about anything else tonight. Except I could not get that voice out of my head. The voice of John Orrack. The Great Orrack himself.

The Great and Evil Orrack.

I had to be imagining that voice. Had to be. It was the only explanation. My father was dead after all; I knew that for a fact.

I knew that because I'm the one who killed him.

Chapter Sixteen

We came along Sunset, Nell behind the wheel of a big Chrysler Imperial. She turned down Mulholland to Melrose, and the next thing I knew we were at the Paramount studio. A sleepy guard in a brown uniform approached and she rolled down the window saying something about Louis Payne. The guard gave us a cursory glance before allowing the car through the impressive gates and onto the lot. No more worrying about voices now. There were other things to consider.

She drove with disconcerting speed through narrow streets twisted between vast stages, finally slowing to turn into the mouth of an alley. She stopped and switched off the ignition. She didn't look at me, just opened the door and got out.

I followed her toward a single lightbulb illuminating a doorway. She pulled the door open and we stepped into another world, one that existed just out of sight of the real one. It was our secret world, only the two of us allowed. I never would have thought of it, but she did: the magic of Nell Devereaux.

Clusters of yellow light flared through a cavernous interior intersected by catwalks dropping long partitions to floor level. Nell again took my hand, the navigator across this new and uncharted realm. We went forward through the light, our shadows thrown across a drawing room of what I imagined was seventeenth-century France.

Huge mirrors framed in gold and gilt reflected an imposing fireplace and lushly brocaded love seats. This history was fake, of course, as it had to be in a place where there was no history and nothing was real. The frames were not of gold but painted wood. The walls were movable and made of balsa. Thick cables snaked across Persian rugs. A vast archway led into a noblewoman's ivory sleeping chamber where a canopied bed draped in silk was watched over by sly cherubs, their dirty little smiles reflected in more gilt-edged mirrors. Beyond the bed rolled endless darkness.

She kneeled on the bed and I floated beside her. "What are you thinking?"

"About you."

"We're going to behave, magic man. Even if you did win a stuffed frog for me."

"A stuffed frog should open all sorts of doors."

"It should, you're right. But we're just going to sleep together because I'm too confused for it to be anything else just now."

Just now? What then of later? Did later present further possibilities? I could not bring myself to ask the question.

"You're going to put your arm around me and hold me tight. But that's all."

"That's enough," I said.

"Am I worth the trouble, do you think?"

I managed a laugh. "Everyone is in love with you. There are lineups. What does it matter what I think?"

"Because it does. Because you don't love me."

"Nell. The irresistible Nell."

"I'll bet you can resist me, Orrack. I see it in your eyes. Steely determination."

"You can see that, can you?"

"With total clarity."

I wanted to kiss her but could not bring myself to do it, so, of course, she did. Our lips were so close by now, I suppose in retrospect it would have been difficult to do anything else. The kiss lingered, her mouth taking its time against mine.

"Lordy, lordy," she said. "Maybe Leslie was right. Maybe you are a warlock at that. Luring away the innocent women of the world."

If only she knew how bad I was at the business of luring. But for the moment, I was willing to allow her to think any way she wanted.

"Except it turns out some of those women are not so innocent, doesn't it magic man?"

"Would that happen to include yourself?"

"It might," she said.

It was my turn to kiss her. Her hand lightly caressed the back of my neck, and the coolness of her skin was against me as I inhaled the aroma of her. Somehow a breast tumbled free of her blouse.

She shuddered, breathing out. "Oh, Orrack, Orrack, you are not playing fair. You promised you'd behave."

"I don't recall any such promises."

"I'm sure there were," she said.

She stretched on the bed and I reached for her; she twisted around so that we lay together spoon fashion, and pressed my hand against her breast. "My magic man," she murmured.

Yes, I was. I was hers. In a matter of hours she had taken possession of my heart. There is the way around a curse and here was the way.

Finally, Nell drifted off to sleep. Gently I turned her onto her back. Her chest rose and fell rhythmically. I felt her stir against me.

Chapter Seventeen

Nothing would please me more than to report that when we awoke the next morning, we made furious love together, Nell and myself, not just lifting the curse threatening my life, but tossing it away forever, totally forgotten in the rushing erotic force of our passion. That's what I would like to tell you rightly enough—but alas I can't do that and maintain an honest chronicle of my adventures. In fact when I awoke, Nell was not even there. She had slipped away during the night, leaving behind a note, folded in two and perched atop my clothes. It stated the following: STAY AWAY FROM ME. I'M NO GOOD FOR YOU. N.

I couldn't believe it. That was all? She was no good for me? How could she say that? What had happened to make her come to such a conclusion? Had I snored in the middle of the night?

I felt terrible as I rose from the bed and began to dress. I had received the first of many lessons about love, apparently, and that lesson as far as I could make out, was as follows: do not believe when it comes to love that anything is ever settled. Just when you think it is, it isn't; love arrives and any kind of certainty disappears.

Here ends the lesson.

At least for now.

I went out into the gloomy morning. Nell had taken the big Chrysler Imperial along with the stuffed frog I had fought so hard to win for her, and so there I was stranded on the Paramount lot, beginning to fill up with poker-faced men in work clothes wearing cloth caps, hurrying to their jobs. Standing there, unshaven in my rumpled clothes, still half asleep, I felt like an absolute fool, played for a sucker by a beautiful woman. But then what did I expect? Well, I guess I expected more.

"Orrack! Brae Orrack," I heard a voice call out. I turned and there was Slim Talbot huffing and puffing toward me.

"You looking for me?" demanded the repairman.

"Just on my way to see you," I said, quick as can be.

"Well, you're headed in the wrong direction," Slim said.

"Easy to get lost around this place."

"Follow me," he ordered, and I duly trailed behind as he turned down a side street, grumbling away to himself as he strode along, a man in perpetual disagreement with the world. "How's Coop doing?"

"Haven't seen him this morning," I said. Truthful enough. "How's Clara?"

"They're letting her out of the hospital today, I believe." He shook his head. "Damn foolish thing to do, you ask me. Thought she had more brains than that. Well, Clara's gonna have a lot to deal with next little while. Hope she's up to it."

Nothing about Nell, though. No curiosity as to why she might have been calling him to get my address. I was not about to complicate matters by asking him.

We went into his office where I once again perched in front of his desk while he sat polishing his glasses. A coffee mug stood guard over an open copy of the *Times*. Slim pointed his glasses in the general direction of the newspaper. "They got rid of the last horse and carriage at the White House. From here on in the president gets himself around in a Pierce-Arrow. Now ain't that a shame? Nothing like a good horse you ask me, but there you go. Just goes to show you, nothing's like it used to be. Don't know whether that's good or bad, but it's sure as hell the way it is. Everyone has to understand that. Me. Clara. Everyone."

He threw his glasses down onto the paper as though to emphasize the point.

"So here's the thing. You've done a pretty good job, Orrack. The way you handled things at Coop's place yesterday and then at the hospital, not bad."

"Thanks," was all I could think of to say.

"You just never know about this business, especially right now with everything up in the air. Yesterday, I figured Coop could start packing his bags. Today, well, the big boys are in the mood to make him a talkies star. So what's the stupid bastard do? He goes and gets himself into more hot water, that's what he does."

I arranged to look exasperated, like one of those schoolteachers I used to have, at the end of their patience with me. "What's he done now?" I demanded in a cross voice.

Slim picked up his newly polished glasses, checked the coffee mug, frowned, then replaced the glasses on the end of his nose, and blinked as though seeing me for the first time. "He's got the president of Cuba himself pissed at him, what he's done."

"General Machado?"

"So you've met him."

"At the premiere the other night."

"Then you must know this Nell Devereaux dame."

"Met her," I said.

"You know Coop's taken a shine to her?"

"He was out at the Malibu with her yesterday," I answered. "I know that much."

"Another one of these dames you could ask a lot of questions about if you happened to be in a suspicious frame of mind." He sighed. "But then I suppose Hollywood's full of dames you should be asking questions about—and steering clear of."

Good advice, the sort I should be listening to. So should Coop. But the plain fact was that neither one of us was listening.

"Anyway," Slim continued, "the general don't appreciate Coop's attentions towards his lady, and the general is no one to mess with in these matters."

"Like Al Howard," said I.

"Yeah, like Al Howard. Only the general he's about ten times as ornery as Al."

"You don't mind me asking, how'd you hear about this?"

"Don't mind you asking." Slim poked his glasses farther up his nose. "I'm the repairman around here, Orrack. Don't you forget it. It's my business to hear things, so I hear 'em. That's how I survive in this town. I hear the things I'm supposed to hear. And I don't hear the things I ain't supposed to hear."

Slim blinked behind his glasses, like an irritated owl. "Here's what I want you to do: I want you to keep on with what you're doing. Stick close to Coop for the time being, see if you can't keep him out of trouble at least till we see if he's gonna be in this Western or not. Pay you another fifty bucks for your good work. How does that sound?"

It sounded better than I could ever have imagined. I said, "It sounds fine."

"Just to complicate things a little more," Slim continued, "I also hear the general's hired his own muscle to take care of Cooper—a pretty tough hombre, I'm told."

"Is that a fact?" I said in a neutral voice. No point telling him I was the tough hombre in question. Not that I was feeling particularly tough this morning.

"What do you think? You think you can handle a fellow like that?"

"He won't be any trouble," I said.

"Well, just in case."

Slim opened a drawer in the bottom of his desk, and the next thing, to my surprise, he was plunking a Colt .45 six-shooter down on his desk. "You know how to handle one of these things?"

I was a fellow used to fists and perhaps the odd crowbar. I didn't know much at all about guns. But I don't suppose that's what Slim wanted to hear. "I reckon you point it at someone and pull the trigger," I said.

"You *squeeze* the trigger, and if you do, make sure you shoot someone worth the shooting. Okay?"

"Good enough," I said.

"You're okay, Orrack. When I first met you, wasn't quite sure what to make of you. But you handle yourself real good, and that's what's needed here the next little while—a fellow who doesn't lose his head where a woman is concerned."

"I'm the fellow for that," I said.

"That's what I want to hear," he said.

Slim gave me a big friendly smile and pushed the gun across the desk toward me. I grinned right back at him and reached for the gun.

Chapter Eighteen

Truth is fine as far as it goes, but the problem is, it doesn't go far enough. Most of the trouble I've found myself in during my misspent life started with the mistake of telling the truth. The lying helps to get around that sort of thing. It allows you to be something you are not— something better—and people like that. This place called Hollywood was built on that kind of thinking, so in a way I suppose I fit right in. If Gerardo Machado thought I was working for him against Coop, and Slim Talbot thought I was working for him so I could protect Coop, then everyone came out ahead, including yours truly.

Let's be honest. If I didn't employ what few wits I possessed, then all the concerned parties wouldn't give me the time of day. I was only the workingman, after all, and who gave a damn about him? For all anyone cared I could be just as easily washing a car as driving it. This morning, as luck, and a little chicanery on my part, would have it, I was driving the car: a rattletrap Ford to be sure, but a real car nonetheless. Not that I owned it or anything, but Slim provided it courtesy of my new pals at Paramount. He also took me back over to the wardrobe department, where the woman who could afford to smoke factory cigarettes outfitted me with a spiffy black suit, a step up from the chauffeur's uniform, to be sure.

This morning as I drove back out to Venice Beach, I had come out unexpectedly on top. I looked the proper gentleman, a long way from the bedraggled character left stranded by an undependable woman who had deceived him as to her true intentions—although what her true intentions were exactly remained something of a mystery. This reversal of fortune was all because I told a few white lies—didn't even tell them so much as I allowed a number of misconceptions to go uncorrected.

I got back to the house, anxious for my fellow boarders to see that overnight I had elevated my status well beyond that of mere chauffeur. Now I was a man in a suit driving a car with a gun in his pocket and money in his wallet. In America, a man with money and a gun is a success and you can't do better than that. But it's a life wherein you take a step forward and someone knocks you three steps back. I came into the parlor, bursting with the news of my unexpected new status. Instead of Eddie the rubber man or Meyer the bootlegger, there was General Machado himself in a white suit I swear did not have a single crease in it. He perched as comfortable as you please under the glowering sepia portrait of the beloved Reillys. Meanwhile, the good missus served him coffee and chattered away.

"Now Bing he likes that new Studebaker President, the Straight Eight, I do believe they call it. He says it can be had for nineteen hundred dollars and he says that's cheap. Well, that don't sound so cheap to me. Does it to you?"

Machado appeared nonplussed by the question. "I'm afraid I do not know much about American automobiles."

The Missus Reilly's face sagged with disappointment. "You being the president of a country and all, I thought you might have the inside track on these things."

"I'm afraid not." The general applied a frosty smile.

I could scarcely believe my eyes. I had never seen her serve anyone anything, and certainly not accompanied by friendly, albeit dim-witted, conversation. Kiki Diaz leaned against the wall a few paces away from his boss, scowling as I made my entrance. General Machado, on the other hand, looked positively delighted.

"Señor Brae Orrack, there you are. Mrs. Reilly has been kind enough to entertain us in your absence."

Mrs. Reilly actually fluttered coquettishly. No sign of a roll-your-own jammed into that foreboding mouth this morning.

"Not every day we have such an important visitor," she said in a voice that carefully pronounced each word as though a grammatical mistake might well cost her valuable social standing. "Brae, you should have told us of your acquaintance with the Señor President Machado."

I couldn't in fact think of a thing to say. I just grinned inanely, aware that I had left the gun in the car. Kiki was a nice reminder that I should not in the future be so careless.

Machado put his coffee cup to one side and blessed Mrs. Reilly with a dazzling smile. "Perhaps I could have a few words in private with Señor Orrack. Do you mind?"

"No, no, not at all." Why the woman was positively simpering as she backed awkwardly from the room. As soon as she was gone, Machado frowned at the coffee as though something black and terrible had just crossed his path, which, if Mrs. Reilly's coffee was up to her usual standards, it had. Kiki straightened and moved away from the wall like he was getting ready to jump me. Abruptly there was a tension in the room that had not been present a moment ago.

"You're wondering where I got to last night," I said, thinking to beat him to the punch.

"Why don't you sit down, Brae?" Machado said in a calm voice. "You know what I hear about this Coop? I hear he is hung like a horse."

"I thought Charlie Chaplin was hung like a horse." I slid into a chair across from him.

"Coop, too. I hear this from a very good source." He looked at me as though expecting some sort of response.

"Maybe everyone in Hollywood is hung like a horse," I said. "Maybe you can't get into Cinemaland unless your penis is a certain size."

"Kiki waited a long time for you," Machado said. The sentence hung in the air like a threat.

"Well, here is the gossip your source didn't tell you, General. Mr. Cooper and Miss Devereaux had a terrible falling out during lunch at the Malibu."

Machado perked up at this news. "They did?"

"Coop insisted on leaving, so I had no choice but to drive him back here."

"Miss Devereaux did not accompany him?"

"Certainly not," I said.

"What did Cooper say about what happened between himself and Miss Devereaux?"

"He didn't say much of anything, except to observe that I wouldn't have to rent a tuxedo because he wasn't going to be marrying Nell Devereaux."

Machado took this in with the serious mien of a man negotiating a peace treaty. "And you are certain he had no further communication with Miss Devereaux?"

"Pretty certain," I said. "Why do you ask?"

"Miss Devereaux seems to have disappeared."

I could have told him where she had disappeared, but that did not seem like a very good idea.

"Where were you last night?" Kiki Diaz moved into my sight line.

"What do you mean?"

"It's a simple question, amigo. Where were you last night?"

"Coop had some problems," I said quickly.

"What kind of problems?" demanded Kiki.

"A female of his acquaintance who had to be hospitalized."

"Not Miss Devereaux?" This from Machado.

I shook my head. "I ended up staying at his place for the night. I had a meeting at Paramount this morning, and then came home when it was finished."

Kiki kept looking at me. It was hard to tell whether he was satisfied with my answer or not.

Machado rose to his feet. He also spent some time studying me before he said, "Continue to keep an eye on Cooper. Can you do that?"

"If that's what you want, although it doesn't seem like he's going to have much of anything to do with Miss Devereaux."

"Nonetheless, let's not take anything for granted. Let's see what happens." He sounded friendly enough, but still I wondered. "Kiki, write down a number where you can be reached, should Señor Orrack come up with anything."

Kiki withdrew a business card from his wallet and quickly scrawled a number on the back of it, then thrust it at me.

"I'll be in touch," I said, pasting on my most reassuring smile.

Machado looked at me curiously before he said, "I'm sure you will."

He went out, and Kiki followed, throwing a dark scowl back at me as a kind of signal, I suppose. But a signal of what? That he didn't believe a word out of my mouth? Most of what I told him was absolutely true. It was the stuff I didn't tell him that could get me into trouble.

I thought I'd best get myself cleaned up, shaved, and over to Coop's place so that I could start protecting him from General Machado as Slim demanded, even as I kept an eye on him for the general.

An hour or so later, I arrived in front of Coop's house, parked the car, and once again inspected the unfolding magnificence of Beverly Hills. Idly I thought about someday having a house on one of these hillsides, Nell and me, living happily in the unending sunshine, the curse a distant, failing memory. Wouldn't that be just swell? Except the woman with whom I hoped to share this idyll was writing notes saying, "Stay away from me. I'm no good for you." A less optimistic fellow might be put off by those words. But not me. I was far too thickheaded, not to mention desperate, to consider anything that smacked of reality.

My reverie was interrupted by the sound of something breaking inside Coop's house. A moment later, the door burst open and out sped Coop himself, naked, smashing right into me, sending me tumbling backwards. Right behind him came a tiny woman in a crimson housecoat waving a kitchen knife. Her jet-black hair was pulled back into a tight bun. Her black eyebrows were like bolts of lightning. She cried out something in Spanish as she threw her small body at the naked Coop, wildly swinging the knife. He ducked and fell back. She came at him again, screaming, "You bastard, Coop! You shit bastard! You deceive Lupe! You play her for the fool! I kill you! I kill you!"

I strode over and grabbed her wrist, twisting until she loosened her grip on the knife and I was able to pluck it from her hand. I seemed to spend a good deal of time in Southern California relieving various individuals of their knives. The young woman reared back, teeth bared, like a small animal intending to lunge. Instead, she burst into tears and ran back inside the house, slamming the door. Coop meanwhile sank to the lawn in exhaustion. I dropped the knife onto the grass. A couple of maids in starched black-and-white uniforms, their dark faces carefully arranged into neutral expressions, came out to inspect the unfolding drama. The Chinese houseboy down the street also put in an appearance. He wore his white gloves, but today did not have his garden hose.

"That must be Lupe Velez," I observed as I got Coop to his feet.

"That's her."

For the first time he appeared to understand that he was standing outside in the sun buck-naked. "Wait out here," he said. "I'll get dressed and come back."

"You can't go back in there," I said. "She's liable to kill you."

"It'll be okay. Once she breaks out the waterworks, that's the end of it. She starts to calm down."

"If you're not back out in five minutes, I'm coming in after you."

He managed the beginnings of a wry smile. "That's right, Orrack. You're my nursemaid, ain't you? One day it's a woman trying to kill herself; next, it's a woman trying to kill me. Keeps you busy, eh?"

"Makes me wonder what's going to happen tomorrow," I said.

"Scares the hell out of me," he said ruefully. "Just hold on there, partner, I'll be back."

I went back to the car and leaned against the hood, listening to the crickets. The houseboy had disappeared. The maids chatted together as if in no hurry to move indoors. Across the street the woman in black I'd seen the previous day came out and squinted at me. The sound of distant organ music once again filled the air. No one paid the least attention to it. Finally, the maids went inside, as did the woman in black. All remained quiet inside Coop's house. Ten minutes later when he still had not reappeared, I thought I'd better go and see if he was all right. I was headed up the walk when he came out wearing a tweed jacket with leather elbow patches that nicely offset his pleated hunter-green trousers.

"Let's get out of here," he said.

I didn't bother to ask him where we were going. I just got behind the wheel of the Ford while he slipped into the passenger side. He issued a huge sigh as we started off down the street. "Well, that's one way to get the day started," he said. He glanced over at me. "Thanks for helping out back there."

"Always wanted to meet Lupe Velez."

"She's a little ticked at me over that situation with Clara yesterday. Suspicious about why she would want to kill herself at my place."

"I guess you weren't too successful at reassuring her," I said.

"I said I wouldn't marry her, and that didn't much help matters."

"Still, the knife seems a little extreme."

"You don't know Lupe. She can come at you with a knife for any number of reasons. Marriage is high on the list, but it's a long list."

"One reason why you might not want to marry her."

"Way I'm feeling today, I don't want to marry anyone, ever," he said gloomily. "The thing is, maybe I do need a nursemaid after all, Orrack, which is probably why I'm not all that sorry to see you—even if I am driving out to the Malibu in this sorry excuse for an automobile."

"Out to the Malibu?" I did not like the sound of that. "What are you going to do out there?"

"I'm going to apologize to Miss Nell Devereaux for the way I carried on yesterday and hope she will forgive me."

"You think that's a good idea?" The notion of seeing Nell again with an apologetic Coop in tow filled me with horror.

"No, Orrack, I'm driving all the way back out there and bearing my soul to this woman 'cause I think it's a bad idea."

"It's just that everywhere you go you manage to get yourself into trouble, so just maybe you should lie low for a time and let things cool off."

That tore it. "Who the blazes are you to be telling me anything?" he shouted. "You're supposed to protect me? Then you damn well protect me and keep that lip of yours buttoned. You got that?"

I was beginning to be sorry I'd kept the knife-wielding Lupe away from him. But I swallowed hard and said, "Yeah, I got it."

"What'd you do with the chauffeur's uniform? I do believe I liked you a lot better in that getup."

"It's back at your place."

"And you still got them evening clothes. Well, I'm gonna need 'em back."

"You'll get them. Don't worry."

"Yeah, well, a fellow who's just a chauffeur, he shouldn't be hanging onto what doesn't belong to him."

I felt the weight of the six-shooter under my jacket. Surely, no jury would convict me if I pulled it out and let him have it right there. But then Nell might not like being involved with a fellow who killed a movie star.

Two hours later, we went through the guard station at the entrance to the Malibu. No one stopped us this early afternoon. In fact no one was in sight. A couple of bulldozers were at odd angles along the side of the road like discarded toys. By the time we reached the house belonging to Louis Payne and Leslie Carter, the gray sky had turned black, a soupy fog descending to hide the Pacific. The little beach house seemed to perch on top of heaven. As we approached, a watery figure drifted at heaven's edges. Leslie Carter, her wide-brimmed black hat flopping in the wind, was a brittle old witch working in the garden adjacent to the house. She straightened, holding a trowel like a gun, which pointed at Coop as he got out of the car. She scowled when she saw me—the Malibu witch sizing up the warlock, I supposed. Coop turned to me and ordered, "Wait here." He sauntered over to Leslie and asked if Nell was about. Leslie waved the trowel in the direction of the house and Coop went up on the veranda, hesitated, and then opened the door and disappeared inside.

I stood there trying to contain my anger over Coop's unflagging certainty that he was the suitor while I was merely the happy driver cooling his heels.

"So you've come back to us, Mr. Orrack."

"So I have."

"And brought the wind and the darkness with you, I see."

"It follows me wherever I go."

She came over. I noticed she still held the trowel like a gun, only now it was pointed at me. She said, "I'm not surprised."

"Well, then, if you truly believe that, I'm afraid you're mistaken about me."

"Am I, Mr. Orrack? I don't think I am. I know who you are, you see."

"And who am I?"

"The darkness that brings the wind and trouble."

I gave her my best reassuring smile. "I believe you have me mistaken for someone else."

"I know about such things," Leslie Carter insisted. "Understand you do not move across this landscape unrecognized, Mr. Orrack. Keep that in mind."

"I will do my best," I said.

I was saved from any further discussion by Coop's sudden reappearance—except the saving was momentary and entirely illusionary.

"You bastard!" he shouted. He was not, it should be pointed out, shouting at Leslie.

Nell Devereaux came out right behind him. She was dressed in brown suede slacks and a white blouse, open at the neck. She looked simple and pure, a white angel on a dark day, an interesting contrast to the black witch of Malibu hovering nearby. Nell said, "Coop, don't do this."

Coop wasn't listening. He came roaring down off the steps, and for a moment I thought he was going to hit me. But he stopped short and contented himself with thrusting his face close to mine. "Why did you let me go in there, you son of a bitch? You're the one she's interested in. You're this mysterious character she's so all-fired worked up about. Why didn't you tell me?"

Because I didn't know. Even now I was having a hard time taking this in. I was the mysterious love Nell talked about? There had to be some mistake. I wasn't hearing Coop properly, something. I looked at Nell. She stood at the top of the veranda, her face pale, showing no emotion.

"You're fired!" Coop hollered.

He stalked past me and got into the car and sat behind the wheel for a while before he rolled down the window and said, "Give me the god-damn keys."

I went over and handed him the key. He grabbed it out of my hand and a moment later the engine coughed to life. He jammed the car into reverse, swung it around and then tore up the road and disappeared into the rolling fog.

"Orrack, come with me," Nell said, coming down the steps and starting for the stables. I glanced at Leslie. She still held that trowel in her hand, poised, mouth open. She looked like an old fish waiting for the hook to arrive.

I followed Nell into the stables. The interior was warm and moist, thick with the odor of horse manure and hay. Nell stood in the shadows and she suddenly came into my arms and kissed me fiercely. "Leslie swears you're a warlock, Coop believes you're a bastard, and I just don't know what to think." She kissed me some more, hard, her mouth panting against mine.

"What did you tell Coop?" I managed between passionate assaults.

"I told him I loved you—except I couldn't love you, could I, Orrack? Because there is no such thing as love, and even if there were I wouldn't have anything to do with it."

"Is that why you went off this morning? Because you don't love me?"

"Or maybe because I do." Her eyes searched mine. "I don't know. Don't know about any of it. Come on. Let's go for a ride. Clear our heads."

Me being the narrator of this tale and all, you're probably wondering what my thoughts were at that moment. But my mind was in a fog as thick as the one outside. All sorts of emotions roiled around inside me, true enough, but I couldn't get a grip on any of them; this was beyond anything I had experienced. Compared to the business of love, surviving the Great and Evil Orrack was easy.

Nell chose a proud chestnut for herself, a palomino for me. She took the chestnut to a gallop as we set out along the beach. The horse leaped along the surf's edge, delighted to be let loose. Nell thundered back to me, and drew to a stop, leaned over, and kissed me on the mouth. "You were bad last night."

"Did you think so?" *Is that why you left?* I thought to myself.

"As I fell asleep, I could feel your hands on me. It felt wonderful. I didn't want you to stop."

"No?"

"So what made you?"

"Second thoughts."

Or fear. Doing something to her she didn't want done, and paying the terrible price of being exiled from her. I wished I knew more about these things, how to better gauge their limits, and then I would have the confidence necessary when it comes to loving a woman. But the depth of what I didn't know was dizzying.

"I hate second thoughts," she said. "They could spoil a good romance."

She kissed me for a long time, me thinking, *Romance?* With Coop angrily gone in a cloud of dust and General Machado nowhere to be seen, was this now a romance?

Out loud I said, "You said you were no good for me."

"I didn't say it. I wrote it."

"You also wrote that I should stay away from you."

"Is that what you want?"

"No, of course not."

"Then don't. Don't stay away from me." She spurred her horse forward and called back, "At least not this afternoon."

Chapter Nineteen

A wood frame beach cabin stood in the shadow of Dias Dorados. Seaside cabins. Empty soundstages. This was a woman who could find a place to love at a moment's notice, not an inconsiderable talent. I vaguely wondered how much time she had spent honing it, but quickly closed down such speculation. She'd sent Coop packing in order to be with me and so here we were at the threshold, so to speak, staring into the dim interior about to go to a place we'd never gone before.

"What are we doing, magic man?" she mumbled, her lips against my neck. "What are we doing?"

She is supposed to know the answer to that question, I thought feverishly as she fitted her body against mine and greedily kissed me. How could I be expected to know? I could barely keep up with her.

I was aware of golden pine walls, and a shed roof ceiling. Comfortable old furniture surrounded a raised fireplace. In the dimness I couldn't see her, but somehow our mouths found each other.

"Don't let me do this," she murmured. "Don't let me." But I could not stop her and she could not stop herself and so the plea was meaningless. Instinctively, I knew there was a bed. Nothing would be done now without a bed close by, no matter how much we protested. She was somehow underneath me, calling my name, opening her blouse. *How did that happen?* I wondered. So much was going on I could barely keep track of everything. The darkness swam up around us.

Then she pushed me away, and fell back against the headboard, most of her clothes somehow gone. Mine as well. How had that happened? True magic.

"I'm such a phony," she said.

In a confused daze, I managed to say, "What do you mean?"

"Suppose I'm not what you think I am? Suppose I can only disappoint you?"

You can't disappoint, you can only save me, I wanted to tell her. But in a darkened cabin, two people learning not to be strangers and having to learn it quickly, the notion that you could save a man's life might be too much. Instead I held her close. She trembled against me.

"I could have gone to the top of Nanga Parbat. I could have done it, Orrack, but I didn't. See what a fraud I am? See?"

"What happened?"

"I chickened out. I was at the twenty-thousand-foot level, at the base camp, and I couldn't do it, couldn't bring myself to go to the top."

Tears ran down her cheeks, and for the life of me, I wasn't sure what to do, so I held her more tightly than I had ever held a living soul.

"It doesn't matter what kept you from the top," I said. "What matters is that you're determined to do it the next time."

"There's something else, too," she said.

"It doesn't matter."

"You'll hate me."

"I won't hate you."

"I've never slept with a man—you know, really *slept* with a man."

For some reason the revelation left me slightly elated. It meant she hadn't slept with Machado, or *really* slept with Machado, as she might say, although I confess I wasn't exactly certain of the distinction between sleeping with a man and *really* sleeping with him.

"You're not saying anything again, Orrack. What's that mean? An accomplished devil like yourself, that's probably it for me, huh?"

"Well, I'm considering hanging on to you, no matter what," I said.

"That's very generous."

"Remarkably generous, I would say."

"I suppose if I were to ask you politely, you might even be able to help me out with my dilemma."

"Of course," I said with more confidence than I was feeling. "There are certain things you should know, and perhaps I can try to show them to you."

"That would be nice," she said.

Lily was right, incidentally. Certain things do have universal appeal, although it turned out I did not know as much as I thought, and it turned out Nell knew more than she might have imagined. Somehow we worked together, and everything fell into place. We were, as she stated previously, a good team. We were a wonderful team.

What Lily failed to tell me was how these things can take on such exquisite depth of emotion when you are doing them with someone you love. And as we finished together, clinging to each other for dear life, I understood finally that here was the true magic. This was what I had come so far to find—what everyone journeys a great distance for and overcomes many obstacles to discover.

I had found that which cannot be found.

Then someone kicked in the door. Kiki Diaz yanked me away from Nell, and slammed me against the wall.

Gerardo Machado stormed in, yelling, "Do you know what you're doing?"

Curious, I thought as Nell rolled away from me. Not that I was so familiar with this sort of thing, but when you come barging in on two naked people, should those really be the first words out of your mouth? Of course she knew what she was doing. How could she not?

Nell said in a calm voice, "Gerry, get out of here."

He came raging across the cabin, moving with ungainly grace. Nell cried, "Gerry, stop this!"

By now I was on my feet, meeting the charging Machado with a surprisingly accurate punch to his jaw. Funny, hitting a dictator was no different than striking any thug back home. The blow sent him reeling, but it brought Kiki and Rodrigo into the fray. I hadn't noticed Rodrigo, and more's the pity, since he had that previously advertised gun and used it to bang me across the head. I collapsed to the floor, which gave Kiki the opening he needed to land a foot into my ribs. Rodrigo proceeded to hammer away with the gun barrel and that made things go blurry. Desperately, I tried to regain my feet, but I was no good against the two of them. Then Nell threw herself on top of me, yelling for them to leave me alone. That gave my assailants pause. They backed off and for a moment there was silence. Machado came into view, breathing hard, his black hair falling in a fringe across his forehead, everything about him startlingly disheveled as though he had not been dressed properly.

"Get her out of here!" he yelled. Rodrigo immediately reached down and yanked an angry, protesting Nell to her feet. Kiki joined him and together they manhandled her away. I tried to rise, but now I saw that Machado also had a gun, and he was pointing it at me. Kiki and Rodrigo managed to get Nell to the doorway. I started after her, but Machado stood directly in front of me, holding the gun at arm's length.

"No, you don't!" he snapped. "I will shoot you, my friend. I swear I will if you take one more step."

So, coward that I was, I came to a stop with the gun barrel hanging off the end of my nose as Nell disappeared out the door. A film of sweat glistened on Machado's forehead; his eyes were like black ball bearings.

"You know what I have to say about you?"

"I'm hung like a horse?"

"You're an idiot. Worse, you are an idiot who does not lie very well."

"So you didn't believe me back at the boardinghouse."

"Of course not."

"She doesn't want to be with you."

"And she wants to be with *you?*" The getting to the summit of Nanga Parbat was more probable if I read Machado's tone of voice correctly. "At that boardinghouse they tell me all about you—magic man." He practically spat the words. "You defraud customers on the pier with your petty little tricks. This is who you are, my friend, a cheat and a charlatan and the worst thing of all, poor."

"And you're rich as they come, General, but it doesn't make any difference. She doesn't want it."

He actually burst out laughing. "What a stupid fool you are. Truly, it is amazing how little you know about anything. I believe I will shoot you right now and the world will be a better place without such stupidity."

His gun arm stiffened and there was no reason to think he wouldn't shoot me.

"Hold on there, General." Coop, of all people, appeared in the doorway speaking in a voice that contained more authority than I had heard in it before. *You would believe the hero of a movie who spoke like that,* I thought vaguely.

"Get out of here," Machado said. Apparently he was unimpressed by heroes with deep voices, for his gun arm did not waver.

"Shooting this character is not worth the trouble it's going to cause you," Coop said.

"You don't think so? Wait a moment and I will shoot you, too. Then it will be all worthwhile."

Coop edged farther into the cabin as he spoke. "Well, that's up to you, but I'm a witness here. With Orrack, no one's gonna ask too many questions when he turns up with a bullet or two in him. Lots of folks might say good riddance. But if I die, too, well, that might be a problem."

"I will take that chance," Machado said.

"You got the girl," Coop went on reasonably. "One of your boys said something outside about going out to the *Johanna Smith* before you return to Havana. That's good. I'll take care of this character for you. He's not worth the bullet it would take to kill him."

Machado lowered the gun a bit. "I will marry her." He addressed the words to me like a challenge.

"She won't do it," I said.

"Orrack! Shut your damn mouth!" This from Coop.

"Yes, you will read about our wedding in all the newspapers. You will read about it and think how stupid you are, how badly you misjudged."

"I'm coming after her," I said.

"Orrack, shut up!" Coop ordered.

"I tell you this," Machado said quietly. "If you come near us, I will kill you."

With the threat safely delivered, he began backing toward the door, and as he did, Kiki Diaz reappeared. Kiki said something in Spanish, and Machado vehemently shook his head. Kiki collected up my clothes and disappeared outside. Machado reached the doorway. His gun arm remained straight, never deviating from my midsection. He paused, and for a single wild moment, I thought he would shoot me, and so did Coop.

"General!" he called sharply.

My eyes began to flutter rhythmically and my mouth again soured with that almond taste. Pain shot through my insides. I sank to my knees, holding my stomach, gasping for breath. The almond taste grew more intense. I thought I could hear Coop's voice calling to me, but could not make out what he was saying. After a while my head cleared a bit, and I realized Machado was gone, the gun, too. I rolled onto my side twitching fitfully.

I could hear Coop yelling. "You stupid bastard! You were only supposed to be the damned chauffeur!"

He worked himself into enough of a fury that he came over, picked me up bodily, and dragged me outside where he proceeded to throw me off the porch. I landed on my stomach, too weak to do much to stop him. He jumped down off the porch and I thought for sure he was going to hit me again. Instead, he was content to watch me flounder around for a while and then said in a resigned voice, "Come on, get up. Let's get the hell out of here."

He grabbed my arm as I staggered up, and then he helped me back up the hill where he'd parked the Ford. He leaned me against its side while he retrieved a red horse blanket from the trunk, and draped it around me.

"What's wrong with you, anyway?"

"Stomach, that's all."

"You're sick, and you should get yourself to a doctor."

"Well, that's a step up from a minute ago when I was going to be dead."

"Good thing I came out here, alls I can say. Get in the car."

"How did you know?"

"Didn't know anything. Machado and his boys went speeding past me. Figured something was up."

"And you came back? Why would you go and do a crazy thing like that?"

"Must have been out of my mind. That Machado was out for blood. I thought he was gonna kill you for sure."

"He kidnapped her. You saw it. He took her away."

"Kidnapped her?" he flared angrily. "Listen to me, you mule-headed idiot. Machado didn't do shit. He went away with the woman he's supposed to be marrying, the woman he caught rolling around on a cabin floor with you—probably because you put some sort of evil spell on her."

"I did what?"

"You heard me."

"Is that what you think I did?"

"It's what Leslie Carter thinks happened. And frankly it goes a long way toward explaining why Nell would go off with someone like you."

"When she could have been with you, I suppose."

"Just get in the car, and start to get a whole lot smarter—and don't think for a moment you're gonna put any sort of hex on me."

"If I could put a hex on you I might just do it."

"You be damn careful with your hocus-pocus, partner. You may be able to put a spell on me, but I can kick your ass."

He threw open the car door. I squelched my fingers so that they approximated claws and made a hissing sound. Involuntarily he jumped back.

"Stop that," he said sheepishly. He pushed me in and then came around to the driver's side and slid behind the wheel. "Don't understand this stuff. You being a witch and all that."

"I'm not a witch," I said. "If I was anything I'd be a warlock."

"What the hell's a warlock?"

"A male witch."

"You one of them?"

"I'm the chauffeur, remember?"

"Well, you don't act like any damned chauffeur I ever knew. If you did you wouldn't be in this mess."

He started the motor and settled in his seat, issuing a deep sigh.

"Here's what I'll do. I'm gonna drive you back to that boardinghouse. I suggest you pack your bags tonight, and first thing tomorrow you get out of town, go back to wherever you come from and forget about Nell and all this other shit you got yourself into. You understand what I'm saying?"

"Coop, she's in trouble," I said quietly.

"No, she isn't, Orrack. Don't you get it yet? You are the one in trouble. Not Nell. *You.*"

He didn't say anything after that, and neither did I. No use worrying Coop with my unconvincing assertions that I was not to be stopped. The fact was I had been stopped, dead in my tracks. I had found what could not be found only to immediately lose it again. I hadn't escaped from anything. My father's curse remained in its place, and it was going to kill me sooner rather than later.

By the time I thought all this through, Coop was pulling up in front of the pink boardinghouse. He turned off the car and sat there silently for a few moments.

"The thing is Orrack, I like you. Can't quite figure out why, but I do. Maybe you cast some sort of spell on me, I don't know. But the fact is I got my career to think of and I can't go running around after you and getting you out of trouble."

"You don't have to get me out of trouble," I said.

"Well, so far you've done a pretty good job of throwing that particular assertion into doubt." He paused again, as though expecting me to argue back. When I didn't he said, "Look, you need money or anything?"

"They said something about taking Nell out to the *Johanna Smith.*"

"Forget about it," Coop said.

"Help me get her back."

Coop snorted with laughter. "Listen to yourself. You sound so damned naïve, it's a wonder they allow you out on the street. I thought I was bad, but I'm positively mature compared to you. You're sick and maybe a little crazy to boot. I don't know what to make of you. But you shouldn't be rescuing anyone, you want my opinion. Someone should be rescuing you."

He leaned across me, and opened the door. "I'll get the car back to Slim. Take care of yourself, Orrack."

I got out, watched him drive away, and then made my way round to the back of the house and went inside. I came out of the mudroom and stepped into the darkened kitchen. For once, there were no dirty dishes in the sink, and only the stale smell of tobacco that clung to everything gave any hint that this was the lair of the good Mrs. Reilly and her evil roll-your-own cigarettes. Unexpectedly, she was absent this evening, perhaps out with that popular man-about-town, Bing Reilly, the two of them kicking up their heels at the local speak. I leaned against the counter, feeling the pain starting to grow in my stomach again. Then it struck me who might be willing to help save Nell Devereaux. It was a long shot, but I was desperate enough to try anything.

I went upstairs, got the number, and then came back to the kitchen, picked up the receiver, and told the operator the number I wanted. My stomach hurt even more. Someone picked up on the other end.

"This is Brae Orrack," I said.

George Raft paused, as though trying to remember if he should know me or not. He decided he should. "Orrack, how are you?"

I gritted my teeth, trying to stop the pain. "In need of help."

Again, there was a pause. "I've got people here. We're just about to go out."

"Gerardo Machado is aboard the *Johanna Smith* with Nell Devereaux."

"Okay," he said carefully. "What's the problem?"

"He's kidnapped her."

"I'm sorry. He's done what?"

"Kidnapped. Abducted. Taken the woman against her will."

"Okay, okay, I get the point. How do you know this?"

"I was with her out at the Malibu when they took her away."

"Keep going."

"You said to call if I ever needed anything. Well, I need help, and I need it now."

"Okay, calm down. You're sure General Machado is on the boat?"

"They're spending time there before heading back to Havana."

"Hold on a minute," Raft said.

There was the sound of the receiver being muffled. A couple of moments later he came back on the line. "Where are you?"

"I'm out in Venice Beach."

Another pause, and then he said, "Okay, here's what you do. You meet me in the lobby of the Ambassador Hotel at ten o'clock tonight."

I'd stashed a couple of dollars away in my room, in case of an emergency. That would give me the streetcar fare I needed. "Yes, I can meet you," I said.

"You're going to need a set of evening clothes. Can you handle that?"

Coop wouldn't be getting his duds back any time soon, but I suspected both he and Paramount would survive. "That's no problem," I said.

"What about your nails. How are they?"

"My nails? I don't understand."

"Your fingernails, are they clean?"

"There's blood on them."

"Then clean 'em up will you? See you at ten, Orrack. And don't be late."

The line went dead. My fingernails?

The pain in my stomach suddenly got worse. The almond taste exploded in my mouth like a small bomb. Once again I found myself on the floor, gasping for breath.

"Hey, Orrack." Meyer Rubin came into the kitchen. His tie was askew and he wasn't navigating very well. By the smell of him, as he kneeled down to me, he once again had been sampling his own product. "What's the matter with you?"

"What makes you think anything's the matter?"

"The fact that you're lying naked on the kitchen floor, that's the tip-off."

"Yes, I can see that," I said.

"Also, it looks as though someone beat the crap out of you."

"Someone did, as a matter of fact."

"If anyone should be lying on the floor, it's me. Had a few drinkies, I'm afraid. I tell myself I'm not going to do this. But every so often, the stuff I tell myself? I don't listen to it." He smiled as though remembering some long-forgotten secret. "Every so often happened tonight."

I eased myself up, clinging to the counter. The pain was not as bad as before. Meyer produced his flask and waved it at me. "You look like you could use a drink."

"No thanks."

"A naked man in L.A. who doesn't drink. What do you know about that?"

What did I know indeed?

Chapter Twenty

My stomach was still on fire when I boarded the Wilshire Boulevard trolley car, but I didn't care. I had nothing left to lose at this point and only Nell to gain. I made a fine sight in Coop's white tie and tails, and drew many admiring glances as the trolley made its way east. However, the driver was unimpressed. He stopped me as I was about to step off. "Hey fella, you want a word of advice?"

"Why not?" I said.

"You dress like a gent, you should act like one. Stay off the streetcars."

"I'm new in town," I said. "I was told gentlemen rode the streetcars."

"I been doing this for five years," said the driver. "Ain't seen a gentleman yet."

"Then your luck's changed tonight, hasn't it?"

He looked me up and down before he said, "I don't think so."

Well, he might be right about that. You could dress up a fellow like me in swell clothes, without necessarily hiding the truth of him. Still, the right clothes could get you into the Ambassador Hotel tonight and so could clean fingernails and that was all that interested me.

Big flower beds adjoined the drive sweeping up to the hotel entrance, and even at night the flowers erupted with voluptuous color, like someone had painted them for the occasion. All sorts of shiny cars floated past as I walked toward the entrance, feeling a trifle foolish and a bit of a fake, the only gent in evening clothes in Los Angeles forced to enter the Ambassador Hotel on foot. The hotel was set back at a distance from the boulevard upon a vast parklike acreage of shrubs and trees. The main building boasted five hundred rooms, a theater, a ballroom, and a dining room that spread more than half an acre. The hotel also contained the town's most famous nightclub, The Cocoanut Grove.

Georgie Raft waited in the dark-wood veneered lobby near the reception desk, his black hair slicked to a bright sheen. He paced the intricately patterned carpet beautifully turned out in a navy-blue dinner jacket, the knot of his tie done just so. Exactly three quarters of an inch of silk cuff showed off gleaming diamond cuff links. Oh, he was a picture was our Georgie. Not a handsome fellow by any stretch, what with that somber ratlike face, and those dead black eyes, but there was something about him. He was like a deep, dark pond whose bottom you could never quite see.

Raft looked uncharacteristically rattled when he saw me. "What the hell's the matter with you?"

"What do you mean?"

"You look like a dead man."

"Pretty close to it."

Raft shook his head. "How are your nails?"

"You're not checking my nails."

"Don't be such a baby. Let me have a look at them."

I gave in and presented my hands like a good little fellow. He scowled. "Christ, what have you been doing?"

"Various characters had it in their mind to kill me today," I said.

"You can't afford a manicure?" Threats to my life seemed far less important in Georgie's estimation.

"I'm a poor lad, hard done by, and like I said, what with one thing and another, there hasn't been a lot of time for manicures."

Georgie rolled his eyes. "Okay, okay. Our friend is waiting inside. I told him you were aces."

"What about Nell?"

"Just be polite. Keep your mouth shut. Let me do the talking."

I was about to tell Georgie what I thought of that particular idea when a commotion erupted behind us. A squad of photographers backpedaled into view, firing off flashbulbs at a beautifully dressed couple. It took me a moment to realize it was Coop with Lupe Velez. I almost didn't recognize her dressed, and without a knife in her hand. Tonight she looked small and beautiful in a beaded evening gown. They glanced neither to the right nor to the left as they swept by and so Coop didn't see me, probably just as well since here I was outfitted in his Paramount evening duds, and him wanting them back so badly. Unseen attendants inside the club seemed to know when important people approached the entrance, for suddenly just when you thought they could not, the doors flew open to admit Coop and Lupe. They appeared not at all surprised; the doors of life flying open automatically for them. How could it be otherwise?

"What's that look on your face, Orrack?" demanded Raft.

"A few hours ago she was trying to kill him."

Raft laughed and said, "Welcome to Hollywood, pal."

The doors opened again so that Georgie could usher me into an *Arabian Nights* oasis beneath a night-blue sky dotted with stars. The oasis featured a waterfall and was bordered by palm trees from the set of that Rudolph Valentino movie, *The Sheik.* I learned later that it cost seventy-five cents just to get into the place, except, I guess, if you were with Georgie Raft and then you just sashayed right on in while the orchestra played "I'll Say She Does." Georgie weaved expertly through the tables, past waiters and enticingly clad cigarette girls, greeting various patrons. Beautiful young women were everywhere you looked. The men with the women were shiny in their black-and-white evening clothes. Surely they employed people to buff them to perfection before stepping out. I could see a maître d' seating Coop and Lupe near a table where Charlie Chaplin held court. He waved at Coop and Coop grinned and waved back. He still didn't see me and even if he did, I doubt he would have waved and grinned the way he did with Charlie Chaplin.

Georgie reached a large table at the back near one of the palm trees. A fake monkey stared down at us from his perch halfway up the trunk. The monkey seemed surprised to see me. Who could blame him? Our table was presided over by a slender, brown-haired man, no more than five feet six inches in height. He had a prissy mouth and large eyes ringed in darkness, like a malevolent racoon. Four other men were with him, also in evening clothes. They were young and tough-looking. Their eyes focused on me, figuring out whether to shoot me or pour me a drink.

"Owney," Georgie said. "The fellow I told you about earlier. Mr. Brae Orrack. Brae, this is Mr. Owney Madden of New York City."

"Georgie, get Mr. Orrack here a seat beside me."

When I was seated, he said, "Orrack, huh?"

"That's right," I replied.

This gent did not take his eyes off me, sitting back like a pint-sized Pacific Island king on a throne surveying his subjects. I didn't know who he was then, but I did not like the look of him, and, of course, it turned out later that Mr. Owney Madden was some pack of goods. If you drank beer on the East Coast of the United States, Owney Madden more than likely supplied it to you. If you made a mistake on the East Coast, it was Owney Madden who would take care of you, which is why, I suppose, they called him "Owney the Killer." He killed the first time when he was seventeen without so much as the blink of an eye; the cost of doing business as far as he was concerned. By the time he was twenty-three, a member of the notorious Gophers gang running Hell's Kitchen, he had killed five men, all members of the rival Hudson Dusters.

Viciousness fueled by a red-hot temper that didn't allow him to take anything from anyone helped put Owney away for nearly a decade. Released from jail five years ago, he partnered with another notorious New York gangster, Dutch Schultz. Together, they had become the most prosperous hoods on the East Coast. But this wasn't the East Coast, now was it? This was the West Coast, begging the question of what Owney the

Killer was doing in these precincts. Well, that wasn't my business; my business this evening was to get out to the *Johanna Smith* before it was too late.

"What brings you out to Los Angeles, Mr. Orrack?"

"I'm looking for true love," I said.

The raccoon eyes widened slightly. "A man comes out to Los Angeles looking for love. There are people who might accuse you of traveling in the wrong direction."

"They might indeed," I said, "but they won't be going out to the *Johanna Smith* tonight."

"No, I guess they won't at that," he said. "What do you do, Orrack, when you're not out looking for love, that is."

"I perform feats of magic. I'm a magic man."

Owney blinked a couple of times before he said, "Feats of magic, huh? Like what for instance?"

"Well, I can turn stones to bees."

Was it my imagination or across the way was Georgie Raft shifting nervously? Owney nodded slowly. "I wouldn't have thought there was a whole lot of call for that."

"I'm sorry to say there isn't."

Gloria Swanson, trailing a swirl of cigarette smoke and an impressive entourage, caused a commotion on the far side of the dance floor. Even at this distance I could see her eyes snapping with light, taking in everything around her. The maître d' held a chair for her at a big round table. The members of the entourage fell over themselves getting her seated, lighting another cigarette, impatiently calling for service. A small army of waiters and busboys descended. Miss Swanson was lost in the chaos. Beyond the Swanson table, a man leaned forward and drew the queen of hearts out of thin air and snapped it between long, elegant fingers. Other guests broke into applause. I could not see the man's face, and now the chaos radiating in ever-widening circles from Miss Swanson's table blocked my view. There was only one man I knew of who could snap the queen of hearts like that.

The Great Orrack himself.

But of course it couldn't be him sitting over there, I reminded myself yet again. Couldn't be.

"Anything the matter?" Owney Madden's voice interrupted my reverie.

I focused on him. "Thought I saw someone I knew, that's all."

Owney glanced down at my nails, and rewarded them with a smile. "A well-turned-out gentleman even if the suit don't fit so well, and those shoes look a little the worse for wear." He turned to Georgie Raft who abruptly looked very alert. "Well, I think we can help Mr. Orrack with his ambitions here in the Los Angeles area, don't you, Georgie?"

"We can certainly give it a try."

He started to get up and that's when I made my first big mistake of the evening. I put a hand on his sleeve. As soon as I did that, Georgie frowned. Everyone else at the table suddenly stopped breathing. Owney inspected my hand on his arm and then gazed at me with those racoon eyes.

"Let me tell you something," he said quietly. "I don't like it when anyone touches me."

I slowly removed my hand and gave him a big smile. "It's just that I'd like to know what the plan is before we go charging out there."

"The plan?" Owney said. "I'll tell you what the plan is, Brae. We're going to the *Johanna Smith* and see if your friend is there. If she is, we'll save her from a fate worse than death."

Everyone chuckled at that, me included. "Well, I appreciate that, Mr. Madden, truly, I do. But if I could make a suggestion."

Owney glanced quickly at Georgie before he said, "Sure, go ahead."

"I go aboard first, make sure the woman's still there. Then when you fellows come storming in, I can ensure she doesn't get hurt."

Those deadly eyes lit with just the hint of humor. "You can do that? Make sure she doesn't get hurt, I mean? One of your feats of magic?"

"Nothing much to do with magic," I said. "Magic won't get me through this, I don't imagine."

"No? Then what do you suppose will do it, Mr. Orrack?"

"Being a rough lad who's learned to handle a tight situation or two."

He paused before he said, "There you go. Good suggestion. Let me think about it."

Owney Madden eased himself to his feet. "All right, boys," he said. "We have our friend Mr. Orrack with us, a real hero it turns out, so let's be off. Brae, you ride in back with me."

I wasn't sure of what to make of the hero stuff, or, for that matter, of my encounter with the notorious Owney Madden. But since everyone had started breathing easy again and Georgie's face had regained it deadpan placidity, I figured everything was okay. I stood and looked over at the table where the gent produced the queen of hearts out of thin air. I couldn't see any sign of him. Could I have been imagining things again?

Owney led the way through the club, and I noticed more than one furtive glance thrown in his direction, evidence that the local crowd knew who he was. You figure that in a club like this just about everyone must be someone, and yet Owney Madden received the second glance. Makes you wonder. At least it made me wonder.

I caught a glimpse of Coop. He held Lupe's hand as I passed. His face went blank when he saw me, and then the doors opened and I exited the club. I half-expected him to come running after me, demanding his tuxedo back.

Outside in the drive a pair of Nashes waited. Owney motioned me into the second auto while Raft climbed into the first. Two of the tough young men from the table sat in the front seat while Owney slid into the back beside me. He smelled of expensive cologne as he settled comfortably against the cushions. He stared out the window. "I don't know about this town," he said to no one in particular. "I'm not sure about this town."

He nodded toward the front seat. "Guy riding shotgun, that's Tony. My man. Mean young kid." Tony did not bother acknowledging the accolade.

"The driver is Vincent. We call him 'Elegant Vincent.' Fellows, this here is Mr. Brae Orrack, who says he's a magic man."

"A magic man?" Tony used a toothpick to clean his teeth. "What do you do, Brae, you pull rabbits out of a hat or what?"

"No, but I can turn stones to bees," I said.

"Always wanted to pull a rabbit out of a hat myself," said Elegant Vincent. "Personally, I'd get tired of turning stones to bees all the time. Okay, here we go, Owney."

"Here we go indeed," said Owney Madden.

Chapter Twenty-one

Y ou see I don't like that," Owney Madden said to Georgie Raft. "I don't mind foreigners, I like a lot of them in fact. I mean we can all learn from foreigners, no question. Although offhand I can't think of anything that foreigners invented, can you, Georgie?"

"The tango, maybe," said Georgie Raft.

"Okay, the tango, you may have a point there. You know about these things. But the point is, I don't like foreigners taking advantage."

"Foreigners shouldn't take advantage," Georgie agreed.

"This Machado, he comes here, and he takes advantage. He sets up a gambling ship offshore, and he rakes in the revenues, and how much of that money stays in the good old U. S. of A.? Not very much, let me tell you. At the same time, his presence prevents legitimate businesspeople like myself from operating. That's taking advantage. That's not good. When that happens, something should be done."

"That's right," said Georgie. "Someone should do something."

An hour or so had passed since we had left the Ambassador Hotel. We were standing around in an open shed just above the docks at Signal Hill, on the outskirts of Long Beach. In the distance, invisible dragons spat mouthfuls of natural gas into the night sky, illuminating momentarily monster oil derricks made of steel pumping deep into the sand adjacent to the ocean. They discovered oil at Signal Hill eight years ago. Now it had been transformed into a modern-day industrial hell by the sea. The oil had brought men, and the men attracted the hookers, and the brothels, and the bootleg joints that housed themselves in the bungalows crawling up around the derricks. It was a perfect hideaway for gangsters, and make no mistake, these were real live American gangsters, and they had the guns to prove it.

Elegant Vincent inspected his distinctive-looking machine gun with its wide diameter cooling shroud around the barrel as well as a top-mounted drum magazine.

"Hey, Vincent," Tony said. "Gonna bite you, is it?"

"Not this baby," said Elegant Vincent in a hushed tone. "No, this baby is the Lewis gun. Look at this. Aluminium barrel casing that uses the muzzle blast to draw air into the gun and cool down the internal mechanism. Fires five-hundred-and-fifty rounds per minute."

Tony laughed and raised up his Thompson submachine gun. "My money's on this here Tommy gun. Compact. Easy to hide. Tremendous firepower—one-thousand-five-hundred rounds per minute."

"The Chicago typewriter," someone said, and everyone laughed.

This would be how gangsters talked, of course, not about the movies they saw or the girls they met, or the music they liked, but the guns they owned and how many bullets those guns could spit out. It was both thrilling and frightening to be part of this, and a little unreal, if you want to know the truth.

Elegant Vincent did not feel compelled to argue with Tony over the merits of their weapons. He continued to rotate the Lewis gun in his hands. "I come from around here," he said. "I remember when they first found the oil. They sank a well, and Jesus, next thing you know, 'bout eight months later, there's this strange kind of growl coming from under the ground and then wham! There's oil spurting up, like some giant black piss, shooting up one hundred and fourteen feet in the air."

"Oil," Owney Madden said, "that's the business I should have gotten myself into. Fellow back there was telling me that they're selling tracts of land, combination of a house and an oil derrick. You get to live, and drill for oil at the same time." He chuckled and shook his head. "Crazy world. But, hey, I'm a kid from Hell's Kitchen. What do I know about oil?"

"No one told us about oil," Raft said. "The hard boys on the street, though. We knew all about them."

"We sure did," Owney said. "Too bad there wasn't an oil man or two in the neighborhood. Who knows? We might have all gone straight."

"Not so much fun though," Elegant Vincent said.

"Not nearly as much fun," Owney agreed.

Georgie Raft pulled me to one side. "You okay, kid?"

He called me a kid? He wasn't much more than a kid himself. "Why wouldn't I be?"

A revolver appeared in his hand. "What's that?" I said.

"From the looks of things, I would say it's a thirty-eight Police Special."

Everyone wanted to give me a gun. He took my hand and shoved the gun into it, grip first. "Just in case," he said.

"Georgie, I get the uneasy feeling there are things about all this you're not telling me."

"Well, you can look at that from one of two perspectives," Raft said. "Perhaps we're going out to the *Johanna Smith* to help out a young woman who's been kidnapped by an evil bastard named Machado, which is personally the way I like to think of it."

"Except these gents look as though they've been getting ready for this for some time."

"That's where the second perspective comes into play. You can also look at it from the point of view that Owney's about to settle a long-standing score and you just happened along at the right time."

"And whose side are you on in all this, Georgie?"

"Owney and me, we grew up together in Hell's Kitchen. So you know from the time you're a kid what side you're on. No mystery about it. Al Howard knew that, yet the guy still thinks he can buy me off."

"Maybe you made him think along those lines, Georgie."

"Maybe I did. But Al shouldn't have been dumb enough to fall for it. Al should have known Georgie Raft don't betray his friends. My old man beat that into me. A poor Kraut immigrant, trying to feed eleven kids, but he taught me all about loyalty to your friends. I was nothing till I met Owney, and I don't forget that. Al should have known. Now he pays the price, and I pay off a debt—and you, Orrack, just maybe you get what you're after. Works out for everyone."

"As long as I go aboard first."

Owney Madden came over. "Everything all right?"

"Brae wants to make sure we're gonna send him onto the ship first," George Raft said.

"Yeah, that's fine. Make sure the woman's okay, and no one's the wiser. Soon as everything is clear you come up on deck, signal to us, and we charge in like the cowboys to the rescue."

"It's the cavalry that comes to the rescue," said Georgie.

"Jeez, Georgie, you always were the history buff," said Owney.

Two high-powered motor launches growled to life by the docks, and the men, as though by previous arrangement, divided themselves into two groups and began to climb down into the crafts. My heart already beginning to pound with excitement, I followed Raft and Owney Madden into the first launch.

No sooner were we huddled in the boats than they were cutting away from the shore. The dragon's breath of the natural gas wells erupted into the night behind us. We slid past moored oil tankers and steamers, their dark hulls occasionally interrupted by the gleam of running lights. The wind at this time of night was sharp, and filled with salt spray. Over the wind, and the sound of the engines, conversation was all but impossible, and these men were through with talking for the night.

The red running lights of the *Johanna Smith* blinked out of the mist. The vessel's searchlight was a pale, uncertain finger stabbing at the sea for a radius of a hundred feet around the ship. Owney Madden turned and looked at me, and broke into a smile that to my surprise transformed his face, turning a gangster into a kid. The wind was in his face; thugs in evening clothes, clutching guns, surrounded him. Owney Madden was in his element.

The pilot of our boat cut his motor and turned sharply to port, swinging around the prow of the *Johanna Smith*. To the right, I saw a taxi boat leave the landing stage. The sound of happy passengers carried across the water over the throb of engines. We waited until the searchlight drifted away, and then skittered around the ship's overhang and came against the hull. The lilt of soft jazz reached our ears. I looked up and saw the double doors of the ship's loading port where they took on lumber during her previous incarnation. The engines were cut. The two boats jostled against the side of the vessel. No one moved. Owney gazed up at the loading port as though willing the doors to open. Sure enough, heavy hinges grated as one of the doors was worked open from the inside. A hazy yellow light showed one half of the open loading port. The light allowed me to see the iron rungs of the ladder bolted to the hull. Owney turned to me and said, "You got ten minutes, Orrack. You haven't signaled by then, we're coming with the guns out. So be careful."

"Right enough," I said.

"All right. Get going."

He slapped my arm, it being okay apparently for Owney to touch you. You just couldn't touch him. I started up the ladder. The rungs were slippery with oil and water and it was all I could do to hang on. Vaguely I wondered how Owney Madden was ever going to do this. Or would he even try? And wouldn't Georgie get his perfect clothes mussed? A couple of moments later I reached the lip of the loading bay and pulled myself in, half-expecting the fellow who opened the door to give me a hand. But no one was in sight. I found myself in a dark hold choked with the smell of engine oil. I could hear the scratch of rats somewhere in the darkness. The yellowish light came from a partially opened hatchway, courtesy of my unseen helper, I supposed. The hatch put me into a narrow, dimly lit passageway. I climbed up a steel ladder at the end of the passageway and found myself on the deck. I could see the spotlight dancing along the waves until it picked out another approaching taxi boat. The sound of dance music reached my ears. It was a busy night on board the *Johanna Smith*.

Pain shot through my stomach. *Not now,* I thought. I could not lose it now. I spent a moment catching my breath, willing the pain to go away, and making sure my clothes were straight. Then I followed the bulkhead past a couple of lifeboats until I reached a metal stairway. At the bottom of the stairway was a bolted door. I tried the latch. The door swung open and abruptly a wall of noise and music hit me. I found myself in a passage leading to the arched entrance of the bar.

Tonight, in contrast to my last visit, the place was packed. The bartenders in their naval whites worked double-time at filling drink orders. What happened? Had they abandoned gambling since the last time I was here? The orchestra struck up a jazzy version of "I'm Always Chasing Rainbows." An audience gave the boys in the band an excuse to show some life. So did the dozen long-legged beauties on the dance floor. They were festooned in feathers as bright as peacocks, kicking and swirling in intricate patterns. The band abruptly cut off, leaving the dancers frozen in place. Patrons seated at the tables crowded around the dance floor erupted into applause. A large man in a white dinner jacket strolled into view. Gerardo Machado allowed his right hand to slap enthusiastically against his leg. The left hand, soft and maimed and with two missing fingers, drooped uselessly. Machado beamed at the performers as they gathered around, proffering cheeks for *el supremo* to kiss. Then the dancers were gone, and Machado adjusted a microphone, causing a screech of static.

"Good evening, ladies and gentlemen," he said. "I want to personally welcome you to the *Johanna Smith* this evening. Is everyone having a good time?"

I couldn't believe he would ask the question, like some lowlife carny barker on the Venice pier. The audience didn't seem to mind at all though. They yelled and cheered acknowledgment that they were having a swell time indeed. Machado beamed at the response and leaned again into the microphone.

"I want to say that in my country there is no prohibition on liquor, gambling, or fun. But why should you have to come all the way to Havana to have a good time? The *Johanna Smith* and the other gambling ships Al Howard intends to launch with my support will bring the fun right here to your communities, and with all the economic benefits—for the towns you represent and for your pocketbooks. So what you see here tonight is just the beginning, my friends."

Everyone applauded and cheered. I took a closer look at the crowd. Most of them men, corpulent gents, escorting beautifully dressed women half their age. I had a suspicion that none of these women were married to the men. From the look of things, I had walked in on some sort of sales pitch promoting the virtues of the gambling ships soon to be operated by Al Howard and his old friend, General Gerardo Machado.

I watched as Machado left the dance floor and navigated his way through the room, shaking hands, kissing every offered cheek. Not far away, Kiki Diaz kept a close eye on his president. Next to Kiki stood Al Howard. People applauded and waved as the general passed. He smiled broadly and waved back. The general was in his element, the man of the moment, *el supremo* supreme, selling sin to a world full of grinning fat cats eager to lap at the same trough as he. Watching this unfold in silent pantomime over the cacophony of music and laughter, I once again found myself filled with admiration. He carried himself like a man on top of the world, indestructible, in charge of a universe that also included Nell, although not at this moment. For the time being, Machado promoted fun all by himself.

Then I saw her crossing the room. She carried a beaded handbag and she wore a simple black evening gown with an appropriately plunging neckline, the wanton who might be a nun. You would never be able to tell for sure. That was the essential mystery of her that men would spend lifetimes attempting to unravel. Not me, though. I knew the truth of her. I was her secret lover, after all. Or did half the male population of Los Angeles believe the same thing?

I came up behind her and touched her arm. Nell turned. Her eyes narrowed, as though not sure what they were seeing.

"Good grief," she said in a tiny voice.

"Good to see you again, Miss Devereaux. It's been a while."

"Well, not that long," she said slowly.

Without saying anything, without having to even signal what was about to happen, we came naturally into each other's arms and turned across the floor. I drew Nell close. Her skin felt warm and smooth, my hand brushing her as she pressed her body against me.

She said, "How did you ever get here?"

"It's a story, no question about it."

"You crazy bastard."

"I would have denied it before, but now I'm thinking you could be right."

"Do you think you have a chance in hell of getting away with this?"

"Well, if I were to be honest, the answer might be no."

"I'm supposed to leave with Gerry in a few minutes."

"For where?"

"Key West and then on to Havana."

"Is that where he plans to marry you?"

"We haven't got that far yet."

"Only as far as Havana."

"Correct."

"Suppose I said I didn't want you to go to Havana. Suppose I said I wanted you to come with me instead?"

"Be sensible," she said.

"It's not in my nature."

"Think of it this way, then. We're in the middle of the ocean and there's no way off this tub."

"Don't underestimate me."

"Then I would have to underestimate Machado, and that's not a good idea."

"Then you just have to trust me."

"Trusting men, I've discovered, is also not a good idea."

"But I'm not like the other men."

"Aren't you?"

"You said it yourself."

"Did I? Well, maybe you are different. No one else ever got himself killed for me. That sets you apart. No doubt about it."

That's when the electricity went out, abruptly plunging the casino into darkness.

"Don't tell me you made that happen," she said.

"For a magic man, it's nothing."

I could feel her lips against my ear, so soft. "You must not ask me to love you, Orrack. Please don't do that, okay? I don't know what the word means."

"Neither do I—except when I see you."

"Stop it. What do we do?"

"You follow me."

"You're asking a hell of a lot."

"Yes."

"Then hurry, before they turn the lights back on and I change my mind."

I took her hand and together we started through the darkness toward the exit. Suddenly, Kiki Diaz was directly in front of me. In other circumstances I would have prepared myself for the worst and thus would have been able to handle the situation. But here I was, giddy as a schoolboy holding Nell's hand as we made our exciting escape, overconfident and thinking nothing could stop us. I failed to take into account that something could.

Kiki raised his fist and I realized too late that it held a blackjack. I ducked, but not fast enough. The blackjack caught me on the side of the head. I saw stars and went reeling back into the crowd. A male voice swore. A woman screamed. I tried to right myself and that allowed Kiki to land another blow that put me onto my knees. The next thing I knew, Nell was gone and someone opened fire in the darkness. That sent the crowd stampeding. Someone knocked against me and I went sprawling across the floor. I finally managed to stumble to my feet, trying to clear my head, pulling out Georgie Raft's gun. But guns in a tumultuous darkness are of little use, I soon discovered. I elbowed and shouldered my way through, and finally reached the staircase, and started up. Around me the crowd surged, people crying and calling out as though a panicky cacophony of noise would somehow improve the chances of getting out of the danger they now found themselves in.

I reached the main deck as a herd of well-dressed passengers bolted out like beans spilling from a spout. More gunfire followed, not from below this time, but from around the corner. My stomach suddenly turned, as though preparing for the arrival of another attack. Around me, passengers screamed and scattered as still more gunfire erupted.

I rounded the corner just as Owney Madden backed across the deck at speed, his gun arm raised. A second man, Al Howard, dressed in a white evening jacket, came after him. Owney pulled the trigger of the gun in his outstretched hand. Nothing came out the end of the barrel. Al Howard looked scared and then when he realized he wasn't about to be shot, allowed the trace of a smile before raising his own pistol. "Try this one, Owney, I think it's still got a couple of bullets in it."

Al Howard was squeezing the trigger when I shot him.

Chapter Twenty-two

Funny, how you just do certain things. I never in my life thought of shooting anyone, wouldn't even have said I could do it. But at the moment a shooting needed to be done, well there I was, like a real American gangster, and just as natural. How does a man shoot another man? He pulls the trigger. No more complicated than that when it comes right down to it. I don't remember even thinking about it. The gun jumped in my hand and Al Howard dropped his pistol, grabbed his arm, and sagged against the wall, his mouth opening as if intending to object to being shot and then thinking better of it.

Immediately, Owney Madden started to slug away at the wounded man, landing awkward blows. I would have expected something a little smoother from Owney the Killer. But then maybe he was used to shooting his victims, not hitting them.

Raft materialized out of the confusion, unruffled by the night's events as always. "You okay, Owney?"

"Yeah, Georgie, yeah, I'm fine," huffed Owney, winding down the ferocity of his blows. "I'm okay thanks to friend Orrack."

Al took his eyes off his wounded arm long enough to see that it was Georgie Raft who had arrived. That made him even more upset. "You bastard, Georgie. You goddamn bastard!"

Owney silenced him with a punch, better aimed than the rest. Al collapsed to the deck, moaning, holding his jaw.

Owney paused, out of breath, glaring down at his victim. "This bastard Al Howard was about to shoot me. Can you believe that, Georgie? Al Howard, and he tries to shoot me."

Al said, "For Christ's sake, Owney, you were trying to shoot *me!*"

"Yeah, well, who could blame me? You come to me, looking for dough to finance this piece of shit idea of yours. The next thing I know you've thrown in with some Cuban greaseball—not even an American, for God's sake. Not even an American, Al!"

"For the love of god, Owney, you didn't want to invest. You said a gambling boat would never make it; they'd close us down."

"It *is* shit, and they *will* close you down."

"Owney," I said.

He ignored the interruption and lashed out with his foot, kicking Al hard in the stomach. "I'm going to burn this fucking floating crap game into the sea, that's what I'm doing, Al. That'll teach you a goddamn lesson or two!"

"Owney, I think Machado got away with Nell," I managed to interject.

Owney looked at me as though I'd taken leave of my senses. "What?"

"Can't do that, Owney," Al Howard groaned. "You can't burn down this boat."

That caused Owney to refocus on Al. "Why can't I?"

"There are two hundred people aboard tonight, and there aren't enough lifeboats."

That made Owney apoplectic. "What kind of cheap, chiseling tinhorn are you anyway, Al? You stick a big ship like this out here without enough lifeboats!"

"We ain't moving anywhere," Howard said in a whiny voice. "Besides, anything happens, we're only twelve miles from Long Beach." He noticed the blood gushing out of his arm. "Jesus, Owney, can't you see I'm bleeding bad?"

"Good! I'll stand here, a big smile on my face, and watch you bleed to death," Owney announced with great satisfaction. Al Howard uttered another despairing cry, and went back to mournfully inspecting his arm. Owney finally turned to me. "You say Machado's gone?"

"With Nell. They must have taken one of the pilot boats."

Owney returned to Al Howard. "Al, where's Machado?"

"Owney, I'm dying here. Can't you see I'm dying?"

Owney kicked him again. "You spineless asshole! Answer the question."

"He's got this broad with him. They were flying out to Key West."

"So there you go." Owney Madden sounded resigned. "We can't get Machado and we can't burn the goddamn boat. Now that isn't much fun, is it?" He stood silent, seemingly deep in thought, and then he smiled. "Where's the captain? Let's get the captain over here."

From his position bleeding on the deck, Al Howard understood before anyone else what Madden was up to. "Aw, c'mon, Owney," he implored. "Don't be crazy. We got some of the most prominent mayors and aldermen along the coast here tonight. You take us in past the twelve-mile limit and the goddamn cops are going to pounce. That's not good for anybody."

"You son a bitch," Owney Madden snarled. "Your friends should have thought of that before they got hooked up with a bag of scum like yourself." Madden motioned to Elegant Vincent. "Get started up. We're taking this tub back to Long Beach."

"Goddamn prick, Owney!" Al Howard screamed. Owney went back and kicked Al Howard some more. That shut him up.

The fact that Machado had escaped with Nell left me despondent. My stomach being on fire didn't help matters, either. Owney Madden, however, was in great spirits, the merry Pied Piper leading us in procession below. The lights were back on in the casino, emphasizing the frightened looks on the faces of a couple of hundred patrons who stood very quietly amid the silent tables, as though a single movement or noise might cause these tuxedoed marauders to open fire with their Tommy guns.

Owney addressed the multitude. "Listen here, folks, sorry about the inconvenience but the fun's over for tonight. Okay? I just wanted to make a point. You deal with scum, you end up in the sewer. You end up in a sewer full of foreigners who don't give a damn about doing proper business in this country. The message tonight is this: Don't get involved with Al Howard and his Cuban greaseball buddy. If you do, well, you see what happens. It ain't gonna be pleasant or fun."

A murmur of concern ran through the crowd. Abruptly, none of the graying burghers, the honorable men of the coastal communities of Southern California, seemed much interested in being anywhere near their lovely and charming escorts for the evening. They looked bleary and drawn, as though they'd been up for a long time while being beaten with sticks.

Owney Madden, unperturbed by the gloom, gave me a conspiratorial wink as he passed. Georgie Raft materialized beside me. Owney paused, abruptly contemplative. "Hey, listen, I understand how you're feeling, Orrack, believe me. Women can make you crazy like nothing else can. Right, Georgie?"

"That's right, Owney. Broads make you crazy if you're not careful."

"Booze, dope, nothing drives you nuts like women. I was on this trolley car once, and I spot this gal I was loony about and she was sitting with another guy. She didn't see me, and the guy's asking her for a date. Right there on the trolley car, in front of me, and he's asking her. Well, I see red. Next thing there's a gun in my hand, and I'm blasting away at this guy. True story. So help me."

"What happened to the guy?" I asked.

"I guess it's fair to say he never went out with this gal. Now isn't that funny? Don't even remember her name, but I sure was loony about her at the time."

We steamed toward Long Beach, the fat cats keeping the white uniformed bartenders busy as they tried to drown their mounting sense of desperation, whispering anxiously among themselves, casting quick nervous glances in the direction of Owney's Tommy-gun-toting men. Almost certainly they were speculating on what lay in store for them back on land, deciding that it wasn't going to be good. By the time the

Johanna Smith crew began throwing lines onto one of the black piers at Long Beach, several pillars of the community had to be helped off by the twenty or so police officers who flooded onto the ship as soon as a gangplank was lowered. A large ruddy-faced inspector with snow-white hair led the cops.

"Owney Madden," the inspector called out in a booming voice.

"Inspector Theodore Dice, good to see you again, Teddy," Owney said.

The two men shook hands heartily. Inspector Teddy Dice's face lost some of its light when he saw the passengers on board the *Johanna Smith.*

"Now who have you got here, Owney?" The inspector's face took on an even darker hue as he started to realize what was happening. "That looks to be the mayor of Long Beach drunk as a skunk over there."

"I wouldn't know about that," Owney said, all innocence. "You can just imagine, Inspector Dice, my friends and I are out for an evening's entertainment during our visit here to Southern California. We discover that gambling is being countenanced on board what we thought to be a simple cruising vessel. Shock and outrage, I believe pretty much sums up our emotions."

Inspector Dice did not seem happy at the news of Owney's good civic deed. Then he spotted Al Howard, and his perplexed face lit up.

"Well, Al, there you are. What'd I tell you? We'd have our day with you fella, and sure enough, here it is."

Howard merely lowered his head as though in abject sorrow. He knew that the jig, for the moment, was up. At least he was still alive, unlike the poor bastard who asked out Owney Madden's girl on a trolley car. In Owney's world it didn't take much to get you killed, and maybe Al understood that and decided the best thing to do was keep a closed mouth until he could get to a lawyer.

"Incidentally, Inspector, I must tell you I confiscated several thousand dollars, obviously ill-gotten gains, from a safe in Al Howard's office," Owney said. "What should I do with that money?"

"Why, you can turn it over to yours truly," Inspector Dice said in his most official voice. "It'll certainly be safe with me."

"I can just imagine," Owney Madden said.

I pulled Raft away. He looked relieved to have the excuse to walk me to the edge of the pier.

"I need to get to Key West."

He regarded me with that enigmatic face of his. "I'm sure she's a great broad, and everything, but there are other great broads around. This town is full of them. Save yourself the aggravation and just put her out of your mind."

"I can't," I said.

"Why not?"

"She's in trouble. Where I come from, it's a little like Hell's Kitchen, I suppose. When a friend is in trouble, you don't back away."

Raft considered this. "Well, in my book that's something, all right. Let me see what I can do."

A few minutes later, the police led Al Howard away to a waiting ambulance. Owney Madden ambled over looking pleased. "One hell of a night, I say. A hell of a night, thanks to you, Orrack."

"Glad I could help, Owney."

"Georgie says you want to go after General Machado."

"I don't have any choice."

"Well, that's fine. I owe you. At the same time, though, I'm in business, so maybe you can help me."

I wasn't sure I liked the sound of that. But Owney wasn't waiting around for any arguments on the subject.

"So happens, I've a business associate down there in Key West. I'm making a little investment in a deal he's got going. He's badly in need of a certain package."

"What kind of package?"

Owney pretended not to hear the question. "The guy flying down to make the delivery for me, well, he's okay, a bit of a blowhard. I don't quite know what to make of him. I wouldn't mind having someone along I can trust and who also knows how to handle himself in a tight spot. What do you say?"

"This man of yours, he's flying directly to Key West?"

"Ain't that all the luck in the world?"

I wasn't so sure, but I plastered on a smile and said, "I guess it is at that, Owney."

Owney motioned George Raft forward. "Georgie here's going to drive you out there. Right, Georgie?"

"Drive me?" I said. "Drive me where?"

"The plane's way out at Mines Field, so we'd better get going," Raft said.

Owney Madden squeezed my arm. "Have a good flight," he said. "Win back the girl of your dreams. Just make sure that package gets there okay."

The way he said it left no doubt about what would happen if it didn't.

Chapter Twenty-three

The papers said the six-hundred-and-forty acres of farmland at Lincoln and Sepulveda Boulevard were to be the site of the Los Angeles airport. You sure could have fooled me. At dawn, Mines Field looked like any other cow pasture in the vicinity, except this one was intersected by a rough runway cut diagonally across it like a scar, skirting the adjacent lima bean and barley fields. A cumbersome chunk of dull metal with wings attached squatted at the runway's edge. It did not look as though it could move, let alone rise into the air.

Not far away from the plane, a couple of guys in coveralls squinted as the lights from Georgie's car caught them having a cigarette beside a battered truck. A slim young man with an open boyish face you might call typically American hopped down from the plane's enclosed cockpit. That American face featured piercing blue eyes topped by short, curly brown hair. The young man wore a leather flying jacket over a turtleneck sweater stuffed into jodhpurs, complete with shiny knee-high boots. He proceeded to vigorously pump our hands like he was running for office.

"Bobby Reedhouse is the name," he announced as though confirming information most of the world already possessed. "This here is the Ford Trimotor." He jerked a thumb in the direction of the plane. "They call my baby 'the Tin Goose,' but don't let the name fool you—or its ugly looks. It's a hell of a fine craft. Mr. Madden's going to be real pleased with me. I'll get his little package delivered for him, you can bet on that."

Raft stepped smoothly in and said, "Uh, Bobby, there's been a slight change of plan."

Bobby looked confused. "Change of plan?"

"Owney wants you to take a passenger along for the ride. Meet Brae Orrack. He has to get to Key West as soon as possible. Owney thinks you're the man who can get him there."

The confusion on Bobby Reedhouse's blandly handsome features deepened. "Passengers. Owney didn't say nothing about no passengers. That'll slow things up. Owney, he didn't want things slowed-up. He wanted that package delivered, and that's the truth of it."

"Well," Raft said quietly, "now he wants you to take a passenger."

Silence. Bobby Reedhouse chewed on his lower lip and appeared to mull this over. Finally, he nodded. "Well, like I say, it slows things down."

Raft touched Bobby Reedhouse on the arm. "Thanks, Bobby. Owney has a lot of faith in you."

"Sure we're going to be all right in that thing?" I said.

Bobby waved his hand dismissively in my direction. "This here, this is the future, sir. And you know who you're flying with? Bobby Reedhouse, hero of the Atlantic, that's who."

"Is that so?" I said.

"That is so. I flew the Atlantic earlier this year."

Raft looked dubious. "I didn't see anything in the papers about it."

"Bad timing is all. My partner, Arne Schwab, he tried to cut back with expenses, and damned if he didn't refuse to hire a press agent. Everyone knows, you going to fly the Atlantic, you got to have a press agent, right? Stupid mistake. That and the fact we had to ditch the plane off the coast of Ireland. It all conspired against us getting our feat into the papers."

"Off the coast of Ireland?" I said. "That's not crossing the Atlantic."

Bobby Reedhouse looked insulted. "Well, it's pretty damned near across the Atlantic. I imagine, for instance, it's a lot farther than you've ever flown."

"Well, you got that part right," I said.

"Look, squirt," Raft interrupted with a rumble that could get necks snapping around. "Let's just get the plane in the air and quit talking about it so much."

Bobby Reedhouse once again looked insulted. "If you say so," he mumbled.

"I'm saying so," Raft said. Bobby Reedhouse scurried up into the cockpit.

Georgie led me over to where he had parked the Nash. He fumbled for his car keys. "Can't say as I trust that little creep."

The trunk flipped up and he reached inside and brought out a package about the size of someone's laundry, wrapped in grease paper and tied with twine. "So here you go."

"What happens when we get to Key West?" I asked.

"A fellow named Billy Ward, well, at least that's what Billy's calling himself these days, will meet you. Just hand this over to him. He knows his way around the town."

"He can help me find Nell?"

Raft nodded. "Let me give you a number where you can reach him."

While Raft wrote the number onto the back of a business card, I hefted the package in my hands, testing its weight. Georgie finished writing and stuck the card into my breast pocket. "Call Billy as soon as you get in. He'll be waiting for you."

We stood together for another moment or so and Georgie knew what I was thinking: something wasn't right here. If I had the brains God gave a gnat I would not be crazy enough to fly off anywhere under these circumstances. His eyes no longer avoided mine. Instead, they bore into me.

"Better be off then," I said. What choice did I have? If I didn't take this ride I could forget about Nell and any chance of getting her back.

He offered me his hand. I let it hang there in the air for a couple of seconds before taking it. "You're quite the parcel of goods, Georgie," I said.

"Every time I have second thoughts, I just think about my old man, the Kraut. The ten other kids still stuck in Hell's Kitchen. I think about those things, and everything gets clear, real fast. Still got that gun I gave you earlier?"

"You want it back?"

"Hang on to it. Machado's a dangerous hombre and Kiki Diaz is worse than dangerous. So go careful."

I crowded into the cockpit beside Bobby Reedhouse, placing the package behind my seat. Through the windshield I could see George Raft walk toward his car, pulling at his shirt cuffs, that ratlike face of his betraying no emotion.

Outside, the two guys in coveralls threw their cigarettes away and moved from the truck toward the plane. Bobby Reedhouse inspected the controls.

"This flying business," I said. "What's involved in it, anyway?"

"You got to be an expert, like myself," Bobby said. "I mean you don't just step into the cockpit here, grab the yoke, and fly off."

Bobby raised his hand in a signal that the ignition was in the Off position. One of the guys outside the plane stepped forward and grabbed the propeller with both hands. He yanked it around a couple of times. Then Bobby turned the ignition on. He signaled again to the guy outside and he again stepped forward, this time giving the propeller a single yank. The engine sputtered to life. The two guys together then went through the same procedure with the two remaining engines.

"That didn't seem so hard," I said as Bobby brought the engines up to two-thirds power.

"Isn't that it's so hard. What counts is experience. You know what I'm doing right now, for instance?"

"What?"

"I'm listening to the sound of the engines. I can tell by their sound if everything is all right. An experienced pilot can tell that."

"They sound fine."

"And you got to make sure the engines aren't smoking or splashing oil."

"How fast do we go?"

"About one hundred miles an hour. Be cruising along at altitudes anywhere from a thousand to fifteen hundred feet, except over the mountains. Higher you get, the thinner the air. Fatigue starts to set in real fast."

Bobby taxied the plane out onto the edge of the runway. I leaned into his ear and said, "Can you stop this thing a moment?"

"Stop? We haven't even started yet. What the hell you want to stop for?"

"Have to take a piss."

Bobby groaned and brought the plane to a stop. He concentrated on one of the gauges, tapping his knuckle against it. I hopped out and ran across the field until I encountered a drainage ditch, its banks lined with scrubby underbrush. I relieved myself, and hurried back to the plane.

"Thanks," I said, regaining the copilot's seat.

Bobby Reedhouse ceased tapping at the gauge. "Never seen the like of it," he grumbled.

He began increasing the plane's speed, so that the engines were shaking and rattling the plane, making a fearsome sound.

"Now what?" I yelled over the whine.

"Now the plane takes off."

Bobby adjusted the wheel so that the nose came up, and a moment later the plane began to lift off the ground.

"What do you think of that?" said Bobby Reedhouse.

A feeling of panic seized me. This loud, vibrating metal box was hurtling up into the sky, being flown by a brash American lad who thought crossing the Atlantic amounted to crashing off the coast of Ireland. I glanced out the cockpit window and Los Angeles tumbled away in streaks of golden morning light. From this vantage point, the city seemed to go on forever, anchored by the gleaming white sphere of the new City Hall building.

"Is that not a sight to behold!" cried Bobby Reedhouse. "Could you not go to your grave saying you seen it all, after you saw this?"

Yes, I could, I thought. *In fact, I might be on my way there right now.*

PART THREE

Sleight of Hand

✴

Chapter Twenty-four

It took three days to fly across California, Arizona, and New Mexico. My stomach settled considerably. I had grown used to the continuous howl of the engines and the soul-shaking rattle of the fuselage. According to Bobby we were now flying over Texas, low enough so that he could see the cows. "If I can see cows, I can tell that I'm still headed east." As much as I studied the cows, I couldn't see how they could provide directions. But they were important to Bobby, that's for sure. Cow sightings at least quieted him for a time. Otherwise, he just kept blabbing away.

"Now as soon as I got myself out of jail—"

"You were in jail?" I said.

"Why, of course I was," said Bobby, as though everyone had been in jail. He yawned.

"What were you doing in jail?" It was not encouraging to know that the man in whose hands you have entrusted your life was behind bars when his time might better have been spent practicing the flying of a plane.

"I shot my girlfriend's husband in Savannah."

"How did you come to do that?"

"The son of a bitch deserved it, that's how it came to be done. It was no big deal. The bullet went right through his arm, never broke no bones, anything like that." He stifled a yawn. "Still, they put me in jail for a couple of years. After I got out, I was determined to accomplish two things. One was to become a pilot, just like Charles A. Lindbergh, whom I somewhat resemble, if you haven't already noticed. The other thing was to win the love of a good woman. A Mexican fortune-teller in Juárez, she once told me I was goal-oriented. Guess she turned out to be right 'cause I'm proud to say I've accomplished both those aims."

He interrupted himself with still another yawn. "Tell you, these long flights start to get to you, huh?"

"You all right, Bobby?"

"Sure, sure, I'm fine. You got to be pretty tough to be a pilot, that's for sure. You're wrestling with the controls constantly. You don't get a moment's peace and quiet. Not just anyone can do this. Takes a pretty peculiar breed of man to fly a plane."

"Someone like yourself."

"Got that right. Let me tell you something. America is tired of the crime and corruption that abounds. Folks don't know what to believe anymore, what with science and philosophy and all sorts of things getting in the way of their simple Christian beliefs."

"I'm not so sure what any of that has to do with flying around in an airplane."

Bobby seemed insulted. "Has everything in the world to do with it, you think about it just a minute. Flying, and the people who do it, represent a simple purity—like Lindbergh. Man taking on nature, and beating nature. Kind of elemental, and back to the frontier."

I settled once more into the rhythms of the plane's gyrations, and drifted off. The last thing I heard was Bobby's yawn, immediately lost in the throb of the engines.

The angels awoke me, whispering in my ear. I found myself at an odd angle, shoved far forward. It took a few seconds to get my bearings, and to realize that the angels were not whispering and it was not me who was positioned oddly, but the aircraft. Nose down it was, and dropping like a rock. I looked over at Bobby. His heroic chin nodded against his manly chest, his curly head rolling about crazily on the stem of his stupid neck. I swatted him and immediately his head snapped up, his tongue snaked out, and he began licking furiously at his lips.

"Whatzit? Where am I?"

"You crazy fool, you're in the air, and you're about to crash this plane!"

Vast stretches of desert tilted at wild angles, dangerously close. Bobby blinked a couple of times, staring out the windshield, coming to terms with what was about to happen.

"Jesus H. Christ!" he said.

"Do something!"

Bobby wrestled with the wheel as though it was attacking him, gritting his teeth and grunting loudly, fighting to pull it back. He managed to get the nose of the trimotor up, and as soon as that happened, the desert tilted away.

"Wow-weee, I tell you, that was a close call," he announced after the engines once again were droning complacently. "I got this tendency to fall asleep on long flights. Or did I mention that?"

"You've talked a lot over the past few days about the various parts of your heroic character, Bobby, but you forgot that particular one. I'm wondering if that's the quality that landed you in the Atlantic off the Irish coast."

"Tell you what happened there. A fuel miscalculation. Nothing to do with my falling asleep."

After our brush with disaster in the air over Texas, Bobby settled down and managed to stay awake when he was flying, a not inconsiderable feat as far as I was concerned. Despite myself, I couldn't help but be impressed with the smooth way he could bring the trimotor through swirling mountains of clouds.

From the vantage point of the cockpit, I looked down onto a sparkling white and floating world, new, uninhabited, and unspoiled. Any connection with the constantly changing landscape below was severed, and

I understood finally what freedom was, although I must be honest and say this was a timid freedom, one that did not allow us to fly at night or chance turning south across open water in order to more quickly reach the Florida Keys. My freedom—and Bobby's, too, for that matter—only took on real confidence as long as we remained in sight of land. Otherwise, with only the wide expanse of the Gulf of Mexico below, I wasn't so much free as plain scared.

Each evening, just before dusk, Bobby landed the plane and then spent the next few hours searching for fuel with which to refill the plane's two-hundred-and-thirty-four-gallon capacity tanks. That accomplished, we camped beside the plane, using the sleeping bags and cooking equipment Bobby had helpfully stored aft. On those nights, the moon stood out against a clear, star-speckled sky. Insects hummed and broke a silence that otherwise heaved up, cathedrallike, around us. Well, cathedrallike until Bobby finished his dinner. That's when he commenced his yammering and not even the beauty of God's earth at nighttime could keep him quiet.

"Amazing what you think of at a time like that, isn't it?" I suspected that the time he was talking about had to do with him nearly crashing the trimotor into the hard-baked Texas earth.

"Now you take me, for instance," he blabbered on. "You know what I was thinking about when that unfortunate situation transpired? It wasn't my life or how my heroic virtues might go unrecorded because I'd be splattered all over that desert down there. No, sir, it was none of that at all. Instead, I was thinking about Ella."

I forced myself not to ask him who Ella was. Not that it stopped him.

"Ella's my one true love," he said in a manner suggesting this was common knowledge across America.

"Gee, Bobby, I wasn't even aware you had a special girl," I said.

"Fella like myself, suppose you thought I had all sorts of girls."

"Gotta confess, I haven't given it much thought."

"Tell you something, a man needs a woman. Doesn't matter how famous he gets or how rich, or how many heroic and wonderful deeds he performs, he needs a woman. It was a long and hard search for me. To be honest, I went up many blind alleys, met many girls who were not appropriate. But I finally found the girl for me, and I am one thankful individual. If there's a god, then he was surely watching over me, I guess, 'cause he just thinks Ella and me, we should be together."

This was not a discussion I much wanted to get into with the lovesick hero, Bobby Reedhouse, particularly if it came to explaining what I was doing on a plane headed for Key West. I was too darned forthcoming about these things, I decided. Actually, I decided this shortly after I met Bobby and understood finally that there are people in the world to whom you should not say a word. I need not have worried about saying too much, however. The last thing Bobby wanted was to hear from anyone but himself.

"Now my plan is to perform heroic flying deeds and make my Ella the happiest woman on earth. Yes, there's nothing like love."

"I'll try to keep that in mind," I said. When in the presence of a superior force such as Bobby Reedhouse, there is, it turns out, a great deal to keep in mind.

By now we'd been traveling for five days. I was tired of the constant shaking drone of engines, the unending swatches of land abutting water, Bobby's self-aggrandizing monologues, as ceaseless as the unfolding earth. Somehow, we had lost the panhandle upon which Florida was supposed to be perched. Not that it made much difference at this point. By now Machado and Nell would be long gone back to Havana. I was a fool on a fool's errand, I concluded. Still, I was a fool with nowhere else to go and so we kept going and that kept Bobby talking. The sound of the engines largely drowned him out, but Bobby didn't seem to mind at all. It was the talking that counted. Who cared if anyone actually listened?

We spent the night outside Biloxi. The fourteen-year-old with a jaw full of pimples we hired to retrieve fuel from a local gas station woke Bobby and me at first light around five-thirty. He said that contrary to anything I might believe, Florida was indeed further east. His own father told him so, and his dad weren't no liar.

We no sooner got airborne than Bobby became lost in a cloud bank. When he finally came clear of it there was nothing but open water. In a flash, all the land in the world had disappeared. Panic choked in my throat, particularly when I saw Bobby's face turn the color of one of those beaches we'd been following so carefully. Worst of all, Bobby stopped talking, a sure sign, in my estimation, that disaster loomed. My inclination was to tell him to turn back, but since everything looked the same there was abruptly no such thing as turning back. Below, the blue-green waters grew increasingly choppy as they continued on to infinity.

"Are we all right?" I asked Bobby, striking a hopeful tone in my voice.

Bobby's Adam's apple bobbed up and down like he was having trouble swallowing. He didn't answer me.

By mid-afternoon the fuel gauge reported that the trimotor was down to a quarter of a tank. Then, just as suddenly as there was nothing, there was something again: a silvery archipelago of islands slipping off to a knifepoint in the southwestern haze.

To my amazement and delight, we had crossed the open waters of the Gulf of Mexico and armed with the luck of small children, drunks, and Bobby Reedhouse, we had reached the Florida Keys.

From the air, Key West appeared in the hazy distance to be little more than a sleepy fishing village huddled at the end of a twist of coral, the Gulf of Mexico to the north, the Atlantic washing up from the south. Curious where you find folks. Now where I come from the place has been around so long it made sense that a few lunatics with nowhere else to go might eventually end up there. But this part of America was new and there was so much of it, hard to imagine why people would ever seek out this flat spit, more water than land, more sky than earth.

Bobby tapped his knuckle against the glass shield of the fuel gauge. "Think we'd better set her down, gas up, and take our bearings."

"Set her down? Where would you set her down?"

"Place below us on Key Largo. We can gas up there before heading into Key West."

"How do you know that?"

"Didn't I tell you? Could have sworn I mentioned it. I hail from around these parts."

Chapter Twenty-five

The land that created the unstoppable Bobby Reedhouse was little more than a wilderness area jutting a few feet out of the water. I caught sight of lime and grape trees as the plane came down on to the hard surface of a narrow stretch of roadway. The air as we taxied to a stop came in on us like a wall; a wall thick with mosquitoes.

Through the shimmering heat waves, I could see a horse-drawn wagon filled with grapefruits pass a fuel pump emblazoned with a Texaco star and a couple of frame shacks amid a stand of palm trees.

A faded American flag hung limply in the still air in front of the sun-blackened shacks. A dirt road ran past the shacks. They had mounted a tire on the road's shoulder, painted it white and hand-lettered WE FIX 'EM DRIVE-IN in black paint. No one currently appeared to be taking up the offer. A copse of mangrove trees partially hid a dock jutting into the greenish waters. Near the dock they had hung four of the biggest fish I'd ever seen; three amberjack, their brownish scales glistening in the sun, and a particularly fierce and toothy barracuda. An impressive powerboat bobbed next to the dock. Farther out in the Gulf Stream the water became a pleasing light blue, intersected by the glistening white hull of a tanker headed toward Key West.

Bobby taxied behind one of the buildings before cutting the engines.

I was feeling weak and cramped as I strained to extract myself from the craft. Bobby was already out, however, seemingly none the worse for wear after our long flight. He came around the plane, stretching his legs as a gaunt man in bib overalls appeared. The man's face was dry and cracked by the unremitting Florida sun. He carried a double-barreled shotgun, the stock hooked into his armpit, the barrels pointing toward the ground. "Howdy," the man said, a deep, guttural twang to his voice.

"Hey, Silas, how are you?" Bobby said.

"Just fine, Bobby, doing just fine."

Another man came into view. He was shorter, and younger than the gaunt man. He wore a jean shirt, filthy dungarees, and scuffed boots. A beaten-up fedora was pushed casually back on his head. He, too, greeted Bobby in the same shy way as his older counterpart.

He looked me up and down, taking in my evening clothes, wrinkled now from the many hours squeezed into the trimotor. "You're a real fancy fella, ain't you?" he drawled in a noncommittal voice.

"I was taught that when you go visiting folks, you always get dressed up," I said.

"Ethan," Bobby said, "where's Ella at?"

The young man known as Ethan kicked at the ground with his boots, and said, "Guess she's getting sort of fixed up for you, Bobby. Big flyboy 'n' all."

Bobby beamed and looked at me proudly. "That's Silas, Ella's daddy, and Ethan, her brother."

"Bobby here, he's fixing to marry Ella," Ethan said to no one in particular.

I noticed the butt of what looked to be a Colt pistol jammed into Ethan's belt.

"What's going on here?" I said to Bobby.

"Silas and Ethan, they're wreckers, the folks you heard so much about," Bobby said.

"I haven't heard anything about wreckers, Bobby."

He looked miffed. "Wreckers, part of the history around these parts you want to know the truth."

"Family's been in the wrecking business 'bout as long as I can remember," agreed Silas. "My daddy and his daddy and his daddy afore him, I suspect."

"See, the reefs around the Keys can be real treacherous," explained Bobby, speaking slowly so even a moron such as myself could understand. "Folks hit on the bright idea of waiting until a ship broke up and then going out there and retrieving its cargo."

"Then the goddamn lighthouses and marker buoys come along," said Silas in a bitter voice that suggested the Black Death itself could not have been worse.

"Used to be a freighter'd hit the rocks up at Key West and its cargo drift right down here into our hands," said Ethan. "Now they got one of them damned lighthouses at Sand Key, gone and done just about ruined our business."

A screen door screeched open and a wild-eyed old woman reeled into view. She scraped against a rusted Coca-Cola sign nailed to one of the posts holding up the porch roof, then bounced away. She wore an ankle-length print dress, faded from too many washings, dark socks pulled up almost to her ankles, and large black shoes. The years had pinched and pulled her face until it was endlessly lined, and set permanently into a look of abject horror. Wispy trails of lank gray hair swirled in the hot wind. That horror-stricken face took in all of us, then her small mouth shot open, and the hag cried out, "Yeh-essss! Yeh-esssss!"

The screen door banged again, and she disappeared, only to reemerge a couple of seconds later, dragging a young, frightened-looking woman onto the porch. She tried to pull away, but the hag, exhibiting unexpected strength, shoved her off the porch into the glare of sunlight.

"Ella!" crowed Bobby, and everyone looked pleased. Everyone, I must say, except Ella herself.

Her face was square and smudged, slanted eyes flaring up against sun-darkened skin. A full mouth hung slightly open, revealing the teeth that next to her long, shiny hair were the best part of her. She wore a plain colorless dress, and being the man that I am, and capable of noticing such things, I could only take admiring note of how it clung to the curve of her.

"Wasn't expecting you 'til tomorrow, Bobby," she said, picking at the skin of her arm, massaging it between her thumb and forefinger.

"Bobby, the flying ace," Ethan said, coming forward. "You go now, Ella, and give Bobby one hell of a big welcome kiss."

But Ella stood stock-still and preoccupied herself by demonstrating how hard she could pinch the skin between her fingers.

The hag staggered off the porch. "Whore-woman! Whore-woman!" she cried out.

"Come on, Ella, give a kiss." Ethan's voice came out harder this time. Still, the young girl stood her ground. Ethan stepped over and slapped her across the face. Ella yelped and staggered back. Immediately, the hag went into a war dance, screaming, "Hit the whore! Hit the whore!"

Now was the time for Bobby to strut his stuff, to provide me with a firsthand demonstration of what he did when someone assaulted his own true love. But he didn't do anything. He just stood there with that silly grin plastered on his face, not at all put out by these events. I could not help but notice the barrels of Silas's gun were no longer pointing directly at the ground. They had raised themselves up, presumably with some help from Silas, so that they were now pointed in the general direction of my midsection.

I said, "Where I come from, Bobby, men don't go around hitting women."

Ethan wheeled on the rounded heel of one of those scuffed boots, squinted his eyes, and peered more closely at me. "Who gives a flying shit where you come from or what you did when you was there?"

The young girl, Ella, tears streaming down her face, scurried over and pecked Bobby decorously on the cheek. He beamed. "Thank you, sweetheart. I love you, too." He looked at me as though to say, "See, I know how to handle these things." Maybe he did.

Ethan jerked a grease-stained thumb in my direction. "This the one has the money?"

Bobby grinned stupidly as he came over to where I stood. Silas had his finger on the shotgun's triggers.

"You sort of messed things up, Mr. Orrack, you want the plainspoken truth of the matter. See, I was supposed to fly a whole bunch of money down to Key West solo for Mr. Madden, and that was fine."

"Ah, money. So that's what's contained in the package. A lot of money, is it?"

"Owney didn't mention anything about money?" Bobby sounded as though he couldn't believe it.

"Not a word."

"Well, just for your information, I overheard one of Mr. Madden's boys saying, 'over twenty-five thousand dollars.' That's what he said. 'Over twenty-five thousand dollars.'"

"That's a lot of money."

"As you've already seen, I'm a pretty smart fellow."

"So you came up with a plan, I would imagine."

"You got that part right. The idea was, the Ford Trimotor would crash in the sea and burn, and me and my future in-laws here would be away with that money without anyone, least of all Mr. Owney Madden, being the wiser."

"Wreckers making the big score. I see. Very clever indeed."

"Yeah, you're not riding across America with no fool, that's for sure."

"Still, wouldn't Owney Madden be just a trifle suspicious if they happened to find the plane, but no body?"

"Yes, sir, he would be a mite suspicious at that. That's why we are going to make use of a family tragedy. My future grandfather-in-law, Granddaddy Raymond, a legendary wrecker out here on the Keys, he passed away about a week ago. Had a terrible heart, I'm afraid."

I glanced at the grieving relatives. They shuffled uneasily, but managed to keep their eyes dry. Such a show of fortitude in the face of tragedy was indeed reassuring.

"Ethan here, and Silas, they packed up Granddaddy Raymond in ice, preserving him till I arrived. We were going to put him in the plane, make it look like it crashed, then set it afire."

"Sounds like you've been planning this for some time."

"You're no fool, Orrack, even if you ain't entirely experienced in the matters of the heart. I'd dearly love to advise you on them matters, so it pains me to have to put an end to you. But you see, we just don't at this point have a whole lot of choice in the matter."

Chapter Twenty-six

Bobby took Georgie Raft's gun out of my pocket, and said, "Let me hold on to that for you. Ethan, you run around and get Mr. Madden's package from the plane."

"Yes, sir, Bobby, that be just fine."

"Save yourself the walk, Ethan."

He regarded me with a quizzical expression. "What?"

"The money's not there."

Bobby's grin went slack. "Now where would that money be, Mr. Orrack?"

"In a safe place."

Bobby and his soon-to-be relatives traded wild glances. "Sheee—ittt!" Bobby cried, and hopped away, disappearing behind the shacks.

Another freighter appeared on the horizon. By now a slight breeze moved the air. It was a nice relief. I noticed Ella watching me, endlessly twirling a strand of hair around her finger. She bit at her lower lip. Then she went over and started to listlessly pitch stones toward the water. I watched the way her lithe body twisted around with each throw. Her father and brother ignored her in favor of keeping their eyes on me. But the old hag watched Ella, and her red-rimmed eyes brimmed with hatred.

"Ella," I said. "Why don't you let me have one of those stones?"

"Don't go near him, Ella!" shouted Ethan.

"It's okay," I said. "It's just a trick, something I want to show you, that's all."

Ella came tentatively forward, biting at that lower lip again, eyes bright with speculative interest. "What kind of trick you got, mister?"

"Magic trick."

Silas tightened his grip on the shotgun. "Ella!"

"What you worried about, Daddy? What's a stone going to do against a shotgun? Just a silly little trick to pass the time."

She swayed over to hand me the stone. "What is it, mister? What do you do?"

"Turn the stone to a bee."

She giggled. "That's the silliest thing I ever did hear."

"Is it?"

"Then let's see you do it."

"You don't touch no stone," snarled Ethan. He was reaching for that pistol.

"That's okay. Ella, you throw it."

Ethan relaxed a bit, but just in case he had the gun in his hand. Ella tossed the stone high into the air. Everyone looked up as the stone reached the top of its arc, and then began to fall toward the ground. I threw up my hand and the stone exploded, sending a fine spray of dust everywhere. Out from the dust emerged a bee, buzzing around Silas, who jumped away with a cry and began to swat at it.

The others now stared at me like I was some strange being newly landed from outer space. Ella particularly looked awed. She bit even harder on her lip, and it seemed to me those eyes became slightly smoky. "Jeez, mister," she said in a breathless voice, "how'd you do that?"

Bobby skittered around the shack, out of breath. He'd left his smile back at the plane. The others watched him charge across the yard.

The bee again buzzed around Silas's head.

"Bobby," Ella said excitedly, "your friend here, he can turn stones to bees. Did you know that?"

Silas swatted at the bee.

Bobby ignored her and pushed his sweaty, boyish mug within a couple of inches of mine. His breath smelled old and stale. No wonder Ella was reluctant to buss our hero.

"All right you, what'd you do with it?"

"Put it this way, Bobby, I'd be real careful about gunning me down since it turns out I'm just about the only means you have of putting your hands on the money."

Ethan leapt in, "Bobby, this fellow here, he's some sort of goddamn witch or something, so be real careful."

The bee shot through the air, on the attack for Silas's head. He ducked, flailing his arms around. "Jeezuz Christ!"

Bobby walked over and yanked the gun from Ethan's hand. Meanwhile, Silas again dodged the bee, swearing loudly.

Bobby came back to me, his arm outstretched so that when he stopped, the gun barrel brushed my temple. He cocked the trigger. The sound of it reverberated across the yard. Lucky Lindy was gone. Bobby's face was soft and puffy, and in its glacial intensity, dangerous. "What about it, Orrack? You want to tell me where the money is? Or you want Ella to see what your brains look like?"

"Go ahead," I said, as casually as I could under the circumstances, "I'm a dead man, anyway."

Ella said, "Bobby, you ain't going to shoot him?"

"Shoot the warlock! Shoot the warlock!" cried the hag.

Bobby gritted his teeth, and I could see him trying to come to terms with the possibility of having to carry out his threat. His gun arm started to shake. Suddenly, he whipped the gun down. He shouted, "Silas, you do it. Shoot him!"

Silas, busy waving wildly at the bee, stopped and looked taken aback by this proposition. "Uh, Bobby, I don't think we should go shooting no one here. I mean, I saw it, fellow turned a stone into a goddamn bee. I mean, where'd you get him from, anyway?"

"Sheee-ittt!" Bobby seemed to call out to the gods who would thwart him in this sun-bleached piece of nowhere. He went stomping petulantly off across the yard, past the crone, now dancing around the gas pump. He kicked furiously at the dirt.

After a couple of moments of this, he bent forward, placed his hands on his knees, and drew deeply on the thick air, willing himself under control. He turned to the group. "All right, here's what we're doing. We're going to calm down, get our heads in order." He nodded toward me. "Orrack, you and me, we're going to have a talk about the money, see if we can't reach some amicable arrangement whereby—"

Ethan was scowling. "Wait a minute, Bobby, that sounds like more partners. I don't like that—"

Bobby leaped on him. "Jeezuz, Ethan, will you keep quiet and let me handle this?"

The bee swirled in the air around us.

Ethan was not about to back down. "Maybe, just maybe, Bobby, I don't like the way you're taking care of things. I mean you come swaggering in here, boy hero and all, and you're going to marry my sister, and make us a whole lot of money. So far, you ain't done diddly-shit."

"Diddly-shit! Diddly-shit!" shrieked the crone.

The bee came straight at Bobby. Before he could do anything, the bee's stinger found its mark. He screamed, and clapped his free hand over his right eye. The gun he was holding went off.

Ethan took two steps backward, his facial expression a mixture of wonder and anger. He looked down at the hole in his chest, and his mouth dropped open as though he was about to address Bobby. Before he could say anything, he flopped forward onto the ground. His fedora went tumbling away across the yard.

Meanwhile Bobby jumped around, holding his eye, screaming blue murder. Everyone else remained frozen in place. The shooting silenced even the crone. Silas stared at me, his face full of fear and confusion. He swung the shotgun up toward me, and as he did, the bee came at him, and he ducked away as the shotgun went off and Bobby's entire back was torn apart in a great spray of blood and flesh. The force of the blast tossed him across the yard, so that when he landed facedown, the heat shimmering off him, he was not far from the lately departed Ethan. He tried to raise his head, and failed. The last word that escaped between his lips was, "Ella."

The bee arced around again, buzzing around Bobby's head.

I thought for sure Silas would carry out his original intention and open up at me. Instead, he let the shotgun drop to the ground, and just stood there, as though trying to figure what chores he had to do that afternoon.

I glanced at Ella, half-expecting her to run to her fallen hero, and take him tearfully in her arms.

It's a good thing I was only half-expecting it.

It was me who went over to Bobby. I bent down and relieved him of Georgie Raft's gun. He wouldn't need it, and it might just come in handy if Silas decided to get nasty.

Ella, in the meantime, didn't move, and she didn't take those smoky eyes off me. She kept biting at her lower lip.

We chose a burial site behind one of the shacks, not far from Bobby's beloved Tin Goose. Silas had not uttered a peep since the shootings. Ella wondered if Ethan should be buried close to Bobby, since Ethan never did like Bobby all that much. Silas did not comment, except to move a few more paces away before he started digging.

There was not a great deal of enthusiasm for the burial. Hard coral lurked a couple of inches beneath the topsoil and it refused to yield itself for these miserable corpses. Thus Bobby and Ethan were not so much buried as covered up with dirt and rock. When we finished as best we could, I turned to Silas. "I could use a ride into Key West."

His eyes narrowed. "You some kind of warlock like Ma says?"

"You give me a ride, you can hang on to the trimotor."

"What would I want with a damn plane?"

"You're in the salvage business, aren't you?"

"Usually the things I salvage is floating."

"Well, this might open a whole new market for you, Silas. Think about it."

Silas did not appear inclined to do much thinking.

"Let me wash up, then I'll take you in by boat."

I went inside the shack where there was a phone on the wall. I gave the operator the number that Georgie Raft had provided me. A formal-sounding female voice demanded without preamble to know who was calling.

"It's Brae Orrack, ma'am," I said.

"Brae Orrack? I know of no one by that name."

I could hear a voice in the background insisting that the receiver be handed over and a moment later a man said, "This is William Ward." He spoke with a soft Southern drawl, smooth as butterscotch.

"Mr. Ward, it's Brae Orrack. Owney Madden told me to give you a call when I got to town."

There was a pause before Billy Ward said, "I was expecting to hear from a Mister Robert Reedhouse." Such a mellifluous voice, almost as though Billy was singing the words.

"I flew down with him," I said. No use saying anything for the moment about Bobby's untimely demise.

"Are you in town?"

"Just south. I'm coming in by boat in a few minutes."

"By boat? I thought you flew down."

"I'll explain everything when I see you."

Another long pause. I could hear the female voice rising sharply in the background. Billy Ward said, "You are arriving at the main docks at the bottom of Duval Street, are you?"

"I guess so."

"Then I will meet you within the hour, Mr. Orrack."

The line went dead.

I went back outside and stood at the dock. The powerboat looked sleek and new, in contrast to just about everything else around here.

"Gets up to forty knots an hour," Ella said.

I turned and there she was standing behind me. "At least that's what my daddy says." The slight breeze flattened the thin material of her dress against her body in a most attractive fashion. "Guess you know I'm of a mind to be pissed off at you."

"Why is that?"

"Thanks to you the one man who could take me away from all this is dead."

"You don't need Bobby. You're a pretty smart girl."

"Not that smart, else I would be long gone from this sorry place. There must be somewhere in the world don't feature mosquitoes."

She eyed me with an open speculation that was as frank as it was slightly disconcerting. "What you gonna do in Key West anyhow?"

"Find the woman I love."

She tried on a smile. It didn't quite fit. "The woman you love, huh?"

"That's right."

"Now here's something you may not have had a chance to think about till now. Maybe the woman you love is right here, and therefore you don't have to go all the way into Key West."

To bring the point home, she insinuated her buttocks against mine so that I could feel the warmth of her.

"I don't think so, Ella," I said as gently as I could.

Give this much to Ella: she was not a woman about to give up easily. Her hand now caressed my thigh.

"Still, it's getting late and there's no hurry about getting to Key West, is there? Why don't you come on in the house? I got my own bedroom and everything."

Silas lumbered onto the dock. He pretended not to notice what Ella was up to. "Better get going," he said. "There's a storm coming."

I looked up at the clear sky. "You sure about that?"

"You got your magic, fella," Silas said. "And I got mine."

He got aboard and looked at me with Ella. "You coming or not?"

I climbed down into the boat. The last I saw of Ella she was standing on that dock, flooded in golden sunlight, raising a hand in sad farewell. Or was it a fist?

Chapter Twenty-seven

We came into the harbor at Key West, passing the one- and two-masted vessels that dotted the choppy waters, skirting a line of dredging pipes mounted on pontoons. The pipes were being used to suck up sludge and deepen the bay. As Silas predicted, the clouds had grown thicker and more ominous, so that the wharfs and docks were all but lost to the fading light. Silas did not look at all pleased with himself for his prescience. That prickly, unshaven jaw of his remained grimly clenched and he steadfastly kept his eyes on the business of guiding his vessel without so much as a glance at me; as though a look might turn him to a pillar of salt. He brought the craft smartly around a sponge boat turning out toward the Gulf Stream, pulling a line of dinghies behind, and put it against the dock owned by the P & O Steamship Company. A big sign advised that steamers left from Key West bound for Havana Monday, Tuesday, Thursday, and Friday mornings at eight-thirty. He let me off without so much as a nod good-bye, didn't even cut the engines. He jerked the wheel around as soon as I was on the dock and started away, staring straight ahead. Undoubtedly, he held me responsible for his son's death and I guess I could hardly blame him.

I came up from the docks and the strong smell of coffee filled the air, all but overwhelming the much earthier odor of the cows tethered near the curb. A fellow in a straw boater sat on a stool working the udder of one of the cows, drawing milk into a tin cup and then handing it to a youngster waiting in line. Not far from the cattle a magnificent Pierce-Arrow was parked beside the La Concha café opposite the Woolworth Building. The café advertised a Sunday chicken dinner for seventy-five cents. The gent leaning against the car's fender didn't seem to be the type much interested in cheap Sunday dinners. He carefully followed my progress without seeing any reason to hurry forward in greeting. He wore a wide-brimmed panama hat and a trench coat, its collar turned up against the wind. His shoes were expensive white buckskin oxfords, trimmed with calfskin. A diamond tiepin gleamed at his collar. His tanned face featured a carefully maintained Douglas Fairbanks mustache.

"Mr. Orrack?" I recognized that butterscotch drawl from the phone.

"I'm Orrack. You must be Billy Ward."

"I am indeed. And what have you done with our friend Bobby Reedhouse, Mr. Brae Orrack?"

"Bobby didn't make the flight."

"I see."

Billy flashed a smile that, matched to his particular brand of handsomeness, could only be described as roguish. He pushed himself away from the Pierce-Arrow, his lively blue eyes dancing with a quality that begged to be called impish. Oh, he was a devil, Billy Ward, and I wouldn't be surprised to learn he'd spent a great deal of time and effort perfecting that particular image of himself.

"Still, I presume you managed to bring along the package Owney sent you out here to deliver."

"I'm afraid not."

The rogue's smile remained intact, but there was much less impishness in those eyes. "That is not the correct answer, old paint."

"Nonetheless, it's the most honest answer that I can give you."

"Since you are here for the express purpose of turning that package over to me, and Mr. Owney Madden will be most perturbed when he discovers you cannot do it, how could that possibly be the honest answer?"

"It's the only one I have to give you, thanks to Bobby Reedhouse."

"Bobby has the money?"

"Bobby is dead."

Billy did not seem particularly surprised by this revelation. "And how did he come to achieve that?"

"He achieved it by first trying to kill me."

"So then you killed Bobby, is that it?"

"In a manner of speaking, I suppose that's right."

"You do not kill people in a manner of speaking, Mr. Orrack. You either kill them or you don't."

"Well, I didn't actually kill Bobby myself. But nonetheless, he is dead and the money is back in Los Angeles."

"Why would you leave it there?"

"Because I didn't trust Bobby."

Now he looked, his blue eyes hard, a man who had heard many stories, and found it helpful not to believe any of them. It didn't matter to me one way or the other. That's not why I was here, and standing around debating money matters with this tinhorn wasn't going to get me any closer to Nell.

"Listen, Bobby's dead. I'm alive. That makes me the fellow who can put his hands on the money. You want that to happen or not?"

"You can get the money?"

"No problem," I said with a confidence I had no business feeling.

"Then for the moment, let us put our differences aside, Mr. Orrack. Why don't you get in the car, and I'll drive you out to your hotel."

"That would be swell, Mr. Ward."

I went around and got into the passenger side. A trolley with a big drum mounted in it went by, spraying water onto the dirt street in order to hold down the dust. Billy slipped behind the wheel and started the car.

I said, "Mind if I ask how you come to know Owney Madden?"

"From New York, Hell's Kitchen."

"Then you must know Georgie Raft."

"Sure, sure I know Georgie. A remarkable dancer."

That surprised me. "Georgie dances?"

"The tango, if you can believe it." The thought made Billy chuckle.

"A German from Hell's Kitchen who dances the tango with more artistry than any Spaniard and yet more than anything else he wants to be a gangster."

"So you've seen him dance?"

"Indeed I have, Mr. Orrack, indeed I have. Amazing to see, thrilling in fact. Drove all the women in New York wild. Personally, I preferred Fred Astaire and his sister Adele who dance at the Tracadero. Much more grace, almost like poetry. Georgie is no poet, more a sexual being, I would say."

I tried to imagine Georgie as a sexual being and could not quite do it. "So you're not from these parts, I guess."

He shook his head. "You must be a bit strange to live down here. I'm a curious fellow in many ways, but not that curious. If you don't make cigars, you smuggle—either rum or illegal immigrants. It's a way of life. Most of it is local and very small-time. I'm trying to get Owney involved, inject a little capital and bring in some organization, do for rum-running down here like what he's done with the beer business up north."

"So you are a bootlegger, Mr. Ward?"

"My goodness, Mr. Orrack, that is a flat-out allegation I would have to reject. No, let's say Owney understands a good thing when it is presented to him. I have presented him with a fine business opportunity and he has responded with some much-needed investment capital. Which you so far have not managed to deliver. Where did you leave it, incidentally?"

"It's safe enough," I said.

"Money is never safe enough, old paint. Reassure me that you can get your hands on it without a great deal of difficulty."

I supposed I could, providing it was still in the shrubs adjacent to the drainage ditch at Mines Field. "No question," I said.

"Here's what we will do. I'll get you settled at your hotel. You'll want to freshen up, I suspect. I have some business to which I must attend forthwith. Later this evening, I'll take you for dinner. By that time you will have contacted Owney, told him what's happened, and made new arrangements for the delivery."

I couldn't imagine how Owney Madden would react to the news that I threw his money away. Nonetheless, I nodded agreement, anything to give me a little breathing room until I could find out if Nell was still in town.

Billy turned left onto a dusty road called Flagler Avenue. The surrounding land was flat and empty save for salt ponds and stands of mangrove trees, not to mention the swarms of mosquitoes that seemed to inhabit every square inch of the Keys.

A couple of flat buildings came into view. Cigar factories, Billy said, run by Cubans who escaped the Machado regime. "So what do they go and do? They establish a regular airplane service between Key West and Havana."

"You can fly to Havana by plane?"

"You can after tomorrow. President Machado himself is in town to inaugurate the service. Why, Pan Am's even calling the Fokker Trimotor out at Meacham Field, *The General Machado.*" Billy laughed some more. "Let me tell you, there are a lot of unhappy *torcedors* at those factories."

"*Torcedors?*"

"The fellows who roll the cigars. You're not a cigar smoker, I guess."

"Afraid not."

"Well, if you were, you would know that the Cubans make the finest cigars in the world. They truly do."

But I was not thinking of Cubans and the cigars they made. I thought instead of General Machado, and the plane they named after him; that he was still in Key West, and I had not arrived too late after all.

Chapter Twenty-eight

The sky had turned black, the wind whipping at the nearby palms as we came under the porte cochere of the Casa Marina, a three-story Spanish-style structure built on a desolate tract of land adjacent to the sea.

"Best hotel in town," stated Billy Ward. "The late Mr. Henry Flagler, the oil tycoon, opened this establishment eight years ago, insisting on the finest beds in the South, and the best food anywhere. You should be comfortable here."

Uniformed employees hurriedly yanked huge amberjack, barracuda, and tarpon off the tables where they had been laid out. "The hotel likes to display the guests' catches," Billy explained. "Afraid we're in for a bit of a storm tonight."

A beamed lobby featured polished teak floors and a large fireplace. Arched doorways opened onto a patio and the beach beyond. Well-dressed tourists, pausing for a few days en route to the wilder pleasures of Havana, perched on wicker chairs waving hand fans before steamy faces worrying over the coming storm.

Billy and I arrived at the front desk. A sly-looking young clerk gave us the once-over.

"Why, Mr. Ward, sir, how are you today?"

"I'm just fine, Evan." Billy flashed the smile that put the world on his side. "I do believe you have a room for my friend here, Mr. Brae Orrack."

"Any friend of Mr. Billy Ward's is certainly a friend of the Casa Marina."

"Much appreciated," I said.

"Besides, you don't look like no federal agent."

"A federal agent? Why would I be a federal agent?"

"Rumors abound that the federal boys are on their way down here from Miami via the Florida East Coast Railway," Billy explained. "Happens every so often. The federals get word we're awash in illegal booze. Of course, nothing could be further from the truth." He gave a knowing wink.

"Around here no one begrudges a man a glass of rum from time to time. Sometimes I am convinced that a drink is all that keeps most of us from joining up with the bugs and losing track of civilization altogether. So the conductor aboard the Florida East Coast signals the stationmaster as the train goes through Homestead. The stationmaster phones down here, and alerts us. Then the taxi drivers go around, collect the booze, and hide it until after the federal agents have departed."

"When are these agents supposed to show up?"

"Could be here now, for all we know," the desk clerk said conspiratorially. "Mr. Ward will make sure you steer clear of any trouble."

"Here's what you do," Billy said as we moved away from the desk. "You get yourself cleaned up—get that tux cleaned and pressed."

"They'll do that here?"

"Paint, I would never check anyone into an establishment that didn't know how to cater to a gentleman. Now get some rest. I'll pick you up about six-thirty for dinner."

I didn't want dinner. I wanted to find Nell. But for the moment, I pasted on my most accommodating smile, and said, "That's mighty kind of you."

"We are the guests of a lovely lady, Miss Irma Curry. Her daddy happens to be the mayor of Key West, a woman soon to be my fiancée I might add."

Billy Ward was right about one thing at least. This was an establishment used to taking care of a gentleman. Thankfully, they did not spend a lot of time figuring who was and was not a gentleman, otherwise I would have been out on my ear. Charlie, the hall porter, a fellow a couple of years younger than myself, had a forehead like the side of a cliff, topped by an unruly mop of straw-colored hair. He took away my grubby duds without even raising an eyebrow and, unasked, returned a few moments later with a complete shaving kit, seeing as how I lacked luggage and thus the necessary implements with which to make myself presentable for the evening.

A herd of cattle would have fit nicely into my room with space for a good-sized party to celebrate the arrival of the cattle. It took me half the day to reach the bathroom, and from the size of the tub I would have said it would require six months to fill. Well, it might be I exaggerate a bit, but then I have a tendency to do that, don't I? In fairly short order I found myself in a warm, scented bath leafing through the *Key West Citizen*. The *Citizen* was a newspaper with nothing but pleasant things to say about the community it served ("Record Tourist Business Next Winter Is Forecast"), but which saw the outside world as a dark and frightening place. In Havana, the paper reported that black voodoo doctors tried to kidnap a two-year-old child "intended for the sacrifice." Three hundred people in Cairo, Egypt, had been killed in an earthquake, while in Alabama it was estimated that so far this year nine Negroes had been lynched. Best stay put, the *Citizen* seemed to advise, and leave the rest of the world to its own sad devices.

I dried myself with a towel the size of a circus tent, and then crawled between fresh linen sheets covering a bed as wide as experience. I lay there only seconds before falling into a deep, dreamless sleep.

I awoke when Charlie returned with my freshly cleaned and pressed clothes.

The wind whipped open the glass-pane doors leading to the balcony. Charlie and I wrestled the doors closed. That's when the lights went out.

Charlie found candles in one of the drawers, lit three of them, and departed. I dressed by the candlelight, tense with the anticipation of the evening. I inspected myself in the mirror. They had done a remarkable job with the evening clothes. A little worn at the edges perhaps, but I could reasonably pass for a young man on the town. I turned Georgie Raft's gun in my hand. The candlelight gleamed off the sideplate as I debated whether to take it with me. Finally, I jammed the gun into my pocket and went out the door. If I was to save my true love from the clutches of the evil Machado, best to be armed. I refused to entertain the fleeting notion that she did not want to be saved, least of all by the likes of me.

Downstairs, the lobby was cast in the yellow glow of hundreds of candles. Ladies in gossamer gowns accompanied by men in white suits floated across the floor, the candles held aloft so that their sputtering light danced off the walls, casting grotesque shadows. We were all lost souls, sharing the moment of intimacy that comes out of danger, and not quite knowing what will happen next.

Billy had changed into evening clothes, although he still wore the panama hat. He sat in one of the wicker chairs near the fireplace, talking to Kiki Diaz. I was across the lobby when I saw them and ducked behind a pillar so they didn't see me. After a few minutes, Kiki rose and Billy followed. The two men shook hands and Kiki crossed the lobby and went outside. Billy sat down again and that's when I came over to him.

"You cleaned up pretty good, I must say," Billy said. "The hotel staff really can pull off small miracles at a moment's notice."

"Not bad," I said. "Been waiting long?"

"A couple of minutes, that's all."

"Sorry to leave you down here alone," I said.

Billy said, "Did you get in touch with Owney?"

"Yes," I said.

"You told him about the money?"

"Truth is, I couldn't get through to him."

"Paint," Billy said unhappily, "you really ought to be doing your level best to put my mind at ease."

"They told me Owney would call back first thing in the morning. He'll get it straightened out then."

"Tomorrow morning it is. Or else I will lose my legendary patience."

"That's what they said. Owney would call in the morning. Get everything straightened out."

He mustered one of his Billy smiles. "Then I guess we'd better be going."

As soon as we stepped outside the force of the wind nearly knocked us over. Billy's hat flew away across the lawn. We struggled to the car and ducked in. He wrestled with the driver's side door and finally got it closed. That's when I stuck the gun into his ribs. I felt a little strange doing it, if you must know, me not having a great deal of experience pulling guns. But I was determined to discover what Billy was doing with Kiki Diaz.

To his credit, Billy did not react with undue alarm, a man who must have had a number of guns jammed into his side over the years and knew enough to stay calm.

"Where did you get that, paint?" he said, glancing down at my weapon.

"Georgie Raft gave it to me."

"I doubt he'll be very happy if you use it to shoot me."

"It's to protect me from duplicitous liars," I said.

"Then, paint, I guess you'd better get about the business of shooting yourself, because you've done nothing but lie to me since you arrived."

"Tell me about Kiki Diaz."

Now he did look surprised. "How do you know him?"

"We grew up together on the streets of Havana. He taught me how to pick my teeth with a knife."

Billy gave me a sidelong glance and then allowed himself to relax a bit. "Let's say I am pursuing a separate business proposition with President Machado."

"It doesn't involve me?"

He sighed and said, "This has to do with the woman accompanying General Machado, that's all. Nothing to do with our business."

The woman with General Machado. Yes, indeed. That would be Nell Devereaux, unless I missed my guess. "Tell me about this woman."

He gave me a curious look. "What possible difference could it make to you, paint?"

"Humor me, Billy."

"You mind if I drive while we talk? Otherwise we're going to be late for this lovely dinner."

"Go ahead," I said.

He slipped the Pierce-Arrow into gear and glided away from the protection of the porte cochere. A gust of wind nearly drove the car off the roadway. Billy tightened his grip on the wheel and concentrated on the road.

"As it happens, I know the lady with whom the general is currently involved, and I thought it advisable to make him aware of that fact. Consequently my meeting with Kiki Diaz that you apparently witnessed."

"What's the lady's name?"

"These days she goes by the name Nell Devereaux. But when I knew her, she was Nellie Bubak from the Lower East Side of New York."

I was having trouble swallowing. "Nellie Bubak? Are you sure it's the same woman?"

"Oh, it's Nellie all right. Up to her old tricks, too."

"And what old tricks might they be?"

"Nellie's a con artist. She was only about eighteen when I knew her, but already accomplished at relieving the rakes of their money."

It had to be someone else. Nell Devereaux might be any number of unexpected things, but she was not a con artist. I could be so accused, certainly, and because I could I would know such a person if I encountered her. She could never fool me.

"She has developed a marvelous scam," Billy continued. "Really, I take my hat off to her. The genius is in its simplicity."

"You must tell me how it works." The words came out between gritted teeth. Billy seemed not to notice.

"Nellie professes to be a mountain climber desperate to reach the top of a mountain in Nepal or some such place. Great passion for it; impossible odds to overcome. She's in town trying to raise money for the expedition. Time is of the essence. Well, naturally, all the rich young swains are anxious to help any way they can. Nellie even has photographs of herself standing on a mountain somewhere. Holding an American flag. Or British or French, depending on the nationality of the mark. All the contributors eventually receive a copy, along with a heartfelt letter of thanks for helping her realize her dream."

I thought of Nell's tears in that Malibu cabin; her frustration and fear at being unable to reach the top of Nanga Parbat. Give her this much: she certainly made it real. Why, a gullible young man could be taken right in if he wasn't careful.

"With most cons, the mark eventually realizes he has been taken to the cleaners and is most unhappy, and that is when the authorities make their appearance. But Nellie sets it up so that none of her marks ever feels cheated. Quite the contrary. They believe they have helped the love of their lives. Truly, it is the most amazing thing. No legal authorities ever enter the picture."

Billy's face took on a slightly wistful expression. I could well imagine that same look on my face.

"One of the many allures she so effectively employs is her supposed innocence. A woman who climbs mountains and flies planes, and yet, a virgin. Like most men, I found the combination highly potent. All part of her scam, of course."

Billy gave a quick look that bespoke the world-weary gentleman forced to learn harsh lessons. "Our relationship quickly ended when she discovered I was that most despicable of all things—poor. But it was lovely while it lasted, I must say."

"How did you know she was here?"

"I didn't." He paused and then chuckled. "Several years had gone by since our brief amorous encounter and my wounds had mostly healed. So here I am in this curious place at the end of the known world. The last place I would expect to encounter anyone I know—which is more or less the idea behind being here. I'm in the lobby of the Casa Marina, arranging for your accommodation, in fact, when who should come sashaying in on the arm of General Machado, but Nellie herself. Only now, she is the remarkable Nell Devereaux.

"She pretended not to see me, but she recognized me rightly enough. After I recovered from my shock, I started thinking. Nellie almost certainly would not want General Machado to know her true identity. Thus, my willingness to keep her little secret might be worth a small percentage of whatever she's about to take from the general."

"What did she have to say about this?"

"I've had occasion lately to discuss the subject with Miss Bubak and she is, as I suspected, most receptive to a partnership arrangement."

"Did you give her any choice?"

Billy gave a vague smile. "Nellie has been around the track a number of times. She knows how the race is run. We will get together later tonight at her hotel suite to discuss our options."

"Is that what you were discussing with Kiki Diaz? Options?"

"Business, I would say."

"So you have told Kiki about Nellie."

"Let's say I commenced negotiations in the lobby," he said. "Much will depend on what kind of an arrangement I can make with Nellie when I show up at room three-ten later tonight." He threw me another glance and a wink. "How cooperative she wants to be with an old friend from her past."

It was not hard to imagine what sort of cooperation Billy was talking about. It was also not hard to imagine that Machado by now was at least suspicious of Nell, and therefore she was in a great deal of danger. That's what I imagined all right: Nell in danger and me saving her, forgiving her for past trespasses and lies because that's what you did when you were in love. You forgave the one you loved. Forgave her everything and saved her life.

All I had to figure out was how to do it.

Chapter Twenty-nine

Curious little houses of unpainted wood with Doric columns and gabled roofs fell into vague outline through the sleetlike rain. Wooden pegs held the houses together, Billy stated, and while the structures looked rickety, their foundations were anchored deep into the coral of the island. On a night like this, that was good to know. By now I'd put the gun away. Billy did not comment one way or the other, but the gun in his ribs and the forced confession that followed had produced a certain tension between us. We rode in silence through the rain and I tried not to think about Nell waiting back at the Casa Marina, and what exactly I might do about that.

Deeper into town, the houses became grander with lovely porch columns and fretwork fences along with ornamental details such as corner brackets and balustrades. The houses sat close together on intimate unpaved roadways hushed by great blooming growths of tropical plants. Billy slowed to turn the car onto Elizabeth. Unlike the surrounding streets, it was paved with bricks to emphasize the prosperity of its inhabitants.

"Here we are," Billy said as he swung the car through a gateway.

Stone walls gave way to exotic-looking shrubbery standing sentinel on either side of a drive that swept to a large, two-story frame house. Verandas ran along the upper and lower floors, propped up by columns and festooned, like so many of the other houses in this part of town, with intricate gingerbread designs. The place was dark, and appeared to be deserted.

Instead of parking in front, Billy turned off the drive and followed a gravel road around to the rear of the house. He parked the car behind a copse of cypress trees and then turned to me.

"You all right, old paint? You look quite pale."

"I'm fine," I said, although I was not feeling fine at all.

"A word of caution, do you mind?"

"Go ahead."

"You and I have had our differences this evening, but my suggestion is we put them behind us for a couple of hours. I'm about to introduce you to a wonderful lady, Miss Irma Curry of Key West. Her father, as I stated previously, is the mayor. Since they are a family out of a long line of smugglers and wreckers, they, of course, have recently put on certain airs in an attempt to cover their dark history. Futile, if you ask me, but there you have it. Thus Irma knows nothing of my current business dealings with Owney Madden, and it wouldn't go particularly well if she did. So if you don't mind, we'll identify you as a business associate from Los Angeles, interested in looking into real estate possibilities in this area."

"A real estate man," I said.

"Thus it will not be necessary for you to go waving that gun around."

"Nonetheless, I do believe I'll keep it in my pocket just in case."

Billy paused before he said, "That's fine. We will have ourselves a good dinner—Irma employs the finest cook on the Keys."

"It's been a while since I've had anything like a decent meal," I admitted.

The rain continued to slash down as the two of us dived through the back door, and stood in a darkened hall shaking water off our clothing. I sensed something behind me. A woman stood silently in the shadows, her arms held straight at her sides. Billy Ward started when he saw her. "Why, Irma, my darling, whatever are you doing standing in the dark?"

The woman said nothing, but continued to stand there, staring at us, a pale ghost in a crimson evening gown, luxurious brown hair falling softly to white shoulders. Her cheekbones were skeletal; her mouth so firmly set it formed a disconcertingly straight line. Her dark eyes burned into Billy Ward as he came forward and bussed her softly on each hard cheek.

"My darling, I hate to throw a surprise at you, but a business associate has come all the way from Los Angeles. I knew you would never forgive me if I didn't invite him to dinner."

"We will be having the bolichi roast this evening," she said in a soft Southern drawl that sounded much more authentic than Billy's. "That is beef stuffed with hardboiled eggs."

"A local dish, very good," stated Billy.

Her eyes inspected me, but except for their burning when they focused on Billy Ward, they seemed somehow dead, as though any life behind them had seeped away. "You did not mention your guest's name, darling."

"This is Mr. Brae Orrack. He's here to investigate real estate opportunities in the Key West area. I thought we might be of help to him."

"Are you familiar with the poetry of Miss Elizabeth Barrett Browning?" she said to me.

"My darling, I'm sure Mr. Orrack—"

"*Are* you familiar with the work of Mrs. Browning?" Her eyes burned even more brightly.

"I am indeed familiar, Miss Curry," I said. Well, I knew who she was, and not much more. But Irma seemed satisfied enough with the answer.

"Follow me, please."

She turned and disappeared, leaving Billy Ward to stare hard and unblinking at the wall. After a moment or two, we went along a darkened hall into a dining room with a crystal chandelier. Candlelight revealed a long table covered in white linen and set with fine silver. Wine was already set out. Behind the table, glass doors were closed to the howling night beyond.

Irma Curry ordered me to be seated. She glared at Billy Ward. "Will you pour the wine for your friend, please? The friend from Los Angeles. The friend who claims to be interested in real estate opportunities in the Key West area."

Billy did not move. "Are you all right?"

"Perfectly fine. Quite excited, in fact. I had a nap this afternoon in preparation for this evening."

I seated myself across from Irma. Billy held her chair as she slid into it. A black waiter in a white jacket appeared carrying a tray filled with small cakes. "These are called *bollos,*" Irma addressed me again. "Usually they are served with coffee."

"The time of day is served with coffee around these parts," said Billy. "We drink our coffee *un buchito*—just a swallow."

I took one of the cakes offered by the waiter.

"The *bollos* are made of black-eyed peas, flour, garlic, and onions, and then cooked in deep boiling lard," said Irma.

I took a bite and said, "They're delicious." In fact, they weren't bad at all. I helped myself to another.

Billy poured wine. Irma made a tent of her slim fingers and said, " 'Accuse me not, beseech thee, that I wear, Too calm and sad a face in front of thine.' What about it, Mr. Orrack? Do you believe my face to be calm and sad, as Mrs. Browning said?"

"There is a calmness," I offered. "The sadness, well, ma'am, I'm not so sure of the sadness."

"You may be assured, Mr. Orrack, this is most definitely sadness you see. Of the calmness, I'm not so certain."

Billy stopped pouring the wine. He looked genuinely puzzled. "My darling, why ever should there be sadness on that lovely face of yours?"

" 'And yet, because thou overcomest so, Because thou art more noble and like a king, Thou canst prevail against my fears and fling, Thy purple round me, till my heart shall grow, Too close against thine heart henceforth to know, How it shook when alone.' What do you think, Mr. Orrack? Do you find Billy to be noble, and like a king?"

"Well, ma'am," I said uneasily, "I don't really know."

"It's funny, because you see, for some time that was how I saw Billy. I was blindly in love, you understand, and like a woman in love, I saw no fault, and I listened to no reason."

"I, too, know what it's like to be blinded by love, Miss Curry."

She looked at me as though she had not heard correctly. "I'm sorry, Mr. Orrack, what did you say?"

"I know what it's like to be blinded by love."

Irma Curry's eyes abruptly shone with life. "My goodness, a male of the species who actually admits to being in love."

"It's love that brings me to Key West." Billy looked stunned when I said this, but Irma appeared quite pleased. Her eyes focused on me, shining even more brightly.

"I was largely unaware love could be found in Key West."

"The woman I love is here," I said. "I must find her before it is too late."

"Too late? Too late for what?"

"If I do not find her soon, I will die."

"My goodness," said Irma Curry in a breathless voice. "I daresay you're a romantic, Mr. Orrack."

She glared at Billy. "You on the other hand are nothing but a scoundrel and a liar."

Billy took a great deal of time before he said, "Irma, I want you to stop this."

From the front of the house came a loud hammering. "What the blazes is that?" Billy demanded.

More pounding reached our ears. Irma seemed unperturbed.

"Your name is James Francis Monaghan," she said in a steady voice. "You've also been known from time to time as 'Smiling Billy' Williams. There is a murder charge hanging over your head. The police on Long Island, New York, want you in connection with a jewel robbery at the home of one Jesse L. Livermore. What's more, when the police tried to arrest you a year ago, they were forced to shoot you. Even so, you escaped their custody. You are a thief and a murderer, William or James or whatever the goddamn hell your name is!"

Billy's face had turned ashen. "God in heaven, Irma, what have you done?"

"I've turned you in to the authorities, that's what I've done. Those are federal agents at the door. They are here to arrest you."

"Mr. Orrack, it appears I was mistaken," Billy said. "Those agents are not looking for local rumrunners after all."

"Apparently not."

"I'm going to have to cut our evening short, I'm afraid."

"So it would seem."

"Now, sir. You can stay here with Miss Curry, if that's what you wish. She may even feed you dinner and her bolichi roast is to die for, no doubt about it. However, she may also turn you over to federal agents, who, to put it mildly, could make the rest of your visit here uncomfortable."

"There is no way out," Irma announced.

"I'm afraid you don't know me well, my darling."

He rose from the table and flung open the glass doors. Wind and rain exploded into the dining room. Billy fought his way forward and disappeared through the doors. The waiter entered and said, "Madam, there are men kicking in the front door."

"That's fine, Otis," Irma Curry said. "I'm expecting them."

"Very well, ma'am. I will hold the roast for the time being."

"I think that's just as well, Otis."

Otis retreated.

Irma sipped her wine. " 'Fast this life of mine was dying,' " she mumbled. " 'Blind already and calm as death.' "

From the corridor, I heard men's voices coming toward the dining room, the federal agents in question, no doubt. Billy almost certainly was on his way back to the Casa Marina to confront Nell. If I stayed here, those fast-approaching agents would detain me, particularly when they found the gun in my pocket. As dangerous as it was to be around him right now, I decided I'd better stick close to Billy.

"Thank you for your hospitality, Miss Curry," I said, getting out of the chair.

"You're leaving, too?"

"Unfortunately."

"You must find your love, I suppose, although I would say the bolichi roast is preferable."

"As a matter of fact that's exactly what I must do."

"My search also continues apparently. So far I am afraid it's been futile. But I remain optimistic. Like you, I am a romantic."

"Good luck to you, Miss Curry."

"And to you as well, Mr. Orrack."

I went through the glass doors. Outside, I found myself on a flagstone patio surrounded by a balustrade. Below the balustrade, I could see Billy disappear around the corner. Now I knew why he took the time to park his car behind the house. I raced down a flight of stone steps leading off the patio. Behind me, voices raised sharply over the wind.

Lightning slashed the sky as I crossed the gravel drive and saw Billy Ward climbing into the Pierce-Arrow. I quickly joined him.

"Decided not to chat with the feds, huh?"

"They don't seem in the mood for conversation. I thought I'd drive back to the Casa Marina with you."

"I don't believe we will be visiting the Casa Marina this evening," he said.

That's not what I wanted to hear, but by now he had shoved the car into gear and shot into the drive. Through the rain, I swore I could hear the sound of gunfire.

"They're not shooting at us, are they?"

"Why not? We're dangerous customers. Who could blame them?"

Of course. Billy was a wanted killer. It had not occurred to me until this moment that they might want to shoot him on sight and be done with it.

I pulled out Georgie Raft's gun and for a moment a hopeful look crossed his smooth face—until I jammed the gun into his side again.

"This is becoming tiresome, paint. Instead of trying to scare me, you might think about shooting an agent or two."

"Head back to the Casa Marina, Billy."

"That's not a very good idea," he said.

"Nonetheless, I want you to do it."

Instead of answering, he made another left past a street sign that said Duval. I caught a glimpse of storefronts, dark against the pelting rain. The watery lights of Pepe's Cafe flashed past and then a billboard advertising Lucky Strike cigarettes. Then more darkness.

I pushed the gun into his ribs. "Billy, do as I say!"

Billy swung the wheel wildly and the car veered past an oncoming car. The rear windshield abruptly shattered, showering the interior with glass. Our pursuers were catching up.

"I keep a small sponge boat at the docks in case of just such a situation as this," he said. "It's the chance we have to get out of this with our skins intact."

More gunfire halted further objections on my part. I got a momentary glimpse of a cypress tree before the wind brought it crashing down on the gleaming hood of the Pierce-Arrow. Billy lost control and the car smashed into a low stone wall.

I could hear the sound of escaping steam, and the thud of the rain against metal. I looked down at my hands. Neither of them held Georgie's gun. They were shaking too hard to hold any gun. I looked over at Billy. He sat up straight, his hands clenched at his throat and I wondered if he wasn't trying to strangle himself to death. Then I saw the blood spurt from the bullet hole in his larynx.

He turned to me, those blue eyes dancing as he tried for one more Billy smile. It surely would have been as brave and roguish as anything he had ever produced. He even opened his mouth, but that was as far as he got. Billy's eyes ceased the dance that I suspect had gone on his whole life. He gripped at his throat and shook his head as though unable to believe his smile could not get him out of one more tough spot. Then he fell face forward against the steering wheel.

I lurched out of the car expecting to be hit by bullets, but I was met only by the sound of the howling wind. I tripped over the low wall, picked myself up again, and tore off into the night.

Chapter Thirty

The lights were still out all over Key West. That probably saved me from the ruthless federal agents who would stop at nothing in their pursuit of Billy Ward. Or maybe the fact that their quarry was dead convinced them to call it a night and go home. Whatever the case, I finally realized no one was chasing me, and slowed my furious run. Not a moment too soon, either. My stomach was aching badly, and I needed to catch my breath—but only for a moment. The thought of Nell, waiting in that hotel room for Billy and Machado turning up instead, soon propelled me forward.

I stumbled through a maze of darkened streets until I reached a roadway, hearing the roar of the ocean beyond. Light flared in the distance, as though a great ship had arrived to hover in the velvety blackness. Well, not a ship exactly, but the hotel Casa Marina. Electric power had returned to Key West.

I passed tennis courts, approaching the seaward side of the hotel, hearing music from inside. Ducking along the loggia, past arcs of light thrown off by the windows, I could make out shadows in the dining-room wing, the sound of the hotel orchestra closer now, playing something smooth and soft for your nighttime dining and dancing pleasure.

I was soaking wet and didn't want to go rushing into the lobby attracting unwanted attention. So I retraced my steps around the dining room, until I came to the metal rigging of the fire escape at the back of the hotel. I leaped up and grabbed onto the ladder that hung suspended above the ground, and drew it down. I climbed to the first-floor landing and then on up to the second floor. Someone had thoughtfully left the window open. I slipped through and went up to the third floor and knocked at room 310. For a moment, I didn't think there was any one inside, then the door opened and there stood Nell, wrapping herself into a robe. She stared when she saw me, looking, of all things, disappointed. "Brae? Oh, God, Brae, what the blazes are you doing here?" she said in an exasperated voice.

"I said I would come for you," was all I could think of to reply.

"No, you didn't," she said.

"I was sure I said something."

"Not a word."

"Well, you should have known I'd come."

She looked nervously up and down the corridor and then refocused those gold-flecked eyes on me, rather unfriendly gold-flecked eyes, I should say. "This is not a good time," she said in a strained voice. "A terrible time, as a matter of fact."

"I understand that," I said.

She was speaking faster now, the way she did when she was nervous. "There are things I have to do and you're going to get in the way. You're an awful mess, you know that? You didn't come here in evening clothes, did you? You came all the way here in evening clothes?"

"How else would you come looking for a lady in distress?"

"Oh, God, Brae." She shook her head in disbelief. "I'm not even in distress."

"You are," I said. "Believe me, you are."

"I certainly will be when Gerry finds out you're here. Are you staying at the hotel? I mean how did you even know I was here? He is going to kill you and he's not going to be happy with me—and right now it's important that Gerry stays happy, do you understand?"

Abruptly, she pulled me into her room and closed the door. "You're

a crazy man, you know that? Absolutely crazy. Soaking wet, too. And so
am I."

"You're not wet at all."

"But I am crazy."

To my absolute astonishment, the next thing she was feverishly kissing me and I was returning those feverish kisses and it was easy to discover she wore nothing under that robe, and that getting out of my wet
evening clothes could be accomplished in remarkably short order.

I will not bother you with the details of what happened next other
than to assert that we attacked each other with a certain animal savagery
I had not experienced before. At least I would say there was animal savagery involved, although please remember I am drawing from a limited
well of experience in these matters. I would further say there was also a
furtive desperation to what we did during the next twenty-five minutes
or so, as though these moments together were finite and not soon to be
repeated.

We finished finally, ending up on a four-poster bed that was, if anything, bigger than the one in my room. She sat up on one narrow elbow,
that golden hair tousled about a blurry and concerned face, and said,
"Now Brae, that's it, all right? You must get out of here."

"Not without you," I said.

"Not without me? What are you thinking? Are you thinking I can
just leave this hotel with you, and not a second thought about it? Impossible. You must not be ridiculous, not now when being ridiculous becomes very dangerous for both of us."

"He knows about you," I said.

She gave me an uncertain look. "Don't be so melodramatic. Melodramatic is not going to work here. Knows about what?"

"You were supposed to meet Billy Ward this evening, right? He's trying to blackmail you, I believe."

Her eyes widened.

"Thanks to Billy's big mouth, the general knows that you are not
Nell Devereaux, that your real name is Nellie Bubak and that you make
a living by convincing men like him that you are mounting an expedition

to Nanga Parbat, even though you have no intention of doing it."

"I wish you had told me this before you allowed me to take your clothes off," she said in a weak voice.

"You didn't give me a chance," I said.

"Incidentally, I am going to get to the top of Nanga Parbat. That is not a con, all right? I am going to do that, I promise you."

"All right," I said. "But we had better get out of here, otherwise it's never going to get done."

"Not that I'm admitting to any of this nonsense."

"You don't have to admit to anything."

"How did you get mixed up with Jimmy?"

"Jimmy?"

"Or Billy or whatever he calls himself. Jimmy, that bastard."

"Well, I didn't know he was also called Jimmy That Bastard. I met him when I got into town and started looking for you."

"You started looking for me and met Jimmy?" Wariness was quickly being replaced by incredulity. "The bastard. He truly is a bastard. Do you know where he is now?"

"He's dead. Killed in a car wreck earlier this evening."

There were a hundred questions she could ask. We could stay up all night interrogating each other, but she knew there wasn't the time for any of it. "All right, let's put Jimmy aside for the time being. If we did get out of here, where would we go? Has your thinking extended that far?"

"The part where you tell people you fly airplanes."

"What about it?"

"Is it true?"

"Yes."

"How about when you rode Outlaw?"

"Outlaw?"

"The horse called Outlaw."

"I'm a pilot, I can fly planes," she said.

"Then you can fly the *President Machado*?"

"Brae, we can't take his plane."

"Why not?"

Those gold-flecked eyes were unblinking, showing nothing of what she was actually thinking, necessary in her profession, I guess—mine too for that matter. Here we were, two people lying naked together, everything showing but our true emotions.

"I'm supposed to meet Gerry in twenty minutes." As though that was the decisive factor in any future decisions. She sat up and ran her fingers through that tangled hair. She issued a long sigh. "We'd better get dressed," she said.

There was nothing to do then but go about the business of accomplishing just that. Silently, Nell dressed in a shirt and slacks, reasonable clothes for an attractive young woman about to embark on a trip. I forced myself into my still damp evening duds. She tore through the trunks and suitcases lining a walk-in closet. I'd never seen one person with so many clothes. Comes to that, I'd never seen a closet the size of most rooms I'd been in. I put aside once again anxious thoughts about how a young man such as myself could be so naïve about the world, and the ways of certain women in that world.

Nell hurriedly put together a small traveling case full of the things she said she would need for the next few days. "I get tired of leaving places in a hurry, you know that?"

Abruptly, she hugged against me, ignoring my wet clothes. I could feel her lips against my ear, so soft, and the electricity that had nothing to do with the storm outside.

"You must not ask me to love you, Orrack."

"You keep telling me not to."

"And you keep refusing to listen."

"We need to find a car," I said.

"There's a car outside."

"You know where it is?"

She nodded. "Let's hurry, before I change my mind."

"You keep saying you're going to change your mind."

"But I don't, is that what you're saying? Very unusual. Ordinarily I change my mind. See the terrible effect you have on me, Orrack?"

She got a trench coat out of the room-sized closet and put it on. Then

I took her hand and grabbed the case on the bed, and together we left the room and went back down the corridor to the window where I had made my entrance. She followed me down the fire escape, ignoring the pelting rain. I could hear the band playing, something livelier now, as though offering musical accompaniment to a couple of rain-swept fugitives. I followed Nell as we ran along the rear of the hotel, dodging mud puddles until we reached a parking area. She pointed me toward a Plymouth roadster and handed me a set of keys. We got in the car and I turned the engine over.

"You are really going to do this," she said, as though she might have expected me to stop suddenly and announce I was just kidding.

"Yes, we are going to do it," I answered, feeling strangely giddy all of a sudden.

I started away, turning out of the parking area onto the drive. As we came around the front entrance I saw someone hurry outside. Kiki Diaz shimmered against the light thrown off by the hotel, hazy and indistinct in the rain. I could have sworn his arm was upraised. Maybe not, though, for the gunshot I expected never arrived. Nell put her hand on my leg.

"My God," she said.

Chapter Thirty-one

In the diminishing rain and the darkness of a Key West once again without electricity, I got lost a couple of times. This did not sit well with Nell.

"If you're rescuing me from a fate worse then death, should you be getting lost?" she inquired.

"I'm not lost," I insisted.

"Then where are we?"

"I'm not sure," I said.

"That sounds like you're lost to me."

Eventually, I swung the car onto a roadway that set the roaring ocean to our right. To the left, I could just make out salt flats and the ivory facade of a hangar. I turned through the gate and headed across the tarmac.

The *President Machado*, ready for its inaugural flight to Havana, sat in the hangar's open mouth, a silvery promise of the future, a great gleaming trimotor, not unlike the one flown by the late Bobby Reedhouse. I brought the car to a halt, and we got out. By now the rain had pretty much stopped. Inside the hangar, rows of chairs had been set up before a raised podium awaiting the guests and dignitaries who tomorrow would send the *President Machado* off on its maiden voyage. Nell looked up at the plane's fuselage. "Well, we got this far."

"Sounds as though you might have had your doubts."

"We should not be flying this plane at night," she said.

More thunder rolled ominously across the sky. Out on the roadway, I could see headlights coming toward us. Who would be out in the rain at this time of night? Only one kind of person, I surmised. A man in search of his missing girl; he would come on a night such as this.

"I don't think we have much choice," I said.

Nell climbed onto the wing and opened the cabin hatch and got in. She eased herself into the pilot's seat, and then leaned out the window.

"Grab the propeller, and give it a yank," she called.

Having gone through this same routine any number of times with Bobby, I was anxious to show off my expertise. I ran around the front of the plane. Nell signaled that the ignition was on. Immediately, I grabbed at the propeller with both hands and yanked it around. The engine sputtered and spat as though it did not like being awakened. Finally, it turned over. I started on the middle propeller, giving it a couple of turns. Nell hit the ignition, but nothing happened. I tried again.

The mystery car, meanwhile, bounced across the tarmac, its headlights waving through the darkness. Another try and this time the center engine roared to life.

Only the portside engine remained. I started toward it. The car picked up speed, rushing toward the hangar.

Frantically, I yanked at the propeller. Nothing. The headlights blazed at the edge of the hangar.

Once more I turned the propeller. The engine caught, coughed, and then roared.

I swung away, but it was too late. The car was on top of me. The edge of the fender clipped my thigh, spinning me into a nearby worktable, sending a toolbox crashing to the floor.

The car plowed through the chairs before it crashed to a stop against the raised stage. I rolled onto my back, amid scattered wrenches and screwdrivers, fierce little explosions of pain igniting along my right leg. Inside the car, no one moved. I tried to get to my feet but before I could, the driver's side door opened and Machado stepped out. In the midst of losing his woman, he still managed to suggest a man who slept soundly each night on expensive bed sheets. But then again perhaps he was not going to lose his woman because he had the gun in his good hand, and I had no gun in either hand.

"Hey, Orrack, you bring some good gossip with you to Key West?" He came sauntering over as if he had all the time in the world.

"I'm afraid I'm fresh out."

"Then I am going to kill you."

"You don't do that sort of thing yourself, do you, General? You must have people who do your killing for you."

"Tonight I'm in the mood to make an exception," he said.

A yelp from the cockpit and Machado cocked his head. "Kiki? Everything okay?"

This was answered with a torrent of Spanish. Then Kiki Diaz appeared around the plane's fuselage with a struggling Nell in tow. *Now where did he come from?* I wondered. Machado looked pleased, a gent in the process of retrieving his lost property.

Except Nell wasn't going along so easily with the retrieval. "Gerry, tell him to let go of me," she called.

Instead, Machado stepped over and slapped her across the face. He didn't look at all angry as he struck the blow; as though this was something he did daily, hitting women who betrayed him.

Nell staggered back, fighting to keep her balance. Machado hit her again. I yelled out something and finally managed to get on my feet, my leg on fire. Kiki's raised gun brought me to a stop. His face was flushed with the tension of a man about to pull the trigger. Hanging on to a limp Nell, Machado yelled something in Spanish and then propelled her outside. Kiki and I suddenly found ourselves alone. The sound of the trimotor's engines filled the hangar.

Kiki edged around so that his back was to the plane and the entrance. He flashed those yellow teeth. "I hear this thing about how you got the *magico,*" Kiki said. "But I guess the magic no help to you now, huh?"

"Never underestimate the power of magic," I advised.

"In this world, guy with the gun, he got the *magico*," Kiki observed. "Makes guys like you stupid—and dead."

"Turn the stones to bees, Kiki," I said.

Kiki cocked his head. "You say what?"

"I can turn the stones to bees."

"In Havana, we got guys in the parks, they take rabbits out of a hat, pull a peso out of your ear. No big deal."

"Ah, but you must understand, there is a great difference between a magician and a magic man."

"Yeah?"

"A magician knows tricks, sleight of hand, how to deceive the eye. A magic man, on the other hand, is a highly trained individual knowledgeable in the dark art of conjuring."

"So how you do that, hombre? How you turn the stones to bees?"

"I'll be glad to show you, Kiki. No trouble at all." I spied a good-sized stone in the gravel adjacent to the plane. "That one over there."

"Hold it," Kiki said.

"It's just a stone. You got the gun. Just step over and pick it up."

For a moment I didn't think he was going to do it. Then he stepped back, closer to the plane, and bent to retrieve the stone.

"Here's the thing," I said. "If you want to see the magic, well, there's a price."

Kiki shook his head. "Hombre, you are amazing. Truly. Don't you get it? I'm about to kill you."

"It's my business, you understand. I have to make it pay."

"So if you do this thing, what do I pay you, huh?"

"You being a special customer, Kiki, you don't pay anything. You just give me something."

"And what is that?"

"My life."

"What if you can't do it?"

"Then you just go ahead and shoot me."

"So what do I do?"

"We have an agreement?"

"Sure, sure. Anything you say."

"All you have to do is toss the stone into the air."

He flashed those yellow teeth again and swung his arm down. The arm shot up, releasing the stone. It arched upward and then began its descent, always with a certain grace that must come from being the center of attention; the stone feeling compelled to provide an artful performance.

As the stone plummeted, everything began moving in slow motion as it does when a fellow goes to the place that allows the stones to be turned to bees. Kiki raised the gun, and began to squeeze the trigger. Ah, Kiki, you duplicitous scoundrel, you didn't want the magic after all. This was merely an amusing distraction for you, a chance to wind up the sucker for a few moments before dispatching him to hell. Kiki's trigger finger tightened some more and that's when I threw the screwdriver. Sleight of hand, Kiki, sleight of hand. Never trust a magic man when it comes down to it. We're duplicitous bastards ourselves, always hovering close to the truth without ever quite reaching it. And sometimes the trick has nothing to do with magic. Sometimes it's just a trick—remembering how to hide an object up your sleeve, like your dad taught you, then producing it when the sucker least expects it.

The stone bounced on the floor. The point of the screwdriver pierced Kiki's left eye. He screamed, dropping the gun, clapping his hands over the bloody mess that an instant before was his eyeball. Kiki staggered back into the trimotor's propeller blade. I could have called out, I suppose, warned him of what he was about to do to himself. I suppose I could have done that. But I never said a word.

And he never saw that blade.

I came out of the hangar with Kiki's gun in my hand. Across the tarmac, Machado was trying to push Nell inside her car. She was resisting, but not very hard. Maybe she was resigned to her fate.

I leveled the gun at him, and yelled, "Let her go."

To my surprise, he immediately did as he was ordered, the obedient lad anxious not to offend those with guns. Nell fell back against the car, and I saw that he had torn at her trench coat and ripped open her shirt. Why the next thing, he might have tied her to the railroad tracks.

"Where is Kiki?" Machado demanded, as though it was his job to keep track of straying employees.

"He's not going to make that inaugural flight."

Nell, preternaturally calm considering recent events, sauntered over like she was joining me for a pleasant nighttime stroll. I had a moment to wonder what she was up to before she grabbed the gun out of my hand. For a terrible instant, I thought she might shoot me; that she had been on Machado's side all along. Instead, she pivoted, and turned the gun on *el supremo*. I managed to hit her arm as the gun went off.

Machado backed up a bit, turning his head as if hearing an unfamiliar noise, and I thought he'd been shot. But he just stood there, staring at Nell in rapt disbelief. I took the gun out of her hand.

"The next time you hit me, I'll kill you," Nell said in a deadly calm voice.

She began walking away. Machado called after her. "I loved you, for God's sake."

"No, you didn't," Nell said, and kept walking. We stood there watching her; the lady's two lovers trapped by their uncertainty over what she would do next. She disappeared inside the hangar.

That seemed to take the air out of him. He sagged against the car. "I am very tired," he said. "I like to have a swim at this time of night. I don't like to be out chasing women around airports."

"There are more than a hundred thousand miles of paved roads in America," I said.

He looked at me in surprise. "What?"

"Something I heard. A statistic I guess you'd call it."

He shook his head. "Why don't you put that gun down?"

"If I do, you might shoot me," I said.

"No, I will not shoot you, not now. What is the point?"

I looked at him, not sure what to say.

He said, "She betrayed me. She will betray you, too."

"She didn't betray you. She tried to shoot you."

He sighed. "You are young and foolish and full of all the wrong notions. So you are not going to listen to me. You believe you got what you want, but you have nothing. I'm being honest with you here."

The trimotor nosed out of the hanger and turned onto the tarmac. Well, at least she hadn't lied about her ability to fly.

"You're wrong about her," I said.

He issued a mirthless chuckle. "You think you know women? Nell will show you how little you know about women."

"Just stay where you are."

"Don't worry. I'm not going anywhere."

I ran to the edge of the tarmac and threw the guns away into the darkness. Machado, true to his word, had not moved.

"Take care of yourself, Orrack," he called. "And when you calm down a bit, and things become a little more clear, try to remember what I said to you."

"A hundred thousand miles," I called back. "I swear it's true."

He looked at me blankly.

Nell had swung the plane around so that its nose pointed down the runway. I climbed into the cockpit. Despite the torn shirt, she managed to look very natural at the plane's controls.

"You really do know how to fly," I said.

"Don't sound so surprised."

I noticed her hand shaking on the controls.

"Are you all right?"

"Sure, Orrack. Kiki Diaz is lying in the hangar without his head on, I just tried to shoot the president of Cuba and we're taking off in the middle of the night. Everything's peachy keen."

"Think of it this way. You didn't shoot him."

"No, thanks to you."

"What will he do?"

"Cover it up. He covers up a whole lot worse than this, believe me."

She straightened the plane on the tarmac, and pushed in the wheel. We began to move forward, picking up speed. A moment later that unbelievable miracle, the one that causes the earth to shake itself loose, leaving the trimotor suspended in air with the two of us in it.

I decided then to say nothing more of what I knew or did not know. What I knew wouldn't fill a thimble. What I didn't know would cover the world. Best to keep my mouth shut. Nell would tell me whatever she had to tell me when the time was right. Until then, it made no difference what either of us had been. We made each other what we were now, at this delicious moment, the trimotor called the *President Machado* lifting away from Key West.

The earth tilted farther away until I couldn't see it anymore, leaving Nell and me finally alone, suspended in the nothingness, shiny new and bright, our love true and destined to endure forever.

I believed that. I truly did.

PART FOUR

South of the Moon, East of the Big Smiling Hot Dog

✳

Chapter Thirty-two

There were times during the unfolding of this chronicle when I'm sure you thought, why, this fellow Brae Orrack, he can't tie his own shoelaces let alone win the hand of a beautiful lady like Nell Devereaux and come out of it alive. Well, I can't say as I blame you, since on more than one occasion I felt the same way myself. But look at me now, the real live hero of this piece. With Brae Orrack around, you can save yourself the cost of a moving-picture show, even if it does have sound. I'm the guy who snatched the heroine off the railroad tracks just before the train came along in those one-reelers. Now you might be thinking, he's talking boastful, just like the late Bobby Reedhouse, and maybe I am at that, but at least I've got something to crow about, unlike Bobby whose achievements amounted to crashing a plane off the coast of Ireland and getting killed by a bee on a sun-baked Florida Key. No, I was the real thing all right, a bona fide heroic being, and here was our lovely heroine, right beside me in the pilot's seat of the Fokker Trimotor, returning us safely to civilization.

And Nell, unlike the aforementioned Bobby Reedhouse, had no qualms about flying over water. Thus when we left Key West, she turned the plane north, making landfall just outside Panama City. We landed, re-fueled, got some rest and me a change of clothes, and then resumed our journey west, crossing Choctawhatchee Bay, passing over Pensicola to spend the night in a rental cabin outside Mobile. We spent more nights wrapped in each other's arms in Baton Rouge, and Tyler, and Lubbock. Outside Albuquerque, we slept beneath the stars. This was the truest magic of all, I concluded, the warmth of Nell as I held her close, the soft caressing murmur of her voice; these surely formed the touchstones of a life that had previously defeated even the imagining. And something else: the lovemaking. Not just once or twice, as I had been led to believe happened between a man and a woman, but constantly. Each time we expanded love's perimeters in the most remarkable ways. Nothing, not Megan's teachings, not local gossip, not even imagination in freefall, prepared me for the ferocity of our coming together. It was as though we had invented something unique, an artistry performed by no other couple in the world.

In feeling so good about everything as I recount our journey back to Los Angeles, there are a couple of moments I should probably skip over, but will not seeing as how this is an honest recitation of events and not one of those phonied-up narratives that you get from other tellers of tales. I'm the hero I always thought I could be rightly enough, but I'm an honest hero, and so I'd better tell you what happened the night we spent outside Albuquerque. Nothing all that important, mind you, a shadow on perfection, you might say, the tiny gray cloud that mars the otherwise beautiful day.

Nell wanted to know more about "this magic man thing." And before I could stop myself, I started telling her about my family, the Serpent Stone, our traveling magic show, the evil of my father, and a number of other things that had I thought more about it, I might have been better advised to keep quiet about. But I was a man in love, you see, and I discovered that night that a man in love is not always a man who can keep his mouth shut.

Nell busied herself poking away at the fire with a stick. Sparks danced, turning the fuselage of the *General Machado* silvery in the firelight, illuminating a lovely face crossed with skepticism.

"Let me get this straight," she said. "This isn't just some tale you use to dazzle the ladies a bit. You really believe you are a magic man?"

"It's not a question of me believing it or not believing it," I said. "It's just what I am."

"And your father, he's a magic man, too?"

"He was."

"Was a magic man. So he's dead?"

"That's right," I said.

"How did he die, your father?"

"Well, if you want to know the truth, I killed him."

She paused a long time before saying, "That's probably not something you should be announcing to a whole lot of people."

"I didn't kill him for no reason at all, you understand."

"No, of course not. So why did you kill him?"

"Because he killed my mother."

The fire flared briefly and then settled again. Nell stopped poking at it. "Your father murdered your mother?"

"I loved my mother very much," I said quietly. "A son always loves his mother, of course, but there was so much more to it because she saved me from him, from becoming what he was. She was as good as he was bad, and that made her very good indeed. My father could not abide that."

"So he killed her?"

I looked at her, my eyes becoming a whole lot more intense than I intended. "As sure as I'm sitting here telling you this story. That's what started him on his way to the graveyard rightly enough. It only took a fellow willing to lay him down and cover him with dirt. And as it happens, that fellow had to be me."

"I see," Nell said in a way that suggested she didn't see at all.

"Although, to be honest, I never really meant to kill him."

"Okay," she said slowly.

"But then I found my mom lying in a great pool of her own blood in a tiny, miserable hotel room, and it was the end of everything she had worked so hard for, trying to hold us together even though he only wanted to tear us apart. Now it was over and she had paid a terrible price for only being good and I was not about to let that stand. Good deserved better, I figured."

"That's terrible," Nell said in a low voice.

"The most terrible thing," I agreed. "Before I knew it, I was at the fairgrounds where my dad was preparing for the night's show. Well, I confronted him and it was as though nothing had happened, like it was the most natural thing in the world that she was gone. 'She wasn't for this world, lad.' That's what he said to me. That's how he justified his action. The man was the devil himself, I swear. Leastwise, he was not my father, nobody who did this could be. He was the killer warlock, the black magician, and such an evil thing had to be destroyed."

She said nothing in response.

"But you've got to believe me here, Nell, it was him that came at me with the athame."

"Athame? What's that?"

"A magician's knife," I said.

"Ah, right. Silly of me. Everyone knows that."

"I swear it's true. Megan who only believes the truth, believes me in this matter, so that should tell you something right there."

"Yes, well, if I only had some idea as to who Megan is."

"Megan's my cousin, a witch—but a white witch, someone who is good, not evil."

"That's reassuring to know," Nell said.

I hurried on as though only the getting to the end of the story would truly convince her. "The bastard was hoping to catch me unawares, see, the same way he caught my mother. But I was ready for the worst, and thus he did not have the element of surprise. Except for the knife. As much as I was prepared for him, I was not ready for that knife sticking out of him."

Nell frowned. "What about this curse?"

"Just before he died, he threw it into me using the power of the Serpent Stone, the only way a warlock such as himself could employ it."

"Then in effect, the three of you ended up killing one another. That's some family situation you got there, Orrack."

"Yes, it is," I said.

"So what did you do then?"

"Stumbled away into the night, Great Orrack's evil digging deep into my guts, knowing there was only one person in the world who could exorcise it—Megan."

"The good witch down the road," said Nell.

"Well, not down the road exactly but close by in a dark castle of gray stone atop a bleak hill."

"Of course," said Nell. "Where else would she live?"

"Megan occupied a room at the back, where she spent most of her time, the outside world being too much for her."

"I can imagine," said Nell.

"I told her what had happened, and she was sad for my mom, but relieved, too, for she hated and feared my father, and thought I'd done the brave thing, proved that I was not like him, that I would not get swept up in his evil ways."

"Yes, I suppose that's good news all right," Nell said dully.

"But what of the curse? I wanted to know. It's bound to kill me. Well, she made me calm down and reminded me that there is always the way around a curse; all you had to do was find it."

"How do you do that?"

"She showed me these magazines she had, all about moving pictures and the people who make them."

"These magazines, they weren't called *Photoplay* by any chance?"

I regarded Nell with surprise. "I believe that's what they were called, all right. You know them?"

"Just about everyone in America does," Nell said. "They're available on every newsstand."

"Well, they all talked about this far away, magical place called Cinemaland."

"What are you saying, Orrack? You knew nothing about Los Angeles or the movies before you saw these magazines that your witch-cousin was hoarding in her hilltop castle?"

I judged by the tone of her voice that lacking this information was not a good thing, at least as far as she was concerned. "Well, I won't say

I didn't know anything," I quickly amended. "But I didn't know as much as I know now."

"Okay. Go on."

"Megan said that Cinemaland was where I would find the one thing that could defeat the curse. That which could not be found could be found there."

Nell went back to concentrating on giving that fire a good poking. "And what is it that cannot be found?"

"Love," I said.

"That would save you from this curse?"

"It being the thing my father wanted to destroy. Therefore, the one thing that would save me."

"Otherwise, you are dead, is that it?"

"Well, I won't be dead now."

Silence for a time, save for the insects and the diminishing crackle of the fire. "So as long as you're in love with someone, you live forever."

"Not forever, Nell. No one lives forever."

"Boy, you sure know how to put pressure on a girl. 'Hey, you'd better love me, sweetheart, or I'm a dead man.' Who can resist a line like that?"

"It isn't a line," I said. "It has to be real or it doesn't work."

"It's not something we have to spend a lot of time on tonight, but, you know, for me, love is right there beside Santa Claus, the Easter Bunny, and magic—lovely cherished myths, but no more than that."

Now it was my turn to be silent.

"In my business, love is what the marks believe in," Nell went on. "If you're going to get what you want, you've got to keep a clear head and stay away from the mythology. I'm surprised you don't know that."

"Why does that surprise you?"

"You being something of a con man yourself, Orrack."

"Yes, I guess that's what I am all right."

She tossed away the stick she had been using on the fire and sat back. "I tell you one thing. Magic is easier to swallow than love."

"So I have fallen in love with someone who can't love."

"Who sees no reason for love, who believes it gets in the way and only manages to complicate things."

For all I knew, she was right. My knowledge of love being limited to my own experience, and that was no experience at all. Nell came over and sat beside me. She put her arm around my waist and I drew her close. Love, I learned that night, could also be a convenient hiding place.

After we were through, we held each other and she said, "Not to belabor this whole curse thing. But let's suppose you had not been able to kick it."

"Well, I have," I said insistently. "There's always the way around a curse, and I found it."

"But supposing you hadn't? How much time would you have left?"

"No time at all," I said.

"And that means?"

"It means I would be dead."

Nell laughed. "Ah, Orrack, you are something else, really you are. You've got the scam down pat, you do. For a moment there, you even had me going, and I'm hard to fool, believe me."

I grinned right back. I believed her all right. She would be a hard one to fool. No doubt about that.

Chapter Thirty-three

A blink—well, it seemed a blink—before we were back at the Malibu, calm Pacific waters rising to embrace a dying sun, the haze settling across Catalina Island, sandpipers bobbing lazily along the edge of the surf, and Louis Payne and, yes, even Leslie Carter greeting us like a popular young couple so recently returned from—what? Our honeymoon? Yes, that's how it felt; Nell and I after the glorious honeymoon, ready to settle down to our happy life together. First however there were necessary embraces and kisses, drinks poured, accompanied by enthusiastic explosions of goodwill. You could believe in the naturalness of it all; you could believe that's how things should be.

I was in love and therefore protected. Love made me strong and would keep me safe. The magic man was gone, and good riddance to him. So was Nellie Bubak, and she would not be missed, either. Suffused in the warmth of our mutual love and snugly returned to Louis and Leslie's beach house, I only dimly heard Louis talk about *The Virginian*, the all-talking Western he was producing featuring my former employer, Gary Cooper. Nell said something about him being more the gigolo type in her estimation. No, no, affirmed Louis. Even though his mother was British and he had spent time in England as a child, he mostly had been raised on a Montana ranch. Gary Cooper was a cowboy. What's more, his voice was perfect for these new talking pictures, very natural, not at all stagy like so many theater-trained actors. If it hadn't been for the arrival of the talkies, Coop would be finished at Paramount. As it was, *The Virginian* would save his career. *Wasn't that nice?* I thought dreamily. *Wasn't that just lovely. Coop was going to be all right. I couldn't be happier for him.* Leslie Carter's voice seemed to come from a long way off, saying something about my father.

"I'm sorry, what did you say?"

"I nearly forgot in the excitement of the two of you returning, but he was around looking for you the other day." Was that a slightly malicious gleam in her eye?

"It couldn't have been my father," I said.

An icicle or two grew on the edge of her voice as she replied, "Your father, John. At least he said his name was John, and that he'd come a long way to find you."

"The return of the warlock," Nell said, apparently without irony.

"He came here?" I said. "How long ago?"

The malicious gleam hardened, as did Leslie's voice. "Three or four days. He's staying at a boardinghouse in Venice Beach. He said you would know it, and that you should contact him there."

I tried to imagine my father renting a room at the pink boardinghouse, dodging the landlord Reilly for the weekly rent, waving off the toxic fumes from Mrs. Reilly's cigarettes, listening to Meyer Rubin's tales of woe in the illicit booze trade. I tried to imagine all of this, and could not imagine any of it.

"I thought you'd be happy to know your father was here," said Leslie Carter.

"Well, my father and I have somewhat contrary views about things," I said.

"Yes, one of you thinks he's dead," said Nell.

"He loves you very much, and is concerned about you," Leslie stated.

"No need for any concerns about me," I said. The words came out lame and left a heavy silence in the little cottage.

Later, Nell and I undressed by a faint electric lamp in an airy guest bedroom at the back of the house, the sound of the surf outside washing against an unseen beach.

"I'm having trouble figuring you, Orrack," Nell said, turning to me, most of her clothes gone.

"Alas, I'm like an open book," I said, touching that fine firm body.

She moved back a pace, just out of reach of my drifting fingers, and wasn't that telling?

"You're a pretty sharp operator. This whole business about the dead mother and the evil father you had to kill, I might almost buy it, except then you go and get careless on me. The father shows up at Leslie's doorstep without a knife in his gut."

"It was never in his gut,' I said. "I swear I left the thing in his chest."

"He's some magic man, your father. Able to come back from the dead."

"Nell, I'm not lying."

"Aren't you?"

More words left hanging. The air was becoming positively crowded with them.

We slept. Or more accurately, Nell slept while I thrashed about, conjuring images of John Orrack. The Great Orrack. The Great and Evil Orrack. No matter how far away I ran, he only seemed to get closer. I told myself that I had nothing to fear. After all, I had found what could not be found. Had I not? I rose on my elbow and looked upon that lovely shadowed face; a face gentle in repose and so endlessly beautiful. How many men could lie here in the dark studying such beauty? In fact there was only one man in the world tonight, and here he was. Yet I was uneasy. Love, instead of making you more confident, acted to make you less so, I decided. You could love, but that didn't necessarily mean the other person could.

Damn love anyway!

I lay back on the pillow, gazing at the ceiling, pondering. This pondering had little effect. Like most pondering in life, it only helped to make me restless and unable to sleep.

Chapter Thirty-four

The next morning I awoke with an unpleasant start. I was not being thrown off the top of a very high wall by the evil General Machado, his equally evil henchman John Orrack cackling beside him. Instead, I lay in the safety of the guest bedroom at Malibu, Nell sleeping contentedly beside me. Outside the screened windows, the sun shone down on a beach rolling into waters stirred by the morning breeze. I stood and dressed quietly so as not to wake her. I needn't have worried. Not only did she not wake up, she never even moved.

I went outside thinking about my dad; thinking that if he could not kill me one way back home, he would work to kill me another way here in Cinemaland.

Unless I stopped him. That was the trick, wasn't it? Stopping him. No way around it.

Above the beach, a small boat sat hull up across sawhorses so that Louis, naked, except for a pair of ragged shorts, could sand away at its peeling bottom. His brown chest had already broken into a sweat.

"Morning," he said cheerfully. "I was just about to jump in the water. Feel like a swim?"

Everyone in Southern California wanted me to go swimming. "Not now, thanks. I was hoping you might be going into town."

"Not till this afternoon. I have to go into the studio about two."

"Then I wonder if I might impose upon your generosity, and borrow a car?"

He put the sander he was using to one side, and grabbed at a hand towel. "None of my business, of course, so feel free to tell me to shut up at any point."

"I'd never tell you to do that, Mr. Payne."

"Ah, but you haven't heard me out. My wife believes you've put some sort of spell on Nell."

"She overestimates my abilities."

"Leslie is a character, no question. And sometimes a little hard to take. But I respect her opinion, Mr. Orrack. She has a good sense of people and who they are. I must says she is deeply concerned about you and what you might do to Nell."

"I have no intention of hurting Nell," I said.

"We're in the midst of a revolution out here," Louis said. "Nobody's fighting in the streets or anything, but it's a revolution just the same. A new magic full of sound and fury is replacing an old magic of lovely silence and elegant images. The upshot is that a generation of magicians is suddenly irrelevant. They are the old magic and no one wants that anymore, and that is a terrible, frightening thing. We are watching the end of something, a civilization quickly disappearing. Everyone wants what's shiny and new, and making noise. I'm not sure I like it, but that is the reality with which we all have to live."

"I suppose you're thinking I'm part of that old magic," I said.

"You are part of something even older than that, I suspect."

"I'm afraid I don't have a lot of choice about it—or a lot of time left."

Louis studied me, as though trying to ascertain how much of me he was going to buy into on a clear morning in the Malibu.

"Tell you what," he said finally. "Leslie's roadster is in the garage. Beaten up a bit, but it works well enough. Keys are under the front seat."

"I appreciate this."

I started away. He called after me and I turned. "Just a thought," he said. "When I was a young man, I came to New York to find my fortune and all that. And I was looking for love, too, I suppose. It was a long time before I realized there was something else I'd been looking for."

"What was that?"

"Myself," Louis said.

"Did you ever find him?"

Louis paused. "After a long and difficult search, I believe I did, yes."

"Will you tell Nell that I will be back?"

"That much she already knows," Louis Payne said.

Lucca's gondola bobbed gently on the canal below the pink boarding-house, a reminder that if you dare to believe everything has changed, you soon learn that nothing has changed at all. The world goes on as it always goes, oblivious to your small plight.

Well, perhaps not quite as it always goes. I expected Mrs. Reilly or perhaps the evil Bing himself, but Meyer Rubin answered the door, gin on his breath, the day's copy of the *Los Angeles Times* in one hand, reading glasses in the other.

He gave me a crooked smile of welcome. "Hey, there you are, Brae. Where you been?"

"Is my father here?"

"He's been looking all over town for you. Kind of worried. Old Bing Reilly was fit to be tied when you didn't show up to pay your rent. 'Course he feels better since he rented the room to Johnny."

"Johnny? He lets you call him Johnny?"

"Why wouldn't he?"

"He doesn't like Johnny."

"Never said anything to me."

"I want to talk to him."

"Bing? I don't think he wants to talk you, pal."

"No, my father."

"I guess Johnny's in his room, I dunno. Hey, take it easy, will you?"

I pushed past Meyer. He called out something I didn't understand, but it made no difference because I was already halfway up the stairs, and nothing was going to stop me from confronting the Great and Evil Orrack, certainly not the ginned-up Meyer. I reached the second-floor landing and went down the hall. The door was unlocked. I stepped inside.

He had removed the picture of Jesus. The roses on the wallpaper were even more faded in the neat square where Our Lord formerly had hung. Photographs and newspaper clippings now adorned the walls around the bed. Pictures of the Venice canal system were displayed from various vantage points, as well as an aerial view of the pier with the Some Kick roller coaster circled in ink. The *Los Angeles Times* report of President Machado's visit to Los Angeles was mounted beside a story of the aviatrix Nell Devereaux arriving in the Malibu to meet her friends, Louis Payne and Leslie Carter. Not far away was another *Los Angeles Times* story devoted to the premiere of *Lilac Time.* On an end table, I found still more clippings concerning the gambling ship, *Johanna Smith,* as well as stories about the notorious New York gangster Owney Madden.

More photographs were piled on the floor, some showing a shadowy George Raft poised to dance. Others featured Gary Cooper in various poses: lounging in a chair wearing a tie and suspenders; holding a gun, lost somewhere beneath the wide brim of a ten-gallon cowboy hat; naked to the waist and waving a saber.

Meyer appeared in the doorway, eyes gleaming, mouth slack, not quite sure what to make of the son rummaging through his father's room.

"Do you know when he's coming back?" I asked.

"I didn't even know he was gone." Meyer seemed to gather himself together. "Look, since this ain't really your room anymore, Brae, why don't you wait downstairs until Johnny gets back?"

"He likes to be called John."

"Okay, but come on downstairs."

I kicked at the photographs, knocking them across the floor. "Hey," Meyer said angrily, "I don't like this, Brae. Let's go. Now."

"I'm leaving," I said.

And then I saw the photograph. "Gee," Meyer said as I picked it up. "Look at that, will you? Your dad knows Gary Cooper, and he never said a word about it."

I reeled out onto the veranda, not at all sure what to make of what I had just seen. He had been watching me for some time, by the look of it, putting together the story of my adventures in Cinemaland, tracking me, getting closer, and preparing to make his move. I was more convinced than ever I had to stop him. Not at the moment, though, because Georgie Raft stood at the bottom of the steps. Behind me at the screen door, I could hear Meyer draw a sharp breath. Obviously he knew who Raft was.

"There you are, Orrack. Wondered if you might show up."

"Just got back last night," I said, calm as could be, as though it wasn't a surprise at all running into Georgie like this.

Georgie noticed Meyer standing behind the door. "Hey, pal," he said.

Meyer managed a nod.

"That's my friend, Meyer Rubin."

"Good to know you, Meyer," Raft said.

"Mr. Raft," said Meyer.

"If you need a drink while you're out here in Venice Beach, Meyer can get it for you."

"Tell you what, Meyer," Raft said. "You think I could talk to Brae alone?"

Meyer bobbed his head up and down before disappearing into the interior of the house.

"I'm in a bit of a hurry, Georgie," I said.

"No, you're not," he stated with infinite certainty. To demonstrate that truth, he took his time lighting a cigarette with a wooden match he pulled from his trousers' pocket. As always, there was not a crooked seam on him, his white fedora worn at just the right angle, slightly down over his right eye.

"You have a good trip?" He sent the match spinning away across the yard.

"It was eventful," I said.

"Eventful." Georgie seemed intrigued by the word. He pulled the cigarette from his mouth and let out a long stream of smoke. "I hear tell you brought the woman back with you. I guess that's eventful, huh?"

"How do you know that?"

"It's my business to know things, and that's one of the things I know," Georgie said.

"Eventful." He said the word again, as though testing it. "It must have been eventful when Machado found out."

"There was a moment or two," I said.

"Well, good for you. You got what you went after. Not all of us can say that. Very few when you think about it. Say, you didn't call Owney by any chance?"

"No, I haven't, not yet."

Georgie took another drag on the cigarette and then dropped it to the ground. "Funny thing. I was talking to him, and he was saying how he was disappointed because he hadn't heard from you."

"Like I say, I just got back into town."

He spent some time using the heel of his perfectly polished shoe to grind the cigarette butt into the ground. "Sure, sure, but he thought you'd be phoning from down there. You know, keeping in touch."

"It turned out to be a pretty crazy situation."

"It did, huh? Because Owney got a wire from Billy Ward saying you'd arrived alone and without the money."

"That's right," I said. Damn that Billy anyway.

"What happened to Bobby Reedhouse?"

"He got himself killed."

"Who killed him? You?"

"No, one of his fiancée's relatives."

"His fiancée's relatives? Didn't know Bobby was planning to marry."

"It's a long story, Georgie, but basically Bobby concocted this scheme whereby they were going to steal Owney's money."

Georgie removed his heel from the devastated cigarette and spent more time inspecting the polish on his shoe, ensuring it had not suffered any damage. "Eventful. That was the word you used, right?"

"That's right."

"Well, that sure is the right word. But the relatives, they didn't get the money because Bobby ended up dead. Right?"

"That was one reason. The other was that I didn't take the money with me."

Amazing how little the matter-of-fact expression on Georgie's face changed, no matter what the revelation. Calmly he said, "What did you do with it?"

"I threw it into some bushes out at Mines Field."

"Okay, so last night when you arrived back, I'm guessing you retrieved the money. Am I right about that?"

I shook my head. "We didn't land at Mines Field. It was an airstrip out in the Malibu that Nell was familiar with."

"Nell was familiar with it, huh?" Georgie kept repeating my sentences, apparently in an effort to convince himself that he was hearing this properly.

"Yes, Nell knew where the airstrip was in the Malibu. That's how we got here. We flew back."

Georgie gave me a baleful stare, the same one he had given his shoe a couple of moments ago.

"Owney likes you, Orrack. You saved his life, and he's appreciative of that. But he is not in a business where he can just walk away when someone takes his money. You remember Owney's boys, Tony and Elegant Vincent? You rode out to Long Beach with them."

"I remember them."

"Well, Tony and Elegant Vincent are still in town. They're staying at the Hollywood Roosevelt Hotel. That's across the street from Grauman's Chinese Theatre."

"I know where it is," I said.

"That's good, because at nine o'clock tonight you're going to go to the Hollywood Roosevelt. They will be waiting for you in the lobby. That's when you'll give them Owney's money."

I started to say something else, but Georgie held up his hand.

"Don't waste your breath. Just be at the hotel tonight with the money. And don't even think about trying to run again. Owney ain't the Machado type. He don't give up and go home because there's always another pretty lady to replace the one he just lost to some kid full of dumb romantic notions. Owney don't forget and he don't forgive. He'll track you to the end of the earth. Okay? So you're gonna see Elegant Vincent and Tony tonight. Otherwise, things are going to get more eventful than you ever imagined."

Georgie Raft turned on his beautifully polished heel and started away. Meyer stepped out, his face the color of writing paper.

"Jeez, kid," he said. "What have you got yourself into?"

"I don't know what you're talking about," I said, lying through my teeth.

"Owney Madden's West Coast boy just threatened to kill you. You'd better be some kind of magic man, pal, 'cause otherwise when Owney Madden threatens to kill you, you're as good as dead."

I gritted my teeth and said, "Do me a favor, will you, Meyer? When your friend Johnny comes back, tell him a dead man came around looking for him."

Chapter Thirty-five

I pasted a big grin on my face and told the guard in the brown uniform at the now all-too-familiar Paramount gates that I was delivering a car for Mr. Louis Payne. The guard's rosy face became rosier at the mention of a recognizable name and let me right in. He even gave me directions where I could leave the car, close to where they were shooting *The Virginian*.

I parked as a big, jazzy-looking LaSalle roadster, driven by a fellow in the same kind of chauffeur's outfit I'd worn, came along, heading for the exit. Clara Bow sat in the back, a hat pulled low over her eyes, all but hidden by piles of suitcases and clothing. The front seat beside the chauffeur was packed with boxes. When she saw me, Clara waved for the chauffeur to stop the car. She rolled down the window as I approached and I saw that her skin, previously so pale and lovely, was now the color of parchment. Large black smudges circled those arresting eyes. The cupid's bow of a mouth looked drawn and pinched, but she still managed a saucy grin. "Hey, Orrack, where you been keeping yourself?"

"Are you all right?" I asked.

The grin did not look quite so saucy all of a sudden. "Well, it's moving day," she said.

"I don't understand."

"It's over for me, what it is. Finished. I'm pulling up stakes at the studio." She tried to say this in her trademark breezy manner, but the breezes failed to sail through her voice.

I looked at her blankly, still uncertain what she was getting at. "How can you be leaving Paramount? You're the biggest star they got."

"That was yesterday," she said. "Today the studio's got sound and I got a s-s-stammer."

"What's that got to do with anything?"

"Just about everything, baby boy. Paramount don't want no actresses with a stammer, I'm afraid. So out I go."

"What about Coop? He finished, too?"

She shook her head. "Hey, no tag days for that boy. He's exactly what they want now. He's gonna be just fine, a big star."

She reached her hand out the window, and squeezed mine. "It's all changing, Orrack. Easy come—and it was so easy—easy go." Her voice choked. "What the hell, right?"

"It's not fair," I said lamely.

"It's not fair, it's Hollywood."

"What are you going to do?"

Her brittle smile widened. "I'm gonna go home and count my money. Listen, I'm feeling a lot better, honest. I went through a bad time there, as you know, but I'm better now—and you're part of the reason for that. So thanks, baby, and be careful okay? If there's anyone more outdated than me around here right now, it's you."

"That's what everyone keeps telling me."

That cupid's bow of a mouth that so entranced all the men of America turned into one last winsome smile and then she rolled up the window and sat back amidst all that luggage. The chauffeur started the LaSalle forward and it went out through the gates. In the hurly-burly of the morning, no one seemed to notice.

I walked toward those same stages I had visited with Nell, passing the same crowds as were present on my first visit, except the people flirting and smoking in the bright morning sunlight were dressed not as seventeenth-century nobility, but as cowboys, saloon girls, and Indians.

A pasty-faced Indian wearing a moth-eaten warbonnet escorted a plump saloon girl with a purple feather adorning the red hair piled high on her head. "I hear tell costs are up fifteen percent since this sound thing come in," the Indian said.

"My sister-in-law works in the front office," said the saloon girl. "She says they've gone crazy cutting costs. No director on the lot is allowed to print more than two takes of any scene."

"It's nuts, what it is," said the Indian solemnly.

I followed them inside, passing a couple of cowboys wearing dark glasses. I stopped to adjust my eyes to the dimness and realized suddenly how quiet it was in here. People passed by as though floating, and I noticed that everyone wore rubber-soled shoes.

Suddenly, the sun itself seemed to explode through the place. I squinted against the light and saw that it came from big kliegs mounted on the catwalk. More extras and crewmen appeared, everyone putting on dark glasses to shield their eyes from the bright light.

"Hold on! Coming through!" a voice barked, breaking the silence. I jumped out of the way as eight workmen, sweating, their sleeves rolled up to their elbows, heaved past lugging a huge black metal contraption that looked like a piece of furniture from hell, but which turned out to be a moving-picture camera. They maneuvered it into a booth surrounded on three sides with glass. They spent more time positioning the camera, while other crewmen stood around, glaring malevolently at the black beast tethered in its cage. Everyone looked like they wanted to poke it with a stick.

Beyond the booth that housed the camera, more kliegs blasted light of such intensity that rather than illuminating things, they had the effect of swallowing them into a drizzle of white. Through that drizzle I could make out a Western saloon, its swinging doors opening onto a painted desert backdrop. Men in chaps and Stetsons crowded the bar. Dance hall girls, in corsets and with feathered plumes erupting from lushly piled hair, moved among the tables. A fellow in suspenders and a bowler hat sat poised at an upright piano. Everyone seemed to have been beamed down from Mars in sunglasses, unmoving, as though frozen by the glare. A hand grabbed my shoulder and spun me around so that I could face an angry walruslike Slim Talbot. "What the hell you doing in here?"

"I'm looking for Coop," I said.

"Get the hell off my lot."

A tiny, mustached fellow in a tweed suit brushed past, followed by two guys in vests wrestling a hamlike black object hanging from the end of what looked to be a particularly long fishing pole.

"What's going on?" I said.

"Sound, that's what's going on." Slim spat out the word *sound*. "So I got enough trouble here today without assholes like you showing up to complicate things."

"Slim, please. I need to see him."

"Well, young fellow, I don't believe he wants to see you. You being nothing but a pack of trouble."

I moved to go past him. Abruptly, his face went blank, and Slim looked not so much like a walrus, but someone who could give you a rough time. "Do yourself a favor," he said quietly, "and get your ass out of here."

That's when he appeared, sauntering out of the light, not quite real for a moment, puffing on a cigarette. I didn't recognize him immediately with the dark glasses he wore and that battered cowboy hat pushed back on his head, the scarf around his neck, the checked shirt, and the jeans. I was more accustomed to the gigolo in the carefully tailored clothes. But then Coop grinned and waved, and sure enough, as unlikely as he appeared in those cowpoke duds, it was him, all right.

"Hey, there, Orrack," he called out like we had just seen each other a few moments before.

Slim, red-faced, shifting back and forth on his stubby legs in case I should make a run for it, said, "Gonna have this fella out of here in just a moment, Coop."

"You trying to break onto the set of the world's first all-talking

Western, is that it, Orrack?" Coop gave a crooked grin; the grin he employed when he didn't have a care in the world. I was willing to bet he used it a lot these days.

"I need to talk to you, Coop."

"Last chance, fella. Start moving out of here."

"It's okay, Slim," Coop said. "You know, Orrack here is a friend of mine."

Slim looked as though someone had hit him with a bat. I probably registered the same surprise. Coop actually threw his arm around me. "C'mon along. I'm on my way into Makeup."

He kept his arm around my shoulder as he ushered me past a clearly befuddled Slim. "Don't pay no attention to Slim. Everyone's a little tense around here. This whole sound deal has everyone buffaloed. Used to be coming to the set was fun, you know? They'd have musicians playing while you did your scenes, and they could move the cameras around real easy, and if you were having trouble with a scene the director could talk you through it.

"Now, with this sound thing, it's like walking into damned church when you come onto the set. See the camera over there? It's locked in that there booth, and it can't move. You have to stand in the exact right spot for that character with the microphone, and if you ain't at the spot, the sound's no good, and it all has to be done over again. Why, I do believe this here sound is the worst thing ever happened to the industry."

"I want to talk to you about my father," I said.

"I met your dad," Coop said. "He's a fine gentleman."

"No, he isn't," I said.

A rugged-looking character approached, well over six feet, with graying hair swept back from a florid face. He wore a tweed jacket, knee-high leather boots, and a scowl.

"Goddamnit, Coop, where you been? We're already behind schedule. We should've had a goddamn shot by now."

"This is Brae Orrack, Vic," Coop said. "Brae, meet Vic Fleming, who's directing our picture."

"We don't get a goddamn shot in the next hour, we'll have Mr. Jesse

Lasky himself over here. Well, I'll feed the goddamn soundman to him. Goddamn this business, anyway. The goddamn sound engineers are taking over. What the hell's Jesse Lasky gonna do about that, I ask you? Why the hell they need a goddamn director around here beats the goddamn hell out of me."

And off he went.

"Vic didn't like me one bit when we started out," Coop said matter-of-factly as he led me out of the lights and into the dim shadows surrounding the saloon. It was like walking off the sun's surface into a mineshaft. I blinked, trying to adjust my eyes to the darkness. Coop paused to remove his glasses. "That's better," he said.

"Why is everyone wearing dark glasses?" I asked.

"So's you don't get klieg eyes. Them lights are so bright they can make you blind. Happens to lots of actors. It's like your eyes are on fire. Only thing you can do is take to your bed with a grated potato wrapped in a cheesecloth over your burning orbs."

"Good God," I said.

Coop grinned. "See, Orrack? And you thought this being a movie star was easy business."

"What did my father say to you?"

He didn't seem to hear my question or, more likely, he chose not to hear it. Instead, he led me into a tiny room containing a long mirror illuminated with lightbulbs and three barber's chairs. Coop sat in one of the chairs so that a heavyset woman with stringy gray hair could attach a bib around his neck. Then she came at him brandishing a cylinder of pink greasepaint wrapped in oilskin paper. She ran stubby fingers gently along the edges and planes of that lovely face before dabbing what she called eye shadow around Coop's eyes. "Not too much," Coop said. "My friend Orrack here, he don't like to see me with too much eye guck. Isn't that right, Orrack?"

The makeup woman responded by waving a velour puff full of something called Stein's white makeup powder and pressing it against his cheeks. To seal the pores, she said.

Dismissed from the barber's chair, Coop's face looked even more shiny and perfect than before. I couldn't help but think again of the wonderful, uncomplicated life he led, and I found myself overwhelmed with a combination of jealousy and envy.

"What about my father?"

Coop studied himself in the mirror. Or was he looking at me? It was hard to tell. "I met your dad a couple of weeks ago out at Harold Lloyd's place. You know Harold?"

"No, I'm afraid I don't know him," I said in a tight voice.

"Your father put on a magic show that night, dazzled us all I must say. But that wasn't what was so amazing about him."

"No? Tell me what was so amazing?"

"It was the way he talked, what the man had to say. He made me see things a lot more clear than I'd been able to see 'em before. Things about myself I hadn't realized. We've talked a lot of times since then."

Vic Fleming appeared, looking very unhappy.

"Coop, we're all waiting."

"Give me another second, Vic."

Fleming glowered and then disappeared. Coop went out of the dressing room and started along the hall, trailing after Vic Fleming. I caught up to him. "Anything my father says to you, it's a lie."

"He knows you're angry with him, Brae, blaming him for your mom's death and all."

"He killed my mother."

That brought him to a stop. "John's a darned good man. He can help you."

"No, he can't, Coop. That's what you don't understand."

"For sure he can help you see this business with Nell for what it is."

That stopped me short. "Wait a minute. You didn't talk to him about Nell did you?"

"Supposing I did?"

"Well, did you?"

Coop looked abruptly uncomfortable. "I may have said something regarding a fool notion you had of finding true love, and maybe thinking Nell was it, and what an addle-brained idea that was."

"You shouldn't have done that."

"Well, for your information, your father completely agreed with me."

"Of course, he agreed with you! Why wouldn't he agree?"

It took me a moment to realize I was yelling. The whole place had gone quiet. Vic Fleming and Slim headed toward us.

"Listen to me, Orrack," Coop said. "Your dad's on his way out to the Malibu right now."

"He's what?" My voice sounded even louder.

"I spoke to him this morning. He only wants to talk. Father to son. Get things straightened out between you two."

I turned and ran down the corridor.

Chapter Thirty-six

Clouds scudded lazily across a lowering sun, casting the quaint little cottage beside the cove in unexpected gloom. *Perfect for my worrying mood,* I thought, parking the car.

I found Leslie Carter inside, as usual draped in black, settled into her thronelike easy chair as though awaiting supplicants. She waited amid lengthening shadows, not willing to raise herself to turn on a light. There was no sign of Nell—or of John Orrack. She scowled as she saw who it was disturbing an afternoon's peace.

"You shouldn't be here," Leslie stated with a snarl. "You're no longer welcome."

"Tell me where she is," I said.

"It won't do you any good."

"Is my father with her?"

"It's too late."

"What are you talking about."

"Your father will protect Nell. Now you can't get her."

"No, he won't, Leslie. He won't protect her at all, I promise you."

"I want you to go away from here, Brae Orrack. I want you to do it now."

"You've got me all wrong."

She came out of her chair, shaking her head, her face contorting with righteous anger. "You are evil," she announced in a loud voice. "I knew it the moment I laid my eyes on you."

"Evil went away with Nell this afternoon and you sat there and let it happen."

"Get out of here!" she yelled and then came at me, crying out, smashing her fists into my body. "Leave her alone!"

Stunned, I backed away. She attacked again. I knocked her to one side and she collapsed to the floor, screaming, "You can't hurt her! You can't!"

There was nothing to say to this crazy, angry woman, so I got the hell out of there as fast as I could.

Dusk again and the same seaside cabins squatted in the familiar shadows of Dias Dorados. Far out in the water the waves were breaking in long smooth curves. Beyond the breaking waves the vastness of the Pacific soon was lost in a falling purple haze.

I parked the car off the roadway on the bluffs above the cabins, and then found a pathway leading down to the seashore. I stepped onto the porch, suddenly dizzy with the sense of betrayal. The pain of the curse or a broken heart? I couldn't tell which was which. It occurred to me, as I hesitated in front of that closed door, that I now knew how Machado must have felt as he stood in the same spot. He had power and money and could have just about any woman in the world, and yet this was how he felt. I, on the other hand, had no power and no money, and I could only have one woman—or could I? I took a deep breath and opened the door.

Inside, the same golden pine walls and shed roof ceiling welcomed me. The same comfortable old furniture surrounded the raised fireplace. In the dimness, I could just make out the shape of her, seated on the bed. She sat dressed in slacks and a blouse, leaning forward, posing for a photograph that could never be taken in this light. Although I could not exactly make out her features, I had the impression she was not surprised to see me, in much the same way she had refused to be surprised at the arrival of Machado.

"There you are," she said with a vague smile. "I was about to start back for Leslie's place."

"Did he hurt you?"

"No, of course not. This is your father."

"Why I asked the question."

"Why would he hurt me?"

"Because he would. Where is he?"

"He's gone back to the city."

Her legs shifted a bit, but otherwise she remained still.

"He wants to see you, Brae. Wants to talk."

"Well, here I am, Nell. Right here."

She gave me a worried look and then reached out to touch my face. I instinctively flinched away. Did I ever imagine a time when I would not want Nell Devereaux to touch me?

"He says you've been troubled since you were a child, that you grew up angry with him."

"Because of the way he treated my mother," I said.

"Where do you come from, Brae?"

"Where I come from? What does that matter?"

"Just tell me."

Her gaze was unwavering. Her eyes demanded an answer. I shrugged and muttered, "A place where always it's the funeral plumes and never the bridal roses, where the curse on souls and the getting of revenge endures over love."

"But where is it?"

"A long way from here."

"Is it in Vermont?"

I didn't say anything.

"Your father says you were born in Vermont. He was a magician working for a small circus traveling through the New England states. Your mother appeared with him. You and your mom assisted your dad with his act. He dressed you up in a little tuxedo. You look at a man in a tux and everyone sees a gentleman. Right? That's what he said. That was as close as either of you ever got to magic."

I turned and went out the door.

She came outside as a flock of pelicans swooped down to inspect the curl of the waves. She found me on the porch, eyes firmly fixed at a point somewhere far out, beyond the purple haze, beyond anything. When she spoke it was in a soft distant voice; a voice that sounded as though it had already left.

"Time I mounted another expedition. The top of Nanga Parbat. No excuses this time. Nothing's going to stop me. I'm going all the way."

"It's lies he tells you," I said, keeping my eyes firmly fixed on that distant point. "He plays everything normal, but it isn't. Not with him, a long way from it, in fact."

I turned and saw that her lovely face was now firmly set. Decisions had been made and she was bound now to follow through on them.

"He says you make up all these wild stories."

"We've all made-up our stories, haven't we?" I said. "But I've made up fewer stories than some others, I'm bound to say."

Those gold-flecked eyes for the first time took on an uncertain cast, and I suppose I had my small victory.

My eyes fluttered and the taste of almonds filled my mouth a moment before the pain dropped me to my knees. A convulsion shook my body. Nell swam in front of me. She had not broken the curse after all.

"Brae," I heard her say. "Let me get you some help."

"Don't need help. I'm going to be all right."

"You're not going to be all right. Quit fooling yourself."

"I'm fooling myself? Your real name is Nellie Bubak. You're not a princess. You tell men you're raising money to climb Nanga Parbat, but in fact you've never been anywhere near it."

Nell abruptly backed up a couple of paces, as though being close to me was not a good idea. "You're mother died of cancer, Brae, that's what happened to her. Your father didn't kill her, no matter what you might think."

She continued to float off somewhere on the periphery of my eyesight. I was having a difficult time bringing her into focus. "You even tell these men, you tell them you're a virgin because they like that, makes you more desirable in their eyes."

She didn't react to my words. Instead, she spoke softly. "Now you're dying, too. There's no curse at all. Just a young man dying of cancer and refusing to believe it."

"It is a curse," I said, shaking my head. "Megan says so. I find that which cannot be found, and I'll be fine."

"Your cousin Megan's not a witch. She's in an institution for the insane back in Vermont. She filled you with all this nonsense—stuff she found in old *Photoplay* magazines."

I wasn't listening to any of it. I swear I wasn't.

She took a deep breath. "Anyway, I tried. I said I would try and there it is, my dumb attempt to talk sense into you. I hope you come to your senses Brae, I really do."

She started walking away. I rose unsteadily, still weak, but determined to finish this. "You think I don't have any money. That's what it is, isn't it?"

She kept walking.

My voice rose unsteadily. "Here's what I'll do. I'll finance that next expedition to Nanga Parbat."

She continued walking.

"This way you can see something for all the work you put into Machado."

That didn't slow her.

"Twenty-five thousand dollars," I said. "It's yours. All you have to do is drive me to where it's hidden."

I didn't think she'd turn. Or maybe I hoped she wouldn't. But then she slowed.

And she turned.

"That's how I got to you so fast. Not magic at all, but Owney Madden, who wanted a package delivered to Key West. That's how much money there was in the package."

"So what are you saying? You never delivered the money?"

I nodded. "It's right here in Los Angeles. I can put my hands on it. Now. Tonight."

"You bastard," she said. "Don't do this."

"Nanga Parbat, Nell. You can finally get to the top of Nanga Parbat."

Her face went cold, her beauty recast in gunmetal.

"Your father's going to be on the pier at Venice Beach later tonight." She threw the words out like a challenge. "He wants you to meet him there."

"Do you want the money or not?" I said.

To her credit, she paused for a while longer before she took another breath and said, "First we have to stop by Leslie's place. Otherwise she'll worry."

Chapter Thirty-seven

You think I can't hear the note of uncertainty in your voice? There's been something suspicious about him from the beginning; saying he was the one thing and as often as not turning out to be something else entirely. But I've told a true tale or at least as true as I'm able to make it, what with one thing and another. My father, on the other hand, is a master at taking little stitches of truth and sewing them into a fabric of lies. He does what he's always done, recasting the darkness as light. But it never changes anything. Where my father is concerned it's always the darkness. You must remember that. It's always darkness. No matter what he says to the contrary. You must put aside what's reasonable and believe in what is not. Hard as it is, you've got to do that for me. Otherwise, I truly am lost.

Nell and I came along Sepulveda Boulevard at day's end. A ranch house was visible in the distance, near Lincoln, but otherwise the surrounding countryside remained flat and lifeless, still waiting to be an airport. I pulled the car over to the side of the road. We had not exchanged a word since leaving the Malibu.

I got out and hopped a low fence while Nell leaned against the fender, folding her arms. Sure enough, there was the drainage ditch. I followed it along until I came to a thicket clinging precariously to the embankment. It was here that I had quickly stuffed Owney Madden's package.

I bent down to the shrubbery, pushed away the lower branches, and there it was, still wrapped in butcher's grease paper and secured with twine, the way Georgie Raft handed it to me that morning. I lifted it above my head as a kind of defiant show to Nell. She didn't react, just kept her arms folded. A night wind grew in intensity, coming from the southeast, creating swirls of dirt, sending them dancing across the field's surface. I brought the package back to Nell in the fading light. That light emphasized the hard lines her face had taken on, and the stiff unyielding quality of her body.

I ripped away at the grease paper and the twine. Wads of bills held together by rubber bands, spilled onto the ground, Owney Madden's failed investment in Key West's crime future. I felt a sickness in my stomach that had nothing to do with my father's curse.

"There," I said. "I can conjure money out of bushes in the middle of a field. How's that for magic?"

She gazed down at the money, and didn't say anything.

"But there's something you must do before you can have it," I said.

She continued to look at the money without saying anything.

A car came toward us. *Well,* I thought, *at least this time we won't have to worry about Gerardo Machado.* Finally, she took her eyes away from the money, and for the first time since we left the Malibu, her gaze met mine. Money changed everything, even the way she looked at me. Now I was the mark, and she waited to hear the mark's opening gambit. You could sense her mind turning, trying to anticipate what would come next.

"What is it?" she said in a dull voice.

"You have to take me with you."

"Where?"

"To where you are going, to the top of Nanga Parbat."

She allowed a rueful smile. "Why should I do that?"

"Because you love me."

Her face went blank, and that blankness was quickly replaced by a look of exquisite anguish, and I couldn't tell whether that was love or the pain of not being in love.

Brae," she started to say, and got no further or if she did I could not hear it.

There was no warning almond taste this time, just the pain returning with red-hot knife-in-the-belly force. Abruptly, I found myself looking up at Nell as she called to this pathetic figure writhing on the ground. How could she love someone so weak and sick? I saw Georgie Raft and cursed myself for not keeping a closer eye on that passing car.

Incongruous in his beautifully tailored suit and shiny shoes, Georgie leapt across the drainage ditch. Behind him, looking even more out of place, were Owney's pals, Tony and Elegant Vincent.

I came back into my body, choking and gasping for breath, in time to hear Georgie say, "Vincent, I want you to take Miss Devereaux back to the hotel."

"No," was all I could manage.

The next thing, Nell was on her knees, so close our faces were nearly touching. Her eyes filled with tears. "Time to stop this, Brae," she said in a pleading voice. "We're just a couple of con artists, aren't we? We both know that. I get the suckers with Nanga Parbat, you bring 'em in with the stones you turn to bees. Right?"

"That's right, Nell, sure. That's what we do. Bring in the suckers."

"Neither one of us is what we seem, Brae, and that's fine. We always keep them guessing, that's what we do and we're both so good at it. Never show who you really are, because maybe we don't know ourselves and if we start to look too closely, that's when we both get into trouble. I'm right about that, aren't I?"

"Sure you are, Nell," I said.

"And we'll always think fondly of each other, Brae, because in the end, we didn't fool each other, did we? We know each other. Don't we, Brae? Don't we?"

I tried to say something, but I was too weak. Her face streaked with tears, she reached out to run her hand along the scar on my chin, tracing it gently. "Tell me we know each other, Brae, tell me it's all a lie and you aren't going to go and die. It's just a story for the suckers. Tell me that, Brae. Please tell me."

"For the suckers, Nell. That's it all right."

"Yeah, that's right." She looked relieved. "Knew it all along. A good con."

"A good con," I agreed.

She leaned forward another centimeter so she could kiss me. Is there finality to certain kisses? I'm not sure, but if there is, this most definitely was a final kiss.

"Tony, you go with Nell and Vincent," I heard Georgie say. "I'll stay here with Brae."

Nell wiped away the tears—*me with them?* I wondered—and straightened up. Elegant Vincent escorted her back to where Leslie's car was parked on the roadway. Tony took one last look at me and then followed after them.

Elegant Vincent also glanced in my direction as he held the passenger door open, but not Nell. She never looked back; she just got in the car and sat there, her head slightly bowed. A moment later, the engine coughed to life and the car drove away down the road. Nell's head never moved.

I managed to sit up as Georgie set about gathering the scattered bundles of cash. He went at the work methodically, stiff-legged, bent at the waist, careful not to get dirt on his perfectly tailored clothes.

"She must have phoned you when we got back to Leslie's place in the Malibu," I said. Georgie continued to retrieve the money packets. "Tell me, Georgie, how did you get to her?"

He glanced up as he worked. "How did I get to her? Like I corrupted Nellie or something. Come on, Orrack, time you grew up a little bit."

"Is it now?"

"Billy and I knew her from the old days. She was Nellie Bubak back then."

"Billy told me."

"So you know. Here's something else you should know: Nell is Owney's girl."

I must have looked dumbfounded when he said this because he sadly shook his head and added, "For a smart guy you can play it real dumb when it comes to dames."

"You mean she loves Owney?" Did the question sound hopelessly naïve? I suppose it did, at least to Georgie's ears.

"Nobody loves anybody, get that through your skull will you?" he said. "Nell works for Owney when Owney needs someone with her particular talents."

"So he needed her talents, is that it?"

"Owney wanted to run booze from Cuba to Key West so he set up Nell with Machado, and then cut Machado's original partner out of the picture."

"That was Al Howard."

"That was Al. Nell was supposed to get the goods on Machado while Owney got things started up in Key West with Smiling Billy. That money you were carrying was going to fund the operation."

"So what went wrong?"

"Machado was a pretty jealous hombre, it turned out, and I guess he got wind of what was really going on—probably from that jerk Al Howard—and he wasn't very happy."

Georgie was right, someone did get to Machado about Nell, but it was Smiling Billy Ward, not Al Howard. But there was no need to interrupt Georgie with the facts, not at this point.

"That's when you came along, our hero," Georgie continued. "Like every other guy on the planet, you fell hard for her, but unlike everyone else, you did something helpful—you got her out of Key West alive. Good for you. Everyone appreciates your efforts. Certainly Owney does, and maybe Nell, too. But now it's time for everyone to move on to other things."

"So what are you going to do with me?"

"You, Orrack?" Georgie straightened, and opened his jacket so I could see the shoulder holster he wore. "Maybe I should put a bullet between those sad lovesick eyes of yours and end the misery."

"Yeah, Georgie, why don't you do that?"

Instead, Georgie closed his jacket and rebuttoned it. "But then again, I've killed too many people already this week. I'm over my limit. No, hopefully you're a little wiser about the ways of the world than you were before. Maybe that's reason enough to keep you alive. A lot of fellas tried to rip off Owney Madden didn't get the same consideration, believe me."

He bundled the money together and positioned it under his arm. "You don't look so good. Whatever's eating away at you, better get it looked at."

I didn't say anything. He stood there with the money under his arm for a couple of moments and then shrugged.

"Can you stand up, Orrack? Here, let me help you."

I used his arm to steady myself as I pulled myself to my feet.

"Think you can make it to the car?"

"Yes."

"Here's what I'll do for you just so there's no hard feelings. I'll give you a ride anywhere you want to go."

I should have told him to go to hell, that I didn't need anything from any of them. But that would have been a lie, and I'd told enough of those for one lifetime. I needed the ride he was offering. There wasn't much time left.

"The Venice pier," I said.

"The Venice pier? You're not in very good shape. You sure that's where you want to go?"

"You going to take me there or not?"

"Whatever you say, pal."

"I'm not your pal, Georgie."

He gave me one of his patented deadpan expressions. "No, I guess you're not at that."

Chapter Thirty-eight

Had there been a time when I didn't know of roller coasters? Did I ever believe there was only one Venice and it was in Italy? As I stood beneath the lights of the Venice sign, I knew the truth of these things. I was a man of the world now, yes I was. I carried so much knowledge in my addled brain it was a wonder I could stand up straight.

Tonight, those Venice lights refused to work for me. If anything, as I started onto the pier, I felt worse than ever. I just wanted to lie down and sleep forever. But I could not do that. No, sir, an appointment had to be kept and so I plowed forward.

The Giant Dipper roller coaster loomed to my left. Eighty-five feet high, someone said, and thirty three thousand long. Why it was the most popular roller coaster on the West Coast! And to make the point, thick crowds milled around its entrance, happy and loud and oblivious.

The clatter of the Great American Racing Derby all but drowned out the quieter demands of skee ball. Young men and women in their summer finery lined up for admittance to the Egyptian Ballroom. There were also long lineups for the Dragon Bamboo Slide and the Over the Falls ride. Only the shooting gallery and the automatic baseball game promised no waiting on this thrilling night.

The almond taste choked my throat. The pain in my stomach twisted into a black knot that now seemed permanent. Somehow I managed to get to the end of the pier, where the biggest crowds massed around the Some Kick roller coaster to hear the swing band dressed in sailor suits mounted atop the ticket booth. Oh, it was a popular attraction tonight, no doubt about it. Behind the musicians, currently taking a break chattering amongst themselves, the ride spread in its clamorous glory across the width of the pier, overshadowed perhaps by the newer Giant Dipper but still formidable nonetheless, a dinosaur's great humped carapace outlined in fierce light. The roller coaster's overwhelming rattle failed to drown out the sound of his voice.

"Well, now you're in luck this evening folks, because here on the pier they don't allow us to tell lies. So, yes indeed, I am a magic man."

My breathing came out in short, rapid gasps, and my hands shook like tuning forks. I tried to push through the onlookers. No one would move.

"I'll tell you the difference between myself and one of those magicians," I heard the voice saying. "A magician knows tricks, sleight of hand, how to deceive the eye. A magic man, on the other hand, is a highly trained individual knowledgeable in the dark art of conjuring."

The crowd had begun to notice this wheezing, perspiring creature in its midst, and retreated in alarm as though I was some evil leper. Maybe they were right to run away at that.

"You ask me where I come from and so I tell you. I come from the land of magic and superstition, a place where the power of Satan and the evil eye transfix everyone, where always it's the funeral plumes and never the bridal roses, where the curse on souls and the getting of revenge endures over love. It is the land that ruined my youth and haunts my life."

His voice rang in my ears, the lights of the Some Kick turning liquid, the pressing crowd full of what observers of these things might call average American faces, the people transfixed, everything moving slowly now.

"And here's a likely young man to do the job for us."

Magically—and what other word was there?—he materialized in front of me, no illusion this time, nothing of the dreaming or the imagining—the real, undeniable thing. Even in my painful delirium, every part of me shaking, I could only think, *Oh, this flesh and blood*

John Orrack, doesn't he cut an impressive figure, tall and courtly as they come, his evening clothes perfection beneath that silken black cape, every piece draped on his frame just so. Even the Serpent Stone, hanging from its chain, positioned an inch or so below that perfect black tie, did not seem out of place. His dark hair, beautifully cut, combed straight back from his forehead, his new mustache—and didn't it add a bit of dash?—precisely clipped so as to emphasize the fine line of his mouth and the straight powerful trim of his ageless jaw. His face was flushed with good health. The dazzling radiance of teeth the size of tombstones only added to the aura surrounding him. Why, with the Great Orrack smiling you could turn off all the lights on the pier. Except as the Great Orrack confronted me, he didn't smile. He opened his palm, revealing the three pebbles it held.

"What do you say, lad? Will you do me the favor of choosing one of these stones?"

The crowd pressed around, alive with anticipation. Orrack held this bunch in his palm, just as surely as he held those three stones.

"There's no such thing as magic," I managed to mumble. "Everyone knows that."

"There you go, then. Prove me wrong and you make some money for your friends and neighbors gathered here. Now come along, lad. Pick a stone for me."

"You're supposed to be dead."

"Of course I am." He turned and grinned at his eager audience. "Some would say I'm dead and born again. Others, well, they'd say I'm just plain not so easy to kill off."

The audience laughed appreciatively. How amusing, trying to kill the Great Orrack—impossible to imagine, a gent like him providing so much free entertainment right here on the Venice pier.

He waved his stone-laden palm in front of me. "What do you say? Don't disappoint these lovely folks. Pick a stone."

I tried to pluck one from his hand, but my fingers would not respond. It went skittering off his palm and dropped to the ground. Calmly, he took another stone and pressed it into my twitching fingers.

"There you go, sir. Now if you'd be so kind as to toss it into the air for me."

"Toss it into the air?" I said in a dull, drugged voice.

"Like a good lad."

Wobbly as I was, I managed to get that stone airborne. It sailed above the lighted rim of the Some Kick roller coaster. A rapturous exhaling was heard from the multitude. The Great Orrack flipped back that cape and flicked his white-gloved hands into the air, slim fingers dancing as the stone arced back toward the ground before exploding into a cloud of gray dust.

And from that dust rose six white doves, wings flapping majestically into the night sky above the crowd, accompanied by great gasps of amazement.

"Well, what do you know!" exclaimed the Great Orrack in a gleeful voice. "It wasn't bees after all. My mistake!"

That brought more admiring laughter accompanied this time by applause. How they loved him here on the pier, what an elegant and unexpected addition he was to the night's entertainment.

The Great Orrack wallowed happily in the attention as he passed through the throng, accepting cash tokens of appreciation. He didn't waste much time with that end of it, not this evening. Soon he returned to my side.

"Brae, lad," he said.

"Been looking for you."

"Or have you been running away? I'm afraid that may be a more accurate description of what you've been up to, son. But that's fine. I've come a long way to find you."

He guided me through the dispersing crowd and I was too weak to resist. Behind us, the swing band mounted atop the ticket booth of the Some Kick returned to musical action. They played that jaunty hit, "Let's Get Together." " 'On a summer evening, what a lovely evening,' " sang one of the onlookers in a loud off-key voice. The band's exuberance caused some of the audience to start dancing. " 'There in the moonlight, oh, what a moonlight!' " A fun night was being had by all. Who would even notice a father and son together heading off the pier? A son who had tried and failed to kill his father, no less; the father even now plotting his revenge against the son.

"Had a time stitching together what happened after you disappeared, believe me," the Great Orrack continued. "Megan wasn't at all helpful at the beginning. Eventually she came around, though, showed me those magazines, and I understood what you'd gone and done—running away to Los Angeles of all places. I never would have suspected it of you. Or maybe I would, you being so crazed after the death of your mother. Madness. But then I never have been able to figure you. Your mother always could, but that's mothers for you. Anyway, I decided there was nothing to do but come after you.

"I had no idea what I would encounter out here. Wasn't even thinking about it. Knew something about the place, of course, cast in myth as it is. But really, it has turned out to be much better than I ever imagined. Fact is, son, I've had quite the time of it in this so-called Cinemaland."

We were moving quickly along the pier now, the lights swirling past.

" 'Course as determined as I was, it still took me a while to track you down once I got here, and then I discovered you'd left town completely, off to chase some girl, I heard, looking for true love, I guessed. More of Megan's mad nonsense filling your head to no good. Well, I could have cautioned you about love, about that particular folly. It's the Holy Grail, the mother lode, the pot of gold at the end of the emotional rainbow, the thing that's always around the next corner, that needs just one more day and you can find it. Ha! Mythology. Fool's gold. Even when you think it's the real eighteen-karat thing, time steals it, and it turns out not to have been real at all. Believe me, I know, son. I know."

He sighed with melodramatic sadness and took a breath. "But no use trying to tell anyone that particular piece of news, least of all your own flesh and blood. It's the sort of thing everyone has to learn for themselves. Right? Well, I'm guessing you've learned a thing or two, because here you are back with your old dad, and not looking so good."

The lights began to fade; the hubbub rising from the crowd on the pier dropped to a whisper. The swing-band sounds of "Let's Get Together" had disappeared. All I could hear now was my father's voice, deep and melodious, his strong hands guiding me.

"Meyer suggested I try out my act here on the pier. Now I know Meyer, and he was joking with me, but in fact it worked out fine. It was on this very pier that Mrs. Constance M. Langford, one of the most prominent hostesses in the city, first saw me. She invited me to her lovely home in Hancock Park where I entertained her and some of her important friends. Ever since that evening, the invitations haven't stopped. Mr. Harold Lloyd had me over to his beautiful estate. Why, the other night I was to the home of Mr. Douglas Fairbanks and Miss Mary Pickford up in Beverly Hills. Pickfair, they call their place—lovely. Do you know them?"

He was not remotely interested in whether I knew them or not so I said nothing, which was how he preferred it.

"A wonderful couple, no question, although Doug's the more outgoing, a real charmer. Little Mary was more reticent, as you might expect from America's sweetheart—and a trifle long in the tooth these days for that role, if you get my drift. Nonetheless, she was quite thrilled with my small act, as was her husband. And, of course, there's the wondrous Miss Gloria Swanson, who I met at Harold Lloyd's, truly one of the great stars of the cinema, and what a loyal friend and guide she has become out here. I believe she finds me most entertaining."

Windward Avenue loomed. The Venice sign blinked overhead.

Together we staggered into the intersection. To the right lay the outlines of the Venice Lagoon, quiet at this time of night save for the whisper of a summer breeze. We came past the hulking exterior of the powerhouse and steam plant, then veered to the right until we arrived at the edge of what I imagined was Coral Canal. Now I saw what brought us to this particular spot—the gondola tied at the canal's edge.

"Belongs to the unhappy Italian lad," the Great Orrack said. "He lets me use it to come over to the pier."

Resentment flared. Lucca never allowed me the use of his gondola. I had to sneak it away late at night. Here he was handing it over to my father so he could ride in style to the pier. The Great Orrack lifted me up with an effortlessness that surprised me, and proceeded to lower me, like a child, into the boat. I looked up into a sympathetic face reflected in the penumbra of light from Windward Avenue and the pier beyond.

"You lied to them," I managed to say. The words came out as though unstuck from my soul. It took just about all the strength I had left in me to free them. "Told them all lies. If they knew the truth, you would be finished."

"Lied?" The word appeared to surprise him. "I wouldn't say I lied to anyone, Brae. I merely allowed certain people to hear what they should hear. There are the things you hear, and then there are the things you should hear, and often as not, those are two different things. Would I be 'finished,' as you say, if people knew certain other things? I suppose I would, but then all of us would be, would we not? There are no innocents, son, just the folks who play themselves as such for public consumption.

"But you're no different, if you don't mind me saying," he continued. "You always wanted things a certain way, and when they weren't, you created other things that put the world in a more understandable light for yourself. I appreciate that, Brae. Truly, I do. Who doesn't want to rearrange events in the simple way that best suits his needs? What we're all looking to do, I suppose. Why those talking pictures appeal to folks. But my thinking is that you took the rearranging too far. Convinced yourself of the factualness of certain wild tales that had no basis in truth. Now it's time for more invention, that's all, creation that puts us both on the right track to where we should have been all along."

"You killed her."

"You keep saying that, son." His words were forced out in quiet, reasonable cadences. "And I keep trying to pretend you didn't. But if you want to know the truth, it's beginning to wear a trifle thin. I loved your mother. You talk about true love? That was it. Beyond any borders of love known or unknown and that's the truth. Your mother and I will be together in eternity. Nothing can get in the way of that, not even our often contrary views of each other. No, not even that, I assure you."

The night wrapped itself around as he pushed the gondola away from shore. He had mounted the stern, using Lucca's long pole to propel us forward. The boat slipped silently along the canal. A nearly full moon gleamed above; the surrounding stars shone bright. The sounds of the Venice pier receded.

"No," the melodious, reasoned voice went on, "you misunderstood what happened between your mother and myself, particularly after she got so sick. That's when it started, I suppose, you rearranging the furniture of our lives in the way that pleased only yourself and didn't take anyone else into consideration. Megan didn't help matters, either, filling your head full of nonsense."

"She told the truth." My voice, finally heard. It was coming back, stronger now. What's more the Great Orrack came more clearly into focus, looming over me, the Serpent Stone twinkling in the moonlight.

"Truth? Megan and the truth? Lord, son, if there ever were two opposite poles in the universe, it was your demented cousin and the truth. Her truth was and is the four walls of the loony bin. Truth enough for her, I'd say! But you're just as damned crazy as she is. Everyone knows it, of course. Something I have to live with, I suppose."

A trace of anger had interfered with the reasonableness of his voice.

The gondola turned into Venus Canal. A bridge lay ahead. Crossing it as we approached was the miniature locomotive that circled the canal area pulling tiny passenger cars, empty at this time of night. The dark outline of the engineer in his square cap bulged out of the locomotive, serving to make the entire enterprise look faintly ridiculous. But then didn't we all look silly out here beneath the moon of Venice, two magic men aboard a gondola navigating a man-made canal circled by a toy train? The engineer must have seen us for he sounded the locomotive's whistle, a plaintive lonely wail.

"Anyway, we're together now, and that's the thing that counts." The calm had reasserted itself.

"Don't do this," I said.

"Don't do what, son? Honestly you do speak in riddles. But then you're sick; I have to understand that, and be sympathetic. That's what I'm here for after all, to try and understand my boy, my only living flesh and blood. To understand and then to find the cure, that's what I have to do. What has to be done."

The Great Orrack's voice had resumed its infinitely reasonable tone. It was the voice I had heard all my life, the voice that said it was light when really there was only the darkness—as there was darkness now, descending with lightning speed, forming itself into a headless apparition draped in the Great Orrack's clothes and swathed in his cape. An athame gleamed as it rose in the moonlight, gripped in the headless oarsman's hand, propelled by the oarsman's arm, its trajectory fueled by the Great and Evil Orrack's true intentions; the intentions I knew were there all along. He had to do this. He'd killed my mother. Murdered his wife. And I was linked irrevocably to that.

He had to cut the link.

Otherwise, there was no telling what the lunatic son who believed in love and curses might do or say. More threatening, no telling who might some day believe him.

So finish it.

The knife whipped through the air faster than I could track it—and then wasn't there anymore because with what little strength I'd been able to hoard, I had forced over the lopsided gondola, heaving us both into the canal. Warm water enveloped me like a soupy bath. My feet hit the bottom. I splashed gracelessly, frantically trying to gain footing on an underwater surface as slippery as a greasy frying pan. The headless oarsman, more agile, lunged out of the darkness, the athame once again upraised to strike. Except now the oarsman was gone, and the true innovator of my death, John Orrack himself, was back. I caught a glimpse of his face, and at that moment, the moment when he would kill, the face was at peace, as though the deed had already been done and he waited on Windward Avenue for the trolley that would take him into Hollywood and his promising future among the swells who adored his magic and would never know the dark truth of him.

The point of the athame sliced along the side of my ribs.

I should have cried out, I suppose, tried to alert someone in the nearby houses to my plight, but I can't actually say the thought occurred to me. It was as though the final conflict between father and son should be played out in silence so as not to embarrass either party.

Orrack slammed himself against me. I kicked back at him, and the next thing found myself rolling across damp grass. He came through the mist raising the athame. There I was on the ground, and here he was swaying above me, knowing there was no further escape, that it was nearly over. A couple more well-placed thrusts and it would be done.

"So sorry, Brae, lad, so truly sorry, but it's the only way. Best for all. This world is not for you, anyway." He had said these same words about my mother and now repeated them in a voice already deep in the requisite mourning for his dead son. It was a voice of regret—and of resignation. What could you do, after all? One could only act, and accept the terrible guilt that inevitably flows out of action.

He should not have said those words. He should not have reminded me.

The Great Orrack lunged again, a trifle awkward, showing his desperation. I found strength in red-hot anger and managed to get my foot up and he went tripping over it, losing his grip on the knife. It dropped into the grass. With a great guttural wail, I grabbed up the knife as he fell upon me, and the next thing I knew, the blade sank deep in his chest.

He fell away, staring in rapt fascination at the thing sticking out of him as though not believing. I yanked it out and he looked relieved until I cried out and stuck it into him again—and again—so as to ensure he would not rise from the dead a second time. Not far away someone yelled. I rose to my feet and saw a man and woman, no more than teenagers, really, out for an evening stroll along the canal. They shrank back in alarm as I loomed in front of them, holding the bloodied knife, while behind me the Great Orrack proceeded to expire.

"I'm dying, Brae," he called out. The young man watching this shouted something that I couldn't make out.

"Do something, Brae," the Great Orrack cried.

I went back to where he lay stretched out in the grass, such a handsome devil in those evening clothes.

"I've done the something that needs doing," I said. "Finally done it, I'm afraid."

"Then the curse will kill you, lad, just as sure as you killed me," he gurgled. "You gain nothing from this. Nothing at all."

"I get this," I said, and reached down and yanked the chain holding the Serpent Stone from his neck.

Nearby the young man had gathered up enough courage to venture closer, "Hey, what's going on there?"

I stood frozen in place. The Great Orrack in the meantime grew still, his head thrown back, his right arm stretched out as though conjuring the bees from the stones. His mouth remained open, preparing a speech that would never be made. Mere seconds after the life departed from him, I was pleased to note, he was already vastly diminished, no longer great or evil, just dead as a doornail.

"Elton, do something!" the woman cried.

"Someone's being kilt!" the young man bellowed. "Help me! Someone's dying here!"

That was enough to induce me to get going out of there. I turned and stumbled toward the young man and woman. She shrieked as I approached. He pulled her away, leaving the way open for me to get up a small incline, dropping the athame in the grass as I went.

I ran along an avenue flanked by one-story frame houses. Lights inside those little houses began to flare on. An old man came out onto his porch wearing a bathrobe.

"Hey, what's going on?" he demanded.

Chapter Thirty-nine

At the outset of this narrative, I believe I mentioned something about my shortcomings, not enough perhaps, although in the telling of this tale, me being totally honest, you undoubtedly have been able to see them for yourself. Yet you wondered, like everyone else, if I wasn't some sort of madman desperate for love, babbling of evil fathers and terrible curses. You thought to yourself, it can't be true, any of it, not in this very real world of 1928. Well, now you know different. Now you know the truth of the Great Orrack. So think what you will of me for destroying him, but remember this: John Orrack was an evil man; there is no getting around the plain fact. With your own eyes, you witnessed him try to kill his son. Why, they might even get you to testify in an open court of law. Go ahead, just make sure you tell it the way it happened. I'd be most appreciative.

I managed to reach the pink boardinghouse without further incident. Inside, Meyer lay on the sofa, snoring softly through his open mouth. No one else was around. I went up the stairs and into what used to be my room, but lately had been occupied by my father. I sat on the bed in the darkness, my head light, mind swirling, taking in the lingering scent of him. The man was dead, but his rich smell filled my nostrils, the way it always had. For a terrible moment I feared that once more I had failed to put an end to him, that he would come staggering through the door, and it would all start again.

Then the moment passed. The Great and Evil Orrack did not appear. He was finally and truly finished.

I stood on wobbly legs, stripping off my blood-soaked shirt and then went down the hall to the bathroom. The cut from the athame's blade wasn't too deep, but it was still bleeding. I got back to the bedroom, pulled a sheet off the bed, tore it into strips, and then went back to the bathroom where I found some tape that enabled me to fashion a makeshift bandage. There was another tux in the closet, my father, well, my late father, never traveling without an extra suit in case of an emergency. It's like he always said, you look at a man in a tux and everyone sees a gentleman. Hopefully you would not see a dying lad on the run.

By the time I finished dressing, my ribs were in flames, particularly when I bent to put on his gleaming black brogues. Whatever strength I'd been able to muster to get this far was gone. I felt terribly weak again and my stomach hurt even worse than my ribs. I ignored all that, though. Feeling sorry for myself wasn't going to get me out of this mess. I concentrated instead on hanging that Serpent Stone around my neck.

From outside came the sound of car doors opening and then slamming closed. I went out and peered through the hall window down to the street. Two Los Angeles police cars had pulled to a stop. A quartet of officers got out and started toward the house.

Downstairs, Meyer stirred on the sofa. He made funny smacking sounds and a moment later called out, "Is there someone here? What the hell's going on?"

I hurried back to my room, closed and locked the door, and then went over and opened the window. With difficulty and a great deal of pain, I squeezed out and lowered myself to the garage roof. I scrambled down the shingles to the gutter. From there it was a short hop to the ground, but even so the weight of my landing sent fire shooting through my body.

A cop with a white face and a startled expression burst through the gate as I straightened up. He yelled, the way all cops do when their man is bound to get away. That was followed by what always follows a cop's demand to stop—a gunshot, aimed, of course, at a poor fellow such as myself, unable to do anything except keep running.

I would like to say that a bullet went whizzing past my ear, I believe it would add to the suspense of our story, but the truth is I had no sense that the cop's bullet came anywhere near me, which shows you what kind of shot the man was. By that time, I was dodging between two houses, lost in the shadows. I paused to catch my breath and to tamp down the pain from both my stomach and my ribs.

Eventually, I got myself together and peered out onto the canal. Not that I could see much, for the pain screeching through me had turned the world misty and indistinct. Wait a minute, though. There was something. I stepped out from the houses and started forward.

As I drew closer, I could see Lucca's abandoned gondola bobbing in the water at the canal's edge. The way of escape.

I leaned down and tipped the craft around, holding it against the side of the canal so that I could slip aboard. The pole lay in the water not far away, and I managed to push the boat over and retrieve it. Then, standing at the back, I poled away and the gondola skimmed gracefully across the placid water.

Uncertain musical sounds from the pier drifted back on the shifting wind, accompanied by the odd scream of delight, patrons having the time of their lives on the Some Kick roller coaster. Or maybe the Giant Dipper. A light went out in a nearby house, its denizens settling in for the night. The world had plodded on. Fellows like myself don't capture its attention for long. Just as well I suppose. The world has more important things with which to concern itself.

As I moved along, the haze deepened and the night grew darker and more silent; it was as though I had entered a long tunnel from which there was no exit. I had a vague sense of turning a bend and there, flashing abruptly out of the darkness, was a huge hot dog with a big neon smile stitched across it. The haze cleared enough so that the diner shimmered uncertainly beneath the full moon. I remembered Lily in her summer dress that night so long ago, rueful about love, and me still hopeful and innocent and undamaged by it. I thought of Nell and those green eyes flecked so enticingly with obscuring gold and how I had lost at love or perhaps lost at something that did not exist. Tears welled in my eyes, turning the world even more opaque than before. I thought of what Lily said that night, "Straight ahead, south of the moon and east of the big smiling hot dog!"

And all of a sudden I felt better.

I had not lost love after all; I just hadn't found it yet. There it was in the distance, straight ahead and south of the moon, not so faraway. All I had to do was keep going and not give up. It's like Megan said, there's always the way around a curse. All you have to do is find it.

I suppose I had a rough ride with love, but then just about everyone does at one time or another, right? But that doesn't make it any less real. How could I have come this far and endured all the things I endured if there was no love? It has to exist; it just has to, otherwise there is nothing. I did not learn so much as I thought during the time I have just related to you, those final moments on an earth where an old magic was dying and a new one starting up, but I did learn that.

So I aimed the gondola's prow at the moon, heading east toward that big smiling hot dog, the canal swirling ceaselessly before me. Now you and me, we've gone a distance with this, and at the finish, even though I've done things that surely raised an eyebrow or two, I do believe you've found me a charming and lively companion and you hate to see the end of me. You never know, I might just show up again when you least expect me. So don't you go fussing and worrying. I'm going to be fine.

Have you ever had reason to doubt me?